RACING THE WIND

WOODY SHERWOOD

For Matt Moran
May your courage and inspiration live on forever

CHAPTER ONE

He stood on his pocket-sized redwood porch, feeling the uneven paint blistering on the ancient railing. His fingers traced the open-grained wood, coming to a lazy stop at potential splinters. The cowboy worked each one loose and watched it freefall past his tobacco-stained boots, every sliver finding the same gravel grave four feet below.

August West—or Augie, as most people called him—appraised each square inch of his hands as he absentmindedly massaged the rail. Like the rings of a tree providing clues to age and weather during its life span, each imperfection, mark, and scar was witness to its own tale of a hard-lived life.

Every crooked wrinkle and sunspot represented yet another year lost to time.

A low-lying, lethargic fog settled into the valley as Augie's gaze drifted from his hands to the amber glow forming behind Sleeping Indian Mountain in the distance. Part of the Gros Ventre Range, Sleeping Indian had a distinct resemblance to a noble Native American proudly stretched out on her back, arms crossed, complete with an Indian headdress. Augie had long ago lost count of the number of times he had observed from this very spot as the Indian came to life under the dawn's shimmering light. Subtle shapes and colors abashedly unveiled themselves in the golden hue, culminating in a final act of perseverance as the perfect ball of hot plasma bloomed above the peaceful Indian's chest.

This day in June was the earliest of the year he had to rise to spectate what he considered the greatest show on earth: 5:41 a.m., the summer solstice.

At fifty years old, his ibuprofen-fueled body fought back most mornings, begging him for a few more moments of slumber before beginning the odyssey of movement. For a hard-living cowboy, fifty felt more like sixty on his battered body. As a wrangler who spent much of his life on horseback, seventy, add in a rodeo career, a bison goring, two knife fights, one gunshot wound, and a cowboy like Augie West probably couldn't calculate that high of a *feels-like* age.

Having spent the last fifteen years working for Mr. Don Lawson as the foreman at Six Dawns Ranch, he figured he had seen over ten thousand sunrises and sunsets from the three-hundred-acre property that sat nestled amid the shadows of the majestic Tetons.

Six months had passed since that fatal Thursday night, twelve hundred miles away, when Lawson's son savagely took his wife's life outside Chicago. For the first few weeks following the murder, dozens of vultures in the form of news media, true crime fanatics, and curious locals had shown up at all hours trying to catch a glimpse of or an interview with the family patriarch. Unbeknownst to Mr. Lawson, Augie had taken it upon himself to minimize his employer's exposure to the miscreants. The heavy wrought iron security gate at the entrance to the ranch's half-mile driveway was enough to discourage most trespassers. A cowboy arriving on horseback and racking a Mossberg 12-gauge shotgun was usually all it took to help an obstinate lingering transgressor rethink their decision to loiter at the gate.

Turning back toward the house, Augie covered the entire trip from the battered railing to the sliding glass door in two well-practiced strides. He paused to survey his reflection in the dirty glass, uncertain if the door or his umber Carhartt jacket was filthier. His black Stetson boasted a dark brown, rust-tipped turkey feather on the left side, secured by a grimy cream-colored ribbon that clung snugly around the hat. Dark stubble covered his weary face. Front and center was a distinctively shaped nose that had been broken too many times to bother resetting and had decided long ago on the contour it would adopt with each successive disfigurement. Nonetheless, Augie was still hopelessly handsome for fifty but no longer the stunner that had won him his high school senior class Best Looking award.

He shuddered in the early morning chill and felt the glass door slide stubbornly in its rusty track, prompting his image to vanish and the memory of a younger self to dissipate as he stepped inside.

The aroma of thick-cut hickory bacon greeted Augie as he crossed the threshold from the porch to the living room and threw open the single kitchen window, hoping to thwart the soon-to-be-riled smoke detector. Not that Augie worried about waking anyone at this hour; he had been primarily unattached his entire life. His only true companion, a white and gray Alaskan husky named Aurora, had been awake since the strips of swine slapped the frying pan.

The bacon fat rendered into a greasy blob of what most people would not consider goodness, yet it was precisely that for Augie West. He would spread it on sourdough bread like it was butter. Globules of artery-clogging fat filled every nook and cranny of the crusty bread as if they were sent to seal a most important dam. He'd add it to peanut butter and jelly sandwiches and even feature it in his trademark cocktail—a Bacon Bourbon Butter Infused Manhattan.

With a diet of bacon grease, bacon, bread, and bourbon, it was a wonder to the community how Augie remained so healthy. *Good genes* was always his stock answer. His morning culinary regimen had become rote, and it nourished him. After spending years without a routine, he'd grown to appreciate a walk on the largely predictable hamster wheel of his existence. Three cups of coffee—black—by 8 a.m. was a normal morning. Anything more or less than that meant a good chance that his day would be off-kilter. Whether it was true or not, who knew—a *self-fulfilling prophecy* is what they'd called it in a course he had taken at the University of Wyoming many years ago.

Whenever he thought back to those courses, his mind drifted far from the four walls that enclosed each classroom. Instead, he wandered to the four football field boundary lines that had framed his existence. As the star running back, his purpose and identity had been unknowingly reduced to that of a ball player.

He dropped the last bite of sourdough on the floor for Aurora, wiped his mouth with a dirty shirt sleeve, and walked back to the sliding door. There she was. Her ghostly silhouette was visible through the valley fog. Twenty paces east of his back porch, a cedar split-rail fence wove along the property, and inside the fence line slouched an old hitching post.

Most mornings, the small girl would appear out of a grove of ponderosa pines to the south, strolling through the dew, carefully choosing the placement of each diminutive shoeless foot as if avoiding land mines. Three thoughtful steps, then a pause. Three steps, then a pause. Her journey from the pines to the hitching post covered no more than two hundred feet but could take upwards of half an hour. One morning after she had departed, Augie methodically retraced her steps, searching in vain for the cause of her circumspect navigation.

On the rare occasion that Augie was still on his deck when she appeared, the little girl avoided eye contact and wouldn't return his smile. He never saw the redhead scramble on top of the hitching post. She would be on her laggard pilgrimage one minute, and the next would be an apparition sitting on the thick, round horizontal beam.

The girl would sit and stare at Sleeping Indian, sometimes for as long as an hour. She seemed particular about the precise spot on the cedar to occupy and would spend several moments correcting the position of her bottom. Always just right of center. Then, she would slip silently over the front of the beam, dangle momentarily, and drop to the dirt below, leaving a tiny cloud of dust to rise just above the cuffs of her faded blue jeans. The proof she was ever there dissipated as the microscopic particles refound their home in the Jackson Hole soil. Her return trip to the pines involved the same painstakingly slow process, and Augie would watch as the forest eventually enveloped the curious girl.

The eight-year-old redhead had arrived at Six Dawns Ranch on June 6, after her emancipation—courtesy of her grandfather Don Lawson—from Whispering Woods Children's Home in Illinois. Her name was Rose, and she had witnessed the gruesome murder of her mother. That's all Augie knew about her. He had tried speaking to her once, but she had looked straight past him with hollow green eyes.

The morning following the summer solstice, Augie finished his bacon and returned to the sliding door. She was there again, but this time lying on the length of the cedar-hitching post; her spindly body appeared no thicker than the wood itself. Rose's head pointed south, her arms crossed over her chest. She alternated glances eastward and skyward, slightly modifying her position each time her gaze returned to the brilliant blue expanse overhead.

She is mirroring the Indian, he thought.

Augie turned toward the back wall of his small, sparsely decorated living room. Years ago, he had won a replica Blackfoot Indian eagle-feather war bonnet in a poker game over Teton Pass in Idaho, and the headdress occupied a proud space on the buttercream wall. Delicately removing it, he adjusted the interior fastener and thought, *Let's try this again.*

As he stepped across the threshold, Augie brought the full weight of each cowboy boot to the decking. Rose's head twitched almost imperceptibly at the sound. She side-eyed him as he slowly descended the three steps, paused ten paces from her, methodically raised the headdress toward his scalp, and then continued toward the hitching post. He extended his arms and motioned for her to take it. She hinged slowly at the waist and cautiously reached for the feather bonnet. Those emerald eyes weren't so much looking past him as through him. Then, they danced back and forth between the sun-baked mountain and the headdress.

When confident she had solved the puzzle, Rose slipped it on and off her head three times before retaking a supine position on the beam and repeating the same pattern of glances east and up. Each time, a minor positioning adjustment was made. The glimpses and corrections finally halted, and Rose closed her eyes, arms hugging her chest, one with the beam. One with the Indian.

CHAPTER TWO

Six Dawns Ranch had been in Don Lawson's family for almost three-quarters of a century. His father, Arthur, had purchased the three-hundred-acre property just after Don was born and long before Teton County held the distinction of being the county with the highest concentration of wealth per household in the nation.

Arthur's work ethic was unparalleled. Rising before dawn, he put in fourteen-hour days, six days a week. His one respite was that he always slept in on Sundays.

He had struck it big in the Permian Basin of western Texas and was one of the youngest multimillionaires in the state; oil and gas would provide the family with generational wealth.

When he turned three, Don and his parents began spending summers at the ranch. Every June, they would make the two-day drive from Fort Worth to Jackson and return at the beginning of August. Eventually, the travel time was significantly reduced with the family's purchase of a twin-engine aircraft after Arthur had earned his pilot's license.

Don had followed his father into oil and gas and married his college sweetheart, Marie, at twenty-seven, and for a time, everything seemed idyllic.

Then, one Saturday afternoon, at thirty years of age, his life was changed forever by a knock on the front door. It was a Texas Ranger, accompanied by a police chaplain.

His parents had perished in a plane crash when the small aircraft went down in poor visibility while approaching Corpus Christi International. Don Lawson had just inherited Six Dawns and a fortune of upwards of twenty million dollars.

He and his bride left Fort Worth a year later and moved to Jackson Hole. A few months into the full-time ranch life, Don quickly recognized the need for a trustworthy foreman. As it so happened, his best friend growing up, Cal West, had recently lost his job as a litter control officer for the city of Fort Worth. Cal and Don had been inseparable through middle and high school, despite having considerably distant familial and financial upbringings. Before Don's move to Wyoming, he and Cal still met every Thursday night at the Silver Leaf Saloon.

Don dialed the familiar 817 area code and offered Cal the ranch foreman position. Within seventy-two hours, Cal, his wife Sarah, and their five-year-old, Augie, packed up their tiny apartment and were on the road headed north.

Their two-bedroom foreman's cottage, tucked snugly on the property's edge, was opulent compared to the Fort Worth digs. It was physically unmerciful work, often seven days a week, and over the years, Cal had supervised some rough and shady characters. Still, he relished immersing his heart and hands in the property and everything that came with it.

But several years into their move from Texas, Sarah's brief love affair with the Teton Valley and ranch life had faded, and with it, her and Cal's relationship. Augie heard his mother's late-night, hushed pleas to move back to Fort Worth—a more suitable place to raise a child. She was tired of the daily grind, the isolation, and the brutal winters.

By twelve, Augie was keenly aware of the strain the lifestyle was taking on their marriage. They eventually divorced in the spring of his senior year, and she moved back to Texas. Her husband's loyalty to Lawson and his love of the land had prevailed over his marital vows. It would take Augie years to forgive him.

Cal managed to handle the day-to-day until he was almost sixty, when his back and knees no longer cooperated with the necessary duties. So he moved to Dallas, where the absence of bitter temperatures would hopefully provide an extension to the borrowed time he was on before needing a double knee replacement.

When Cal retired, Mr. Lawson talked a thirty-five-year-old Augie into returning to the ranch he had grown up on. Augie had led a peripatetic life for the last ten years, all while chasing his aviation dream. But making a living from flight instruction proved elusive, no matter the airport. Inevitably, he would land a gig training wannabe pilots for a few hours a week in the evening and pick up ranch hand work full time.

His wanderings had taken him to Elko, Nevada, then north to Pendleton, Oregon, followed by a stint in Cody, Wyoming. Eventually, he'd come almost full circle, returning to Driggs, Idaho.

Augie toiled over the decision and turned Mr. Lawson down twice in the same week before relenting as conflicting memories of the ranch life clashed. While currently single, the toll the job had taken on his parents' marriage was not lost on him. Nonetheless, Augie packed up and made the forty-minute drive over Teton Pass back to where it all began.

One of Augie's earliest memories of Jackson was from when he was around seven years of age. It was late summer—his last week before the start of second grade. His father had hitched two horses to a vintage covered wagon. He watched from the barn as his old man and Mr. Fogel, a ranch hand, loaded a collapsable card table, followed by two mahogany folding chairs, a shovel, fly-fishing rods, an olive-green canvas tent, and two goose-down sleeping bags. Finally, the two men hauled what looked like a considerably large and weighty burlap sack up into the wagon. Mr. Fogel's teenage daughter sat on a milking stool, her baseball cap pulled down low, attempting—and failing—to hide her black eye.

Fogel shook hands with Lawson, returned to the barn, and, taking his daughter's hand, climbed the stairs to their second-floor apartment above the stalls.

Hickory spokes and iron rims made for a ragged ride as his father guided the horses slowly from the barn toward the Snake River. To a seven-year-old, the journey seemed to take hours, though, in reality, it took under forty-five minutes as Cal navigated an unnecessarily tangled route toward the river to stretch the trip for the boy.

An outgoing summer sun stubbornly hovered low in the sky, willing the cool evening air to embrace its fading offer as father and son worked to unload the wagon under the shade of a single black cottonwood. Setting up the campsite was a familiar ritual to Cal; there was no pondering precisely where each article would be placed or the direction it would face.

The site sat on a slightly elevated gravel bed on the western side of the Snake. A fifty-foot Colorado blue spruce provided the southwestern backdrop, casting its shadow over the camp and running unbroken nearly across the river. His father unfolded the two rickety chairs and patted one wooden seat. Augie sat as instructed, observing as his pa untied a red bandana from his neck and wiped the summer sweat from his brow. The boy did the same.

They watched in silence as an otter scent-marked rocks along the river, rubbing and rolling as he left an olfactory message for his pals. Cal pointed south and skyward to a pair of bald eagles soaring effortlessly as though running downhill. They seemed to be able to anticipate the invisible drafts, changing direction to catch the next current that would keep them aloft without expending any energy. Unexpectedly, one raptor turned toward the camp and broke from its lazy flight into a piercing dive. Like horse-racing spectators with seats on the finish line, they watched as the eagle fine-tuned her descent toward the unseen prey just below the river's surface, her sharp yellow beak visible against her white hood. Mustard brown talons that, to

Augie, looked like witches' fingers advanced from her underbelly. The eagle was so close now.

Splash.

A brown trout glistened and flopped as it was seized and carried skyward before the adversarial predator and prey dissolved into a pine across the river.

"Speaking of dinner, the fish ain't gonna catch themselves, son. Why don't you gather our rods from the wagon?"

Augie placed the two Orvis rod tubes at his father's feet and watched as he deftly assembled the nine-foot poles. He fed a few inches of tippet through the hook eye of the insect-resembling dry fly, made five turns with the tag end, and pushed it through the small loop, snugging it tight. The second rod was readied similarly, and they marched to the water's edge, finding a pocket carved into the riverbank.

He observed as his old man used his left hand to pull a rod's length of neon green backing from the reel, letting it drape below the Orvis. The rod rose high into the sleepy Wyoming sky as the sunset drained what was left of the summer evening. He whipped the pole overhead, back and forth, creating a rhythmic dance in the air. With each pass, a bit more line slid from the reel and through the guides, liberated into the pale-orange sky.

Augie was mesmerized as he watched the dry fly trip the light fantastic on the end of the line as his father hummed an unfamiliar tune. Then, after the fourth overhead pass, he broke his ritual of motion, extended his right arm forward, and allowed the fly to land feebly on the water upriver.

It free-drifted downstream with an occasional twitch effectuated by a tug on the backing held loosely in the fisherman's left hand. On the second cast, a rainbow trout hit the lure, and the rod tip snapped high, setting the hook firmly in the fish's jaw. The chase began as she ran upriver, looking for the first underwater boulder to snap the line on.

Snatching the net, Augie followed his father north along the river's edge, carefully navigating the rocks. As the fish tired, Cal gradually put more tension on the line. *Too much, and the leader would snap*, Augie recalled his father saying. As he closed the gap with the tuckered rainbow, he stripped in line with his left hand. The defeated trout finally surrendered, and Augie dipped the net below the water and, with a proud grin, brought the three-pound fish to the surface.

Back at camp, Cal began building a small fire ring with dusty, mismatched river rocks. Next, he pulled an eight-inch Bowie knife from its sheath on his belt, strode to a nearby birch tree, and, like a chef de cuisine, expertly worked the blade along the bark as if filleting a delicate fish. Wispy shavings fluttered to his feet. He collected the handful of snippets and returned to the fire ring where Augie had pridefully piled kindling and larger pieces of driftwood next to the small circle of rocks.

Cal worked, methodically arranging the firewood as Augie's gaze shifted from his father's lively hands to his face, imploring their eyes to meet. The boy waited impatiently for an opportunity to prove his mettle to the hardened outdoorsman he so desperately desired to imitate.

Once the birch bark and small pieces of kindling had found their proper positions, Cal asked Augie to choose the best three logs. After careful deliberation, he singled out a fitting triad of logs, and his father instructed him to set the pieces in the shape of a teepee. Following a few minor adjustments, the boy looked up and nodded. A match was lit, and the flames languidly nibbled at the birch before engulfing the shavings. Augie was then instructed to take the red potato foil packets from the wagon and carefully place them at the base of the fire as his father sank cans of warm soda between rocks in the chilly river.

Augie watched as two slits were deftly cut under and behind the fish's bottom jaw, creating a V, through which Cal inserted his thumb into the opening and pulled down forcefully, unzipping the trout's guts, gills, and internal organs. Once satisfied that the rainbow was clean, he pulled a small bag of thyme, oregano, and garlic from his jacket pocket and packed the seasoning into the newly vacated cavity. The fish was then handed over to Augie to wrap in foil and deposit on the gray masses of hot ash.

Aside from the glowing embers of the dwindling fire, darkness encased the campsite. The river knew neither day nor night and continued its trespass of sound across the valley as the crisp evening air waded deeper in. A silvery shard of the moon rose in the western sky, and stars began to poke brilliant holes in the darkness above.

The foil packets were removed and set away from the fire to cool. Then, with a nod from his father, the boy added more wood to the surviving live coals, bringing life to the blackness.

They carefully extracted tiny, translucent bones from the flaky white flesh, stuffed chunks of trout and salted potatoes into their mouths, and washed it down with cans of cherry cola pulled from the cold river. Other than the boisterous gurgle of the Snake and an occasional neigh from the horses, the land was drowsy.

Shadows from the fire crept low up the trunk of the cottonwood as Cal rooted out a silver Roy

Rogers Riders harmonica from the wagon. The reeds vibrated in the stream of air forced across them with a pattern of inhales and exhales. Augie thought the melodies sounded sad, but he wasn't sure if that was because of the instrument or the musician. A final note lingered in the air before Cal carried the sleepy seven-year-old to bed.

Augie woke to his heart racing and beads of sweat on his forehead. He'd dreamed that someone was drowning in the river, and he was too small to save them. The vision had tormented him before. He clicked on his penlight, swept it low across the tent floor, and found the sleeping bag beside him empty. He soon mustered the courage to crawl to the canvas flap opening and cautiously peek out.

His head followed a sound south down the riverbank toward a reverberating rhythm, where a silhouette came into focus, barely lit by the waxing quarter moon. The figure was shoveling. He squinted, trying to discern the man's identity. Trembling, Augie receded from the tent's opening, backed deeper into the shelter, and dove into his bedroll headfirst, curling tightly into an impenetrable ball.

Augie held his breath as he heard what he hoped was his father entering the tent. After several minutes of quiet, he decided that if a stranger had accessed the camp with ill intentions, he would be dead by now. He drifted in and out for hours before a brilliant sunrise infiltrated the thin sleeping bag and wooed the boy from a fitful sleep. It wasn't from bravery but rather his bladder's necessity that he emerged from his cocoon—the sleep sack next to him was empty again. Outside, he could hear the crackling of bacon and smell the mouthwatering aroma of pork drifting in the morning air.

Relieving himself by a tree adjacent to the tent, he watched as a red-tailed hawk landed in the cottonwood and surveyed the awakening land for a meal. Augie approached the campfire, where a cast-iron skillet sizzled, capriciously splattering bacon grease.

"Morning. How'd you sleep?" asked his father as he reached for a soot-stained white kettle resting on the edge of the fire. Augie didn't respond; he eyed his dad's dusty blue overalls and scanned the ground for a shovel.

"Breakfast will be ready in a minute, and then we'll head out. Sound good?" Augie nodded.

The boy knows something, thought Cal.

They took a more direct route on the ride back to the ranch. His father guided the wagon down the drive to the barn, and Mr. Fogel appeared from the large red door. As his pa stepped from the wagon, he nodded, and Fogel returned the gesture. Augie watched as they worked silently to unload the table, chairs, tent, rods, shovel, and sleeping bags. No burlap sack materialized.

CHAPTER THREE

While Six Dawns harvested hay and, for a time, raised cattle to hold a tax-favorable agricultural status, it had never been a working ranch. For an outdoorsman, it could be considered one of the country's greatest and most scenic playgrounds. Within spitting distance were world-class fly-fishing, breathtaking hikes, Class V whitewater, and extraordinary hunting grounds—not to mention the winter activities.

The estate consisted of a 10,000-square-foot lodge, a guest house, the foreman's cottage, a barn, and outdoor and indoor horse arenas. The lodge's architecture was Western contemporary, blending traditional Western rustic materials with modern elements. Lawson desired a remarkable view from every room, so massive, custom-made floor-to-ceiling windows were prominently featured throughout the home.

Meticulous attention had been paid to the interior, as no detail was left undone. Exquisite carpentry, scarred hickory floors, reclaimed wood ceiling beams, and intricately carved mahogany banisters collaborated to create an unrivaled residence. The first-floor, western-facing, twenty-five-foot-long living room glass wall was retractable. It had a hand-cranked leather pulley system, enabling the entire wall to slide open, allowing the short but spectacular summer season to enter the home. A movie theater and a pub with stools adorned with actual saddles—courtesy of the Million Dollar Cowboy Bar in downtown Jackson— beckoned from the basement.

The five-bedroom, four-bath, one-of-a-kind structure housed a gym, a yoga studio, an indoor lap pool, and a five-thousand-bottle wine cellar.

Nestled adjacent to the lodge were the horse arenas. Two American Quarter Horses resided on the property year-round, one being Augie's. Another four would join from May to October, when the equines would trek with the wrangler from Fort Worth in the spring and return when the hostile Jackson winter was on the doorstep.

The barn's second floor housed a quaint, two-bedroom apartment. The wrangler's quarters currently accommodated Cassidy, who was sporadically on the property as Mr. Lawson allowed her to chase her dream—barrel racing at rodeos. Cassidy was the latest in the revolving cast of part-time horse wranglers who pursued prize money and the elusive championship belt buckle across the country.

The barn's western end had been constructed with something other than equines in mind. A sizeable hydraulic door provided access to Mr. Lawson's Piper Super Cub. The canary-yellow, two-seat plane had minimal comforts and almost no modern technology, but it was an aviator's dream machine. With its oversized twenty-six-inch tundra tires, the Super Cub could land on everything from sandbars to mountain tops.

Lawson's flying days had been recently shelved after an unexpected ground loop upon landing on the grass runway next to the barn. Just after touching down, a gust of wind spun the plane violently to the left before he could take corrective action. The centrifugal force was enough to cause the starboard wing to contact the ground and the right landing gear to collapse. The incident shook the old pilot enough to transition from captain to passenger. Now, whenever Mr. Lawson flew, Augie was in command.

The foreman's cottage, where Augie had lived for the past fifteen years, was a simple two-bedroom, one-and-a-half-bath accommodation. The basic, open floor plan suited him well. In addition, it had an attached, two-car garage—all he needed. Out back, a small barn contained two horse stalls. Most of the time, Augie's horse, Winston, had the camaraderie of the other ranch equines over at the lodge, but on occasion, he kept him more accessible at the cottage's stall.

No longer having a tolerance for the bone-chilling cold, Mr. Lawson would depart the ranch a few days after his annual holiday party in mid-December for his second home at the prestigious Colonial Country Club in Fort Worth, Texas. While the frosting the Wyoming pines received courtesy of over thirty feet of snow per winter drew thousands of visitors, Lawson was inclined to escape for the one inch of annual snowfall in Fort Worth.

Augie's cell phone vibrated in his pocket, fracturing the serenity of an otherwise perfect horseback ride. His disdain for the Motorola had nothing to do with the device itself; it was what it represented. It meant being constantly tethered to something other than what made him happiest—the natural majesty of this hallowed land. But when Lawson was in town, the phone was a necessary evil.

"Mr. Lawson, good morning."

"Morning, Augie. Can you stop by the lodge when you break for lunch today?"

"I'll see you around twelve," Augie replied.

Neither enjoyed spending any more time on the phone than was necessary. Their conversations would appear laconic to an outsider, but there was no discourtesy behind the brevity.

Augie returned to his methodical voyage around the property. He enjoyed the weekly routine. Fence lines were checked for fractures, trails were surveyed for anything that could impede movement, and occasionally, the corpse of an unfortunate moose or elk that had been shot off the property and staggered across the ranch boundary was discovered.

This could present two potential issues: an armed, trespassing hunter searching for his wounded prize or a hungry grizzly bear. In these cases, Augie would need to dispose of the carcass quickly before it became problematic. He would periodically receive a call from Game & Fish, which had been alerted by a responsible hunter that their prey had absconded, possibly injured. In those situations, he would gladly meet the sportsman and authorities at the gate to the ranch, where they would begin a targeted search until they found or didn't find the animal.

While patrolling the property, Augie carried a Colt Python .357 Magnum on his right hip. The double-action, six-round handgun was a staple for cowboys needing stopping power in an unfortunate encounter with an overly aggressive animal. Coming across a carcass with a feeding bear was a potentially deadly situation for a rancher, hunter, or hiker. So whenever he was on horseback, he also kept a Mossberg 500 standard pump-action shotgun tucked in a leather scabbard hanging from the D-rings on his saddle.

In his fifteen years at Six Dawns, Augie had only needed to fire the .357 on one occasion. Mr. Lawson had friends come up from Fort Worth for a week with their two grandchildren, and Augie had taken the group on a morning hike around the property. The expedition proceeded as usual, stopping at the edge of the Snake and then at one of the ranch's ponds, where the Teton Range reflected perfectly off of the water. Augie had been wrestling with a canoe in the brush on the water's edge when a grizzly came crashing through a blueberry thicket. The two kids screamed and started to run, triggering the bear's predatory instinct to give chase. Augie fired a round from the Colt at the caramel-coated bruin's feet. It wasn't so much the projectile that stopped the animal but rather the 165 decibels of sound from the blast. Rearing up on its hind legs, the massive bear momentarily dwarfed humans and shrubs alike—then it dropped back down and scurried off into the brush.

CHAPTER FOUR

Augie's view of humanity had been shaped far differently than that of most men. He had witnessed things others had not, and to him, the world was undeniably a harsh place. By fourteen, Augie had seen more than his share of fistfights between ranch hands, a stabbing over missing cash, and a poker game outside of the Whiskey Wheel among intoxicated cowboys, ending with a night in the drunk tank for several after one accused another of cheating before all hell broke loose.

On his sixteenth birthday, he earned his driver's license in the morning, only to have the joy replaced by anguish when he was instructed to euthanize a lame horse. He'd paced for fifteen minutes, fighting nausea, before summoning the courage to fire the lever-action Winchester.

At thirty-five—when Augie had taken over at Six Dawns and met a stunning brunette named Chloe—he had briefly courted the idea that the tough existence of a foreman could exist in harmony with a family before cynicism had crept back into its place in his cerebral cortex.

That same year, he had watched Mr. Lawson point a 12-gauge shotgun at a depraved seasonal hand, threatening to paint the driveway with his gray matter if he ever set foot on Six Dawns again. The following day, Augie had surrendered, in frustration, the notion of ever living a version of life with white picket fences, an impeccably manicured lawn, and 2.5 kids.

Augie's morning progressed in a suspenseless fashion. In his youth, he had craved the unpredictability of the wild. Now, it was an unnewsworthy day that he sought.

The early morn chill eased by the time he completed the loop on the eastern side of the property. Riding south, paralleling the Snake River, he silently listed the vegetation to himself as he passed. Milkweed bloomed with its rose-purple clusters; bittersweet nightshade blossomed with indigo flowers and red-orange berries; and yellow-green leaves with tiny white hairs broadcast the presence of a rubber rabbitbrush shrub.

He dismounted under the shade of a single black cottonwood, wrapped the halter rope around the tree three times, and tied a bowline knot, double-checking its security. As equines went, Winston was especially intelligent and had been known to unfasten a tie—thus, reviewing the knot was doubly important.

He looked south about fifty paces and recalled the camping trip with his father over forty years ago. The bank's contours had changed due to erosion, but he could still picture the scene from that night. The burlap sack. The shovel.

When he turned fourteen, his dad took him back to the same campsite. That evening, sitting in the fire's orange glow, Cal decided it was time to explain to his son what had occurred several years earlier. He felt the boy already partially knew something sinful had transpired.

Ever since returning to the barn and watching the wagon unload that morning seven years prior, Augie had looked at him differently, almost warily at times, and the mystery of the first camping trip was part of a subtle strain in the father-son relationship. So, sitting around the fire, his dad had spoken.

"Do you remember the first time I took you to this spot? You were about seven." Augie nodded. "You were too young to understand back then, but I feel it's time to tell you…and I suspect you already know something. This life I've chosen…our life, it's not for everyone."

Cal continued, "There was a drifter I hired in late July to help harvest hay from the fields, and I gave him a small cash advance and allowed him to stay in a tent next to the barn while he fulfilled his two-week commitment to the ranch.

"Early one evening, a week into his employment, I found him drunk, asleep at the wheel of a parked, still-running tractor. I fired him on the spot and told him to be off the property by 8:00 a.m. the following morning. He took a swing at me before getting dragged back to his tent by a couple of the ranch hands to sober up.

"Just before sundown, he noticed Mr. Fogel's fifteen-year-old daughter locking the gate to the paddock for the evening. He held a knife to her throat and forced her back to the tent."

Cal omitted the violent details but made it clear to Augie that a brutal assault had occurred. The girl had screamed, alerting her father and some ranch hands. Within a few minutes, the drifter was bound and tied to a hitching post behind the barn before Fogel, his daughter, and the ranch workers walked hastily to the lodge to speak with Mr. Lawson. The girl shook as she formed partial sentences between gasps of air, trying to explain what had occurred before vomiting and running to the restroom.

Lawson excused the ranch hands and spoke with Cal and Fogel privately. Mr. Fogel lobbied for a different kind of justice than Cal had suggested, while Lawson mediated the heated discussion for several minutes before holding a hand in the air for silence.

"That's enough for now. Check on your daughter," he said to Fogel, who disappeared down the hallway.

"Abigail." Fogel's voice echoed from the corridor. "Abigail!"

Boots pounded down the hardwood, and Fogel emerged from the hall.

"She's gone," he said, his mouth and eyes agape.

"Abigail has to be here somewhere," said Cal.

They called out her name. Each shout grew more urgent.

"Maybe she went back to the apartment," offered Cal.

The trio hurried out the door toward the barn, continuing to yell the girl's name. Cal arrived first and took the stairs to the loft two at a time.

"She's not here!" he yelled.

Lawson walked quickly around the side of the barn and spotted her. She moved methodically as if in a trance, walking from the hitching post toward the stalls.

"Please drop the gun, Abigail," Lawson said as calmly as he could, almost in a whisper.

She looked up with a wrinkled brow, confused, as if not understanding what he was saying, and tumbled to her knees, her face dappled with curious crimson freckles.

Mr. Lawson heard the shuffling of boots behind him suddenly stop.

"What did you do?" gasped Fogel.

Abigail didn't respond. She curled into the fetal position, released the nickel-plated .22-caliber revolver, and wailed as her father held her. Behind her, the drifter's body hung lifeless from the hitching post.

Augie strode down the bank to the river's edge and tried to shake the dark memories of his father's story and the drifter's body, buried long ago in the burlap sack. On Mr. Lawson's advice, the Fogels had disappeared from the valley, finding a safe harbor in Southern California, last Augie's dad had heard.

As he dropped to a knee on the course pebbles, his weary joint capsules stretched, releasing an all-too-familiar symphony of pops. He tugged at the worn fingertips of the buffalo-leather glove on his right hand, pulled it off, and did the same with the left. Like his hands, the gloves had scars that told stories—stories of encounters with barbed wire, shifty rogue flames, and ropes that had been yanked hell-for-leather through the mustard-yellow gloves. Coffee, tobacco, and gun oil each announced their presence as if in a competition of eminence.

Augie removed his Stetson and cupped his hands, crossing the left over the right as if in the act of Communion. He paused, pressing to remember the last time he had even set foot in a church, concluding it was probably the time he had ridden a horse, slightly inebriated, directly through the chapel doors in a futile attempt to romance Chloe—the one that got away. He was too late, off by one wedding that day. Augie had left the church, returned home, grabbed his guitar, and written a sad love song—"Here We Go Again."

Just this morning, well, it came with no warning
But it came, oh it came all the same
You're leaving for him; you're leaving again
And nothing, oh nothing has changed
But my soul's on fire, burning only with desire
And still, that plane will land
Like water on the beach, that soon will reach
Just melting those castles of sand
Just melting those castles of sand
Well, if they only knew what I'm going through
Maybe they could lend a hand
But the words they hear well they don't ring clear
So here alone I stand
Oh here alone I stand
But my heart is growing weary, and my eyes they
are a tearin'
So here I'll rest tonight.
The answers I find may not be so kind
But maybe they'll shed some light
Oh maybe they'll shed a little light
You're leaving for him, and here we go again
And here we go again
And here we go again

Lowering his cupped hands, he broke the water's surface and watched it pool in the makeshift chalice. He herded the small body of water quickly up toward his face, halting at his chin, allowing the cool liquid to explode upward. He did this two more times. No matter the season, this was always part of his routine. Augie liked wondering where these particular molecules had come from and suspected they called the Jackson Dam home at some point. His brown eyes tracked a cluster of water-blown scarlet trumpet flowers, their bright red lobes pointing proudly skyward as they rode the Snake River down to the next town.

There was something spiritual in the self-baptism. He relished the collision and the briskness, but most of all, he craved the connection to the river, the land, and something much more significant than himself. Reinvigorated by his river ritual, he returned to Winston, reversed the bowline knot, and unwound the rope.

He was keenly aware of having counted and named the three different types of vegetation, taken three splashes from the river, and circled the black cottonwood three times with the rope. Augie had shown these proclivities at an early age. Kids at school had made fun of him, while his parents mostly ignored his quirks or spoke in hushed conversations about his unusual patterns. These oddities were part of why he liked the serenity and isolation of ranch life.

He rode leisurely further south before turning west back toward the lodge, making mental notes about the particulars he would add to the small, color-coded spiral notebook on his kitchen counter. He observed some fencing needing repair, and a problematic beaver dam appeared to have progressed to an enormous resort-like structure, presenting an issue for irrigation downstream. Stopping at a creek that dissected the property from north to south, Winston lowered his head to the water and siphoned through pursed lips, a sucking sound audible in the wilderness far removed from the raging Snake River.

Augie reached down and withdrew his homemade beef jerky from the saddle bag. He preferred making his own, fashioned from strips of flank steak with a marinade of soy, brown sugar, Worcestershire, and smoked paprika. The cowboy fed the echoes in his stomach, intent on hushing the sounds before meeting with Mr. Lawson, as Winston picked up his gait, exited the grove of pines, and turned for home.

CHAPTER FIVE

Lawson sat on his porch in a sheeny teak Adirondack chair, a white ceramic coffee mug with the forest green Six Dawns Ranch logo balanced on one of the wide arms. Augie tipped his hat.

"Good afternoon, Mr. Lawson," he said, slipping from Winston.

"Augie," Lawson replied, nodding in his direction. "Thanks for coming by. Morning ride okay?"

"A couple of repairs added to the list, and the beavers are at it again. Same spot. Otherwise, good shape," Augie replied.

"Are we going to try to relocate this group?" asked Lawson.

"Yes, sir. I know beavers don't have a great survival rate when being moved, but I'd prefer not to shoot them if possible. If the creek stays blocked too much longer, we will have a major irrigation issue on our hands."

"Well, let me know what you need from me, Augie. On a different note, I know Rose has been coming to your place in the mornings. She's been drawing pictures of you and the Indian. Pretty good drawings, I might add. Now that she's settling in, I wanted to speak to you about her." Lawson paused, staring off toward the Gros Ventre.

"We've talked about many things but have never spoken of the deal with Dennis in Chicago six months ago. I appreciate how respectful you've been regarding my privacy about that night, even though I'm sure you read a bit about it and probably had some questions." Augie nodded.

"Fortunately, I had enough connections here in the valley to limit the media coverage, aside from a few small initial articles. The news folks obliged my wishes not to run any follow-up stories.

"As I think you know, Rose witnessed my piece-of-shit son, Dennis, beat her mom to death with a claw hammer in a motel room in Illinois. A claw hammer…The coroner couldn't count all the strikes. A terrible thing it was. Meth, mental illness. Don't know and don't care. Thirty-year sentence. With good behavior, he'll do twenty and still have much of his life in front of him. I'll probably be long gone when he gets out, and that's fine by me.

"The state took Rose and placed her at Whispering Woods while my lawyer worked to get me custody. She hasn't uttered a word since the night in Chicago. Psychogenic mutism, they call it—brought on by trauma. Whispering Woods's psychologist also said she has OCD and night terrors. I haven't heard or seen any of the terrors as of yet. The shrink over there thinks that based on the context of her drawings in art therapy, her life before the murder was bleak as well.

"I'd visited her a few times when she was little, but then Dennis began making excuses as to why I couldn't come to see her…It's been a long time since I raised a kid, and my first run-through didn't seem to work out. But I just couldn't let that angel spend her days trapped in some home. Sorry to dump all this on you, but I figured you should know."

Augie's wheels turned as he processed Mr. Lawson's words. During his first year working at the ranch, Dennis had visited for a few weeks just after graduating from college. He remembered the tension between the father and son but never saw Dennis again, and Mr. Lawson barely spoke of him.

He stared at the ground thoughtfully, then looked up.

"I don't even know what to say, Mr. Lawson. That poor girl…what she's been through…"

"The staff did say that despite her lack of verbalizing, she befriended several other children up there and connected with a few kids through drawing and writing. I think a couple of her sketches are of her with some of those other kiddos."

"Anything I can do to help, please let me know, Mr. Lawson."

"Thank you, Augie. I'm taking her to Salt Lake this afternoon. We've been going to Teton Valley Psychological Services once a week, but they suggested also seeing this specialist. We have an appointment tomorrow morning. We'll be back early Monday evening. Stop by for dinner."

"Sounds good, sir. And, Mr. Lawson…well, Rose is lucky to have you."

Augie traded in Winston for an orange ATV Kubota back at the barn, and Aurora joined him in the passenger seat. Packing some fencing timber and a spring-loaded animal trap in the rear bed, he headed for the eastern side of the property. An hour was spent methodically mending the split rail fence before moving on to the problematic beaver dam. What had been a two-foot-high structure three weeks ago now stood level with the cowboy's 6'3" frame.

The property had an ingenious irrigation design for the hay fields, using only the creeks. Trenches had been dug, complete with makeshift barriers, allowing Augie to route water to almost any meadow. However, the log and mud beaver dam had shut down the flow and was on the verge of initiating a serious drought threat.

He pulled the large trap from the Kubota, tugged on his camouflage hip waders, and cautiously entered the cool water. Augie set the baited contraption on the pond side of the dam, just in front of a worn trail the beavers used to cross their blockade, and then he climbed from the creek.

As he sat on the ATV's bed, removing his waders, Augie heard the distinctive crack of a sonic boom created when a rifle was fired. Then, a second shot. It had come from the northeast, near the Snake, and sounded too close to home. Starting up the Kubota, he followed the trail to where it dead-ended at the river, climbed out, dipped under some wire fencing, and began to make his way north along the Snake, with Aurora following at his heels.

Along the western bank, he spotted two hunters staring across the water. On a sandbar in the middle of the river was a downed elk. Having just launched one hundred yards upstream, a boat full of horrified whitewater rafters floated by with mouths agape.

As he approached the hunters, it became clear they were now in over their heads. A seven-hundred-pound lifeless elk lay on the gravel island, accessible only by boat, and the men, decked out in recently purchased high-end outdoor gear, had no skiff in sight.

"What's the plan, fellas?" asked Augie.

The two were speechless. In the excitement of spotting the eight-point elk, they had fired with no strategy.

"We, uh, don't have one," said one of the tourist hunters.

A crowd was gathering, including a furious rafting company employee who had just dropped off a load of whitewater enthusiasts upstream at their launching point. Augie feared a full-on beating might be in store for the negligent duo, so he called Wyoming Game & Fish with an urgent warning that they may want to get there sooner than later.

The cavalry arrived just in time to spare the hunters from more than humiliation. Technically, while unsafe, the two were still within their rights to shoot the animal. WGF launched a metal-bottom river skiff, took the pair across the water to the sandbar, and two hours later, with Augie's reluctant but necessary help, they had field dressed and quartered the elk and headed down the road posthaste.

CHAPTER SIX

Augie took the long route home on the Kubota, checking the beaver trap on the way. Nothing indicated that the dam's architects had been active in the hours since he had chaperoned the hunters' sideshow.

The low afternoon sun fought a losing battle with the thick forest canopy as he motored laggardly through the fading light. A few lonely, milky shafts snuck through the stronghold of the giant pines as the ATV bumped along the trail before announcing its departure from the forest with a windshield-dousing splash dispensed by the meandering creek.

A hardened cowboy's shower customarily persists longer than the average man's. Between the washing away of a day's worth of grime and a life's worth of sins, it was common for Augie to outlast the small hot-water heater—not to mention this particular cowboy's bathing rituals, as virtually every appendage was subjected to a particular scrubbing pattern. As expected, the heater lost its battle and gave in to circulating tepid water. Augie quickly shut off the shower, drawing an aching groan from deep within the pipes, toweled himself dry, and shaved. Fresh charcoal jeans, a black button-down—embroidered with an elaborate floral motif design on the chest—and his copper saddle bronc champion belt buckle were momentarily laid on the bed for inspection.

His everyday cowboy boots would be temporarily retired for the evening, and he slipped into what he referred to as his *dress boots*. The black Laredos sported a decorative silver toe protector and had lived a far more pampered life than his work footwear.

He appraised his appearance in the mirror, poured two fingers of Four Roses Single Barrel, and walked to the sliding door, absorbing the limestone crest of the Gros Ventre range shimming in the distance. A red hawk sat perched, facing east in Rose's seat on the hitching post; it shuffled left, then right, and grew still before disappearing on the western wind. Augie grew pensive. *How long will this land be protected?*

He gently slid his Martin Shadow guitar—one of only fifty produced—from the whiskey barrel stave wall hanger. It featured a Sitka spruce top, quilted maple back, and sides with a translucent black sunburst finish. Augie had quite a repertoire of original songs he had written, and those were his preference to play.

(Scan to play)
Will a river run through my town again
Watching the earth burn at both ends
A red hawk is still, up on that perch
Watching the sun as it scorches her earth
A gray whale beaches, he'll be the first to fall
People all gather, learning nothing at all
Forests grow silent, as progress prevails
Glaciers are melting, leaving no trails
Deserts will burn, streams will run dry
As men in high castles, never wonder why
Scarecrows grow lonely, acid rain in the soil
Birds in the Gulf, they're drowning in oil
Inspired are some, outnumbered by most
Voices grow silent, dying like ghosts
Photos are all, the witnesses left
But one man marches, medals pinned
to his chest
Ninety-four years, lost all his friends
Now he watches his planet as it burns
at both ends

> *Deserts will burn, streams will run dry*
> *As men in high castles, never wonder why*
> *Will a river run through, your town again*
> *Or will you watch it with me*
> *As it burns at both ends*
> *Burns at both ends*

Augie replaced the Martin in the wall hanger, offered his chin for a quick bath from Aurora's slippery blushing tongue, and climbed into the matte-black Ford Super Duty F-250 pickup, headed to the legendary Whiskey Wheel bar. A landmark in the valley since 1942, it was three right turns away—all of one mile—and Augie had made the responsible walk home many times.

He pulled into the lot in front of the bar, an unassuming one-story, green tin-roofed structure with faded barn-red siding. Once a true rodeo cowboy, bare-knuckled brawling joint, it was now an amalgamation of hippies, tourists, ski bums, laborers, cowboys, and millionaires.

Sunday night meant only one thing at the Whiskey Wheel—*church*. At least that's what the Wheel's band called the Sunday evening live music and dancing ritual that had been a staple in the community for over fifty years. It was one of the few places where diverse social classes and contrasting cliques became one. Attending was truly a unifying spiritual experience.

The saloon was already in the evening shadow of the Teton Range when Augie walked in through the side door. A solitary seat remained open at the bar, the furthest stool from the stage. He preferred this type of spot: not too close to the music and a fine place to people-watch. Harmonica, electric guitar, and drums quickly joined an acoustic guitar as the band whipped the patrons into a fury with Willie Nelson's "Whiskey River."

Augie was halfway through his beer when the bartender slid two shot glasses his way.

"Courtesy of the lady in the Grateful Dead trucker hat, Augie."

One was amber, and the neighboring glass held a transparent liquid best described as an altercation between yellow and green where yellow had prevailed. He used his hand to waft the scent of each his way. Jameson whiskey and pickle juice— or, more specifically, a pickleback shot. He hadn't had one of these in almost fifteen years. His heart raced as he scanned the bar, intent on confirming a suspicion—only one person would have ordered that shot for him.

There's no way, he thought.

Yet there she was. The one that got away. Chloe smiled a wink from under a pale-blue trucker hat with a dancing bear. Slowly, she came his way.

"It's been a long time, Augie West."

"Fourteen years and two months, Chloe O'Connor." Augie smiled. He couldn't recall her married name. "Where's Mr. Perfect?"

"How about the shots first?" she said as she made eye contact with the bartender, pointed a finger at the two glasses, and nodded.

Augie's eyes traced her familiar curves. Dark brunette hair was captured in a ponytail that emerged from the hole above the closure in the back of her hat, and Chloe's hippie days were apparent in the boho chic, flowing floral print dress that finished at her ankles. She was still stunning.

Growing up in Boulder, she had stayed local for college and been a First Team All-Big Twelve selection at the University of Colorado in track. Upon graduation, she and her college roommate spent four months backpacking across Europe, where she had fallen in love in—and with—Barcelona. After a two-week whirlwind romance, it was time for her next stop, Marseille. Chloe promised to stay in touch with the dashing Spaniard, but the affair did not survive the nomadic journey.

The youngest of six children—five girls—she had been her mother's last hope for the sisterhood. A devout Catholic, her mom prayed Chloe would find her way to the convent, not the University of Colorado, but she was far too free-spirited and adventurous to even consider a life in a habit.

Augie recalled the first summer he worked at the ranch and the torrid love affair that lasted well into the winter. Though ten years younger, she had been in the twilight of her carefree phase, and she wanted something more serious—marriage and children. He hadn't been ready for that, so the romance fizzled, and she moved on.

Augie believed his world was an inhospitable place for a family and questioned his ability to raise a child. However, there were moments recently— often kneeling at the Snake—when regret slithered through his mind. A splash of frigid river water was usually all it took to eradicate the thought until it inevitably surfaced again.

Chloe had become a fixture at the ranch that summer and fall, and Mr. Lawson had come to look at her like a daughter. Lawson was brokenhearted to see the relationship end, but the two had stayed sporadically in touch, exchanging Christmas cards over the years as well as the occasional phone call.

The bartender lined up two more glasses as Augie offered Chloe his barstool. There was a clink of glass over the booming band, and the sharp, briny-sweet juice chased the shot of Jameson. The pickleback ceremony was complete.

"Well, as far as 'Mr. Perfect,' *Steve* and I left Jackson six months after the wedding when the bank transferred him to San Francisco. We moved again to Portland two years later, and he began traveling regularly for work. Only, not all of those trips ended up being for business…I had my suspicions about something going on with Steve and his secretary, which were confirmed when he came clean about it one night. I was completely devastated. My world…well, it went dark in an instant. It took me a while to climb from that hole."

"I'm so sorry, Chloe. I can't imagine what that was like."

Moments passed as they watched the band in silence.

"Do you still like drawing pictures on your computer?" he asked.

"If you mean, *am I still a graphic designer,* then yes." She smiled. "It's how I'm able to move here for the summer. I have my own business and a loyal set of clients. So as long as there is internet, I can work from anywhere."

"That must be great having all that freedom—nothing tying you down," Augie replied.

He signaled the bartender for another beer.

"So, if you don't mind me asking, what brings you to Jackson?"

"Certainly not you." Her tone was playful as she leaned a shoulder into his. "I just thought it would be good for me to clear my head in a place like no other. I've rented a cabin for the summer in Wilson, behind the post office."

The band broke into "Remember When" by Alan Jackson.

"Care to dance, Miss Chloe?"

"Why I'd love to, Mr. West."

They moved gracefully to the music, their bodies in complete rhythm, as if one hundred seventy months hadn't passed. For several hours, they caught up on the missing years before the band played its last song of the night: "Keep on the Sunny Side."

"I think that's my cue to get home, Augie," she said, hugging him goodbye. "I have an early morning trail ride scheduled across the pass."

"You'll need to come by the ranch sometime and meet Rose," he replied.

"Rose? All that catching up we just did, and not a word was said about any Rose." Chloe smiled.

"Oh, it's nothing like that. She's Mr. Lawson's granddaughter." Chloe nodded.

"While we're on the subject, do you have anyone special in your life, Augie?"

He looked down at the scarred pine floorboards before shaking his head.

"I don't…I just don't know that I can ever be enough for anyone…" He trailed off.

Chloe kissed him on the cheek and smiled.

"You were always enough. I'll see you around, cowboy."

A light rain had begun to fall as the bar's screen door clapped shut behind her.

He walks to the bar, throws down some dough
Turns to the door, just a little too slow
Out in the rain, on Route 22
Waits the dark-haired girl, he once knew
Standing so still
Oh she's standing so still

CHAPTER SEVEN

Augie tossed a cooler into the bed of the Ford and headed south toward the lodge for dinner. In the container were three elk tenderloin steaks he had promised Mr. Lawson he would bring—courtesy of the prior incident on the gravel bar. Augie had also packed a bag of frozen chicken nuggets, unaware of Rose's culinary disposition.

He wore dark jeans and a long-sleeve white cotton dress shirt with the cuffs folded back three times, exposing half his powerful forearms. His *dress* boots made their second appearance in as many days, and he substituted his championship belt buckle for a more restrained pewter-plate buckle with a stamped Six Dawns Ranch logo.

Rose was picking wildflowers from around the flagpole when Augie parked the three-ton vehicle and moved to the rear passenger door, allowing Aurora to jump from the seat to the driveway.

Upon seeing Aurora emerge, Rose moved behind the pole, creating a fruitless barrier. Her wide eyes darted between the dog and the lodge. It seemed she was calculating whether she could reach the front door before the beast struck when Augie commanded Aurora down, and she melted into the pavement.

He approached Rose, explaining that this was his pet; she was friendly and well-trained. Blood returned to her fingers as she released her grip on the flagpole and exchanged it for her notebook. On an already-used piece of paper, she wrote four letters: *WOLF*. This wasn't the first time a husky had been confused with a wolf. Augie clarified that huskies have fluffy, curled tails, and wolves have straight tails. He went through a few other comparisons, and when the girl seemed convinced, he asked her if she would like to meet the canine. She nodded a hesitant yes.

"Aurora, come."

"Sit."

Augie instructed Rose to let Aurora come to her. Once the husky was familiar with her, he indicated she could pet her, and the fifty-pound hound responded with a sloppy kiss on Rose's cheek, drawing a smiling giggle.

The canine lay down at Rose's feet before rolling over.

"I think someone wants a belly rub," remarked Augie.

The husky had all four legs extended skyward as she wriggled on her back. Rose lowered to one knee and began kneading the soft gray fur.

"Do you know what it means when a dog rolls onto its back, Rose?" asked Augie. She shook her head from side to side.

"It means she trusts you. It's a very vulnerable position for a dog to be in. Do you know what trust is?" Rose turned to the cowboy and nodded.

Like the Pied Piper, Rose led Aurora around back, past the rope swing, down the flagstone patio through the rear door around the fireplace, out the front door, and returned to the starting line.

"Rose, why don't you take Aurora out back and keep an eye on her for me?" She nodded excitedly.

Augie took all three stairs at once, landing at Mr. Lawson's front door in a single stride. He gave a quick knock, paused, and then entered.

"Augie, glad you could make it," said Lawson as he approached with a smile, his hand extended. Simple blue jeans, a forest green golf polo, and loafers made up his ensemble.

"Thank you for the invite, sir. How was the trip to Salt Lake?"

"It was good. The doctor said she would probably speak at some point, but no one can predict when that might happen. She's been communicating through her drawings, which they said is fine. Her odd counting quirks and repetitive behaviors are nothing to worry about."

Augie wondered if Mr. Lawson had ever picked up on his similar idiosyncrasies.

"I mentioned that Rose has been drawing you and the Indian."

He walked from the bar to the kitchen table and returned with a piece of unlined notebook paper. A picture of a man on a horse wearing a black hat was illustrated rather well, followed by a redheaded girl on a pony. Sleeping Indian and the rising sun composed the backdrop.

Lawson walked around the reddish-brown, highly polished mahogany bar.

"Bourbon?"

"Yes, sir, that will be fine."

Mr. Lawson pulled a bottle of Weller 12 Year from the shelf and poured two glasses of amber liquid.

"Neat or a rock?"

"Neat, thank you. I see we're drinking the good stuff tonight."

"I believe in splurging on three things if God has graced you with wealth, Augie: good bourbon, good wine, and good coffee."

The cowboy glanced at Lawson's twenty-thousand-dollar Siphon Bar coffee maker sitting on the polished mahogany. He had seen it in action a few times. It was as much a work of art as an instrument to deliver a once-in-a-lifetime java experience—at least that's what the salesman had told Mr. Lawson.

Pointing back at the drawing, Lawson asked, "What would you think of seeing how Rose does on Scarborough in the arena? I think she'd like that."

"She ever ridden?" asked Augie.

"Nothing more than a bicycle, as far as I know. Whispering Woods had some kind of equine therapy program where the kids were driven to a farm and interacted with the horses. But, no, I don't believe she made it to the riding stage."

"Well, let's go see what Rose thinks," said Augie.

As they went through the family room toward the back door, the bell chimed, interrupting their trip to discover Rose's interest in riding. Lawson returned to the foyer, and the heavy door creaked open, revealing Chloe.

"Chloe?" Augie said, one eyebrow raised high.

Lawson beamed as he embraced her in a bear hug.

"Chloe?" the cowboy said again.

"I invited her for dinner, Augie. I hope that was okay?"

"Of course, sir…it's just…how…"

"The secret's out." Lawson chuckled. "Chloe and I've stayed in touch a bit over the years. She let me know she'd be spending the summer in the valley."

"Well, let's introduce you to Rose," said Lawson. "Has Augie filled you in on her?"

"All I know is she's *not* his wife, and she *is* your granddaughter."

Rose swung lazily from an aspen, her rear planted securely on a saucer swing seat, the tree's Dalmatian-spotted trunk disappearing into the branches high above. The rope had circular plastic handholds embedded every few feet for the adventurous to climb. She was looking down, fascinated by a baby dust devil that had kicked up under her feet, when the back door opened. Mr. Lawson took the lead, strolling toward her. Rose dipped one barefoot toe in the dust, halting the swing's pendulum rhythm and fracturing the small tornado's swirl.

"Rose, I know you have seen Mr. Augie around, but I wanted to introduce you formally."

The cowboy forced an awkward smile and nodded in her direction.

"Also, this is our dear friend, Miss Chloe." Chloe's smile formed more naturally.

If the little girl heard or understood any of that, she didn't permit herself to express it.

Chloe approached the swing. "Mind if I try?"

Rose slid from the disc's edge and stepped to the side as Chloe kicked off her sandals and reached high for a handhold on the rope. With the grace and power reserved for a gymnast, she pulled herself up, her bare feet settling on the swing's seat. She reached for the next handhold and hauled herself one position higher as her feet operated more like hands, grasping the lowest block to secure her position. She climbed two more rungs before reversing the process and returning to the dusty ground.

"You wanna try?"

Rose successfully navigated the ascent before Mr. Lawson said, "That's high enough. Come on down." The redhead complied. "Say, Rose, would you ever want to go horseback riding with Mr. Augie?" She looked toward the barn, pointed, and started walking. "Well, I think that's a *yes*. No, not today, Rose. Maybe tomorrow." She paused midstride, then returned, poorly hiding a slight pout.

They spent the evening out back by the grill and fire pit, sharing stories from another lifetime. Augie served up three elk tenderloins, one order of chicken nuggets, and four loaded baked potatoes. Chloe brought out a tomato, mozzarella, and basil salad. Mr. Lawson's contribution would be dessert— Nilla Wafers dipped in peanut butter.

Rose pointed to Augie's tenderloin and then to the barn, shaking her head from side to side. He looked at Mr. Lawson quizzically.

"I'm not sure either, Augie," said Lawson.

The redhead picked up her fork, mimed eating a piece of the cowboy's elk, then pointed to the barn again.

Chloe filled in the blank. "I think she wants to know if you are eating horse, Augie."

"Oh, God! No, no, honey. This isn't horse. It's elk. An elk is kind of like a deer, a little bigger," said Augie.

Her mouth turned down, and her eyebrows furrowed. She was between anger and confusion when she picked up her drawing notebook, grasped a pencil in her left hand, and wrote, *BAMBI*.

"No, no, no, we aren't eating deer. An elk just looks like a deer. They actually like to be eaten." Augie was now in over his head.

"What?" said Chloe, laughing. "Did you just say *they like to be eaten*? Have your reasoning skills been effective in the past with children? Wait, don't answer that. Have you ever met a child before? Let's start there."

Mr. Lawson laughed loudly, while Rose just stared.

What is wrong with this man? Inside, Rose was holding back a mischievous grin.

Mr. Lawson cleared their plates and brought out a crystal decanter with a sterling silver stag's head stopper. He set four brandy snifters on the table and poured an ounce of Grand Marnier into three glass tumblers, while fruit punch filled the final snifter.

"Here's to old friends," offered Lawson as he handed his smiling granddaughter her glass of bright red sugar water.

"And to new." Chloe looked over at Rose.

Their glasses clinked. The sweet orange liqueur burned as it traveled down Augie's throat.

"Time for a shower, little girl. And that's not a suggestion," said Mr. Lawson.

She set her notebook down and headed for the wide, ornate staircase that ran to the second floor. Once the water came on, Augie spoke.

"Mr. Lawson, do you have a plan for Rose? I mean, will she stay here with you indefinitely? And what about schooling?"

"At this point, it's day to day, but yes, I plan on having her here with me as long as I can and as long as the doctors think it's okay. I haven't been in touch with the school system yet. They did some cognitive and academic testing in Salt Lake, and her scores show she's in the ninetieth percentile for her age in English and math. There is no doubt that she is very sharp. They also said that when she uses her notebook to communicate, she can be quite witty for an eight-year-old. Clearly, learning took place at Whispering Woods.

"One concern from the physicians is her isolation. They said interacting, even with adults, and sensory experiences are incredibly important. Augie, you wanna stop by in the morning when Rose returns from your hitching post and we can see about walking her around the arena on Scarborough?" asked Lawson.

"I'll be over after she leaves," he replied.

They finished their nightcaps and said their goodbyes. Augie walked Chloe to her car, catching a scent from long ago. *Same perfume.* He flashed back to their fire pit dates at his cottage, snuggled close against the sharp mountain air. His movie reel played through slow-dancing at the Whiskey Wheel and fly-fishing side by side in the mist.

They say smell has a stronger link to memory and emotion than any of the other senses. At that moment, Augie could taste the coconut chapstick on her warm, soft lips. Fortunately, his departure was ephemeral, and he returned to the present day before she recognized his detour. Chloe kissed him on the cheek and was gone.

CHAPTER EIGHT

Augie's Tuesday began like most others, with coffee, bacon, the Indian, and Rose. Once she had danced her way back to the lodge, he and Aurora boarded the Kubota and made the three-minute drive. He had to hold the speedometer at precisely ten miles per hour to make the half-mile trek to the front door in exactly three minutes. At nine miles per hour he would arrive in an unacceptable three minutes and twenty seconds, and at eleven miles per hour, two minutes and forty-four seconds. Three minutes it was. He reached the lodge on time and continued to the barn, finding Rose on her rope swing.

"Who wants to ride a horse?" asked Lawson from the patio door.

A small, pale hand climbed skyward.

Upon entering the barn, Augie looked at Rose and pointed to a stool outside of Scarborough's stall. Of the Quarter Horses, she was the smallest and had the best temperament for the test they were about to undertake.

Augie guided Rose through the process of tacking up the majestic creature as she watched intently from the stool. First, he brushed her out and laid a black blanket over her back. Next, he placed a western saddle on the blanket, then attached and buckled the girth, securing the saddle. Rose's emerald eyes never left the cowboy as he continued the lesson, slipping the halter over Scarborough's nose and ears and securing the nine-foot lead line.

"Mr. Lawson, any chance we have a small riding helmet around that I don't know about?"

Lawson pondered momentarily. "No, but I have an idea that will do for now."

Returning from the garage, he tossed Augie a pink children's bicycle helmet over the stall door, evoking a quizzical look from the cowboy. Her grandfather had purchased Rose a bike and helmet for her birthday, which was quickly approaching. However, the high-end Trek would remain hidden inside the garage for now.

Lawson slid the stall door fully open, allowing Augie to lead the equine toward the mounting block. Rose stood from the stool, scrunched every muscle she could, and compressed her body as the enormous gray beast brushed by, her thick, powerful muscles flexing in a flashy show of self-assurance.

With the helmet secure, her grandfather walked her to the block on the horse's left side, made some adjustments with the stirrups, and instructed her to place her foot into the ring. She followed that movement by throwing her right leg over the saddle, her toe finding the other stirrup's ring and settling in. She wiped the moisture from her palms on her faded jeans as the horse shifted under its rider's weight, startling Rose momentarily.

Augie held the lead line firmly and marshaled Scarborough from the barn to the adjacent outdoor arena as Rose clutched the western saddle's pommel, grasping the raised knob tightly with both hands. They entered the ring, and the ride was on. Rose's shoulders gradually relaxed downward, her facial muscles loosened, and tension left her tiny body. Round and round they went, with Augie reversing the circle's direction every three trips. She was immersed in the entire experience as her body found its cadence in time with the horse's movement.

"Well, that's all you get for five dollars, Rose. Looks like time's up," said Augie.

She looked longingly at her grandfather and pointed to her back pocket.

"Rose, I'm sorry, honey. I don't have my wallet on me."

She tucked her chin down and gave him the meanest stare she could muster. He raised his arms in mock surrender.

"Augie, you know I'm good for it, right?"

The calculator buttons punched quickly in the cowboy's brain.

"If my math is correct, sir, you could afford approximately twenty million of these at five dollars apiece." Lawson shook a smile onto his face.

"Rose, I think I just got you another ten minutes," said the cowboy.

Augie led Scarborough from the arena back to the stable. Rose carried a broad smile from the barn, past the saucer swing, through the patio, and into the lodge.

"That look tells me all I need to know about how it went," said Lawson. "Thank you, Augie. You went above and beyond, as you always do."

"I don't know for sure what it is, Mr. Lawson—I don't have a lot of experience with kids—but I feel like she *trusts* me, if that's the right word. We… *share* something, I suppose."

"I think you and I know what you share, Augie."

The cowboy looked down.

"Augie, I don't mean that in any negative way. I've known you and your quirks for your entire life. I understand you at a level most people probably don't. I mean, I think she connects with you somehow differently. It's like you two speak the same language, one that none of us understand."

Augie smiled. "Thank you, sir. I appreciate all you have done for me and the opportunity provided by the ranch. I truly do."

"Augie, I could not have asked for a better caretaker of Six Dawns than you. You're like a son to me."

"Thank you…Sir, I don't mean to overstep here, but can I ask how your son ended up a…"

"A murderer?" Lawson said, tilting his chin skyward and exhaling deeply. A long pause hung heavily over the conversation.

"No, it's alright. We may never know what went wrong with Dennis. I attribute it to a couple of things, but then again, I'm no psychologist. From the beginning, when he was young, he and animals did not get along. I remember him dousing a kitten in 10W-40 engine oil at eight. We cleaned the young cat, and she was fine, but it was disturbing as hell, as you could probably imagine.

"Marie and I sent him to a behavioral psychologist, who warned us that he might have an antisocial personality disorder. We made him see a counselor all through high school. Then, junior year, his mom died in the kayaking accident, and he shut down. After that, the thoughts he did share were dark." Lawson paused again.

"He went off to college, and for a while, things seemed better. I encouraged him to schedule an appointment with the counseling department, and he said he would. He was eighteen, so I had no legal right to force him. I'm really not saying all this to assuage my guilt; that will never leave me. I just go back in time and constantly try to find what I did wrong. It's never-ending."

Augie hadn't planned on this earnest of a response; he doubted he was equipped for the current conversation.

"I certainly don't know anything more than you do about how to raise a kid, so I'll just say to you what my grandfather used to tell my dad. *No matter how much we try to be perfect fathers, the guilt will always find us.* We do what we can. Then…well, life happens. Dennis became Dennis. You are a good man, Mr. Lawson. Check that. You're a great man."

Lawson's breathing became labored and his face distressed as he dropped to one knee.

"Mr. Lawson, are you okay?"

"I feel…pressure on my chest…something's wrong," he gasped.

Beads of sweat formed on Lawson's reddening forehead as his facial muscles contracted.

Augie reached quickly to the inside pocket of his denim jacket.

"Nine-one-one, what's your emergency?" He provided the address and requested an ambulance immediately.

Mr. Lawson's chest stopped rising and falling as he lost consciousness. The 911 operator asked Augie if he knew CPR. One of the prerequisites for managing the Six Dawns Ranch was to be current in CPR. After assuring that there was no pulse, he began chest compressions.

Please do not let Rose come outside, he thought.

On cue, Rose appeared on the patio; confusion and fear momentarily met in her expression. She had seen this before. A man performing chest compressions on someone she loved. That person had been her mother, and the individual pounding her chest that day was a paramedic trying in vain to save her.

She watched without expression as the cowboy pressed mercilessly on her grandfather. A sickening sound pierced the air as the first rib cracked.

The Teton County Hospital ambulance arrived in under eight minutes, and two paramedics rushed from the vehicle, each with a black backpack. The medics found them in less than a minute.

"Please step aside, sir," said one of the uniforms as the two professionals moved in coordinated unison.

"He's not breathing, Mark," said the older of the duo. "And I can't find a pulse."

Mark pulled the automated external defibrillator from his bag and powered it on. He quickly peeled the backing off each pad. One was placed below Lawson's right collarbone, while the other was positioned on his left side, slightly below the pectoral muscle.

"Charging. Stand clear," said the automated female voice. "Press shock button now." The paramedic hit the flashing red pad.

"Shock one delivered. Begin CPR," the device robotically responded.

"Eddie, check for a pulse," said Mark.

"It's faint, but I have a pulse."

Mr. Lawson's chest rose and fell ever so slightly. "He's breathing."

"County, Jackson Med 2," Eddie barked into the radio microphone that hung from his chest pocket.

"Jackson Med 2, go ahead," was the immediate reply.

"Med 2 is on scene. One patient. Probable heart attack. Request Life Flight."

"Roger Med 2. Standby."

Eastern Idaho Medical Center in Idaho Falls had world-class cardiac care. It was a two-hour drive, even at high speed, with a siren wailing. The paramedics felt the best chance to save Lawson was to get him to the first-rate facility as soon as possible. This meant traveling by helicopter, which would shorten the trip to under forty-five minutes.

"Med 2, County. Life Flight is on the scene of a rollover accident and unavailable."

"County, contact Teton Search and Rescue and see if they are willing to assist. We need to get the patient to Idaho Falls right now."

"Standby."

After several minutes, the radio crackled back to life.

"Med 2, be advised, Teton Search and Rescue is scrambled. Will be on scene in fifteen."

"Copy that," said Eddie.

They heard it before they saw it. The *whup-whup-whup* of the Bell Jet Ranger broke the mid-morning silence as the cherry-red helicopter streaked low across the Wyoming sky.

Eddie changed radio frequencies. "SAR 1, scene is clear. No power lines. I suggest the car parking pad on the south side."

"Roger that. Dropping in," radioed the pilot.

Rose stood beside the gurney, holding her grandfather's pointer finger. She wiped away the tear trickling down her cheek with the back of her other hand.

The downwash from the enormous rotor blades spawned a tempest of dust before the helicopter settled unsteadily onto the driveway. A nurse and flight doctor emerged, received a quick briefing from the paramedics, and transferred Lawson to the helicopter's stretcher—they were in the air within two minutes of landing. The red Bell Ranger disappeared over Teton Pass, and all was quiet. Quiet, except for the soft whimpering coming from Rose as they walked back inside.

"What happened?" Chloe burst through the front door. She had seen the air ambulance come in low over her house and land on what she surmised was somewhere on Lawson's three hundred acres.

"It's Mr. Lawson," said Augie. "They think he had a heart attack. He's alive, and they're taking him to Idaho Falls."

Rose sat motionless at the kitchen table while Augie rummaged through the pantry, finding the ginger snaps. He piled a plate high with the cookies and slid it toward the whimpering girl. She reached for one and held it between her thumb and forefinger, rolling it back and forth on the table like a wheel. Bits of the treat dropped to the floor as she nibbled her way around the edge.

"Your grandfather is going to be okay, Rose." But as it left his lips, Augie wasn't sure if he should have made this promise.

CHAPTER NINE

At 2 p.m., Augie phoned the hospital. After three transfers and a long hold, a nurse came on the line and explained that Mr. Lawson was stable after undergoing angioplasty surgery to open up an artery blockage. She indicated it was still too early to tell if there were any complications from the cardiac arrest or the procedure, took his phone number, and promised to call with an update in a few hours.

Augie sat, eyes closed, elbows resting on the kitchen table, while his thumbs traced slow circles over his temples. He thought of the ranch being gone in an instant. Of Rose being sent back to Whispering Woods…or somewhere worse. He suddenly considered his mortality. His head jerked up in response to the light pressure on his left shoulder; the depth of the rabbit hole would not be tested.

"Sorry. I didn't mean to scare you," said Chloe softly.

He reached his hand across his body and caressed her fingers.

"You doing okay?" she asked. He nodded.

"Let's get some air," he said, standing.

Rose was balanced on a low branch of an apple tree, sketching, when Augie and Chloe walked outside, crossed the flagstone, and approached her. Anticipating a drawing of Mr. Lawson laid out on a stretcher with medics working on him, they were relieved to observe instead a rather accurate rendering of Princesses Elsa and Anna from *Frozen*. A redhead sat on a horse next to the royals.

"Rose, I spoke to the hospital, and your grandfather just came out of surgery," said Augie. She didn't look up from her notebook. "He's doing well, so hopefully I'll be able to pick him up in the next few days. You doing okay?"

She blew a tuft of scarlet hair from her face, looked up at the cowboy, and fractionally nodded.

"Chloe, I have to run an errand. Could you possibly stay with Rose for an hour?"

"Of course."

Chloe pretended to read from the comfort of a patio lounge chair, but over the top of her book, she watched Rose draw. After thirty minutes, the redhead cautiously approached her with puffy eyes. Rose pointed to the words written on her pad. *Is Augie sure?*

"Sure of what, Rose?"

The redhead put pencil to paper. *Grandpa.*

"Is he going to be okay? Yes, Rose. Yes. Augie talked to the nurse in charge. He is definitely going to be fine. You'll be seeing him real soon." Rose moved closer.

Chloe set her book on the side table and knelt next to Rose. She extended her arms outward, and the redhead fell into her embrace, burying her head in Chloe's shoulder.

The pair spent time trading climbs on the rope swing before moving on to the barn, where Chloe taught Rose how to hand-feed a carrot to a horse without forfeiting a finger. Her hushed giggles grew marginally louder with each gobbled-up root.

Rose straddled a hay bale in front of Scarborough's stall and opened her notebook. What sounded like a growl emanated from her throat. She had a stern look as she raised the booklet above her head, directing it toward Chloe, void of any more pristine pages.

The F-250 kicked up a cloud of dust as it turned into the property and transitioned from pavement to gravel. Augie parked, carried two bags inside, and hollered for the girls before spotting them by the pond.

"Rose, come here. I have a few surprises for you," said Augie. She wasn't afforded many surprises and came bounding over.

The first item produced was a proper children's horseback riding helmet, which earned a smile. Next came a cardboard box. Rose opened it and dug out a pair of genuine leather cowgirl boots embroidered with colorful wildflowers. Her smile blossomed as she pulled them on. The final gift was an artist's sketch pad—including a set of colored pencils—and each page was stamped with a small rainbow in the top left corner. Rose could hardly contain herself. She wrapped her arms around Augie's waist as far as they would reach and excitedly stomped her boots on the dusty ground before vanishing back into the barn to the bale of hay and Scarborough.

"Did you know Rose was about out of blank canvas in her sketchbook, Augie?" He nodded.

"Mr. Lawson and I were looking through it a few days ago, and I noticed there were only a few pages left."

"That, along with the boots and helmet, just might put you in contention for a Father of the Year award, cowboy," said Chloe with a wink.

Augie's cell phone vibrated just after 5 p.m. It was the nurse from earlier in the day.

"Mr. West, I have someone here who would like to say hello," she said.

Augie was relieved to hear Lawson's groggy voice on the other end of the line. He sounded exhausted and complained about discomfort in his chest from the compressions—including a broken rib—but he had survived.

The nurse took back the phone and explained that Lawson should be able to be released in the next forty-eight hours. She advised Augie to begin making arrangements and promised to call him the next day to confirm the discharge time. He thanked her, disconnected the call, and collapsed on the leather wrap-around sofa.

"Would you like a coffee?" Chloe asked.

"That machine costs more than some cars. I don't see either of us working out that puzzle," quipped Augie.

"I think I can figure it out," said Chloe.

"Okay, but if you break it, they don't sell those things at Walmart, so we sure aren't going to be able to replace it before Mr. Lawson returns."

Chloe followed the three-step instructions on the Siphon Bar and had two steaming cups of java ready in a few minutes.

"So, you think he's really going to be okay?" she asked.

"I do. Based on that call and how the angioplasty went, I think he'll be tired, maybe a bit scared, but fine. He did have one request for the day after tomorrow, though, and that request tells me all I need to know about how well he is feeling." Augie let the statement hang playfully.

"*So,* what did he say?"

"He wants to fly home."

"As in charter a private plane?" asked Chloe. "He certainly can afford to."

"No, more like I'll go get him in the Super Cub. Idaho Falls Regional Airport is a short drive from the hospital."

"You have to be kidding."

"I'm as serious as a heart attack, Chloe." She shook her head.

"Too soon?"

"Yes, too soon," she replied.

"The nurse was right there when he told me he wanted to fly home. She didn't seem to have any issue with it."

They sat in comfortable silence for several minutes, each recalling the events of the surreal day.

"Will Rose stay with you tonight?" asked Chloe.

"No, I think I'll sleep here at the lodge. The last thing she needs is a change in her routine."

"Would you like me to stay over and help with anything?"

So many ways to interpret that, thought Augie. *But only two ways to answer it.* The pause was too prolonged, but if Chloe was growing restless, she didn't show it. *How long can I keep drawing in one sip of coffee?*

"I would like that, Chloe. I'll make up a bed in a guest room." Chloe smiled.

"Great. How about I head home and pick up some things for the night? I'll also swing by the grocery for burgers, hot dogs, and onion rings if that sounds good for dinner."

"Maybe a side of mac and cheese for Rose?" said Augie. "And how about picking out a couple of nice cabernets? I don't want to select one from his wine cellar and accidentally choose a thousand-dollar bottle." Augie removed his American Express Centurion Black card and handed it to Chloe. "On the ranch tonight."

"These Amex Black cards don't have a limit, do they?" asked Chloe.

"Correct. But I will find you if you get any ideas." They both grinned.

"I might be the first person ever to buy hot dogs using this," she said as she held it up, waving it in the air. "I'll see you in a few hours and check on Rose on my way out."

Augie lit the ultra-high-end Hestan grill as Chloe appeared with two glasses of wine. As the stainless-steel grates heated, Augie drew in a sip and swirled the deep-red velvet over his taste buds. Chloe watched, hopeful that she hadn't just blown two hundred dollars that was not hers.

"I detect earthy blackberry and currant notes with a floral-tobacco finish," Augie said, trying to keep a straight face. "Actually, it's quite delicious, but I can't pick out certain flavors like Mr. Lawson can."

Chloe swirled her goblet, held it up to the daylight, and observed the viscosity and the rich, raspberry-purple color as the syrupy legs crawled slowly down the sides. Unlike Augie, Chloe did know a thing or two about vino. While living in San Francisco, she and her ex-husband made the fifty-mile trip to Napa several times a year. She had done tours and tastings at Stags' Leap, Beaulieu Vineyard, Cakebread Cellars, Nickel & Nickel, and Far Niente. Chloe had taken a three-day sommelier course, completing the first designation—Introductory Sommelier.

"You know, I think your observations are right on, Augie. Not so much the blackberry and tobacco commentary, more the quite delicious statement." Chloe always seemed to be smiling.

Rose was buried deep in her new sketchbook but seemed to be, at least physically, less distant from Chloe and Augie than she usually would be. As they moved around the patio, so did she—ever so subtly. Augie leaned in toward Chloe and suggested they test a theory.

As he whispered the plan in her ear, he gathered the same scent as the night at the Whiskey Wheel and was transported back in time. The romantic nights on his bearskin rug in front of a blazing fire. The steaming hot winter baths together, candles providing the only light. Her soft caress. *Oh God, how long is this going to last?* Augie had no idea if he had just whispered the plan or verbalized a soft-porn scene in Chloe's ear.

Chloe responded, "Let's do it."

Well, that's no help in figuring out what I just said, he thought.

"Okay, so what do you think we should do?" asked Augie.

"We should go with your plan and move to the rope swing. Let's see if Rose follows us."

The pair strolled toward the swing, carrying on an intentional, artificial conversation during their short passage. They laughed at faux jokes, making no eye contact with Rose as she side-eyed them again. The couple then moved past the swing to the apple tree and looked further, feigning interest in the barn. Augie reached down and grabbed a small stone from the edge of the pond. He released it with a flick of his wrist and watched as it skipped four times across the glassy water. When they turned, Rose was sitting on the saucer swing, not facing the home as usual but facing the pond.

"I think she likes us," Chloe whispered.

Augie returned to the grill and placed the burgers and dogs in their respective places, ensuring a healthy distance between them, as he was always a bit neurotic about raw hamburger meat touching other food. Chloe had taken care of the onion rings and the mac and cheese. She felt pressure to provide the proper sustenance to a growing child under their brief watch. Carbs and protein were accounted for out of the four food groups, and onion rings loosely fit in the fruits and vegetables band, although likely under a technicality. Chloe searched the refrigerator, trying to find the fourth representative—dairy—the easy way. *How on earth does this man not have milk?* The closest thing was cream.

Chloe stepped out onto the deck. She was panicked. Having never raised a child, she felt compelled to get this right.

"Rose, honey, would you like a nice glass of cream with dinner?"

Rose looked up and then back down at her sketchbook, ignoring the ridiculous question.

The mac and cheese has cream! Chloe thought with some relief and decided to count that for dairy.

Augie took requests from the two girls, and he plated accordingly. They sat outside at the rectangular glass table, set immaculately by Chloe, and Augie poured what remained of the wine before giving a simple but thoughtful toast. He acknowledged the two ladies, Mr. Lawson, and the horses.

Rose shook her head. *You aren't done.*

She and Augie were in a stare-down, but only one knew what it was concerning. Rose pulled her sketch pad from the empty chair to her left and wrote, *WOLF.*

"Yes, of course, I was about to include Aurora in the toast. And to Aurora," he said, raising his glass higher.

Rose broke a small piece off the hot dog and subtly slipped it to the comrade at her feet. The mood around the table was complicated. Mr. Lawson had almost died. Rose was, well, Rose. Augie and Chloe were yet to be determined. Their individual emotional watersheds were drained by the day.

Chloe uncovered a surprise offering of cupcakes, and the redhead's eyes lit up at the tasty iced snacks.

"Rose, have you ever seen the Harry Potter movies?" asked Augie. She shook her head.

He looked at Chloe. "Mr. Lawson loves the series and has the box set in his media cabinet. Let's introduce Rose to the famous wizard."

"Okay, Rose," said Augie. "We're going to watch an hour of the movie, and then it will be time to get to bed. Agreed?" She nodded.

The redhead was absorbed in the action. She lay on her stomach against the bearskin rug, her chin propped up and nestled into the V created by her palms. Every few minutes, she would belly crawl a few more inches toward the large-screen TV.

Upon Harry and Ron's successful takedown of a troll in defense of Hermione, Augie paused the movie and announced it was time for bed, prompting another stare-down. The cowboy won.

Chloe and Augie shared a nightcap of decaf coffee on the sofa. Her hand brushed against his outer thigh, sending a surge of electricity through his spine.

"Can I ask a personal question?" he said.

"Of course."

"I always thought you'd be the perfect mom. So why didn't you and Steve ever have kids?"

"We tried," Chloe paused. "A pair of miscarriages later, I just couldn't go through it again. A piece of me died with those two little girls. I believe we probably would have tried again if we both hadn't felt the relationship changing for the worse."

"I'm so sorry, Chloe. I shouldn't have asked."

"No, Augie, it's fine." She rested her hand on his knee. "We would have talked about it at some point."

They sipped slowly, neither wanting the night to end. When their mugs were dry, Chloe announced it was time for her to get some shut-eye. She kissed Augie on the cheek and slowly made her way up the grand staircase, looking back with a fading smile. Augie thought he recognized an offer in the gesture but was unsure. If he read this wrong, it would be beyond embarrassing and potentially decimate their relationship. He pulled a throw blanket from the ottoman and stayed put.

Safest way to play this, he thought.

Thankfully, sleep came effortlessly.

CHAPTER TEN

Almost forty-eight hours had passed since the heart attack, and it was time to retrieve Lawson. The hospital had called the previous day and confirmed arrangements for pickup at Idaho Falls Regional Airport.

Augie left the lodge and went through his morning routine, taking the Kubota for a general property check and on to his cottage. He loaded a soft-sided Yeti cooler with an ice pack, three bottles of water, two colas, a bologna sandwich, a zip lock of ginger snaps, and a bag of pretzels. Finally, he snatched the two Bose aviation headsets from their hooks on the living room wall and headed out to the F-250.

Augie's flight planning software indicated that the highest obstacle on his route would be 10,400 feet and include a short stretch where he would need to climb above the Teton's peaks. Due to unseen and potentially deadly updrafts and downdrafts that occur over mountains, it would be advisable to cross two thousand feet above the ridge, low enough not to require oxygen.

Rose wrestled with a formidable hay bale, trying to position it in just the right spot to sit and watch the cowboy preflight the airplane. Augie worked through the checklist, draining small amounts of fuel from the tanks and holding the liquid up to the morning light. Checking for any condensation that may have contaminated the avgas, he nodded with slight satisfaction before topping off the oil and circling the plane counterclockwise, carefully inspecting the ailerons, flaps, and rudder.

"Hey, Rose, wanna help me push the Cub out of the hangar?"

She eagerly sprung to her feet and waited for instruction. Augie pointed to the wing strut on the plane's port side, then moved into position on the opposite flank.

"Ready? One, two, three, push!"

The plane rolled smoothly through the large opening. He took one last loop around the aircraft—the *dummy check*, he called it.

He walked back into the lodge, finding Chloe doing some light cleaning in preparation for Mr. Lawson's return. The housekeeper wasn't scheduled for another three days.

"I'm heading out. I should be back in about three hours or so. Keep an eye on Rose when I start the engine so she doesn't get too close."

"Fly safe, Augie, especially over those big hills," she said.

"'Big hills?' Is that what you call a range whose highest peak is over fourteen thousand feet?"
He smiled.

He checked his seatbelt, doors and windows, circuit breakers, and fuel selector before pushing the throttle in half an inch, yelling, "Clear!" and turning the key, commanding the 150-horsepower engine to roar to life. Augie reviewed the information he had programmed into his iPad for the flight and released the brakes.

The Super Cub was airborne in less than four hundred feet. He climbed and circled back over the ranch, giving a wing waggle to Rose and Chloe below. Then, keying the microphone, he contacted Flight Service and opened his flight plan.

He needed to reach the 12,400-foot crossing altitude quickly, as the towering mountain rose only three miles from his departure point. The strategy was a circling climb west of the ranch until reaching the required height before proceeding with the crossing. As he completed the first 360-degree climbing turn, he glanced at Grand Teton in the distance and briefly watched in awe as snow billowed like smoke from the peak, caught in the brutal winds.

Augie battled the stick, losing four hundred feet of altitude in just a few seconds as the Cub fought through its first downdraft just before reaching the range. He turned slightly, approaching the ridge at a forty-five-degree angle. This provided a safety measure, as he would just need to turn another forty-five degrees to fly away from the high terrain should things become too hazardous with the drafts. The crossing could only be done safely in a small plane like the Super Cub in the morning due to the nausea-inducing drafts coming off the mountains in the afternoon. At their worst, they could force an aircraft into the granite below, leaving only a debris field.

Mr. Lawson better be on time, he thought.

Augie white-knuckled it over the range, finding smooth air in Idaho. Alternating sections of forest and farmland below played a perpetual game of leapfrog as rudderless rivers meandered unknowingly through their competition. A crop duster opened its nozzles a few thousand feet beneath the Cub, blanketing unsuspecting prey in a smokey mist.

He tuned his radio to 135.325 and picked up the Idaho Falls Airport weather. With a southwesterly wind at fourteen knots, he suspected the tower would give him runway 21. Ten miles out, he contacted air traffic control.

"Idaho Falls tower, good morning, Super Cub niner, eight, whiskey, sierra, ten miles to the east, inbound with information alpha." Augie had provided the controller with his type of plane, tail number, and location and confirmed that he had picked up the current weather and altimeter setting.

"Super Cub niner, eight, whiskey, sierra, good morning. Report a two-mile left base for runway 21."

"Wilco," replied Augie, acknowledging the controller's order.

Five minutes later, he reported the two-mile base.

"Super Cub niner, eight, whiskey, sierra, you are cleared to land runway 21, number two, following a Citation. Caution, wake turbulence."

Augie repeated the landing clearance back to the controller, lowered the flaps, and turned final. The Cub touched down on its enormous tundra tires, then settled onto the tail wheel with a shudder.

He brought the plane to a stop at the general aviation terminal and was relieved to see an ambulance parked on the tarmac. *He's on time.*

Mr. Lawson had refused to lie on the gurney in the back and emerged from the passenger seat. Moving slowly, he extended his hand as the cowboy approached.

"I'd hug you, Augie, but let's skip that on account of my broken rib," said Lawson with a slight smile as they shook hands.

"Yeah, sorry about that, sir."

"Are you kidding me, Augie? You
saved my life."

The paramedic provided Augie with some
papers and instructions for the next few days of
recovery and indicated they had coordinated with
Mr. Lawson's cardiologist in Jackson, whom he
would see in three days.

"Let's kick the tires and light the fires," said
Lawson, ready to put Idaho Falls behind him.

"Sounds good to me. Just so you are prepared,
we will probably have a few minutes of healthy
bumps crossing the range."

Augie helped his passenger into the Cub before
entering the cockpit and securing the door. He
went through a similar start sequence as before,
contacted Idaho Falls ground control, and received
taxi instructions. They were number one for
departure and airborne less than three minutes from
engine start.

"How's Rose doing with everything?"
asked Lawson.

The Bose headset's noise-canceling feature did
their jobs over the roar of the Cub's engine.

"She seems to be doing very well, near as Chloe
and I can tell. We all stayed over at the lodge last
night. No problems."

"All?" Lawson repeated slowly. "Is there something between you and Chloe again?"

"It was nothing like that last night. She's leaving in less than two months anyway, so I don't see how anything could work out." Lawson grinned, and Augie changed the subject.

Eventually, they found themselves approaching the mountain range at the same forty-five-degree angle, this time with the wind on the plane's tail, and aside from two minutes of moderate turbulence, the crossing was smooth. After clearing the Tetons, Augie pulled the power back, allowing the plane to descend quickly toward the valley floor. He overflew the ranch, observing the American flag flying on the pole in the front drive. The Stars and Stripes indicated a southwestern wind and a landing from the north.

"A greaser, Augie," said Mr. Lawson upon touchdown. The cowboy received the compliment with a smile.

When the propeller had stopped, Rose ran toward the plane, and her grandfather climbed out, greeting her with a monumental hug despite the probability of triggering rib pain. Chloe acknowledged Augie's safe return likewise, holding the embrace for what some would say was awkwardly long, but not the cowboy.

They rolled the Cub into the hangar and buttoned it up.

"I could use a nap," yawned Lawson.

"Before you do, any special requests for dinner tonight?" asked Chloe.

"How about a taco bar?" he answered, looking at Rose. "Let's take a vote. All in favor."

Hands went up.

"One, two, three, four, five. Wait, there are only four of us here. Rose, you can only vote once," Lawson chuckled.

When the foursome reconvened in Mr. Lawson's kitchen that evening for dinner, sitting front and center on the dining room table next to the carry-out bags from La Taqueria was an orange five-gallon Home Depot bucket. Inside it was a stack of index cards.

Mr. Lawson spoke. "Before we start in on dinner, let me explain the orange pail's significance. This near-death experience has got me thinking…I don't want to get too philosophical on you all, but instead of waiting until something like this happens, everyone should start on their bucket list while they are still healthy. It seems people wait until the end to tick things off that they always wanted to do.

"After dinner, I'd like all of you to fill out three cards, each with a different idea for something on your bucket list. Give it some thought as we eat. And don't consider the expense," he said with a smile.

Rose drew a question mark on her pad and pointed to the orange container.

"Well, a *bucket list* is a term for things you want to do or accomplish before you…before you get too old to be able to do them," her grandfather explained. She nodded slowly.

Rose had never seen so many options for a taco. The kitchen table was bursting with choices. There was lettuce, diced tomatoes, cilantro, jalapeños, green onions, avocado, mango, two kinds of shredded cheese, queso, and three different salsas, one of which was green. For shells, Rose's choices were much more spartan, hard, or soft, and the protein selections were: rotisserie chicken, ground beef, skirt steak, and chorizo.

Augie took a soft shell, applied a dollop of queso to the pliable flour, and used the back of a spoon to evenly spread the golden, cheesy goodness. He then moved on to a hard shell that he proceeded to stuff without discretion. Multiple types of meat were layered in, veggies were compacted to maximize room, and shredded cheese overflowed. Two of the three salsas made their way into the mess. Finally, he reached for the queso-covered soft shell and wrapped it around the hard shell. Rose's mouth hung open as her fascination with the taco-building process turned to something between bewilderment and horror. Then he repeated the process with a second taco.

What is wrong with the cowboy?

Rose picked up her sketchbook and wrote a question. She pointed to the meats and flashed the book toward her grandfather. *Which one is horse?*

"Nice try, Rose. We've been through this. You know none of these are horse. We don't eat them. We ride them."

Sure, you don't. She nodded in faux belief.

The redhead showed significantly more decorum in constructing her taco than Augie. She trusted the chicken was chicken and went with that, adding avocado and mango scooped from their ramekins and daintily placed in the shell. She topped it with queso and red salsa. Below her question about the horse meat, she wrote a new question: *My wine?* She knew this would generate an anxious response and delighted in it.

A somewhat concerned Lawson looked at Augie. "What's been going on since I left? Only two days ago, might I add."

"Mr. Lawson, let me clarify," said Chloe, eager to clear up the misunderstanding. "Yesterday, when I went to the grocery store to get a nice bottle of wine for your return, I told Rose I would get her some sparkling cider to celebrate with. That's what she means by *wine*."

"Thank God," said Lawson.

When everyone's plates had been satisfactorily prepared, Augie poured himself and Chloe a glass of cabernet and filled Rose's goblet with cider. Lawson would be drinking water this week.

"Welcome home, Mr. Lawson. It's great to have you back," Augie said, raising his glass.

"Thank you again for saving my life, Augie, and to you both for caring for Rose the past two days. On that note, I could use some help around here for the next few weeks. Chloe, would you be interested in some part-time work to help around the ranch? You can stay in the guest room if you're interested. And I completely understand if you want to pass."

"I'm glad to help with anything you need, but no payment is necessary," she replied.

"Thank you, Chloe. Let's talk in the morning."

Augie reached for his taco, triggering Rose to slam her ubiquitous sketchbook on the table. The cowboy froze, mouth open, taco suspended between his chin and the table.

"What is it, Rose?" asked Mr. Lawson.

She wrote, *Grace.*

"Would you like to say grace, Rose?" questioned Chloe.

She pointed at the cowboy. *There is no way he knows grace.*

Rose wasn't doing this with any villainous intent. On the contrary, she was beginning to fancy him and was putting him on the spot for her entertainment.

The chance of Augie remembering a formal grace was remote. He winged it with *Thou's, Lords, Thanks*, and a *baby Jesus*. A *blasphemy* made it in there; although he had no idea what it meant, hopefully neither did Rose. He lifted his head, avoiding eye contact with the girl, and pointed skyward.

What is he doing? thought Rose.

He had played college football with some guys who seemed pretty religious, and upon scoring a touchdown, those players would look up toward the heavens, raise an arm high, and extend their index finger. Augie figured there must be something sacred about the ritual back then, so he added it to the grace. He could feel the emerald-green stare coming from the redhead to his right.

"Thank you, Augie. That was, uhm…lovely," said Lawson.

The sketchbook hit the table again. She wrote, *Gloves?*

"What do you mean, Rose?" asked her grandfather. She pointed to the plates of sloppy tacos and back to the word in her book.

"You want to wear gloves while you eat tonight, honey?" She nodded. "I don't think I have any food service-type gloves in the house." Rose crossed her arms and stared at him.

"Augie, do you mind going out to the hunting supply cabinet? I think you'll find what Rose is looking for," said Lawson.

Augie returned through the garage door less than a minute later, holding a fresh pair of black nitrile gloves from a box Mr. Lawson kept with his gun cleaning kit.

Rose nodded in appreciation, slipped the size large gloves on her size extra small hands, and worked her way through the taco like an expert. Aurora gave up on the possibility of her accidentally dropping any morsels and moved on to a sure thing—Augie.

When taco night ended, Rose produced her sketchbook and flashed a drawing at the adults. It was a young wizard with a lightning bolt scar on his forehead.

"Harry Potter?" Mr. Lawson asked. Rose nodded.

"We introduced Rose to the Hogwarts School of Witchcraft last night. I'm betting Rose wants to finish the movie," Augie said, producing a nod from the girl.

"Magnificent idea! To Hogsmeade Station we go. But first, everyone needs to add their index cards to the bucket," Lawson shouted.

Pens and lined cards were passed around the table. Three sets of eyes turned skyward in thoughtful consideration, the wooden ceiling beams garnering the most attention they had received since the builders had constructed the home. Rose raised a fist, slowly unbent one finger at a time, then finally extended her thumb. Mr. Lawson knew what she was asking.

"No, Rose. Three things for the bucket, not five. Nice try. We'll talk about possibly adding more later."

After fifteen minutes, the large pail contained twelve cards.

"Okay. We're going to pull one now, then we will put on the movie," said Mr. Lawson.

"Rose, you do the honors, please. Close your eyes, and no peaking."

The redhead's lids closed, and the orange bucket swallowed her scrawny arm. Her latched eyes ripened into a squint as she fumbled through the cards.

"Any day now," quipped Augie.

Rose's hand retreated from the bucket, coincidentally revealing one of her index cards.

"Hmm, are you sure your eyes were closed?" asked her grandfather. A furious nod said *yes*.

"Well, let's see it."

Pet eagle was written on the paper.

"Rose, that would be illegal. I'm afraid you cannot keep an eagle as a pet," said her grandfather. She shook her head.

Rose reached for her pen and inserted an *an* between the two words. The three adults exchanged calculating looks.

Mr. Lawson spoke. "That could be a tough one." Rose's head dropped. "But, let me give it some thought."

With that, Chloe pressed play on the DVD, and the wizarding world reawakened.

"Shh!" Rose produced the closest thing to a word she had uttered since arriving at the ranch. She glared at Augie and her grandfather, who had been carrying on a hushed conversation during the movie.

"Sorry. We'll try to keep it down," said the cowboy.

"As I was saying, Augie," whispered Lawson as he covered his mouth with a hand. "Feel free to take over the other empty guest bedroom upstairs. You've been here a lot helping with Rose late into the evenings, and with me somewhat laid up, it might be easier for you to have a room and some of your clothes here."

"Thank you, sir. I just might take you up on that."

CHAPTER ELEVEN

It was late afternoon the following day; Chloe and Rose had just returned from grocery shopping when the home phone rang. Lawson was recuperating in the recliner, covered with a beige cashmere throw. He pressed the speaker button, and an automated voice came on the line.

"Hello, this is a call from…" The robotic message paused while a recording from a human said, "Dennis Lawson." Then, the automation picked back up. "…an inmate at the United States Penitentiary at Marion. Press 1 to accept the charges."

Rose spun toward the sound, mouth agape, her face turning ashen. Mr. Lawson was frozen as the recording repeated. With a sudden heave, the contents of Rose's stomach splattered on the floor. Lawson immediately disconnected the call.

Chloe grabbed the little girl's hand and walked her to the sofa. She wet a paper towel, filled a glass tumbler with cold water, and sat beside Rose as Mr. Lawson moved to the couch. They sandwiched the redhead between them, neither sure of what to say, while Lawson dabbed the towel at Rose's lips and chin, his hand shaking. Her hollow stare from several weeks ago had returned. The redhead's eyes began moving randomly at breakneck speed; her breathing was shallow and rapid. She was back in the hotel room in Chicago.

Once Chloe and Lawson had Rose settled on the couch with pillows and a blanket, they walked out to the back patio.

"Have you spoken with him since he was sentenced?"

"You know about the situation with Dennis, Chloe?"

"I'd heard a little from some friends still in the valley, and Augie filled in the rest last week."

"I assume way more people know about Dennis than let on," said Lawson. "But, no, I haven't spoken to him. No interest either."

"Any idea why he would be calling?" she asked.

"No, but I'm sure he'll call back. I just need to decide if I'm going to answer," he paused briefly, then continued, "Rose seems to be doing better since coming to the ranch. It's a million miles from the horror she experienced in Chicago."

"This is probably going to be a setback, but something triggering was bound to happen at some point," offered Chloe. Lawson nodded, then pulled his cell phone from his pants pocket.

He called Teton Valley Psychological Services and moved Rose's next counseling appointment up two days before making a second call, this one to Augie, who was somewhere working on the property. He prepared the cowboy for what to expect when he returned to the lodge.

Mr. Lawson woke up early and decided he would confront the call from Dennis head-on, assuming if it came again, it would come at the same time as yesterday.

He and Chloe met over breakfast to discuss her new ranch role, and she reluctantly consented to receive payment. Her first job was to drive him to his cardiologist appointment that morning, and her second task was to ensure Rose was not in the lodge later that afternoon when the call from Dennis might come.

His doctor's appointment was routine. He was cleared for light activity and could begin moving around the property, but there would be no heavy exertion or lifting for the next few weeks. Chloe received a grocery list from the physician assistant for permitted healthy provisions: vegetables, fruits, beans, nuts, salmon, and sardines.

"Where's the sausage?" Mr. Lawson asked.

"Sausage is not your friend," fired Chloe. "You've eaten your last one, I'm afraid." Lawson pouted playfully.

They left the hospital parking lot at 11 a.m. and returned to the ranch.

"Let's stop at the Heart Attack Grill for some burgers and fries," Lawson said. Chloe ignored him.

"How about King Sushi, Mr. Lawson?"

"Fine," he said begrudgingly.

"I'll get Rose out of the house this afternoon," said Chloe. "She'll help me grocery shop for you."

"I've got another idea as well," said Lawson, "and it will also check the box on the card Rose pulled from the bucket. Let me call the Teton Raptor Center. I've donated enough money over the years to The Raptor Fund that I should be able to get you two in for one of their private hands-on experiences, and they're bound to have an eagle of some kind."

They stopped for carry-out sushi, picked up some extra for Rose, and returned to the property.

"Rose, we're home," hollered her grandfather. The redhead appeared at the top of the stairs, mounted the banister, and slid down.

"Yikes, Rose!" her grandfather said with a disapproving look. "You're either going to kill yourself or give me another heart attack." She shrugged, offering a weak apology.

Mr. Lawson was still shaking his head when Chloe set up three placemats and laid a sushi platter on each.

"Have a seat, Rose. We brought you some lunch," said Chloe. "Have you ever had sushi?" Rose shook her head, eyeing the three plates uneasily.

"It's fish, rice, vegetables, and seaweed. One has shrimp." Mr. Lawson added.

You expect me to eat this?

She inspected the first plate more closely.

A ball of rice rolled in mouse droppings? These people cannot be serious. Did she say seaweed? No way the cowboy would touch this.

Rose headed to the refrigerator, removed a hotdog from its pack, and bit off a piece. Then she wiggled the remaining dog in their direction. *Now, this is lunch.*

The redhead observed from a safe distance as the two adults worked their way through the Japanese cuisine.

Why are they eating with sticks? Are we out of forks? She opened the kitchen drawer, looked in, counted, then counted them again before moving on to the spoons and knives—twelve of everything except only eleven forks. She looked in the dishwasher. It was empty. She removed all the utensils from the drawer and laid them on the counter.

Three, six, nine, twelve. Three, six, nine, twelve. Three, six, nine, eleven.

Chloe and Mr. Lawson watched her as they ate, and he whispered about obsessive-compulsive counting behavior.

The redhead removed one fork from its neatly arranged formation and held it in the air, waving it dramatically like a wand over the others. Her lips moved, but no words surfaced. Her eyes fluttered closed.

"Harry Potter," Chloe said softly.

"Hermione?" he offered.

Lawson picked up the fork under his napkin— he usually became impatient with chopsticks. With Rose mid-spell, eyes still closed, he silently deposited the utensil on the counter in front of her. The redhead's lips came to a stop, and her eyelids swept open. She counted. *Three, six, nine, twelve!* Rose shrieked. She looked at the arrangement before her, then at her grandfather and Chloe.

Are you all not seeing this?

"What's going on over there, Rose?" asked Mr. Lawson.

I'm clearly a wizard is what's going on over here! She shook her head. *Muggles.*

Mr. Lawson had secured a 1 p.m. private encounter at the Teton Raptor Center for Chloe and Rose, where a force of energy named Meadow greeted them. She was Chloe fifteen years ago. A red paisley bandana formed a knot holding her high ponytail, and vintage mauve-tinted octagon glasses sat perched on her nose. A floral halter top, retro army green surplus jacket, and bell-bottom jeans completed the ensemble. She seemed more suited for an incense and candle shop than the raptor center.

A shrill descending whine ripped from an opening door behind the receptionist's desk. Belle, an eastern screech owl, sat perched on the falconer's closed fist. Rose stared, transfixed by the mesmerizing reddish-brown bird. With each subtle movement, Belle's elaborate banded and spotted plumage patterns changed like a kaleidoscope.

"You must be Rose," said Jack with a wide smile. She nodded, still staring at the owl.

"Follow me, and we'll get started." They walked through the swinging door and into the barn.

"We do three things here at the center. Education, research, and rehabilitation. When it comes to the education piece, our best teachers are our rescued raptors. Each of these majestic birds has a story: car strikes, train strikes, vision loss, broken wings, orphaned. Some cannot be released back into the wild and stay with us permanently, but we aim to rehabilitate as many as possible and return them to their natural habitat."

They met a barn owl, a red-tailed hawk, and a great horned owl before Jack's partner appeared behind them with a large brown and white, gold-feathered raptor.

"This is Misty. She's a golden eagle, about ten years old, and came to us with a right-wing injury," she said.

An eagle! thought Rose.

She continued, "I heard you wanted to pet an eagle someday, Rose. Is that true?" Rose nodded excitedly.

"Okay, well, here's your chance. Come stand by my side, and you can gently touch her feathered wing."

Silky softness saturated Rose's tiny fingertips as she followed the raptor's plumage down her wing to her tail feathers.

The magic orange bucket really works!

"Rose, do you want to hold Belle for me?" asked Jack.

She looked at Chloe, who nodded her approval.

"Okay. We're going to slip this gauntlet over your hand and arm. It will protect you from her talons. She is so tiny, you probably don't need it. But to be safe, we'll have you wear it."

Jack gingerly placed the owl onto the brown leather glove, and Rose's eyes swelled.

"Is she a baby?" asked Chloe.

"No, she's about eight years old. The screech owl is one of the smallest owl species in North America. Rose, what do you think she likes to eat?" She shrugged.

"How do frogs, salamanders, and insects sound?" She wrinkled her nose, a grimace taking over her face.

Rose watched in awe as Belle rotated her head two hundred seventy degrees, surveying her environment. The owl whined. *Almost like a horse*, she thought. Softly, Rose tried to mimic the sound. Belle turned toward her and mirrored Rose's version.

"Again, Rose," said Jack softly, staring intently at the owl. He reached for his phone and tapped on the camera to record what was playing out for the first time in his fifteen years working with raptors.

Rose recreated her own whine. Belle copied.

The cardiologist had told Mr. Lawson to begin walking for at least thirty minutes a day. He spent almost a half hour pacing his living room, not so much to comply with the doctor's orders but to burn off the nervous energy in anticipation of a call from Dennis.

At two o'clock, it came.

"Hello, this is a call from…" The robotic voice paused while a recording from his son said, "Dennis

Lawson." The automation picked back up. "…an inmate at the United States Penitentiary at Marion. Press 1 to accept the charges." He punched 1.

"Hello," Mr. Lawson said hesitantly. The line was momentarily silent.

"I wasn't sure if you'd pick up. How are you?" asked Dennis.

"How am I? I'm fine, Dennis."

"Matthew told me you had a heart attack." Matthew was Dennis's second cousin.

"You talked to Matthew?"

"Yeah, we catch up from time to time. He just thought I should know."

Silence.

"And how's my little girl doing? Man, do I miss her."

"You mean your daughter, whose mother you murdered in front of her? She's doing great. Witnessing a homicide had very little effect on her. How do you think she's doing, Dennis!"

Mr. Lawson could feel his heart pounding in his chest.

"She's mute, and her best friend is a hitching post."

"Can I talk to her?" Dennis asked.

"Absolutely not. It'll be her decision when she turns eighteen, but right now, it's mine."

"I could be out in less than twenty years. I want to rebuild a life with her in it."

"Dennis, you didn't care for her when she was a child, and now, after murdering her mother, you're looking forward to some kind of reconciliation? Are you delusional?"

"Look, Dad, we all make mistakes. I want Rose back in my life."

"A mistake, Dennis, is leaving a carton of milk out to spoil. You didn't make a mistake."

"Well, the guard is pointing at his watch, so I will need to get going. One last thing. My cellmate was asking me about growing up on the ranch. He was asking how much I think all that land is worth. What do you think?"

"What?" asked Mr. Lawson.

"The ranch. I was just wondering what it's valued at now."

"Dennis, don't call here again." With that, Mr. Lawson ended the call.

Rose and Chloe finished up the raptor experience and headed to Whole Foods, where Chloe worked through Mr. Lawson's list while Rose went on a scavenger hunt for food-sampling stations around the store. She delighted in her kiwi find. The sweet and salty uncured pepperoni slices were more than acceptable. However, a blue cheese-stuffed olive triggered her gag reflex, causing her to spit it back into its tiny cup and hand it over to a store employee.

No, fine sir, those should not be for sale.

Rose found a cheese board that met her culinary standards.

The pepperoni would go nicely with this.

She spotted the coffee sampling station and glanced left and right. This was her chance; she had four options. She eyed the dark Columbian roast, and the description on the chalkboard mentioned *chocolatey*. Rose needed not to look any further. *Here goes.* She spat the mouthful onto the floor. *Does this store understand what chocolate even is?*

Chloe emerged from an aisle and spotted Rose standing by the small puddle of dark liquid.

"Rose, tell me you didn't just try coffee."

Okay, I didn't try coffee. The redhead attempted to wait out Chloe. Chloe stared. Rose then went with the *but* argument.

She frantically pointed to the word chocolate on the board.

"So you tried it but thought it was hot chocolate, Rose?"

Yes, that was it. Exactly. She nodded feverishly.

"Get some of those napkins from the counter and clean that mess up."

Chloe texted Mr. Lawson from the car to confirm it was alright to return home. A yellow thumbs-up emoji flashed on her iPhone.

A short drive later, they pulled into the lodge's parking pad, and Rose immediately sprung from the car to help with the grocery bags.

I hope Chloe does not tell Grandpa about the chocolate coffee.

"So, Mr. Lawson, did you know Rose is fond of Columbian dark roast?"

"Huh?"

"Oh, nothing."

Lawson shook his head, returning to his crossword puzzle. Chloe winked at Rose.

Rose was sketching her whittled owl when Augie returned from town, having picked up some fencing supplies. He looked at Mr. Lawson, trying to decipher any sign of a conversation with Dennis. Lawson stood and nodded at Augie to follow him outside. They crossed the flagstone patio and continued to the barn.

"He called?" asked Augie. Lawson nodded.

"His cousin Matthew spoke to Dennis and told him about the heart attack…I can't quite believe it, but the man actually thinks he can have a relationship with Rose when he gets out of prison. Dennis only wants a relationship with her for one reason—money. I'm sure he has some scheme about getting his hands on an inheritance Rose might be left with. His final question was asking about how much the ranch is currently worth. This was asked under the pretense of a cellmate's *curiosity* about his family. He can't even hide his greed." Augie slowly shook his head in disbelief.

"So, how did you end it with him?"

"I told him never to call here again and hung up. Part of me is concerned that Rose will want to reconnect with him on some level when she gets older. I know he's my son, and as hard as this is to say…he's evil. Despite that, I can't help but think there is a chance she will want to believe he has changed and can fill a void that a parent can only fill. I could see him trying to brainwash her into believing her mother was at fault."

"I understand your fear, sir, but I'd give Rose some credit for making the right decision when the time comes. She's a smart girl, and what she saw in Chicago is never going away."

"No, it's not…Augie, remember when you told me Rose was lucky to have me?" The cowboy nodded. "She's lucky to have you."

CHAPTER TWELVE

Mr. Lawson's recovery was progressing, and his cardiologist appointment provided positive news. Aside from taking a nap every afternoon and limiting some of his physical activity, he had returned to much of his prior lifestyle.

Chloe had undertaken additional responsibilities on the ranch and stayed more than busy when not keeping tabs on the redhead. Rose had broken in her new helmet on Scarborough, and Augie had transitioned to riding Winston while leading her; thus, the pace had slightly quickened. Rose felt an even greater sense of independence as she proudly sat high in the saddle, no longer needing a walking escort.

During one ride, Augie noticed her constantly looking down.

"Rose, you should be looking where you're going." She glanced up and nodded before lowering her head again. It wasn't due to poor riding technique; Rose just couldn't take her eyes off the intricate floral pattern of her new cowgirl boots.

Augie took Rose to one of the Six Dawn's ponds and began her indoctrination into the refined art of fly fishing. He explained that to many, it was an almost religious experience and required technique, patience, strategy, and detailed observation. Augie pointed out several mayflies, with yellow wings upright like sails, floating on the pond. He opened the fly box and had Rose choose one that most replicated the insects he had just shown her. She meticulously ran her eyes up and down the rows, looking for a match, eventually selecting a Blue Dun fly.

"Excellent choice, Rose! I'd have gone with the same."

Augie removed the fly and demonstrated how to tie it to the line.

A much too complicated process for just tying a knot, thought Rose.

The cowboy explained the purpose of the small loops and circles that secured the delicate fly to the tippet material at the end of the fishing line. During those first few outings, Rose caught far more iris petals and sagebrush than she did fish. As the braided nylon whipped overhead, it would lose momentum as it passed behind her, tumbling toward the earth, the hook lodging in some unsuspecting vegetation.

Once the morning fishing interest dwindled, they would walk to the Snake River, where Rose would lie on her back, hands cupped behind her head, scanning the sky for bald eagles. On a good day, she would spot a raptor and feverishly search for its mate. On a great day, she would spy multiple eagles soaring like a loose squadron of fighter jets.

They would always end their excursions just before lunch with a contest—Augie had taught Rose how to skip a stone across the water. He had explained that it all started with the perfect rock. It had to be flat, light, and fit in her palm. Augie curled her index finger into the proper position and drove her arm along the correct plane. Her first dozen attempts concluded with a total of zero skips. She tucked her upper lip inside her lower one and blew in frustration, her scarlet bangs momentarily defying gravity. He made a few changes to her wrist position and demonstrated the technique himself. She tried again. The compressed mineral matter hit the water at the perfect angle and darted forward twice before disappearing below the surface. She squealed.

Again, again!

Augie held several assorted stones in his hand, and she took them like ginger snaps, one after the other, each proceeding to skip at least one time.

By the third day, the competition had grown fierce. They both chose five stones and agreed that the total combined skips would determine the winner. Augie asked Rose what the prize would be; she drew on her pad for several minutes, then flipped it toward the cowboy. He stared at the rather accurate sketch for a moment, thinking.

He nodded. "If it's okay with Mr. Lawson. But Rose, before you get too excited, no one has ever beaten me."

It was a heavyweight bout. According to the tally on Rose's sketch pad, they were tied at ten skips apiece, entering the second to last round. Rose's heart raced as Augie opened the fourth with a triple, and she followed with a deuce—thirteen to twelve. Rose initiated the final round, flicking her wrist and leaning after the stone, willing it to glide across the still water. It slapped the surface, rose once, fell, then ascended a final time—thirteen to fourteen. Augie stepped to the water's edge, and the redhead held her breath—rosy cheeks puffed out. The cowboy swung his arm, and at the last second, he warped his wrist ever so slightly downward.

Dunk. The sound of second place. He hung his head in mock anguish as her emerald eyes grew heroic. She ran back to her sketch pad and pointed to the drawing.

"Yes, Rose, I'll ask your grandfather if I can take you up in the Super Cub."

The drawing of the Cub had been torn from the book and accompanied her everywhere. Any opportunity she had to remind the cowboy of his failure on the pond and the ensuing consequences, she did. Augie had asked Mr. Lawson privately about the possibility of taking Rose flying, and without hesitation, he had provided an emphatic yes.

"Rose, I'm sorry, but your grandfather doesn't want you flying. You know, for your safety and all."

She flipped the drawing over and wrote one word: *LIAR*. He stared at the letters, then at the expressionless girl.

God, she's good, he thought.

"Rose, the thing is, it's a lot of responsibility taking a child up in an airplane. I mean, things can go wrong. Do you understand?" Augie had some natural trepidation about taking her up and something disastrous happening.

She didn't crack. Her green eyes had stopped looking through him and now looked into him. Augie fumbled with his phone, checking the following day's weather.

"Okay, a bet is a bet. We'll go up tomorrow at 8 a.m. If you're not awake and ready at that time, no flight. Got it?"

She nodded. *I got it, cowboy. You make sure you're up.*

Morning came, and unfortunately for Augie, the forecasted valley fog that would have canceled the flight had not appeared. *Maybe she won't wake up on time*, he thought.

At 7 a.m., he descended the staircase, started the coffee, and headed to the hangar to preflight the Cub. She was sitting with her book on a hay bale directly in front of the large sliding door.

"Well, I see you're up early." Rose nodded.

The horses stirred as the heavy door slid along its tracks, permitting the sun's rays to wake the Super Cub inside. Augie went through his checklist methodically, with Rose following every step. He called out each item on the list, allowing her to partake in the process. Augie had Rose check the fuel sample for water, explaining that if condensation was in the tube, the clear water would separate from the blue-tinted fuel. Next, she stretched tall on her tippy toes and tugged on the flaps, ensuring a solid connection. They inspected the propeller to be sure there were no significant nicks, and when the pair was satisfied the airplane was in good flying condition, they pushed it out of its home and squeezed in; Rose sat in the back seat and Augie in the front.

The plane started on the first turn of the key, and Augie taxied out to the grass strip. They bumped along the rough runway, and when the airspeed reached forty knots, Augie pulled back on the stick. A cackle met a giggle and exploded through Augie's headset.

He banked the aircraft softly left, away from the mountain range, and they followed the Snake River south. Then, crossing Hoback Junction, he descended to five hundred feet.

"Look out your window, Rose. Do you see all that whitewater just below you?" She nodded. "Keep an eye on that section as we circle it, and you're bound to see some tourists go for an unplanned swim." Augie was orbiting over one of the most famous rapids in this section of the river—Lunch Counter. Then, on cue, a yellow, urethane nine-person raft appeared above the rapid. The guide sitting in the back strained to get the correct entry angle, but the powerful river had other ambitions.

He had misjudged the rapid and unintentionally set up for a hero line—the route with the lowest odds of success. The bow rose skyward on the first large swell, crashed down into the following trough, and then climbed again, now at the mercy of the river. The raft kicked forty-five degrees left, forcing the side tube into the next oncoming wave. Reversing his starboard paddle, the guide tried to force the bow back downstream, but the raft reared up, and the dominoes began to fall. One after the other, blue-helmeted tourists flailed over the side and into the strong current.

Rose was delighted by the action down below. Her forefinger was up against the glass, counting the rafters, and once she was sure all eight, plus the guide, had made it to safety, she smiled. *What's next, cowboy?*

They continued south, chasing and overtaking a cattle hauler down US 89. Reaching Alpine Airpark, nestled on the banks of the Palisades Reservoir, the Cub banked west and turned for home.

"Rose, see the pole between your legs?" Augie swiveled his head in time to see her nodding.

"That's called the stick, and it controls the turns, climbs, and descents. Lightly put your right hand on it, and we'll make some turns." With some trepidation, she cupped her palm around the top of it and felt the left and right motions as Augie moved the controls.

"Okay, you try now, real gentle."

Rose applied slight pressure left, and the Cub started a soft bank.

"Great job. Now, the other direction."

She moved the stick to the right and giggled as the aircraft followed her input perfectly.

"I want you to pull back and see what it does."

The Cub started to climb.

"Very good. Push forward."

Rose applied more pressure this time, and her stomach dropped with a tickle as the plane started to dive.

So much fun, this flying stuff!

Augie took back the controls, and the redhead settled in for the scenic flight home. The Cub touched down perfectly, and Augie complimented himself on his landing. "Greaser."

Grease her? she repeated to herself. *What a strange thing to say. The cowboy certainly isn't referring to me, I hope.*

The following morning, Rose requested another stone-skipping contest, with the desired prize being a pony. "Absolutely not," Augie answered. She had settled for *breakfast for dinner*, and they headed out to the Snake with Aurora hot on the heels of the Kubota. Rose took her time collecting the perfect rocks that would win her a banquet of French toast, scrambled eggs, and a cheesy hash brown potato casserole.

Augie chose the most substandard stones he could find—he loved breakfast for dinner and fully intended to lose. He walked south down the riverbank past the black cottonwood, searching for a final few rocks. In the distance, Aurora seemed to be trying to unearth some kind of rodent. Augie returned to the competition site and hollered to

Rose that he was ready. She turned and waved, then held one finger in the air.

"Okay, take your time. I'll be ready when you are," he yelled back.

The cowboy lowered his stiff body onto a large piece of granite as Aurora returned with a broken birch limb, wanting a game of fetch. Augie reached for the stick as he watched the river tumble by. He froze. In his hand was no piece of timber. Instead, it appeared to be a human femur with a rotten fragment of burlap embedded in the bone.

He was as close to panic as a seasoned cowboy could be.

"I need another minute, Rose. Gotta find a few more stones down the river," he shouted.

Augie walked as casually as he could over to the Kubota and set the bone in a large toolbox strapped to the bed.

It was all coming together. Aurora had been digging at the spot where Cal had buried the body of the drifter who had assaulted Fogel's daughter so many decades ago, and years of opening the Jackson Dam had eroded layers of sand, silt, and gravel, most likely exposing the bone.

This is going to be a problem, he thought.

Augie sped through tanking the competition, raised Rose's hand in victory, and made up a story about needing to return to the lodge.

When they pulled in, Lawson was sitting in an Adirondack chair on the front porch. Rose ran inside to report the news of her securing a second stone-skipping title to Chloe. Augie had some time before she would emerge again through the door.

"Mr. Lawson, we have a problem," Augie said, jerking his head in the direction of the Kubota.

Lawson rose without a word and met him at the ATV, where the cowboy opened the metal box and pointed at the weathered bone.

"It's from the…situation…with the drifter," Augie said. "I think erosion has finally exposed the…" He paused. "It's probably only a matter of time before animals spread this mess up and down the riverbank."

Augie's father had told Mr. Lawson of his son's knowledge of what had happened so many years ago, but the two had never spoken of it.

"I'll need to take care of that, probably tonight," said Lawson.

"No, sir, I will handle it. I just needed to let you know."

"That will make you an accessory to covering up a murder, Augie. I'm not sure you want any part of that, son. There's no going back."

Augie's pulse quickened—his stare fixed on the human bone as he weighed the gravity of Lawson's words before finally looking up.

"We've got a beaver currently in the trap. I'll manage the situation with the drifter tonight and take both of them to the Gros Ventre." Lawson nodded appreciatively.

After everyone had retired for the evening, Augie walked to the barn, where he pulled a dirty black duffel bag from the shelf and emptied its contents of extra bridles and halters. Next, he grabbed a pair of leather work gloves, an LED headlamp, and a shovel.

The Kubota bounced along the trail, its headlights casting a haunting beam into the settling fog. He found the black cottonwood, killed the engine, and grabbed his supplies as a haunting chill ran deep down his spine.

The eerie haze along the river thickened as he worked the shovel meticulously around the edges of the decaying burlap sack, unsure if each crunch was gravel or human remains. Burlap, denim, and bone were all that remained.

The skull was missing a small portion between where the eyebrows would have been, and as he transferred it to the duffel bag, something rattled inside. Distorted lead, no longer recognizable as a .22 caliber bullet, slid from the back of the skull, falling to the earth, spawning another chill and shiver.

He completed the gruesome task in thirty minutes and scanned the hole with his headlamp for any telltale evidence before repositioning soil from other areas and filling in the one-time grave. He slung the duffle over his shoulder, hiked back to the ATV, and headed to the beaver dam.

Once back at the ranch, he moved the duffel and the trapped beaver into the bed of his Super Duty and pointed the truck toward the Gros Ventre. It was midnight when he left the bright lights of Jackson and turned onto Cache Creek Drive, immediately triggering a set of flashing red and blue police lights. He knew instantly why he was being pulled over, and it had nothing to do with the remains in the back.

Before starting the pickup truck at the ranch, he had manually turned off the headlights to prevent Chloe or Rose from seeing him leave at an odd hour. But, coming through the well-lit town, he hadn't noticed his lights were still off. As soon as he had made the turn onto a pitch-black Cache Creek Drive and noticed this, it was too late.

"Evening. License and registration, sir." The officer had his right hand resting on a 9mm Glock. Augie moved slowly to not alarm the patrolman and produced both documents. The policeman eyed the logo on the Ford.

"You work for Mr. Lawson?"

"Yes, sir," answered Augie.

"Well, as you probably know, he's a big supporter of the FOP. We sure appreciate all that he does."

Augie had no idea. *Thank you, Mr. Lawson.*

The officer went back to his car, observing the pickup truck's bed contents.

He returned several minutes later.

"Is Six Dawns in the beaver Uber business now?"

Augie forced a laugh. "Just doing some relocating."

"Odd hour for that, Mr. West," the officer replied.

"I was planning on waiting until the morning, but the grunts and whines from the pickup bed were disturbing my little girl's sleep. I figured I might as well just get it done."

The cop paused, then handed Augie's documents back to him.

"You have a good evening, Mr. West, and turn your headlights on."

"Thank you, officer. You do the same."

Augie's hand trembled as he fumbled with the key. After starting the truck, he ensured his headlights were on, continued down Cache Creek, and turned left, transitioning to an unimproved fire road and making his way into the mountains. The cowboy hiked the final quarter mile to a secluded pond that wasn't displayed on any topographic map. What should have taken five minutes took fifteen as he struggled with the beaver's weight as it rattled the cage. After releasing the rodent, he returned to the truck for the bag of bones and hiked back to the pond.

Augie scoured the shore for a few heavy rocks, loaded them into the duffel, and stripped off his jeans and shirt. Then, wading into the pond up to his chest, he submerged the bag in the murky black water.

CHAPTER THIRTEEN

The cowboy slept fitfully that night and spent the day busying himself with small projects around the property, attempting to keep his mind from wandering back to the bag of bones. It was late afternoon when he finally stopped by the lodge to tell Lawson that the issue with the drifter had been taken care of.

"Another favor, Augie," said Lawson.

"Anything, sir."

"Ms. St. James is asking if I can meet with her in the morning. After the scare with my heart attack, she implied we must button up a few loose ends with my will, but Rose has an appointment tomorrow in town with her psychiatrist, Dr. Mahoney. Would you be able to take her at about 9:30?"

"If Six Dawn's lawyer needs to meet, I won't stand in the way of that, sir. The last thing I need is to be on the wrong side of a legal eagle. Of course, I can take her," Augie quipped with a smile.

The day of Rose's appointment, Augie returned to the lodge from his morning rounds and watched through the picture window as she disappeared into the stalls.

He froze when he first entered the barn and saw her hinged forward at the waist, sitting bareback on Scarborough, arms drooping down over the horse's front shoulders in a hug. Her head was turned toward the stall window and rested awkwardly on Scarborough's mane. A mounting block sat by the equine's side.

"Rose," said Augie softly. She stirred.

He withheld the lecture on the tip of his tongue about what a dangerous thing she had just done.

"It's time to go see Dr. Mahoney."

She laggardly sat up, reached for Augie, and fell into his arms.

They climbed into the Super Duty and headed for the medical center, where Dr. Mahoney's assistant escorted them to an office, pausing at the wet bar to see if they would like water or coffee. Rose pointed to the Keurig.

"We're fine, but thank you," said Augie.

"You must be Augie," said the child psychiatrist as she entered the room with a smile and an extended hand. "I've heard a lot about you from Mr. Lawson."

"All good things, I hope, doc," replied Augie.

"Yes. All good things. I've known Don Lawson a long time and can't say I've ever heard him speak unkindly about anyone. I've yet to meet Chloe, but he certainly appreciates how you two have stepped up to help out with Rose."

Dr. Mahoney had seen Rose once a week for the past month, and those sessions had been designed to build Rose's trust and create a safe space. She had reassured the redhead that things would get better; it was now time to pick the trauma's scab.

Helping children through disturbing and painful experiences was a challenge on its own. Add mutism to the equation, and it becomes colossal. Dr. Mahoney lowered her chair and was now eye-to-eye with the little girl.

"Rose, I'd like to start with you drawing me a picture." The redhead's eyes came into focus. "Let's have you sketch a family picture. It might be hard, but I want you to draw your family as you remember them living in Chicago." Rose squeezed and released her balled-up hand.

She hesitated, reached for her colored pencils, and her face hardened as she drew. A few minutes later, the family portrait was done. Augie glanced at it and saw two adults and one child, but Dr. Mahoney observed more. The three figures stood noticeably apart, and Rose was unusually dwarfed by her parents. In each silhouette's chest was a heart; the woman's was filled in with pink and gray, the man's was black, and Rose's was gray. The girl's mouth was downturned. Her father's face revealed anger, and her mother's showed fear—her mouth open as if screaming.

"That's very good, Rose," said Dr. Mahoney. "You're quite the artist. Do you like to draw?" She nodded.

"What's your favorite thing to draw?" Rose threw the peace sign.

"Okay, your favorite two things to draw." She wrote, *Horses and the Indian.*

"Do you have any drawings in that sketchbook you can show me?" Her head bobbed excitedly.

Rose flipped through her book and found a drawing of Scarborough tied to a hitching post under a large oak tree. She looked at the doctor for any signs of approval, and the psychiatrist nodded warmly. Next, she turned to a sketch of Sleeping Indian.

"Well, Rose, those are impressive. Can you draw something for me right now?" A single, hesitant nod.

"How about a picture of you, your grandfather, Augie, and Chloe?" The muscles in her face relaxed as she began outlining more figures. "I'll be back in about ten minutes, and we'll see what you drew." Rose didn't look up.

She sketched energetically, changing out colored pencils and occasionally cocking her head to slightly change her view as she assessed her progress.

Dr. Mahoney returned. "Let's see what you have so far."

It's not ready yet, thought Rose.

She clutched the pad to her body.

"I'm guessing you're not done. Can I take a look while you work on finishing it?"

She slowly lowered it from her chest to the table as she pulled an orange pencil for the sun.

The four characters were easily identified and bunched significantly closer than in the first drawing. The girl stood nearest the bearded cowboy—the largest of the foursome—and each held the end of a short rope. Next to him was Chloe, and on the other side of Rose was Mr. Lawson. All had versions of a smile on their faces, and all had hearts outlined on their chests. Rose reached for a red pencil and, one by one, filled in the hearts. She pulled a gray pencil from the box and drew a heavy line around her own heart.

"Rose, I'm going to speak with Augie outside for a few minutes. You keep sketching, and we'll be right back."

Augie spoke before they came to a stop. "So what did you make of the drawings, doc?"

"First and foremost, interpreting drawings is not a science. I have some theories on what we just saw, but I cannot say definitively that they are correct.

"But the first drawing did tell me that her family life in Chicago was possibly chaotic and unstructured. She probably wasn't nearly as close as a child should be to either parent. The physical distance between the three and her diminutive size indicate this."

Augie nodded, waiting for her to continue.

"And I'm sure you noticed the color of their hearts. As we would probably suspect, knowing her father is a murderer and, I'm told, an avid drug user, he was likely disconnected and cold in Rose's eyes. That said, I'm less concerned with how she felt about her parents; it's the gray in Rose's heart that worries me. It's how she feels about herself. Our goal is to bring her out of her seemingly indifferent detachment. She needs to *feel* things that kids should feel. She must do and see things that bring life back to her soul. She needs to trust before she will open up."

"What about the second family picture you had her draw?"

"She may see you all as her family now. Your size in the drawing indicates that she looks at you as the group's patriarch," said Dr. Mahoney.

"And what about the rope Rose and I were holding?"

"That's an interesting thing. I believe it's indicative of some kind of connection she feels with you. Something stronger than with Chloe or even her grandfather. What it's based on, having only known you for a short time, I can't say. I assume Rose still isn't speaking, even to you?"

"No. An occasional sound but never words, although I have seen her whispering in Scarborough's ear. At least that's what it looked like to me."

"Scarborough?" Dr. Mahoney asked.

"Oh, that's one of our quarter horses in the barn."

Dr. Mahoney fielded a few more questions before returning to collect Rose—she was mid-drawing when they entered. Pausing, she looked down and away from the pair as they peered at the sketch pad on the table. It was a man with a hammer looming over a woman on the ground.

"It's okay, Rose. You've done nothing wrong," said Dr. Mahoney comfortingly. "Do you want to keep drawing?" Rose shook her head side to side, then massaged her right temple.

The psychiatrist walked out with them, slowing her gait and allowing Rose to move slightly ahead. Augie followed suit, pacing the doctor.

"I saw the concern on your face with the last drawing," she said softly, "but that's a positive step. It's allowing her to move from a passive role in the trauma-healing process to an active one. It's a necessary stage in her treatment."

They shook hands, and offering his thanks, Augie and Rose climbed in the Ford.

CHAPTER FOURTEEN

A few days before Rose's birthday, the three adults gathered to discuss the possibility of a party and what that might resemble. Mr. Lawson had the means to put on a grand affair with no expense spared, but they kept coming back to the same conundrum. Kids' birthday parties customarily had other kids at them, and through no fault of her own, Rose hadn't made any friends during her short time in the valley.

"I have an idea. Let me make a call," said Mr. Lawson. "You two give some more thought to what Rose might like at her party." He disappeared upstairs.

"Chloe, I'll be honest, I haven't been to a children's birthday party, ever," said Augie.

"Augie, you were a kid once. What are some things you remember enjoying?"

"Shooting squirrels with my .22 rifle, egging the neighbor's house, stealing cigarettes from my dad's dresser, stuff like that," he answered.

Chloe stared at him and tried to process what he had just offered. Finally, she rolled her eyes and, hiding a smile, said, "Okay, that sounds good. We'll get some rifles, ammo, and a carton of unfiltered cigarettes. Then, we'll send Rose out into the woods for some fun. When she returns—sorry, *if* she returns—we'll drop her over at Harrison Ford's property with two dozen eggs. Even better, if Mr. Lawson rounds up some other kids, I'm sure their parents would be thrilled with the birthday party activity choices. Augie, are you serious?" Chloe was doubled over laughing.

"Well, I answered the question, didn't I?" said Augie. "I didn't necessarily mean that's what we *should* do for her big day."

"What about a bounce castle?" asked Chloe. "Those seem to be a big hit with kids. And I know you can rent characters. Wait, we could get Princesses Elsa and Anna! Remember, she was sketching them?" Chloe's cadence accelerated with each excitable image. "A puppet show! We must have a puppet show! Followed by a magician, one with real rabbits."

Lawson appeared on the staircase. "What's all the commotion, Chloe?"

Regaining a semblance of control, a slightly embarrassed Chloe replied, "Just planning the big day, Mr. Lawson."

"Possibly some good news on the guest front," he said, coming down the stairs. "I just got off the phone with Whispering Woods. They are going to send a few of Rose's friends and will call to confirm tomorrow morning."

"What exactly do you mean by *send*, sir?" asked Augie.

"I mean, I'm dispatching a chartered jet for them. They'll arrive the morning of the party, along with a chaperone, and return the next day. We have plenty of room, right?"

Augie and Chloe stared at each other, momentarily expressionless, then broke into sincere smiles.

"That's a great idea, Mr. Lawson." Chloe was the first to applaud the over-the-top decision.

"I agree. Outstanding, sir," Augie added.

The budget was now out the window. A bounce castle, magician, characters, and puppet show were all on the table.

"We better start making some calls. July 5 is coming," said Chloe to Augie.

They soon realized they had two parties to plan. Independence Day was in forty-eight hours, and Rose indicated that she had no idea what this holiday was all about, so Augie felt the first order of business was to educate her on the holiday's significance. He knew the date celebrated the passage of separating the colonies from Great Britain but did not have the background to explain the historical events in any significant detail. Nonetheless, Augie felt giving Rose the full meaning of the holiday was important.

It seemed the Six Dawns' checkbook was currently open, so he asked Chloe to hire a period actor to come in and explain to Rose what the Fourth of July was all about. The company that would send the two princesses on the fifth agreed to add a Thomas Jefferson actor to appear on the fourth.

"Fireworks!" Chloe announced. "We obviously need a big fireworks show."

"Teton County doesn't allow the big ones without a permit," said Augie.

"I think we both know someone powerful enough in the valley to secure a permit, even on short notice," Chloe retorted. Augie paused for a moment, then nodded.

"We'll need to move the horses out for the evening. Fireworks and equines don't necessarily get along," said Augie.

"I'll go speak to Mr. Lawson on both accounts," Chloe replied.

"And, Chloe, remember, if Mr. Lawson seems reserved, it's because his wife Marie died on July 4, a long time ago."

She nodded somberly.

"If we're going to do fireworks, we might as well invite all the neighbors within five miles. If they're here, they probably won't call in a noise complaint on us," Lawson said in response to Chloe's request. "I'll make the calls. In the meantime, ring Nora's Inn and see if they can pull together some catering for us, maybe for two dozen. The party starts at five."

The next day was filled with last-minute preparations for the dual affairs. Deposits were paid, equipment rentals finalized, catering confirmed, and logistics for the air and ground transportation for the lot from Whispering Woods were organized.

The morning arrived, bringing with it a rare gloom to the valley. A low layer of thick, gray stratocumulus clouds blanketed the sky.

Hopefully, it's not a harbinger of a doomed fireworks show, thought Lawson.

A lost deposit was the furthest thing from his mind. Over the past several weeks, he had come to realize just how devoid of joy Rose's upbringing had been before she arrived at the ranch. He was intent on filling every day with all that an eight-year-old should have experienced in life, and fireworks seemed to be near the pinnacle of the list.

Sleeping Indian was obscured; thus, there would be no diversion to the hitching post. Rose eagerly greeted the staircase to the family room, descending two steps at a time. Mr. Lawson cringed with each launch and landing. *All we need is a broken arm.* She went right for the coffee pot, testing the limits as usual.

"I don't think so, Rose," said her grandfather. She stared at him, turned her palms skyward, and raised her shoulders, much of her neck vanishing.

"Because it will stunt your growth, and you're small enough as it is. Plus, that's caffeinated, and I don't need you bouncing off the walls this morning."

Defeated, she abandoned her coffee quest, theatrically caromed off the kitchen wall, and arrived at the table in front of her sketchbook. Her brow rose slowly, just above the book held firmly in front of her face. Her grandfather stared back at her before shifting his gaze around the room.

I don't appear to be in too much trouble for that, she thought, lowering her head like a periscope back to the safety of invisibility behind the sketch pad.

Mr. Lawson stood, looking around the family room as if searching for something. He dialed back in on Rose.

"Come here," he said sternly. She obliged.

Lawson leaned in toward his granddaughter and drew a deep breath through his nose.

"I need you to be honest with me. Have you gotten into the perfume bottle I keep on my nightstand?"

Rose looked at the floor, uncertain if she was now in trouble. She nodded.

"It's okay, honey. That perfume belonged to your grandmother, Marie, whom you never met. I keep it because it reminds me of her. Sometimes, I'll spray it on her…on *the* pillow. Do you like it?" She nodded. "It's called Camile. The scents you smell are bergamot and vanilla, and they take me back to another time."

The front door opened, fracturing Lawson's reflection on an era long gone.

"We caught a second one at the dam," said Augie. They all walked outside.

The little girl's mouth dropped open. *This is the largest mouse I have ever seen.*

She looked at the cowboy, then back at the rodent, then back at the cowboy. *Are you seeing this? I feel like you should be more excited. You know this is a mouse, right, cowboy?*

Augie didn't know what to make of Rose's astonishment and confusion.

She knows this is a beaver, right? he thought.

Rose continued to stare, dumbfounded.

Look at those huge orange teeth! Something is definitely wrong with its tail.

A broad, flat, scaly tail grew where she felt a thin, skinny one should be. She had seen enough of the zombie mouse and high-tailed it inside.

"I wonder what that was all about," said Chloe.

"I'm going to take this one to a pond in the Gros Ventre, then reset the trap. I'll be back in an hour or so," said Augie.

Lawson returned inside, walked into the den, and closed the door.

Dearest Marie,

Today marks the 25th anniversary of the cruelest day of our lives. Words cannot describe how much I miss your tender smile, our sunset rides, and your gentle touch. I feel you looking over us every day.

As you probably know, the ranch has been graced with the gift of a beautiful redhead you could never meet. Your granddaughter has been here for less than a month but has already made an impact. She takes after you, Marie. She's intelligent, curious, brave, and has the same affinity for horses that you did. I pray daily for her and ask God to shine His light on the darkness she has witnessed.

Tonight will be the first fireworks on the ranch in 26 years. I hope you enjoy the show.

Until we meet again,

Don

Lawson trudged up the staircase, entered his bedroom, and slipped the note under the unspoiled pillow where it would remain until the following morning, when it would join the prior twenty-four in an old shoe box.

The fireworks team was the first to arrive, and their setup would take several hours. A safe location was agreed upon, and the workers began situating racks, each containing ten tubes. An explosive was then carefully lowered to the bottom of each cylinder by its two-foot fuse. Late in the afternoon, the fire marshal arrived to inspect and sign off on the evening's display.

A caterer from Nora's showed up at four and set up stations where burgers, chicken-fried steak, prime rib, and local trout would be served. Chloe readied a water balloon toss, a limbo covered in red, white, and blue streamers, and a giant Tic-Tac-Toe game for the local ranch owner's kids.

At 5 p.m., neighbors began trickling in; the vehicle theme seemed to be white Ford pickups, each with a liberal coating of dust. "Thomas Jefferson" arrived via a historically inaccurate means—a motorcycle—and provided Rose with a private history lesson before mingling with the crowd.

A gold Aviat Husky with black trim made a low pass above the grass runway—one of Lawson's pilot friends. The plane had been outfitted with a colored smoke system similar to aerobatic planes at airshows, and after circling to the north, it released tight red and blue streams that quickly morphed into thick lines of cloud. Raucous applause greeted the aviator as he landed on the strip and taxied to a stop.

At 9 p.m., a single skyrocket launched into the clear Wyoming sky, and a burst of red dappled the full moon. The show had commenced. Color, light, and sound painted the heavens with fickle patterns. For fleeting seconds, night turned to day as rockets sizzled, departing the valley soil and burning holes in the cool evening air. Purples, greens, reds, whites, and blues materialized as the mineral elements responsible for each color burned. The cadence of the rocket reports grew quicker, and with it, the night became brighter as the finale fractured the prior launch pattern. Finally, the cascade of lights climaxed, replaced by a heavy fog of lingering smoke and cheers.

CHAPTER FIFTEEN

The following morning came far too early for Augie, as he had worked late into the evening, ensuring no smoldering hot spots from the fireworks. Rose was already downstairs sketching the rising sun from the front porch when he lumbered down the steps. She looked up and smiled, waiting patiently for what should be the first of many birthday greetings.

"Oh, Rose, I meant to tell you…hap… haphazardness won't cut it on a ranch. There are just too many things going on, and everyone should have a plan," said Augie.

What is he talking about?

"And, hap…happiness is loving and being loved."

Where is Chloe? I think the cowboy has a fever.

"Rose, sincerely, hap…hapless people deserve our charity."

Maybe it's a stroke. I hope they won't need to land another helicopter in our driveway.

"Happy birthday, Rose!" yelled Chloe from the second floor.

"I was getting to that, Chloe. You interrupted my prank," said Augie. "Seriously, Rose, happy birthday. What are you, like six now?"

Very funny cowboy. She drew a large nine on her pad. Augie grabbed the sketchbook and flipped it upside down, revealing a six.

"Yes, six. That's what I thought." This elicited a low growl from the redhead. She snatched the pad back and resumed her sketching.

The Gulfstream 500 was scheduled to land at noon. Onboard were three of Rose's former housemates at Whispering Woods and one chaperone. Augie rolled through the security gate at Jackson Hole Airport's private terminal just as the jet touched down. Three beaming girls emerged carrying matching forest green backpacks and descended the plane's nine stairs, where they were deposited onto a red carpet that had just been rolled out. The Whispering Woods staff member stepped from the aircraft door, pausing to take in the magnificent view.

Introductions were made, and arrangements for the following day were confirmed with the two pilots.

"How's Rose doing?" asked the chaperone.

Augie filled her in on the basics as they walked to the pickup truck. The three children had yet to speak.

"Are the kids nonverbal like Rose?" he asked.

"No, they all talk. I think they're in shock from having just been taken to an airport, put on a private jet, and now seeing mountains for the first time in their lives."

Back at the lodge, Chloe was working on putting the final touches on the birthday party setup. Colorful streamers and signs adorned the family room; birthday hats resembling upside-down ice cream cones were laid out on the oak table, along with goody bags; and a red and blue bounce castle with a twelve-foot-high slide rose from the back lawn. The magician was to arrive at 1 p.m. and the princesses at 2 p.m.

Rose was out back by the barn when she heard the pickup return from the airport. She dropped her sketchbook and started to run toward the front of the lodge, stopped halfway, and returned to collect her book and pencils. Then, out of breath, she greeted her old friends with a broad smile, and the group of four formed an amorphous hug, the orb eventually tumbling to the ground in laughter. The foursome made a failing attempt at dusting off before Rose led them inside to meet Chloe and her grandfather.

Their chatter came to an instant halt as they slowed their gait, gawking at the interior of the enormous home. Chloe showed them to the theatre room that had been converted to a bedroom/recreation room for the evening, where they deposited their backpacks and returned upstairs to the main level.

"What's it like now that you're rich, Rose?" asked Taylor, the oldest and blondest of the girls. The redhead stared at the floor, shifting her weight from side to side. "I'm sure Rosie Rich gets anything she wants now. Rose, can you make your grandfather buy me a pony?"

Chloe looked up from the kitchen island, pausing mid-slice as she quartered an apple.

"Girls, why don't you head out back to the pond? Rose needs to help me with something, and then she'll be right out." Taylor signaled for the other two to follow her.

When the door shut behind the last girl, Chloe waved Rose over to the kitchen.

"Try to ignore her, honey. She's just jealous."

Rose set her notepad on the island and wrote, *Why did she say that?*

"Sometimes kids struggling with their feelings don't know how to deal with them, and they say mean things…But if you're open to a few suggestions, I have just the way for you to handle Taylor." She nodded slowly.

Rose was smiling confidently as she walked across the flagstone and toward the threesome sitting on the edge of the pond. Setting a foil-covered paper plate on a large rock, she flipped her pad toward Taylor, making direct eye contact.

Did I do something to make you mad?

The blonde responded defensively, "No…why?"

Rose wrote, *Rosie Rich?*

Taylor forced an uncomfortable laugh and looked at the other two girls, who quickly diverted their eyes. Rose remained stolid as she watched Taylor begin to squirm.

"I…I'm sorry, Rose. I was just playing around. I didn't mean anything…" She looked down, kicking at the soil with the toe cap of her shoe, her body rigid. Rose extended her hand, and Taylor looked up, relief visible as her shoulders relaxed.

The next order of business was the paper plate. Rose slowly peeled back the foil, drawing out the anticipation as the three girls cocked their heads, trying to catch the first glimpse of the shroud's secret.

A perfectly quartered apple appeared, drizzled with caramel, dusted with crushed graham crackers, and finished with gummy bears. Three pairs of eyes swelled as taste buds were tantalized. Rose offered the plate to the smallest of the Whispering Woods lot first, who took far too long deciding which apple to snatch. Taylor chewed on a fingernail, fighting the urge to coerce the little girl to make a selection.

The treats vanished in much less time than it took for them to be selected. Sticky fingers found shorts and T-shirts, adding a layer of varnish on top of the Wyoming soil embedded in the cotton fibers.

"Girls, come on inside and help me with a few last things before people start arriving," yelled Chloe from the back door. "Last one in is a rotten egg!" They bolted for the lodge amid squeals and shrieks.

While no live rabbit appeared, the magical display by the man in the black tuxedo was first-rate. Rose demanded that he teach her a card trick, and after some talk about a magician never revealing his secrets—and Chloe having none of it—he obliged. The princesses arrived to much fanfare, singing and dancing their way to rock star status among the four girls. Much to Mr. Lawson's relief, no one emerged from the bounce house with bones pointing in the wrong direction.

Games continued until it was time for presents and dinner. The three guests vanished downstairs to the makeshift bedroom before reappearing holding wrapped gifts, courtesy of a wire transfer by Mr. Lawson to Whispering Woods for the girls to choose presents for Rose. A 130-piece art set, an Exploding Kittens card game, and the *Magic Treehouse* box set were all unwrapped. Rose wasn't quite sure what to make of the second gift.

I know the kids at Whispering Woods all have issues, but exploding kittens?

Lawson emerged from his den holding a small gift wrapped in colorful Happy Birthday paper and handed it to Rose.

She tore at it frantically, revealing a blue box. *Paris* was the only word she recognized. Rose slowed, opening it carefully, and withdrew a familiar-looking bottle with a sapphire blue stopper shaped like a fan. She held it above her head, showing the other girls.

"Now, you have your own bottle of Camile," said her grandfather.

The redhead pranced toward Lawson and embraced him in a hug. She immediately returned to her friends and coated each with a liberal dousing of the French perfume.

"A little goes a long way," said Chloe, cringing at the sheer amount of fragrance now suspended in the air.

After grilled cheese sandwiches and tater tots, a raspberry vanilla ice cream cake made its way to the table. Rose requested gloves, and Mr. Lawson returned with a pair from his stash in the garage, also rolling in the new Trek bicycle. She galloped to the hot-pink beauty and tried it on for size before attempting a lap through the room, only to be corralled back to the table by Aurora.

The night ended with the children tucked snugly in sleeping bags and Harry Potter flying through towers and turrets on the one-hundred-inch screen in the theatre room.

Rose accompanied her friends to the airport the following morning as tears stained her face. She tried to swallow the lump in her throat when they boarded the plane. Then, once the Gulfstream had become just a speck on the northern horizon, Augie opened the rear passenger door for Rose. She climbed in, and they headed for the ranch.

Rose was staring out her window when Augie asked her if she would like to go for a ride in the arena when they returned. Her scarlet ponytail answered for her.

"Okay, well, maybe tomorrow," he said.

Back at the lodge, Chloe watched from the sofa as Rose climbed the stairs dispiritedly, dragging herself step by step with the help of the banister. When she disappeared at the top of the landing, Chloe waited five minutes and then headed up.

The door to Rose's room was cracked when Chloe knocked lightly and entered the bedroom.

Rose was staring out the window while picking at a pale pink gum eraser from her new art set. Small pieces of rubber speckled the top of the mahogany dresser.

"Hey, honey," she said softly. "Mind if I come in?" The redhead nodded as Chloe walked to the foot of the bed and sat. Rose turned to face her, the remnants of tears still visible on her cheeks.

"Come sit with me," she said, patting the comforter. "Let me guess; you miss your friends?" Her head moved up and down.

"Well, in two short months, you'll be able to start school, and think of all the kids you'll get to meet then."

Rose walked back to the dresser and picked up her pad and pen.

2 whole months!

"I know. It seems like a long time, but it will go faster than you think…and…I have a story about a little girl about your age when her parents decided she would spend the entire summer with her grandparents. But they lived on a farm in a tiny town in Colorado, with the nearest neighbor five miles away. Five miles away! Wanna guess who that little girl was?" Rose pointed to Chloe.

"That's right. I was eight years old, and my only friend was a cow. A cow." Chloe smiled, and Rose's frown softened.

"After two weeks of chasing chickens and walking my cow"— the redhead giggled—"I missed my friends so much. My grandmother sensed my sadness, and she came up with an idea. We set out to make the perfect chocolate chip cookie, and once we perfected the recipe, we took them, along with Mabel, to the county fair." Rose looked quizzically at Chloe and wrote, *Mabel?*

"Mabel was my grandfather's prize hog." Confusion was still evident on Rose's face.

"His pig…he raised hogs to show at the fair." Incredulous, the redhead began a measured side-to-side head shake.

Where is this going?

"Anyway, we loaded up Mabel, a table from the stable, and some bagels."

Rose giggled.

"Okay, no bagels. We brought three dozen cookies…and we headed to the fair, where my grandmother set out the table and a hand-drawn sign in front of the hog pens that said *Kid's Cookie Club*. I met a bunch of children my age, and over the next few weeks, I had so many play dates. That summer ended up being one of my favorites ever.

"So, here's what I was thinking. An old friend of mine owns a store in town called The Bookshelf. On Wednesday afternoons, she hosts *Storytime*, where staff or guest authors read parts of a book to kids.

We could bake the world's greatest cookies, and you could give them out to the kids. You're bound to make friends. Who doesn't like chocolate chip cookies? What do you think?"

Rose was bouncing on the foot of the bed as her hands met in frenzied clapping. Mid-bounce, she launched into Chloe, arms spread wide, pinning her to the bed in a makeshift hug.

"I'll take that as a yes," gasped Chloe, under fifty pounds of redhead.

After dinner, Rose indicated she was going to bed early and headed up the stairs. Chloe reached for the TV remote on the coffee table and noticed an envelope addressed to *Grandpa, Augie, Chloe.*

"Mr. Lawson, do you know what this is?" she asked.

He looked up from the recliner. "Not a clue."

The red flap had clearly been opened, then resealed sloppily with glue. Chloe slipped the card from the envelope. What had once been a *Happy 9th Birthday* card had been transformed with paper, tape, and glue into a *Thank You* card. On the inside, Rose had handwritten a short note of thanks for throwing her the birthday party. She signed it with her name inside a red heart.

Chloe was on the patio, halfway through her second cup of morning coffee, when Rose darted from the back door, balancing her grandfather's laptop precariously in the palm of one hand and her notepad in the other. *World's best chocolate chip cookies* filled the Google search bar. Two small fingers slipped up on the trackpad, revealing an endless list of recipes. Rose dipped her chin and raised her eyebrows, encouraging Chloe to join her frustration with the overwhelming compilation of choices.

"So many options… Not to worry, honey. I have my grandmother's recipe saved in my phone."

Rose stood behind Chloe, resting her chin on her shoulder, as she skimmed through the iPhone Notes app and finally found the list of ingredients.

"I'm guessing your grandfather doesn't have anything other than the butter and eggs. Let's go inside and see what we need; then we'll head to the store."

Rose snagged Chloe's hand and pulled her from the wicker chair.

Once inside, they rummaged through cabinets, building a list of what would be needed.

"What, might I ask, are you two up to?" asked Lawson from his chair.

"We're on a quest to bake the best cookie you've ever had…You don't happen to have a stand mixer by chance?"

"A *what* mixer?"

"Never mind…I know I've seen an electric hand mixer around here somewhere…Rose and I are heading to Whole Foods. We'll be back soon."

Forty-five minutes later, a brown grocery bag arrived through the front door with a redhead buried behind it. She carefully laid the items out on the kitchen island, changing their order several times until she was satisfied. Chloe set her keys on the counter and eyed the tidy row of ingredients. A small handful of semi-sweet chocolate chip morsels spilled from the corner of their yellow package.

"I don't suppose you know how the chips ended up opened?" she asked Rose.

The redhead's eyes widened, feigning surprise. Her eyebrows rose as she pointed suggestively toward Lawson, currently napping in his lounger.

"You think maybe your grandfather sleepwalked to the counter and opened the bag?"

She nodded.

"Mm-hmm…Sure he did. How might you explain the dab of chocolate currently resting in the corner of your mouth?" Chloe cocked her head, withholding a smile.

Rose held up three fingers.

"You ate three?"

She slowly nodded.

"I found the hand mixer." Lawson awoke from his nap and broke the mock tension. "Third drawer down on the left, next to the fridge. I'll be out at the barn if you need an extra pastry chef."

"Thanks, Mr. Lawson. Rose, you ready to get started?" asked Chloe.

She clapped enthusiastically.

After mixing the flour, baking soda, salt, and baking powder, Chloe showed Rose how to cream the sugar and butter together.

"A chef's secret: don't overmix the dough. Blend the butter and sugar only as long as needed."

"Now for the hard part."

Chloe picked up two eggs and handed one to Rose.

"I'll demonstrate. Eggs can be tricky. We want to make sure no shell falls into the mixing bowl. We'll give the egg one tap on the counter. Like this.

"Next, I'm gonna hold it over the bowl and press my thumbs into the little crack I just made."

Chloe gently separated the shell, and the egg slipped from its cocoon and plopped into the mixture below.

"Okay, now you try."

Rose focused intently as Chloe walked her through the steps. She shrieked as her golden yolk toppled triumphantly into the bowl.

"No shell! Great job. You must have done this before."

Rose shook her head, drawing an approving nod from Chloe.

When the dough was properly mixed, they used the quarter cup measurer to form the balls and set the first batch in the oven.

"Now for the not-so-fun part…the cleanup. But first, I need to introduce you to an age-old tradition—the licking of the beaters!"

She detached both stainless steel beaters and handed one to Rose, who daintily began working her way around the metal, nabbing small pieces of dough with her tongue as she went.

The kitchen timer went off precisely eleven minutes after the cookies were loaded into the oven. Rose donned an oven mitt and helped Chloe remove the first batch before adding a final pinch of sea salt to the treats.

"Pour us each a glass of milk, and we'll have a taste test to see how they turned out after I put the second batch in."

Rose did as instructed, filling both tumblers to the top. Chloe broke apart a cookie and waved the two halves in the air to cool, then handed one to the redhead.

Chloe watched as Rose's carnation pink tongue surfaced, testing the temperature of the chocolatey goodness before committing to a nibble and then a bite.

"What do you think?"

Rose scribbled on her pad before reaching for a second one.

World's Best Cookie!

"I agree! You're quite the baker."

Rose picked her pencil back up.

When can we go to the bookstore?

"Let me call Kasey and see if this Wednesday will work."

Rose looked at the calendar hanging on the pantry door and flashed Chloe two fingers.

"Yep. That's two days from now."

We should probably bake fresh cookies tomorrow, she wrote.

"You think so? This wouldn't have anything to do with you making plans to eat this entire batch in the next few days, would it?"

Rose shook her head sternly from side to side and snagged three more cookies from the cooling rack before heading for the back door.

"Rose. That would be four and a half cookies for you. You're going to get a tummy ache."

She returned to the counter and her notebook.
1 for Grandpa
1 for Scarborough
1 for me

Kasey loved Chloe's idea about Rose giving out cookies at *Storytime* and invited them to arrive early on Wednesday. They brought a fresh batch— still warm—small scalloped paper dessert plates, a package of cocktail napkins, and a hand-drawn sign proclaiming the *World's Best Cookie*. A folding table beside the store's fireplace made for an ideal serving station.

Rose's first potential new pal arrived in the form of an adorable boy, no more than ten, dressed in khaki pants and a navy blue polo.

Perfect, thought Chloe.

She looked at Rose and watched as the plate of cookies vanished momentarily under the table. The boy walked by, smiled at the redhead, and followed his mother to the children's section.

"What was that?" asked Chloe, with a hint of exasperation.

He didn't look hungry, she wrote.

Chloe folded her arms across her chest.

"You thought he was cute and didn't want him to come to the table, didn't you?"

A warmth began to grow from her neck to her cheeks.

"You're blushing," Chloe blurted out a bit too loudly.

A single finger quickly moved to Rose's lips as her eyes darted around the room, searching for anyone taking a newfound interest in Chloe's words, especially the dapper boy.

"Sorry, honey," Chloe whispered. "Come on, admit it, he's cute."

Rose fought the full smile trying to take over her mouth, picked up her pen, and with a soft giggle, wrote, *Maybe a little.*

"Oh, to be nine again…Okay, no more hiding the cookies."

Rose nodded as the door swung open. A sleek, candy-apple red, wheeled mobility walker rolled through the store entrance. Behind it stood a mahogany head of tightly coiled, bouncy curls. Rose stared as she moved the frame with unexpected self-assurance directly toward her.

"Hi. Are the cookies free?"

Rose slowly nodded, transfixed by the girl's hair.

"I'm Maya."

The redhead slid her eyes down, inspecting the contraption parked in front of her.

"Usually, when someone introduces themselves, the other person does the same," her tone more playful than aristocratic.

The redhead flipped open her notepad and wrote, *Rose.*

"Pretty name."

Rose smiled.

"You don't talk?"

She shook her head and held the pen up in front of her with her left hand.

"That's okay. My mom says I talk for two." Both girls giggled.

She bit into the soft cookie, considered the sign hanging from the table, nodded, and then devoured what remained in her hand.

"You sure make a good cookie, Rose. I haven't seen you at *Storytime* before."

First time. I just moved here.

"From where?"

Chicago.

The blue gel ink from the prior sentences smeared as she wrote.

"What's Chicago like?"

It's OK. Big city.

Why do you have that? Rose wrote, pointing to the walker.

"I have spina bifida. Do you know what that is?"

Rose shook her head.

"My spinal cord didn't grow right when I was in my mom's tummy, so I need this to get around. I call her Ruby."

The boy in the navy blue polo lingered just out of reach, peering at the pair from over the top of a book.

"Hi, Charlie," said Maya. "He's probably trying to impress you by hanging out in the Young Adult section, but he's only nine."

"Charlie, come say hello to my new friend, Rose."

The tray of chocolate chip cookies stayed put as the boy approached with a shy wave. Rose's hand barely lifted from the table and then pivoted vertically, sheepishly returning his greeting.

"Can he have a cookie?" asked Maya. Rose nodded, sliding the tray forward.

Charlie's brown side-swept bangs drifted in front of one eye as he reached for the platter.

He nodded his thanks and awkwardly backpedaled away.

"He's low-key cute, right?" whispered Maya.

Rose shrugged her shoulders.

"Seriously?"

OK. Yes. Don't tell him, she wrote, the blush returning to her cheeks.

"Your secret's safe with me."

A dozen children between the ages of eight and twelve filled the three rows in front of the fireplace as Kasey began reading from a Percy Jackson book. Ten of the twelve had bits of crumb on their clothing or remnants of chocolate on their faces tantalizingly out of reach of their tongues.

When the reading concluded, a solitary cookie remained. Rose could feel the pitter-patter in her chest as she approached Charlie, broke it in half, and offered it to him. He paused, giving her time to ponder the potential rejection. Her heartbeat quickened. Finally, he grasped it and inserted the cookie, three fingers, and a thumb into his mouth.

"Thanks, Rose," he said with a smile. "See you next time?"

She nodded as casually as possible, turned, and spotted Chloe giving her a thumbs up.

CHAPTER SIXTEEN

Rose requested an adventure into town with Augie and Chloe. Some of the kids at *Storytime* had talked about all of the fun activities in Jackson. She wanted to fly in. After explaining the lack of runways in downtown Jackson and that the ranch did not currently have access to a helicopter, they drove.

Arriving in the late afternoon, the dust-covered Super Duty found a primo spot one block south of the square. The first stop was the famed Elk Antler Arches, and four sets of these guarded the corners of George Washington Memorial Park, commonly called the town square. Augie chose to enter the set at Cache and Broadway.

Rose paused, staring intently at the massive structure of sun-bleached antlers, while Augie and Chloe watched and waited. She was doing more than just taking in the tourist attraction as her eyes moved slowly in a pattern known only to her.

"What's she doing?" whispered Chloe.

"Counting," replied Augie.

As much as he would love to allow Rose to stand and count for hours, they did have a schedule to keep.

"Two thousand thirteen," said Augie. A year earlier, he spent a half day at each arch, trying to calculate the correct number and verify his tally at the Chamber of Commerce office.

"Come on, Rose, there are three more of these to see. Then we've got a date with the Cowboy Coaster," he said.

Once they had successfully navigated passage through all four arches, Augie steered the group south toward Snow King Resort. They arrived at the base of the mountain, greeted by a giant monster of a contraption Rose had certainly never seen before rising in front of them.

"It's called a chairlift, Rose. We're going to ride it up the hill," said Chloe.

Rose stood still, eying the sizeable horizontal wheel and gears that made the seats turn. She traced the thick cable as it exited the open-air building, ran up the mountain, and disappeared over the crest of a hill.

Chloe purchased tickets from a skinny man in a small shack, and the threesome boarded an empty chair as it swung through the station. The seat rocked forward, then back, and settled into position. Ten feet, fifteen feet, twenty feet— the distance between the chair and the ground continued to increase until the lift came to a predetermined agreement with the earth as to an acceptable breadth.

Rose observed tourists passing their carriage in the opposite direction, no doubt on their return from riding the beast. Their seats appeared to be more secure. She looked directly overhead.

Are either of you considering pulling down the safety bar on account of the nine-year-old?

She nudged Augie in the ribs with a sharp elbow and peered up.

"Real cowboys don't need a safety bar, Rose."

Real cowboys don't need the death of a child on their conscience. She continued staring at him.

Augie shook his head, reached up, and lowered the bar in front of them.

They rode mostly in attentive silence, observing the natural beauty from a different perspective high in the canopy of the pines. The five-and-a-half-minute ride terminated at a lift station similar to the one at the base, where they stepped off the chair and walked down the platform to the next adventure— the Cowboy Coaster.

A two-person sled was attached to steel tracks and descended forty-five stories, following a mile of roller coaster track. Rose and Augie boarded one vehicle and Chloe another. Holding her hands at nine and three, Rose gave the *I'm driving* signal from the rear seat. The coaster attendant provided the mandatory safety instructions, and they were off. Speeding along at twenty-five miles per hour, they soared above hikers below, then down through wildflower meadows as curves, drops, and steep turns all provided breathtaking views of the Tetons in the distance. Plunging down the final hill, Rose screamed her loudest yet and pointed back to the top of the mountain.

Augie shook his head. "Rose, we have to move on to our next stop. It starts at six back at the square."

Upon returning to Washington Memorial Park, a large crowd had gathered on the northeast corner. Chloe let Rose know that what they were about to see were just actors and that there was nothing to be concerned about when the show started.

A cowboy thespian from the Jackson Playhouse appeared from a storefront and regaled the crowd with tales of gold and a stolen woman. Within minutes, the Jackson Hole Shootout was on full display.

Rose had been startled by the first gunshot but soon became more settled as the scenes played out. Eventually, she worked her way through the crowd, staying as close as she could to the action. She delighted in the costumes, the sounds, the movement, and the fuel the spectators poured on the performers. Once frontier justice was served, an actor removed his hat and passed it around the crowd. The black Resistol transferred hands in front of Rose as an appreciative tourist dropped a five-dollar bill into it.

She searched for Augie, finally found him, and patted the wallet in his back pocket. He pulled out a single and held it toward Rose. She shook her head and motioned skyward with a closed fist, thumb extended. He put the dollar back, handed her a five, and she took off, pursuing the black hat like a hawk on a field mouse, dodging in and out of adults and children alike. Finally, she converged on her prey as the cowboy actor in all black welcomed the hat back from its passage through the legions of tourists. She slipped the bill in over the black brim.

Bowing his head, the cowboy acknowledged her. "Why thank you, Cattle Kate. Appreciate your kindness, ma'am." Rose was smitten.

Chloe walked up behind Rose and put her hand on the little girl's shoulder.

"Well, what did you think?"

She smiled widely and signaled a double thumbs up.

They stopped at Moo's, where Rose ordered a double scoop of chocolate marshmallow graham in a waffle cone. Chloe and Augie split a dish of praline pecan as they walked around the square, savoring the creamy goodness. Rose made a valiant effort but could not get through the last scoop. She pointed to Chloe's purse, shifting her cone toward it.

"Rose, you aren't seriously asking if we can keep that in my purse for later, are you?"

I guess not. It was worth a try.

Rose deposited the treat in the next garbage can they passed and noticed the milky mess now adhered to her hands. She held both palms up toward Augie, implying he needed to help solve this.

"Should have worn gloves," Augie said, smiling slyly.

The cowboy is right. I should have worn gloves.

"We'll get you washed up when we find a place for dinner," said Chloe.

Halfway through their trip around the square, Rose paused in front of Snake River Rafting. A large video screen took up the entire window and played a highlight reel of summer rafting trips. Boats splashed, families paddled, the sun shined, and smiles adorned every face. She tugged on the hem of Augie's black denim jacket, eyes wide and shifting from the cowboy to the video screen. *We must do this,* was written on her face.

"I take it you want to go whitewater rafting, Rose?" he asked.

The response was a voracious nod.

"Do you know how to swim, honey?"

She looked down at her boots. Then her eyes returned to the screen. She pointed excitedly to a sodden but blissful Meriwether Lewis wannabe, targeting the life jacket he was wearing.

"It's a lot of money, those trips," said Augie.

She pulled her notepad from her jacket pocket and wrote.

Chores. I'll clean Scarborough's stall for a month.

"We'll talk about it with your grandfather, okay?"

They continued down the block until Rose stopped, staring up at a particular restaurant's circular hanging sign. A facial profile drawing of an attractive woman with a flower in her ear had earned her attention.

I know that flower! thought the redhead.

The jacket tugging began again. Pinky G's Pizzeria it would be.

After agreeing on two small pizzas and a basket of cheese fries, Augie ordered at the counter, and they found a small table in the corner of the cozy eatery. The redhead disappeared twice during their wait; on both occasions, it was to ogle the beautiful woman on the sign with the pink rose in her hair. Half an hour later, they had put only a small dent in the jumbo basket of fries but had fared better with the pizzas.

Leaving the restaurant, Rose pointed in the direction of Moo's.

"Hell no." Augie immediately regretted his language.

"Can we stop at the Cowboy Coffee Company on the way home?" asked Chloe. "I've got a caffeine withdrawal headache, which hurts something fierce."

"Rose, how about a hot chocolate instead of ice cream?" queried Augie.

Hot chocolate is for kids. How about a coffee, cowboy?

Rose nodded indifferently.

"Okay, Cowboy Coffee it is. Actually, there's a Mike's Car Wash next door. We'll give the old girl a bath first," said Augie.

I hope he's not talking about me, thought Rose.

Augie punched his code into the keypad, inciting multicolored lights to flash from the wash bay, enticing the Super Duty to enter. Rose's face was plastered against the glass as the soapy suds came to life, backlit with a montage of colors. Augie winked at Chloe and pressed the rear passenger window, unleashing a sustained high-pitched squeal from the depths of the Ford.

In one motion, Rose unbuckled her seat belt and tumbled onto the relative safety of the floor as detergent and water doused the interior. An angry face rose in the rearview mirror, revealing slick red bangs cemented to the little girl's forehead.

Not funny, cowboy. Not funny.

"Rose, if you would just shower more often, we wouldn't need to give you a bath at the car wash," chuckled Augie.

Chloe leaned into the rear compartment and gave Rose a quick inspection. Other than a soggy mop, she was declared dry and intact.

An espresso, decaf, and hot chocolate were ordered at Cowboy Coffee, and they made the fifteen-minute trip back to the ranch uneventfully. Rose's sugar-high comedown and the pizza-french fry food coma resulted in her hibernation five minutes into the ride.

Augie lifted Rose from the pickup and carried her through the front door, up the stairs, and into her bedroom. Gently removing her shoes, he tucked her in snugly before descending the grand staircase and being absorbed by the leather couch. Chloe's silken hand found Augie's calloused palm. His heartbeat quickened as she traced the creases, following the broken pattern of alcoves until the pathway exited at his wrist, where her thumb worked in a circular hover, barely connecting with his skin.

"You did good today, cowboy," Chloe said, heading up the stairs.

CHAPTER SEVENTEEN

The following evening, an advertisement came on television for the "Snake River trip of a lifetime." Rose looked up from her sketchbook. Some of the same video clips she had seen on the screen at Snake River Rafting played on the TV. She looked at Augie, then pointed to her grandfather.

You said you would ask him.

"Say, Mr. Lawson, I've been meaning to ask you. Rose seems to have gotten the idea that a whitewater trip would be great fun. Any thoughts on that?" asked Augie.

Lawson looked at the TV and then sternly at Rose. "Well, I know the doctors won't let me do something that cardiac stimulating—if that's even a phrase—but you, Chloe, and Rose should do it!"

The hard *no* that Augie had predicted was an emphatic *yes*.

"I think you all should make the overnight trip. I did one over a decade ago with some of my golf buddies, and it really was the river trip of a lifetime," Lawson added.

Augie recalled when he and Chloe made a two-night float trip so many years ago. He still had such wonderful memories of those forty-eight hours. The summer tourists were gone, leaving the river devoid of the snarls of rafts and endless howls echoing off the canyon walls. They stayed up so late the first night that all their firewood was burned through. Augie had navigated thickets of thorns the second evening, scavenging dead wood in an attempt to repeat the romantic mystique brought on in part by the previous night's fire.

Chloe looked at Augie and shrugged. "It'll be fun," she said.

Rose was now on her knees, with prayer hands extended toward Augie.

Please don't make me beg, cowboy.

Augie conceded, and the redhead shrieked. Chloe opened her laptop to begin planning; within an hour, she had the overnight adventure organized.

The sun was high overhead when they piled into the Ford and headed to Snake River Rafting. There, they completed the registration process, signed their lives away, and were fitted for life jackets and helmets. Next, they were directed outside to board an aging baby-blue shuttle. Rose ran her hand along the side of the van, feeling the textured dripping ridges of the poorly applied spray paint. They climbed in the fifteen-passenger vehicle, along with their guide, Marcus, two bankers from Chicago, a recently divorced art teacher from Minneapolis, and a dark-bearded, antisocial serial killer, who most likely escaped from prison. At least, that's how Chloe had pegged the final rafter.

The bankers, Stephen and Jonathan, were former college swimmers who had committed to taking an annual trip together until one of them married. They alternated between domestic and international travel each year, and the streak stood at seven years. Margaret, the art teacher, was forty-eight and appeared an unlikely candidate for a Wyoming outdoor adventure. She dressed like she would be more at home in a senior citizen community center craft room than on the Snake River. Chloe's least favorite, the serial killer, would not say where he was from. In the raft shop, he offered little more than a strong jawline, a firm handshake, and a single word, *Kane*. First or last name, he didn't say.

Twenty minutes later, they pulled into a turnoff, exited the van, and watched as Marcus and the driver undid the tie-down straps on the trailer. The eighteen-foot raft was carried down a small grass hill to the water's edge, where two extra-large, red dry bags were loaded with the rafter's personal effects. The water-tight packs would keep things safe from moisture should the raft flip or poor weather move in. After fifteen minutes of instruction and a safety briefing, Augie approached each rafter and quietly let them know of Rose's mutism. Life jackets and helmets were secured, and they were off.

The early portion of the trip was leisurely paced by design as the Snake offered up its tamest stretches—class one and class two rapids—during the first two miles. This allowed the rafting companies to teach the ABCs of navigating the river in a controlled environment with no threat of panic or capsize; those terrors would come later.

During the first hour, joy and wonderment collided as meditative scene after scene played out in three dimensions. Marcus was seasoned enough to read each band of rafters independently and provide the appropriate level of facts, humor, and instruction accordingly. This group was clearly entranced by their surroundings, and he remained mostly quiet.

Osprey, bald eagles, and moose made seemingly scheduled appearances along the swath of flowing water. Massive boulders, some as large as houses, swelled from the river. Awe-inspiring rock formations loomed on each side, closing the river in. It was a geologist's dream. Layer upon layer of basaltic volcanic rock climbed proudly in a threatening rage, only to retreat and give way to flourishing mint green sagebrush and chromatic wildflower meadows.

The flow picked up in the second hour as the river began to drop. Class one and two rapids morphed into class three as gravity incited the Snake. The roiling water demanded additional effort from the rafters, and Marcus's instructions took on a more earnest tone. A palpable mixture of excitement and trepidation pervaded the boat. They paddled hard with Rose at the bow on the port side, following every command flawlessly, while Chloe swept hard on the starboard side. Neither exhibited fear as the raft hit a brick wall of wave, sprung up, crested, and crashed back down. Rose delighted in the full-on shower provided by the swell.

The itinerary called for a three-hour first leg of the trip before setting up camp for the night. A calm stretch of water arrived, and Marcus commanded the crew to the bank, where they beached the raft on a sandy stretch of shoreline. Each rafter collared a D ring, and they carried the boat further onto dry land. Snake River Rafting owned the riverside camp with multiple six-person canvas lodges and bear-proof storage containers. They transported the dry bags, cooler, and freshwater jugs twenty yards to the site and took their time setting up as nightfall would not arrive for another two hours.

Kane took it upon himself to build a fire rather expertly. Chloe elbowed Augie when the serial killer dropped to his left knee to add more wood to the blaze. His right pant leg rose several inches, exposing a six-inch Ontario MK 3 Navy knife buried in an ankle holster.

"There's something off with this guy. Why does he need that knife?" whispered Chloe.

Marcus readied dinner. A couple of foil packs stuffed with yellow potatoes were nestled into the hot coals, welcoming a twenty-minute head start. Next, he pulled two zipped bags of browned ground beef from the cooler and deposited them in a skillet to warm. Cans of refried beans found their home in a saucepan by Margaret's hand. Chloe and Augie diced up avocados and fresh tomatoes, and a large stack of soft shells wrapped in foil was placed in the fire.

The bankers sat on the river's edge, sipping whiskey from mini 50-ml bottles before tossing the empties into the Snake. Rose grabbed Augie's hand and pointed toward the two men as another empty one flew into the river. Marcus unlocked a storage cabinet and removed eight stainless steel dinner plates and an equal number of plastic forks as the cowboy stood.

Augie calmly strolled toward the bankers on the river's edge.

"If I see one more bottle enter this majestic river, both of you are going after it without a life vest."

One of the bankers moved to stand, but Augie placed a hand on the skinny man's shoulder and hastily redeposited him back in his seat.

"Got it?" asked Augie—less of a question and more of a statement.

Silence.

"I'm going to need an audible response from both of you boys, and I'm not going to ask again."

"Got it," came the dejected joint reply.

Everything was laid out on the table, and the rafters lined up to construct their version of dinner. Kane sat alone by the campfire with no use for a fork. He ate like an animal, and it seemed to come naturally to him.

The sun dipped below the canyon wall, bringing an immediate shiver to camp. More wood was added to the fire as sweatshirts were pulled from the dry bags, and, one by one, the rafters moved to the fire ring.

Stephen and Jonathan mostly talked about themselves and the Windy City. Then, after shooting another whiskey, they retired to one of the spacious tents, and Kane drew his knife from the ankle scabbard.

"Oh God, this is it. He waited for those two to head off to make the odds more manageable," whispered Chloe as she grabbed Augie's hand.

Kane turned the blade's focus to a piece of pine driftwood and began whittling. Augie shook his head and smiled. He knew her well enough to know that she was only half serious. The humor helped her diffuse the slight concern she had bubbling up in the back of her head.

Margaret tried to engage Kane with beauty-parlor chitchat that drew some expressionless head nods and shakes sprinkled in between laconic replies. Not rude, not interested. The quiet man intrigued Rose. She had been watching him intently throughout dinner. Kane paused paring the driftwood, and looked up as Rose approached, producing a deck of cards and fanning them out in front of him. He stared.

You know how "pick a card" works, right?

He chose one from the deck, and Rose motioned for him to show it to the others as she buried her head in a sleeve. Kane showed the jack of diamonds. *One, two, three.* She slowly peeled her forehead from the arm of her sweatshirt. He reinserted the card into the middle of the deck, and Rose momentarily moved the stack behind her back. She returned the cards forward and began slowly sifting through them one by one. There it was, the only card facing up, the jack of diamonds. Rose beamed as the soundless man nodded.

That's it? Did you just see what I made happen?

She turned to the audience around the campfire. *What's with this guy?* Delayed applause began from the fireside, and Rose bowed.

Kane moved confidently from the fire, down the bank, and to the river's edge while Marcus prepared the raft for the following morning's launch.

"Augie, if he's not here to kill us—which we won't be sure of until the morning, by the way— what is he doing on this trip?" asked Chloe in a hushed voice. "He doesn't seem like he's in a good place and isn't talking to anyone."

"I learned long ago not to judge a book by its cover. He has his reasons for being here. I presume those do not include murdering a group of rafters," Augie smiled.

The art teacher was next to go, bidding goodnight to all and retiring to her tent. Chloe put Rose to bed and dug through her bag, finally producing a compact LED mirror and a small travel makeup case.

She flipped the light's teal cover open, drew it close, and braved a glimpse of her bare face. Folds and creases took on the appearance of tiny scars as she traced their roadmaps underneath her eye and down her cheek. She sighed a deep breath of insecurity, reflecting back on a time when foundation and concealer were something other women needed—a time when she had first been with Augie.

Chloe glanced at the simple makeup bag and reached for the pull tab. The zipper purred as the slider body freed the metal teeth from its grasp. Staring into the case, she paused. A final sigh escaped her lungs. She guided the tab to the stop, closed the lighted mirror, and returned to the fire.

"Do you remember that night we spent along this same stretch fourteen years ago?" she asked.

"No. When was this?" said Augie.

She cocked her head, unsure if he was serious or not.

Augie's defense mechanism with intimacy was humor, and as cowboys went, he fit the mold— tough on the outside and tough on the inside.

"Of course I remember," he conceded.

Chloe, on the other hand, was a romantic at heart and had no trouble reminiscing.

"We made love under the stars with nothing but the sound of the river and an occasional coyote howling. Or maybe that was you, Augie?"

He smiled and tried to fight off a coming blush, remembering it vividly. They had grilled filet mignon in a cast iron skillet, reheated homemade cheesy au Gratin potatoes in foil, and shared a bottle of Quintessa cabernet. If he closed his eyes and thought hard enough, he could savor the wine's smokey sweetness that bathed his taste buds. Dessert was chocolate-covered strawberries, followed by Chloe.

She reached for his hand and caressed it, sensing something so sensual about such a benign act. He leaned in to kiss her, and she offered her lips and tongue without resistance. He tasted sweet coconut as the kiss played out like a piano player's final note, with the sustain pedal pressed hard to the floor until their lips slowly parted.

"Don't get any ideas about recreating the last river trip, cowboy. Rose is a light sleeper." Chloe smiled. As Kane returned from the river, Augie took her hand and led her to the tent.

"Kane, do you want me to put out the fire, or are you staying up?" Marcus asked.

"I'll be up for a while and can take care of it," he replied. Those were the most words he had used at one time since arriving at the rafting shop six hours prior.

Marcus found his tent and settled into the cot, his book illuminated by a headlamp. He would remain awake until the dark-bearded man turned in for the evening.

The river campsite begrudgingly accepted the early sunrise, even less so the still half-drunken bankers. It was 5:55 a.m. when the light encroached on the tents perched west of the river. Marcus emerged dutifully and went straight for the fire ring, but he was too late; Kane was already there, having set a log on a foundation of sticks, twigs, and paper. He flicked the lighter, and the pyre slowly came alive as the small flames fought for their breath, soundlessly coughing for precious oxygen. The men acknowledged each other's presence with a nod.

Marcus walked toward the cooler and withdrew eight foil packets. He laid the bundles on the edge of the fire before setting a large water kettle on the grate and heading back to the storage cabinet, where he removed an industrial-size French roast coffee press and a bag of ground beans. When the water was scalding, he poured it into the French press's glass vessel and stirred. Then, inserting the plunger into the device, he forced the beans down and the piping hot dark roast—freshly filtered—up.

Now, for Marcus's favorite part. He removed his bugle from its case and blew reveille, the morning wake-up call. Kane turned and stood motionlessly, staring solemnly at the bugler as Chloe, Augie, and Rose emerged from their tent.

Yawns and shivers greeted the chilly morning. The bankers woke last and stumbled from their shelter as the sleepy rafters drifted in search of the dark roast's captivating aroma.

"Fill her up, Marcus. If I don't get my three cups in, I'll have a headache even this beautiful river won't cure," said Augie.

Rose grabbed a paper cup and held it up to Marcus.

"How old are you, Rose?" he asked.

She set her cup down and signaled a one and a six with her fingers.

"Sixteen?" the guide queried. She nodded.

"Show me some ID," he replied.

Rose shrugged and returned to the tent, apparently no longer interested in coffee.

The egg, ham, and cheese foil packets were removed from the fire, and breakfast burritos were served. Other than the serene flow of the river, all was silent.

"Rose, come on out. Breakfast is ready," hollered Augie.

She joined the others at the table and began unwrapping her burrito. The scent of vanilla and bergamot reached Chloe and Augie at the same time.

"Rose, did you put on perfume by chance?" asked the cowboy. She nodded.

"You brought your bottle of Camile on the rafting trip?" Another nod.

"Can I ask why?"

She shook her head from side to side.

Once the nourishment and caffeine kicked in, the rafters showed signs of life. Margaret began asking what to expect regarding rapids, and in response to that question, the boozy bankers inquired about the likelihood of vomiting. Chloe wanted to know if the Department of Natural Resources regularly patrolled the river and if they were armed.

"She's just kidding," came the response from Augie.

Kane had disappeared, emerging from the woods a few minutes later.

"Hopefully, that was just a bathroom break, not him sharpening his knife on a rock," said Chloe.

They broke camp, loaded the raft, and pushed off onto the river's next challenge. The first stretch checked the scenic box. Paddling was easy. The group again fell into the trance of the river and its surroundings. They alternated white water for calm and pulled over for an early lunch on a driftwood-coated sandy beach. Marcus produced turkey and ham sandwiches from the cooler and an array of canned sodas and bottled water. They watched silently from the shore as the occasional raft floated by with a friendly wave and holler.

The final two-hour stretch would be the most challenging. Marcus prepped the crew, intentionally avoiding any possible discernment of alarm in his message, before leaving the safety of the sand and setting out for the journey's last leg.

With a confident air, the rafters navigated treacherous stretches of river with relative ease. Marcus indicated that the last major rapid would be one of their biggest challenges, and on cue, it appeared on the horizon. The rapid snarled and churned, almost daring the raft to attempt floating it. Marcus barked commands. The river had other ideas as they hit the first swell head-on and were tossed sideways down the wave. As the raft crashed into the next wall of water, Rose's feet slipped from the foot cups attached to the boat's floor. Chloe lunged desperately for the redhead's leg as she fell over the bow toward the seething water. Her tiny ankle slipped through her grasp, and she disappeared over the side.

"Man overboard!" came the call from Marcus.

All eyes turned frantically to the enraged river. Heads swiveled, trying to spot the small yellow life jacket that would most likely be easily visible in calm water, but the turbulence of the class 4 rapids made it almost impossible to see anything other than chaos.

"Where is she?" screamed Augie. "Rose!"

What felt like minutes passed as they desperately scanned the river.

"There!" yelled Chloe.

The redhead floated motionlessly on her back fifteen yards downstream.

Augie paddled hard. Kane quickly removed his life jacket and slipped over the boat's bow, immediately transitioning into a freestyle swim. While extremely dangerous, he could move faster without the life vest. He reached Rose well before the raft did and grabbed the neck of her vest, kicking hard to drag her to shore. Kane could not find a pulse. Quickly removing her life vest, he watched her chest remain motionless. He began shallow compressions on the small girl before transitioning to rescue breaths. She gurgled and convulsed; the Snake River spewed from her mouth as she regained consciousness and vomited.

The raft hit the rocky shoreline hard, and Augie quickly jumped from the bow onto the rocks, kneeling to hold her hand. Their eyes met. She was smiling as if in a dream when he noticed the crack in the back of her helmet.

Kane walked toward the tree line, peeled off his shirt, and wrung it out. Augie noticed it before anyone else—not the multitude of scars covering much of Kane's back but the bone frog tattoo on his right scapula. It was a hallmark of an exclusive club. This man was no serial killer; he was a Navy SEAL.

Kane returned to Rose, gently removed her helmet, and conducted a basic physical and neurological assessment. At first, Chloe intervened when he knelt over the redhead, but Augie softly guided her by the elbow backward a few steps.

"He knows what he's doing, Chloe. Let him work."

"We don't know that, Augie. We just met him, and we know nothing about him," responded Chloe.

"He's a Navy SEAL. He'd have had to attend a six-month Special Operations Tactical Medic course as part of his training. So he's our best option," replied Augie.

"How do you know that?"

"The tattoo on his back and the blade he kept in the ankle holster. Both are reserved for SEALs. Did you see how he stood at attention when Marcus blew reveille?"

Kane shined a flashlight at Rose as he checked her slightly enlarged pupils. He then had her follow his finger, sliding it left, right, up, and down. She tracked slower than he would have liked and had some unexpected muscular weakness in her arms and legs. Her reflexes were normal, but she squealed when he assessed her right elbow. There was already some swelling, most likely from an encounter with a submerged boulder.

"Marcus, what's the final hour like in terms of rapids?" Kane asked.

"Some class ones and twos, that's about it," he replied.

"Okay. I don't think we need a medical evac. She'll be uncomfortable, but our best option is to meet the van at the pickup site and then get her to a hospital for a full checkout. She appears to have some head trauma. Let's go. We're Oscar Mike."

Chloe looked at Augie with confusion.

He responded, "It's a term often used by the military for *On the Move.*"

Margaret and Chloe each held one of Rose's small hands for the last part of the float. The redhead pointed out wildlife with her left hand whenever a curious creature appeared in the air or on the shore.

Marcus had texted the rafting company, and they had two vans waiting at the takeout—one to immediately get Augie, Chloe, and Rose back to their vehicle and the second for the boat, equipment, and other paddlers.

Once they hit the beach, Marcus handed the threesome their gear from the dry bag. Chloe was the first to approach Kane and extend her hand in thanks. Augie followed suit, and Rose embraced his lower body with her left arm. After quick goodbyes, they were off.

CHAPTER EIGHTEEN

Augie drove the Super Duty directly to Jackson Medical Center, where Mr. Lawson met them. He filled the medical team in on the field evaluation of Rose, including the crack in the back of her helmet, elbow pain, and Kane's neurological and muscular exam findings. She spent the next two hours alternately waiting and testing.

The CT scan ruled out any skull fractures and brain bleeds, but it did show an abnormality the doctor wanted to take a better look at with an MRI. Augie paced in the small hospital room as Chloe did her best to distract Rose from all things medical.

There was a light rap on the door, and it opened to reveal Kane.

"Kane?" said Chloe.

"Sorry to barge in unannounced, but I have something for Rose," he said.

Rose's face lit up as Kane approached her, holding the piece of carved driftwood, which had now morphed into a strikingly majestic owl with large eyes, a pronounced beak, and finely textured feathers. It was a work of art. Rose reached down for the pad of hospital stationery and wrote, *Thank you. I love it.*

"How's she doing?" Kane asked.

"We're still waiting on some tests, but thanks to you, she's alive," answered Augie. "Kane, I don't mean to pry, but I saw your bone frog. Safe to assume you are, or were a SEAL?"

He nodded. That was all they would hear on that subject.

"How long are you staying in the valley?" Chloe asked.

"Been here three days, and I have two more left. I just needed to breathe some mountain air and forget some things I've seen recently." He paused. "I grew up in the New Hampshire wilderness. Family's still there, but it was too far to go from Coronado for only five days."

"Well, if you need anything while you're in town, or if you ever get back, come by the ranch," Augie said, handing him a business card. "We're ten miles west of town; it's called Six Dawns." Kane nodded his thanks.

"Rose, take good care of that owl for me. Do you know what a totem animal is?"

She slowly shook her head.

"In Native American culture, a totem animal is the spiritual symbol of a person or a family. It's a guiding spirit that stays with you for your lifetime and in the afterlife. If an owl is your spirit animal, it means you find wisdom in silence. I think it fits you, Rose."

With that, Kane was gone, replaced by a nurse who wheeled Rose down the hall for an MRI.

An hour later, there was a quick rap on the door, and Dr. Barrett entered. He handed Rose a small notepad with six facial emojis running left to right. The first one was colored green, and the face offered up a broad smile. As the row ran on, the faces became less happy, turning shades of yellow, orange, and finally red—a grimacing emoji with a teardrop falling from its right eye.

"Point to the one that represents your pain level and where you feel it, Rose." She selected a shade of yellow and touched her elbow.

"Where else?"

Next, she pointed to an orange face and the right side of her forehead.

"Is that the exact spot, Rose? In the front, not the back?" She nodded.

"Has that been bothering you before the rafting accident?" She nodded again.

Dr. Barrett looked at Mr. Lawson and subtly motioned him outside.

"I'm just going to cut to the chase, Mr. Lawson. We identified a tumor in Rose's right frontal lobe. We'll need a biopsy to determine if it's malignant or benign."

Lawson stared at the doctor. "No. She hit her head on a rock. Could it be some kind of swelling?" he asked defiantly.

"This isn't swelling. It's a mass growing inside her skull, and her helmet was cracked in the back. This is up front," Dr. Barrett countered.

Augie walked from the hospital room into the hallway, and Lawson repeated what the physician had just told him. A hostile glare materialized on the cowboy's face as he stared at the doctor.

"That little girl doesn't deserve this," he said with a clenched jaw. "Are you sure?"

"There is a tumor there, but we won't know until the biopsy if it's cancerous."

"When would the biopsy take place?" asked Augie.

"I'll need to check with the neuro team, but most likely in the next twenty-four hours. I'll give you and Mr. Lawson a few minutes to talk while I call upstairs."

Chloe appeared in the hallway. Her eyes darted between the two men, waiting impatiently for an explanation. Augie broke the news to her. Chloe's mouth opened as if to speak, but no sound emerged as her palm rose to cover her horror.

The doctor returned with positive news from neurosurgery. She would stay the night for continued observation, and they could handle

Rose's case the following morning at 7 a.m. The four of them huddled for a few minutes, discussing the best way to explain the procedure to Rose before entering the room.

"Rose," began Mr. Lawson, who had taken a seat on the edge of her bed. "Dr. Barrett has requested us to stay overnight. Because of the accident, they must do a small procedure on your head."

Dr. Barrett took over. "It's nothing to worry about, and you'll be asleep while we handle the operation. Again, it really is minor."

The redhead just stared.

Operation? That sounds scary.

The physician continued, "And once it's done, they bring you ice cream, so I will need to take your order now if you don't mind."

Ice cream?

"Rose, the ice cream here is genuinely the best any hospital offers in Wyoming. I've even been known to sneak some off my patients' trays if they fall asleep."

The redhead held up two fingers, followed by prayer hands. "Peace to you, too," he responded.

What is wrong with this doctor? Why would I be giving him the peace sign? This is the universal symbol for two scoops, please.

"No, Dr. Barrett, I think Rose is *asking* if she can *please* have two scoops," said Chloe, looking at Rose. She nodded.

Rose picked up the hospital notepad and wrote down her order:

- One scoop chocolate
- One scoop strawberry
- Hot fudge
- Whipped cream
- A cherry

The nurses woke Rose at 6 a.m., followed by Mr. Lawson, who was folded up in the lounge chair beside the hospital bed. The redhead signaled that she was both hungry and thirsty as a nurse provided an oral sedative and apologetically explained that she would need to wait until after the doctors finished the procedure to eat or drink.

A steady stream of medical personnel flowed in and out as they readied the little girl for the operation. A tourniquet was applied to her left arm, and the nurse deftly inserted the sharp needle tip of the IV catheter, puncturing the skin and vein wall. Blood flashed back into the catheter, and the nurse separated the needle.

As complicated as the redhead was to read, Mr. Lawson detected an understandable fear. He had to fight to keep it together. She looked so vulnerable and defenseless, hooked up to tubes, a blood pressure monitor, and an oxygen detector. Lawson stiffened an otherwise quivering lip as he leaned over and kissed Rose on the forehead.

"Easy-peasy, Rose. I'll see you real soon. You'll do great. Love you."

Rose looked around, flustered. *Where's my notepad?* She lifted her right arm, causing a jolt of pain from the rafting injury, and signaled for a pen. The nurse looked at Mr. Lawson and nodded. He turned over the pen and paper to her, and she drew a heart on it.

"Count to ten, Rose," the anesthesiologist said.

Her lips moved. The redhead was out at three.

"Here we go, team," said the lead surgeon.

She drilled a small hole into a shaved portion of Rose's skull and used a stereotactic navigation system to determine the precise position for the tissue extraction. Then, guided by the computer-generated coordinates, she inserted a thin needle and advanced it into the lesion. Once the needle and tissue sample were removed, a small titanium plate was used to cover the burr hole, and the skin was drawn back over the plate. Sutures and a bandage completed the procedure.

Rose woke up in recovery with her grandfather by her side. Augie and Chloe were summoned from the visitor waiting room. Other than some confusion and grogginess, Rose was doing just fine. It took her a few tries to successfully request a mirror.

Where is my hair?

A small shaved patch, now covered with a bandage, drew her ire. She clumsily pounded a closed fist into the bed before reaching for her notepad.

Rose drew a simple cowgirl hat and flipped the pad around, glowering at the three of them.

"Okay, honey, we'll get you a hat this week," said Mr. Lawson. She shook her head—an emphatic no.

Rose pointed to Augie's Stetson.

"Rose, I'm sure the doctor won't want this dirty hat on your freshly bandaged head. So let's get you a new one and one that fits."

Augie pulled the truck around as Rose was wheeled out of the main entrance, and a nurse handed Mr. Lawson a wound care instruction sheet with some dos and don'ts. As they exited the hospital lot to the west, Rose growled, pointing east. When no one understood the issue, she pointed to Augie's cowboy hat, then to her head.

"Now, Rose? You want to go now?" asked Mr. Lawson. A nod.

"I don't think the medical team would be very keen on us going directly from your procedure into town for a hat-buying outing. Let's see how you feel in a couple of days."

The following morning, Rose skipped her walk to the hitching post. Chloe had made her world-famous breakfast casserole; the grand title had been self-proclaimed. Sausage, red and green bell peppers, eggs, cream, onions, and cheddar cheese amalgamated into a food-coma-inducing dish. After two servings, Rose watched Harry Potter and fell back asleep on the couch. This would be her morning routine for the next few days.

Augie removed the turkey feather from his Stetson and walked to the sofa. He lightly brushed the tip against the bottom of Rose's bare foot. It squirmed away blindly, finding a flap of the throw blanket. He introduced the feather to her other sole. Rose woke with a sleepy smile on her face.

"The train is leaving the station, Rose. It's been three days since your procedure. The doctor said you could resume normal activities. Next stop, Beaver Creek Hat and Leathers," announced Augie. Her eyes sparkled as they came to life.

She tugged her brown boots on and stood, flowing directly into a long, arms-over-head stretch.

"Mr. Lawson, will you be joining us this afternoon?" asked Augie.

"No, I think Rose is in good hands with you two." Lawson smiled.

"Last one to the truck is a sausage, bell pepper, onion, cheese, rotten egg casserole!" Chloe exclaimed. Rose took off.

Chloe realized her mistake as soon as the redhead started running. A fall this soon after surgery could be catastrophic. Augie slipped around the corner of the kitchen island and scooped her up before she could do any damage.

"Sorry about that," she said to Mr. Lawson.

"Chloe, it's fine."

They found a spot right on the square and parked. Piles upon piles of cowboy hats crowded the store; racks and stacks filled every square foot of the shop. Chloe located the children's section and guided Rose in that direction.

"Careful with the bandage, Rose," Augie said.

She tried on cowgirl hats for a half hour, settling on three: a rustic-tan straw hat, a white Stetson, and a hot pink rhinestone-covered hat. Rose carried the stack to Augie.

I'll take these, she signaled.

"No, no, no. You get one hat."

It was worth a try.

She chose the classic white Stetson with a black string hat band and three venting eyelets on each side.

"A Stetson. Outstanding choice, Rose. That's what I wear," said Augie.

I know, cowboy.

Augie flagged down a Beaver Creek employee.

"She'd like this Stetson," he said.

"Perfect! I'm what they call a 'hat shaper.' Follow me, and we'll get this ready for you to rodeo in."

Rose trailed her to a counter, where she used a steamer and her hands to mold the hat just right. When everyone agreed that perfection had been reached, they checked out.

"We have one more surprise for you, honey," said Chloe.

Rose looked up expectantly.

"Do you know what day of the week it is?"

She thought for a moment, then gave up with a shrug.

"Wednesday. Do you remember what happens on Wednesdays at four?"

Her eyes grew wide as she scanned the town square, trying to recall which side The Bookshelf was on. She pretended to open a book and read out loud.

"That's right! *Storytime*," said Chloe.

Rose grabbed each of their hands and began to lead them in the wrong direction.

"Other way, Rose," said Augie.

"Rose!" screamed Maya as she deftly navigated her walker through the folding chairs of the bookstore. "Charlie's here somewhere…His mom put a bow tie on him today. If you can get past the nerdy part, he looks regal," she said as she embraced the redhead. "Do you know what *regal* means?" Rose shook her head from side to side. "Neither do I, but that's what Miss Kasey called him."

Rose instinctively reached for the shaved spot on her head before realizing she had her new Stetson on, avoiding any potential embarrassment.

"Hi, Rose. No cookies?" Charlie said with a smile.

Her face flushed as her head shook in apology.

"That's okay…I like your cowgirl hat."

She looked down at her shuffling feet and allowed a small smile to form.

"Rose, Augie and I are going to take a walk around the square. You okay staying by yourself for *Storytime*?"

Her eyebrows raised, then tightened as she tucked her chin.

"Okay, just checking," said Chloe. "We'll see you in an hour."

They walked clockwise around the square, stopping occasionally to pop into a store. As they turned left out of High Country Outfitters, Augie wiped the moisture from his palm onto his jeans and slipped his hand into Chloe's.

"I've missed that kiss from the river all these years," said Augie, catching her by surprise. "You know I've never stopped thinking about you?"

Chloe squeezed his hand and swallowed a quick-witted wisecrack sitting on her tongue about cowboys and feelings. She turned to face him, bringing the pair to a stop.

"Augie, I always held you in my heart…in my darkest days and most joyful times…a piece of you was there…I just wished all of you were."

He reached for her other hand and tucked her close to his body. "I'm really glad you're back, Chloe. I've missed your contagious smile and the wave of nausea that comes over me when I'm close to you, and—"

"Nausea? As in I make you sick to your stomach? You wanna explain that in a bit more detail, cowboy?"

"I can see how that sounds, Chloe," said Augie with a smile. "I guess the less manly version of what I'm trying to say is that I get butterflies in my stomach when I'm around you."

"You're going to get your cowboy card pulled if anyone finds out you just referred to butterflies in the context of your emotions," said Chloe, grinning.

"You won't tell." He smiled and checked his watch. "We better head back to pick up Rose."

Chloe leaned in, kissed him on the cheek, and they headed to The Bookshelf.

CHAPTER NINETEEN

It had been five days since Rose's biopsy when the hospital called. Dr. Barrett's secretary informed Mr. Lawson that the results were back, but she could not confirm the conclusions of the procedure on the phone. She indicated that Dr. Barrett would like to speak with him in person and made it clear that Rose was not to attend. A wave of nausea overcame Lawson as he agreed to a 1 p.m. meeting the following day.

When Augie arrived at the ranch after evening rounds, Mr. Lawson was in the den with the door partially closed, his head in his hands. He approached his boss cautiously.

"Sir, everything okay?"

"Bad phone call, Augie."

"Dennis again?"

"No." Lawson paused. "The hospital. Dr. Barrett wants to meet with me tomorrow to review the biopsy results."

"Okay…Where's Rose?" Augie asked softly.

"She's out by the pond on the swing."

"Sir, did they give you some indication that concerns you?"

"They told me not to bring Rose. I think that's a pretty good indication of something not being right, wouldn't you say?" Augie agreed, but he didn't want to acknowledge it. He looked at his boots, then at the ceiling. Lawson took his silence for agreement.

"Augie, would you mind coming with me to the appointment tomorrow?"

"Of course, Mr. Lawson. What time do we need to leave?"

"Let's plan on twelve thirty."

"I'll pick you up then, sir."

Rose had taken to sleeping in since the procedure. She woke each morning with a slight headache and, having heard Augie and Chloe's reasoning for the same condition, attributed it to a lack of morning coffee. In reality, Rose had been dealing with headaches for the past several months.

The hitching post and headdress remained part of her routine, albeit at a later arrival time than usual. Augie turned onto the gravel drive paralleling the field Rose took to and from the lodge and slowed to watch her drift back toward home. Her arms were out wide as she banked an imaginary airplane through the vibrant yellow knee-high wildflowers. Then, as the redhead approached the tree line, Augie saw them. Rose was blissfully unaware of the thousand-pound moose and her calf grazing on the branches of an aspen to her left. She closed the distance to twenty yards.

Augie slammed the Ford's gas pedal and immediately jerked the wheel left off the road and into the field. He instinctively braced himself as he plowed through a split rail fence, sending cedar logs sailing and causing beauty and beast to turn toward the sound of the exploding barrier. The startled mother moose immediately perceived the nearest human, Rose, as the most imminent threat. She charged. The redhead was still oblivious to the danger behind her as the Ford's needle hit sixty, and the truck bucked wildly over the uneven terrain.

Why is the cowboy speeding his truck at me?

Augie turned the wheel left and then right, setting up for the correct intercept angle. He missed Rose by just a few feet as he jerked the wheel to the right and hit the brakes hard, allowing the truck's back end to swing toward the moose and make contact with a solid thud. Augie turned his head and watched the animal and her calf scamper into the woods. Rose stood motionless, seemingly oblivious to the near-death encounter.

"Hey, Rose," he said as calmly as he could. "I thought you might like a ride to the lodge."

She stared back at him, mouth agape. Her eyes then moved to the destroyed section of cedar fencing and the front-end damage to the pickup.

This driving thing looks to be more fun than I thought. Let's go smash up some more fencing!

Rose nodded, climbed into the back seat, and buckled up, ready for the ride of a lifetime.

The short drive back to the lodge was far too uneventful for Rose as they stuck to the driveway, cruising along at a nap-inducing fifteen miles per hour. After no surprise attacks on fences or people, she raised both arms to shoulder level, flipped her palms skyward, and shook her head as he watched in the rearview mirror.

"What's the matter, Rose? Am I driving too fast or something?" She grimaced.

Augie returned to the lodge at noon after repairing the split rail from the morning's excitement. Chloe and Lawson were in the home office paying bills online, and Rose sat sketching.

Chloe looked up from the computer. "Augie, care to tell me what happened this morning?"

Had she seen the damage to the fence or the Ford? he thought.

"Have a look at what Rose is working on right now," she said.

He walked over to the redhead. She was putting the final touches on another masterpiece, including a shattered fence, a banged-up black truck, Rose with her hair pointing straight up, and two moose standing by the tree line.

Did she know the moose were there the whole time? he thought. *And she was going right toward them. Fearlessly.*

"Rose, you saw the moose and her calf today? Before I drove through the fence?" he asked.
She nodded.

"Honey, moose are responsible for injuring more people in Wyoming than any other animal. They are very dangerous." She shook her head in disagreement.

Rose flipped a page in her sketchbook backward and showed him a drawing of her and a pair of moose. She had her arm extended, touching the calf's nose.

Augie's blood pressure rose. "You haven't been that close to one of these animals before, have you?" A nod.

Chloe and Mr. Lawson had stopped what they were doing and stared in disbelief.

"Have you actually touched one? Be honest, Rose," said Lawson. She nodded again.

Her grandfather raised his voice and said, "Rose, Augie is right. They can be extremely dangerous. You cannot approach them. Do you understand me?" She crossed her arms and frowned before pointing at Augie.

Do you know that the cowboy wrecked the truck?

Augie and Mr. Lawson headed to Jackson Medical Center for the appointment in the Ford. Not a word was spoken.

Based on Dr. Barret's office requesting Rose not to attend the meeting, both assumed there would be bad news—but the *degree* of bad news weighed heavily on the men as Augie pulled into the first open visitor parking spot, and they made their way to reception. After a short wait, they were led down a narrow corridor to a physician's office. Augie's thumb repeatedly worked the chrome button on the Ford's fob, releasing and then folding the key back into its shell as Lawson paced the small room.

Dr. Barrett entered with a quick handshake and greeting.

"Dr. May is on her way down and will join us. She is the neurosurgeon who removed the tissue during the biopsy."

Dr. Jennifer May entered after a quick rap on the door. Introductions were made, and the neurosurgeon spoke.

"I'm just going to cut right to it. The biopsy revealed some bad news. Rose has a glioblastoma." Neither of the men had any idea what that meant.

"It's aggressive cancer that forms from cells called astrocytes that support nerve cells. We usually see it in older adults, but it can occur at any age." May paused to let the men digest her words.

"Treatment?" asked Mr. Lawson softly.

"There is, but this type of cancer is difficult to treat, and a cure is often impossible."

The room was momentarily cloaked in silence as a tear trickled down Lawson's cheek.

"I would suggest having the neuro team operate and remove what they can. Unfortunately, because the glioblastoma grows into normal brain tissue, full removal of the cancer is not achievable. Keep in mind, the procedure itself has risks." Augie stared at the floor.

"After surgery, we would use radiation treatments to target the remaining cells. From there, we may move to a combination of chemotherapy and TTF therapy. The TTF treatment uses an electrical field to disrupt the tumor cells' ability to multiply."

Augie hadn't heard anything past *full removal of the cancer is not achievable.*

"Is this a death sentence?" Lawson said, barely above a whisper.

"Not at this point. We won't know until the surgery is complete and the radiation effects are measured. There is the possibility of Rose living a fairly normal life." Dr. May paused momentarily. "It's just the odds of that are low."

"And if we do nothing?" asked Lawson.

"In large part because Rose has been nonverbal, we don't know how long she's been dealing with headaches, memory loss, speech difficulty, or muscle weakness. If these things have been going on for a year or so, she may only have weeks to months left to live. I can tell you that the tumor is rather large, indicating it has been growing for some time."

"Dr. Barrett and I will give you two a few minutes to talk." With that, the physicians left the room.

A heavy cloud of silence hung for several moments before Lawson spoke.

"I don't think we have a choice, Augie. Her only shot seems to be surgery and radiation. I think it will mean a terrible daily existence in the short term, but maybe it extends her life?"

"I would have to agree with you, Mr. Lawson. As much as things could go wrong with the surgery, it gives her a chance. Sounds to me like without it, she has none."

When the doctors returned to the office, Lawson asked when surgery could be scheduled. Dr. May indicated that her team could operate as soon as Monday morning.

"I'll have my assistant come in and walk you through everything you need to know in preparation. She'll provide you with the paperwork for Sunday evening and arrival instructions for Monday. You'll want to take the weekend to explain to Rose that we need to do another procedure.

"We will be doing MRI-guided laser ablation. It's far less invasive than you probably think when you hear *brain tumor removal*. As a result, there is less postoperative pain and a quicker recovery than with a traditional craniotomy. Rose will most likely be able to return home on Tuesday." Dr. May paused, allowing the pair to absorb the information. "Do either of you have any questions for us?"

"Do we tell Rose she has cancer? asked Lawson.

"Yes," said Dr. May. "And it's best to come from a parent or loved one, not a physician. My assistant can provide some helpful suggestions on how to speak with Rose."

After a brief meeting with the physician assistant, they solemnly departed the hospital. On the drive back to the ranch, they agreed that Rose would be told about Monday's procedure on Sunday.

Augie put the truck's left turn signal on a hundred yards from home.

"Keep going," said Lawson.

"Sir?"

"Take me up to the top of the pass. I need some air and some time."

Augie continued west on Route 22 past the entrance to the ranch. The truck wove up the steep curves before finding a small parking lot at the summit of Teton Pass. They parked and took a short hike further up the mountain along a well-worn dirt path.

Two stumps connected by a planed log made for a primitive bench. Augie could make out Mr. Lawson's property in the distance as the men stared silently down into the valley below. The three hundred acres looked puny from the pass. Augie's eyes rose slowly from the valley floor, spying Sleeping Indian twenty miles to the east.

Mr. Lawson drew a deep breath of fresh mountain air, allowing it to escape with a long sigh.

"There is something different about the air here, Augie. It's like nowhere I've ever been." The cowboy nodded in agreement. "You can taste the clean crispness. If I could bottle this, I'd be a rich man."

"You are a rich man, Mr. Lawson."

"You've got me there, Augie. But my wealth seems to mean very little at the moment."

After several minutes of quiet reflection, Lawson stood. "Let's head back. I think we need to move our bucket list activity up."

CHAPTER TWENTY

ose helped Chloe set the dining room table as Augie laid a platter of grilled salmon and asparagus in the center. She stiffened at the sight of the dish.

That is definitely not for me. I wonder what I'm having.

Mr. Lawson stood from his recliner and moved to the dining room, taking his seat at the head of the table. Rose's eyes shifted from the platter to the kitchen island and back again as she walked to the stove.

Maybe they've forgotten to get the chicken nuggets or mac and cheese from the oven. The oven was off. She pulled the stainless steel handle, and the door swung open. It was empty.

"Rose, what are you doing? Come join us," said Mr. Lawson.

She shook her head, pointing toward the bronze-orange fish. Lawson glanced at the platter.

"Augie, could you have at least removed the head?" he asked.

"That's the tastiest part," Augie answered. Rose shuddered and moved to the pantry.

She returned to the table, theatrically dropped a piece of white bread onto her plate, and reached for a pad of butter.

"Rose, bread and butter are what they serve inmates. Augie has prepared for you a delicious grilled salmon with asparagus. You're going to try some of each. No excuses," said Lawson.

If they even think about giving me the head...

Chloe cut a piece of dark pink flesh and laid it on Rose's plate, joined by a single stalk of asparagus. The redhead played with the salmon, moving it from side to side on her plate.

"Who would like to say grace tonight?" asked Lawson.

"I will," said Chloe.

Heads were bowed, and eyes were closed as Chloe went through a short prayer of thanks while Rose channeled her inner Harry Potter and tried a quick Evanesco spell, but the food did not vanish.

"Amen" echoed through the dining room when Chloe finished.

Rose was chewing, staring at a now-empty plate, when grace concluded.

"Did you eat while Chloe said grace?" asked Mr. Lawson skeptically. "Rose, open your mouth for me."

She shook her head.

"I can tell there's no food in your mouth. You are fake chewing."

She swallowed hard. *All gone.*

Her grandfather continued, "Any chance if I look under the table, Aurora would be at your feet licking her lips?"

Augie slowly bent sideways and cocked his head. The dog was right where Lawson suspected, lapping at invisible morsels on the floor. Augie nodded at Mr. Lawson.

"What do you have to say for yourself?" her grandfather asked.

She stared back at him, patting her belly. *That was delicious?*

"Rose? I asked you a question."

There's only one way out of this.

She held up two fingers, then reached for the platter of salmon and sliced off another piece of fish.

So good, I would like seconds.

"You liked it, Rose?" said her grandfather warily, going along with the ruse for the time being. She nodded excitedly.

"Well then, why don't you plate a third piece and maybe a few more stalks of asparagus?"

"Let me help you with that," Augie said, popping an eyeball from the salmon's head and planting it on her plate before scooping out the other one and swallowing it after two chews.

A combination of nausea from the tumor and the grotesque display from the cowboy caused Rose to expel the remnants of the mozzarella tomato appetizer she had eaten before dinner. This triggered Chloe to begin dry heaving and run for the bathroom.

That's one way around me having to eat three servings of fish and asparagus.

Rose walked sheepishly into the kitchen, tore off several sheets of paper towels, and began cleaning up the regurgitated, partially digested food.

Augie moved his plate to the island and went to check on Chloe before returning to scarf down his fish and vegetables. Mr. Lawson had decided he was no longer hungry and had settled into his recliner. The redhead downed her slice of buttered bread and grinned mischievously.

Once everything was tidied up and the leftovers put away, Mr. Lawson spoke.

"Rose, please run into the den and get the orange bucket."

She set the pail at his feet.

"Okay, ready to pull another one?"

This time, her grandfather pretended to close his eyes, fishing for an index card at the bottom, and when he was confident he had found a certain redheads, he plucked it from the bucket.

"This is one of Rose's. It says…" He paused for dramatic effect. "*Go to the rodeo*. It's your lucky day, young lady. The Jackson Hole Rodeo operates on Wednesdays and Saturdays. I think Cassidy is riding this week. We'll go tomorrow." Rose broke into a smile and unleashed an enthusiastic round of fast clapping.

The Ford rolled into 447 Snow King Avenue's dusty parking lot at 7:45 p.m. Showtime was 8 p.m., and it was a perfect night for a rodeo under the clear Wyoming evening sky.

Rodeo ran generations deep in the cowboy town. It was in the fabric of the locals and became embedded in the tourists, travelers, and holidayers. The latter took a piece of it with them when they abandoned town as the leaves began falling.

Augie, Chloe, Rose, and Mr. Lawson breathed it before they saw it. Rodeo has a distinct scent where funnel cake and buttercream meet leather, wet hay, and manure. It's dust, sweat, and pageantry. It's rodeo.

Rose had never even been to a zoo, let alone a rodeo. Other than a sprinkling of National Geographic television, squirrels, horses, moose, and enormous mice were the extent of her in-person wildlife experience.

"Rose, wait 'til you see the goats, bulls, broncos, calves, and clowns," Mr. Lawson said.

Clowns. That will be fun, thought Rose.

An announcer's voice boomed over the speakers. "Ladies and gentlemen, boys and girls, welcome to the Jackson Hole Rodeo. Please stand for the national anthem."

The action commenced with the calf roping event as a bovine was liberated from a small chute. It ran hard, with a cowboy on his mount and in pursuit. The denim-clad wrangler spun his lasso counterclockwise above his head and released it for a ten-foot float, targeting the calf's head. It descended perfectly. The rider simultaneously brought the horse to a stop and dismounted, landing and transitioning immediately to a sprint. With the lasso tied to the saddle horn, the calf came to a quick and violent halt. The roper added to the violence by lifting the two-hundred-pound animal into the air and taking it hard to the ground. He reached for his back pocket and pulled a tie-down rope, then, using a "wrap and a slap," the cowboy tied the mandatory three legs together. All of this occurred in 10.5 seconds.

The crowd cheered, but Rose did not. Inside or out. The redhead was mortified at what had just occurred. She looked at Chloe and shook her head from side to side, narrowing her eyes.

"Augie, I'm going to take Rose to get something to eat. We'll be back in time for the barrel racing." Augie nodded.

Chloe knew she could kill twenty minutes weaving through the metal pens housing bulls and horses searching for the concession stand. An order of fried Oreos and a jumbo corn dog were delivered across the counter to Rose. They walked along the outside of the grandstand past pens of fifteen-hundred-pound Brahman bulls, broncos, and calves. Rose slowed, moving ever so slightly away from the bull's fencing, shocked by the horned creature's sheer size.

"Ladies and gentlemen, that concludes the calf roping. We will begin the barrel racing in five minutes," said the P.A. announcer. Rose looked up expectantly at Chloe.

"Heck yeah. Let's get going, Rose. We don't want to miss this."

They returned to their center section, fourth-row seats just in time.

"Rose, keep your eye on the opening at the end of the arena," said Augie.

The announcer introduced the first rider, and a coffee-brown quarter horse burst through the open yellow gate at forty miles per hour. On the saddle was Six Dawn's own—Cassidy. The horse broke right for the first of three barrels set up in a triangle.

Cassidy turned her partner two hundred seventy degrees on a dime and exploded straight across the arena for the second barrel.

Another tight turn, and she was on to the final one in the cloverleaf pattern. Coming around the last barrel resulted in a mad dash for the finish line; Cassidy's dark mane flew wildly in the wind.

"Thirteen point three five seconds," hollered the voice through the public address as Rose stood and clapped eagerly.

Now, this I like. A giddy smile and frenetic nod replaced the scowl and head shake. Riders continued to gush from the yellow gate, each drawing a standing ovation from at least one redhead in the crowd. She loved the strength, power, confidence, and elegance.

Steer wrestling was up next, and Chloe got ahead of this one. Rose would undoubtedly be unsettled watching a cowboy jump from his horse onto the back of a fleeing steer, grab it by the horns, and wrestle it to the ground.

"Rose, let's see if we can meet some barrel racers. Maybe they'll sign your notepad," said Chloe.

Yes, yes, yes!

They wound through the maze of stands, fencing, and stalls, arriving at Autograph Alley, populated by a dozen racers. Rose produced her small notepad and sheepishly handed it to the first rider. She signed *Cheyenne* with a smile and asked a question.

Where are we from? thought Rose. The redhead wasn't sure. Such a simple question with such a complicated answer. Her new family of four didn't have a common geographic thread.

Chloe saved her. "We're from the good old U.S. of A!"

"Welcome to Wyoming!" said Cheyenne.

Rose couldn't take her eyes off the cowgirl. An intricate peach-stitched floral pattern wove its way up her dark denim sleeve and disappeared under shoulder-length hair. The buttons on her shirt matched the color of the stitching perfectly, while rhinestones and studs adorned a black belt that sparkled in the arena lights.

"Hey, Rose," came a familiar voice. "What did you think about the barrel riders?" asked an animated Cassidy.

Rose smiled and formed a heart shape with her thumbs and pointer fingers that Chloe had taught her.

"I love them too," said Cassidy, mirroring the symbol. "How about I introduce you to some cowgirls?"

The redhead looked at Chloe. *Can we?*

She broke into a soft smile and nodded her approval. They spent most of an hour in Autograph

Alley—escorted by Cassidy—followed by another trip to the concession stand. Chloe ordered, and Rose grimaced at the request.

This could be worse than the fish with its head on that the cowboy grilled.

Chloe tugged a piece of the savory treat off and immediately gulped it down. Then, she pulled another portion and handed it to Rose.

"Trust me, Rose. You'll love it."

She took a slight nibble, then a bigger bite.

This could not possibly be an actual elephant ear.

The warm fried dough, coated in cinnamon and sugar, disappeared from the plate in seconds, except for one small piece.

They returned to Autograph Alley, where Rose hugged Cassidy and offered her the final bit of elephant ear before returning to their seats for the last event—bull riding.

Rose listened intently as Mr. Lawson provided the basics.

"In a minute, you will see a cowboy climb up over the railing of that bucking chute down there." Lawson pointed. "He'll jump right on the bull's back and wrap a rope tightly around his hand. He tries to stay on the bull for eight seconds as it bucks around the arena. Oh, and he can't touch the bull or himself with his other hand." Rose nodded in understanding.

The first contestant boarded an enormous beast named Voodoo Loco and securely wrapped the braided nylon rope around his gloved hand. A few minor adjustments and tugs later, the rider nodded to the cowboy operating the door before a tidal wave of energy screamed from the chute.

The bull was airborne instantly, spinning left in a whirlpool of movement. Voodoo Loco's hindquarters seemed to move independently from the rest of his body as the enraged animal kicked in a furious attempt to remove his rider. Four point three seconds later, the helmeted cowboy was flung into the air, landing hard on his back.

Three rodeo clowns moved in quickly to distract the bull as the rider scampered to his feet and climbed up and over the fencing next to the chute. Voodoo got ahold of one unlucky bullfighter with its horns, hurtling the helpless clown like a rag doll before the others corralled it out of the arena.

These are the clowns Grandpa was talking about? Where are the juggling and balloon animals?

Rose left the rodeo more confused than she had ever been. She jerked up in her seat multiple times during the ride home, turned both palms skyward, and shook her head. The universal sign for, *what was that?*

"Rose, did you have a good time?" Augie asked.

She conceded with a gentle nod.

Yes, cowboy, it was fun.

A gold Denali with an Enterprise rental car sticker on the bumper passed the Super Duty at a dangerous rate of speed, crossing the double yellow line and drawing Augie's ire. He raised his fist out the window, laid on the horn, and gave the guy the middle finger.

"Tourists!" he grumbled.

Rose looked at Chloe.

"It's just a greeting we use out here in Wyoming. Augie's saying hi or bye. He probably knows them or something." Chloe covered poorly for the cowboy.

CHAPTER TWENTY-ONE

A slow, rising ball of fire lit up the Gros Ventre, but this particular Sunday was different. Three of the four felt it when they woke. A sense of trepidation permeated the breakfast table, knowing Mr. Lawson would need to tell Rose what was in store for her on Monday. Augie was the first to break the silence in an attempt to restore normality to a situation that was anything but normal.

"I was thinking maybe I'd go to church this morning if anyone would like to join me."

What's church? was Rose's first thought. She drew a question mark on her pad.

Augie looked at Lawson.

"Rose, your parents never took you to church?" asked her grandfather. She shook her head. It was more of a sign for *I'm not sure what you are talking about.*

"I'll be leaving at 10:45 if you would like to join. They have coffee and doughnuts," he said.

All three were out front when Augie pulled the pickup around from the side parking pad. Crossroads was a non-denominational megachurch on the outskirts of Jackson. None of the crew had been there before, but the laid-back, easily understood sermons had created quite the buzz around town.

Mr. Lawson and Augie had both been raised Protestant, while Chloe was a twice-a-year Catholic. But, whether out of guilt from her mother or hoping that God would speak to her, she always managed to attend Easter and Christmas Mass.

On the ride over, Mr. Lawson had done his best to give Rose a quick tutorial on religion. He explained that Protestants believe salvation can be found through faith in Jesus, and Catholicism is similar but also emphasizes good works.

Crossroads was a coffee lover's paradise. The voluminous three-story lobby had multiple java stations, each attended by an almost too-congenial barista. Rose pondered sneaking off to give coffee a second chance but thought better of it as the crowd swelled through the four sets of doors. The three adults each filled a Styrofoam cup with piping-hot java and headed into the main auditorium.

The setup rivaled any small-scale concert venue. Huge overhead lighting bars lit up the stage with a myriad of colors while giant speakers piped house music into the arena. The stadium seating could accommodate over two thousand worshipers.

Four church band members walked on stage to polite applause as an organ began to fill the room with one of the most iconic rock song introductions of all time. The drummer layered in a pattern on the symbols, followed by a repeating guitar arpeggio running through a delay pedal. The house lights flashed on momentarily as "Where the Streets Have No Name" woke the church walls and any members who may have just rolled out of bed.

The pastor strolled onto the stage wearing jeans and an untucked flannel shirt, an iPad mini in his hand. He introduced a guest speaker who talked about how he found God at the lowest point of his life. Next, a five-minute educational segment shot in Bethlehem appeared on the massive video screen.

The preacher returned to the stage. "Do you doubt God's goodness? His willingness to work miracles in our lives?"

We'll soon find out, thought Lawson.

The pastor continued for fifteen minutes before he concluded his sermon; the band returned, and a small pail was passed down the aisle in front of the foursome and wound its way to Augie, who handed it to his right to Rose. She peered inside.

They give you money to come to church? Rose reached into the bucket and withdrew a five-dollar bill.

"Rose!" Mr. Lawson barked quietly. "That's not for you. It's for the church."

She dropped the bill back into the pail and passed it to her grandfather, who deposited a large wad of cash.

The service wrapped up with a moment of silent prayer. Rose could see most of the congregation's chins dip toward the ground in the semi-darkness.

What could they be looking for on the floor? Money that spilled from the buckets? She searched.

There was no doubt as to the intentions of Rose's chaperones. With heads bowed and eyes closed, each pleaded to spare the nine-year-old's life before the band closed with a moving rendition of "Hallelujah." A tear streamed down Chloe's cheek as the lights turned on and the gatherers filed out.

The drive home was quiet. A pit in Mr. Lawson's stomach grew more significant with each mile that passed under the Ford's tires. Augie and Chloe sensed that he was still wrestling with how exactly to tell Rose about the operation the following morning.

They approached a well-known orange and pink sign.

"Let's stop at Dunkin' Donuts." Lawson broke the silence, and Rose's eyes lit up. "Go to the drive-through, Augie."

The cowboy swung the truck into the parking lot. Rose scrambled to get her pad, and she scribbled feverishly. *Vanilla Frosting with Sprinkles. Powdered Sugar. Jelly. Strawberry Frosted.* She tore the page

from her book and handed it to her grandfather
in the front passenger seat as they approached the
menu board.

"Rose, you cannot eat four donuts."

I would have given you eight if I had more time.

"Welcome to Dunkin'. May I take your order?"
cracked a voice through the speaker.

Augie looked at Mr. Lawson.

"We'll take a dozen donuts, assorted flavors,
and three large coffees, black." Rose tapped her
grandfather's shoulder and flashed two fingers.

"Two dozen?" he said, shaking his head
a firm no.

The voice from the speaker materialized again.
"Okay, so two dozen assorted and three coffees.
That will be twenty-eight dollars and fifty-two cents.
Please pull forward."

Her grandfather grunted and motioned for
Augie to drive. Rose calculated that if each adult had
one donut, she would be left with twenty-one. She
figured those would last her three days.

Rose removed the top of one of the boxes and
eyed her choices. The first decision was always
the hardest, and there would be only one way to
decide fairly.

*One potato, two potatoes, three potatoes, four,
five potatoes, six potatoes, seven potatoes, more.*
Powdered sugar it would be.

"Rose, please don't make a mess of the truck. We're almost home," Augie requested.

Rose had managed to keep the rear seat and floor free of donut debris, but her black Johnny Cash t-shirt and jeans were another story. A small powdered sugar handprint was visible on the shirt, and enough remains of the sweet fried dough rested in the crevices of her denim pants to form a donut hole at the very least.

"Honey, get changed into something with less sugar on it and meet me at the barn. I need some help brushing out Scarborough. Okay?" her grandfather asked. Rose nodded and started up the staircase. "The donuts stay down here," Lawson added.

She returned to the kitchen island, deposited the two boxes on the counter, and headed up the stairs.

"Mr. Lawson, would you like Augie or me to be with you when you tell Rose?" Chloe asked in a hushed tone.

"No, but thank you. I think the mood may come off as more serious than I'd like if we're all around for the conversation. She might pick up on that." He headed for the barn.

Rose skipped across the flagstone with her sketchbook and slapped the rope swing seat, sending it into a pendulum of motion. Although Scarborough had been thoroughly brushed out the day prior, her grandfather had set out two soft bristle brushes. This would just be an exercise to keep Rose's mind from becoming too focused on the seriousness of the chat.

Mr. Lawson had Rose begin on the horse's chest and powerful front legs. She worked the brush in the direction of Scarborough's hair growth, freeing fine dust particles. Dr. May's assistant had suggested writing down what he would say, and he took a quick look at the notecard in his pocket.

"Rose, the doctor would like to see you back tomorrow." Her brush slowed. "They need to do another procedure…Dr. May assured me it won't hurt at all and will help with your headaches and nausea." Her brush stopped.

"Honey, have a seat on that hay bale for a minute."

Rose sat, staring down at the brush in her hand.

"Have you heard the word cancer?" Lawson had been told not to avoid the term. She shook her head a curious no.

"It's stuff in your body that's not working as it should and can make you sick. You might also hear the word tumor when you are at the hospital. That's a lump that isn't supposed to be there, and Dr. May is going to remove it."

"Rose? Can you look at me?" Her eyes met his as he dropped to a knee and reached for her hand.

"I want you to know that Augie, Chloe, and I will be with you every step of the way. Okay?" She gave a slender half-nod. "Do you have any questions you'd like to ask me?"

She removed her cowgirl hat, grasped a lock of hair, and tugged on it.

"Yes, they will probably need to shave a small patch of hair again." Her jaw clenched as she shook her head.

"Rose, I want to show you something." He gently guided her from the bale. She knelt in the dust and hay.

Lawson pointed to a long scar along the horse's abdomen. Rose had never noticed it before.

"Scarborough had almost her entire belly shaved off by the doctor three years ago. He had to perform emergency surgery. Some intestines had gotten twisted, and it was very dangerous for her. She had to stay in the horse hospital for two days, and I know for a fact that some of her barn mates made fun of her hairless tummy when she got home. But look at her now. She's the queen bean around here."

A thin smile appeared. Rose traced the rough scar through her gray coat with two fingers before standing and moving to the horse's head, lifting an earflap and whispering in the equine's ear. Scarborough turned toward Rose and nuzzled the side of her face.

"What did you tell her, Rose?" She just stared at her grinning grandfather.

It's what Scarborough told me.

Rose's surgery required her to arrive at the hospital at 5:30 a.m. A waxing gibbous moon lit up the chilly Jackson morning as Augie carried the still-sleeping girl to the pickup.

"I'll follow you over, Augie. I think we should have two vehicles since I'll probably be staying overnight."

"Yes, sir," replied Augie.

Rose slept with her head resting in Chloe's lap as they silently drove to town.

Upon arriving, Mr. Lawson filled out several pages of paperwork for the hospital as Rose, Augie, and Chloe sat idly in the waiting room. Augie tried to distract Rose with a hidden pictures game in a *Highlights* magazine. Either the tumor was turning Rose into a savant, or the age range for this game was not the right fit. She completed the first one in under thirty seconds, while it took Augie three minutes.

They moved on to kids' riddles.

"What's bright orange with green on top and sounds like a parrot?" Augie asked.

Rose thought for a minute, then wrote, *A carrot.*

"Very good!"

"Next one. A girl fell off a twenty-foot ladder. Why wasn't she hurt?"

Rose pictured the tall ladder in the barn that went up to the hay loft. She would definitely get hurt if she fell from the top of it. She shrugged her shoulders in defeat.

"The girl fell off the bottom rung," said Augie.

I should have gotten that one.

They went through a few more before a nurse appeared between the double doors and introduced herself as Mary. She escorted them back to a pre-op room, had Rose change into a surgical gown, and provided an oral sedative.

"Comfortable?" The redhead nodded.

"Rose, we're going to put an IV in your arm now so the doctors can administer the medicine. I know you had one of these before. Remember, there is just a little prick."

Mary swabbed the inside of Rose's elbow, found a suitable vein, and inserted the IV catheter, drawing a grimace. She placed some sticky ECG leads on her chest, wrapped a blood pressure sleeve around Rose's left bicep, and put a pulse oximeter on the tip of her index finger. Mary entered some readings into an iPad, asked Rose if she needed anything, and disappeared through the door.

Dr. May knocked and entered with a warm smile a few minutes later.

"Rose! You're still here. I thought you might try to sneak out a window or something. I know how much kids *love* being in hospitals." Rose was far too nervous to acknowledge the humor.

The neurosurgeon clasped the young girl's hand, pressed gently, and assured her everything would be fine.

"And I know what you're thinking," said Dr. May. "How soon can I have a double scoop of ice cream after the procedure? Right? Dr. Barrett told me how much you love ice cream."

Actually, that wasn't close to what I was thinking.

Rose went with it and nodded.

"I'll be sure to have some for you in recovery when we finish."

Dr. May indicated that two nurses would be in shortly to complete more preoperative procedures, followed by an introduction from the anesthesiologist. Once everything was readied, Rose would be wheeled down the hall to an operating room, and the family would be directed to the OR waiting room.

Rose's attention was drawn to the blue vital signs monitor at the side of the gurney, flashing colorful numbers and squiggly lines. The lime green numeral in the screen's top right corner read sixty-five and had a red heart next to it. She pointed and looked quizzically at Chloe.

"That's your heart rate, Rose. It's telling us that your ticker is beating sixty-five times per minute. Believe it or not, you can somewhat control that number." The redhead tilted her head skeptically.

Chloe continued, "Take a deep, slow breath over five seconds, then hold it for three seconds before exhaling. Do that three times."

At the end of her final exhale, Rose checked the monitor. The green number had dropped to sixty-two, and a slender smile formed. She pointed at the green, wavy line with sharp vertical peaks at regular intervals and looked at Chloe again.

"That's showing your heartbeat. Each one of those mountains rising straight up represents a heartbeat." She nodded and then worked her way through the other readings with Chloe.

The redhead held her breath as long as she could, attempting to drop the yellow respiration number from twenty to zero before Mr. Lawson intervened.

"Let's try not to pass out before surgery, Rose. We would have a lot of explaining to do."

You're no fun, Grandpa.

She turned her attention to a red box mounted on the wall with a key.

That looks interesting. She reached toward it.

"No, Rose. That's a sharps disposal container for used needles," said Mr. Lawson.

The anesthesiologist entered as a nurse exited.

"Rose, this will be similar to your previous procedure. I will administer something called Propofol once you are in the operating room, and you will have the best nap of your life." The anesthesiologist continued, "If you're ready, the nurses will take you down now. I'll show your family to the waiting room."

Rose glanced quickly at her grandfather before turning back to the doctor. Augie noticed.

Are they leaving me?

"Doc, I think Rose is nervous about us leaving her," said Augie.

"I'll tell you what, I'm going to see if Dr. May is okay with me providing the general anesthesia while you all are still here. I'll be back in a few minutes."

He returned with a smile. "Rose, they can stay with you until you fall asleep."

This sounds better.

"Count to ten, sunshine," said the anesthesiologist. She was asleep by six and was wheeled down the hall as the threesome walked somberly to the waiting room.

Once in the operating room, a nurse sterilized the exposed skin, and a 3mm hole was drilled into her skull. Using a real-time MRI for guidance, Dr. May navigated a thin fiber-optic laser applicator toward the area of the brain where the tumor was located. She then applied laser heat to destroy the cancerous tissue. It was a meticulous process that required a steady hand and tremendous teamwork.

Two hours after arriving at the hospital, Augie and Chloe walked outside, finding the mid-morning sun taking the chill from the air. Chloe slipped her arm through the bend in Augie's elbow as they strolled through the hospital's grounds. They paused, looking west, and took in Grand Teton rising above its brethren's summits with its sky-piercing snow-covered peak.

Augie's phone vibrated, and he tapped the green icon for messages. *It's done.* Their pace quickened as they reached the main entrance and wound through the hospital's corridors until they located the OR waiting room.

"She's in recovery," said Mr. Lawson. "The nurse didn't offer many details but said Dr. May would be out shortly."

The neurosurgeon appeared in light blue scrubs, having forgone her lab coat.

"It went well, and she's still sleeping. It will be a bit more challenging to determine any impairments from the procedure due to her mutism, but I'll assess that later today. We'll go after the part of the tumor intertwined with the healthy brain matter using radiation once Rose recovers. I'd say that will be in the next four to six weeks."

"Can we see her?" asked Augie.

"I'm sorry, but not until she's out of recovery and moved to a room in the ICU. That should happen in the next two hours. You are welcome to wait here, but I'd suggest going to lunch, and you may be able to visit her when you return. Off the record, our cafeteria isn't that great, but it's in the east wing if you're interested." Lawson nodded.

"Mr. Lawson, if you want to stay, Chloe and I can pick you up a sandwich."

"That would be nice, Augie."

The pair exited the hospital and headed for the Super Duty.

"Let's walk," said Chloe, and they turned toward town.

"Do you think you'll die here?" she asked, catching him by surprise.

"As in here at this hospital, Chloe?"

"No, I mean in this cowboy town. Do you ever see yourself leaving?"

"I guess I haven't given it all that much thought. Planning anything unrelated to the ranch more than a month in advance would be uncharted waters for me."

"I won't hold you to anything, Augie."

"I guess I'd give it a seventy-five percent chance of me living out my final days here."

"And where would the remaining twenty-five have you end up?"

"Somewhere warmer. That's about as specific as I can be. These Teton winters become harder and harder to manage. Heading out at seven a.m. when it's minus ten degrees is something I would not miss. And my office isn't heated. Mother Nature has its own thermostat settings. What about you, Chloe? Where might you want to live out your final years?"

"I don't know. I like the West Coast, but the more time I spend here, the more I miss it. Florida or Texas would be too hot for me. Colorado would be nice; maybe Boulder. That's the great thing about my graphic design career. I can do it from anywhere."

The line at Pearl Street Bagels was out the door—nothing unusual for Jackson's famous bagel and sandwich shop. A PB&J on pumpernickel was ordered for Mr. Lawson, and Chloe requested a cinnamon raisin bagel with honey walnut cream cheese, while Augie asked for chicken salad with pepper jack cheese on a plain bagel. The three bundles of parchment paper were dropped into a sack, Augie paid, and they headed back toward the hospital.

"Do you think Mr. Lawson will stay here forever?" Chloe asked.

"I think he'll start spending more time in Fort Worth. He'd have a hard time selling this place, though. It has so much history and nostalgia; his soul is in this land. Rose will, of course, factor in as well."

They walked the final two blocks in silence. The reality and gravity of Rose's situation grew with each step as they closed in on the Jackson Medical Center.

"Any news?" Augie asked as he sat beside Lawson and pulled the sandwiches from the bag.

"Nothing yet. Every time I look at the clock on the wall, I feel like fifteen minutes have passed, but it's never more than four or five."

Lawson bit into his bagel.

"Peanut butter and jelly on pumpernickel," he said after a big swallow. "How'd you know, Augie?"

The cowboy laughed.

"Sir, in all the years I've known you, that is the only sandwich you've ever ordered at Pearl Street."

"That's not true. Once, they were out of pumpernickel. I had to substitute an everything bagel." Lawson grinned.

Each time a set of scrubs entered the waiting room, their heads rose quickly in unison. Then, just before noon, a familiar nurse appeared and walked toward them.

"Rose is awake and in one of our ICU rooms if you'd like to see her. She is still under the effect of anesthesia and pain medicine."

The nurse led them down a hallway to the Neuro Intensive Care Unit.

She looks so brittle and vulnerable, thought Augie.

Tubes and leads entered and exited various portions of the redhead's gown and body. The vital signs monitor danced with colors. A sterile dressing covered the incision on the front of her skull, and an IV drip trickled Gabapentin into the port on Rose's arm.

Her eyes had to work to focus on each visitor as she shook her head, trying to clear the fog of lingering anesthesia.

I know you, she slurred to herself, pointing at each of them.

Mr. Lawson sat on the edge of the hospital bed.

"How are you feeling, sweetheart?"

A drunken smile crossed her face.

I'm sorry, did you say something?

"Rose? Can you give me a thumbs-up or a thumbs-down? How are you feeling?"

She went with a nonpartisan sideways thumb, and all three visitors nodded.

I don't see any ice cream, people.

She began a movement resembling that of an orchestra conductor. Lawson looked at Chloe and Augie.

"Honey?" said Lawson.

She flailed her right arm in the air again, then pointed to the paper pad on the side table.

Augie delivered it to her with a pen.

An unsteady hand wrote, *Ice cream?*

On cue, Dr. May entered with a hospital food service employee.

"Chocolate and strawberry, right, Rose?" said the surgeon.

She managed a bite of each before the pain medicine nudged her back to dreamland.

"Rose should be able to head home tomorrow, provided nothing unexpected occurs with her recovery. She'll be sleeping a lot over the next twenty-four hours, and if any of you would like to stay tonight, unfortunately, the only thing we can offer you is the waiting room. Our intensive care unit isn't set up to host visitors."

"Thanks, doc," said Lawson. "Augie, why don't you and Chloe head back to the ranch? I'll stay overnight with Rose."

CHAPTER TWENTY-TWO

Augie turned right on Route 22, transitioning from the strip of fast food restaurants, hotels, and gas stations to a more soothing pastoral scene. Wildflowers blanketed a field on the north side of the highway, and the Teton range filled the truck's windshield as they rounded East Gros Ventre Butte. Augie reached overhead and pressed the button for the Ford's sunroof, allowing the afternoon breeze to flood the cab with the scent of pine and hay.

"I feel like a horseback ride to clear my head when we get back. Care to join me?" Augie asked.

Chloe smiled softly and nodded.

"It's a date, then," he said.

Augie saddled a reddish-brown quarter horse named Copper for Chloe and prepared Winston for himself. He put a few supplies in his saddle bag and led the horses from their stalls. Chloe had changed into tight, dark denim jeans, a scarlet flannel button-down, and light brown riding boots. She donned a gray Stetson. Standing on the mounting block, Chloe placed her left foot in the stirrup and effortlessly floated onto the saddle.

The horses walked leisurely from the barn, through the arena, and down a single-track trail leading to the tree line. They picked up the pace to a trot as the path widened in the woods. The only sounds were birds, hooves, and the horses' heavy respirations. The pair splashed through a creek, up a soft incline, and parted ways with the dense pine canopy, emerging on the riverbank. Passing the single black cottonwood, Augie couldn't help but scan the land for any trace of the former makeshift gravesite, but the gravel and sand had melded seamlessly, covering any signs of the foggy night and the bag of bones.

They followed the river south until the cottonwood was out of sight, and the spooky chill slowly left his spine.

"Let's stop here for a picnic," said Augie.

"A picnic? Do cowboys do picnics?" asked Chloe. Augie smiled.

They dismounted and lashed the equines to an aspen. He opened the saddle bag and removed a half bottle of Prosecco, two plastic wine glasses, a zip lock of sliced gouda cheese, and another with wheat crackers.

"What's the occasion?"

"Do I need an occasion, Chloe?" He grinned.

Augie popped the sparkling wine bottle and filled each glass as fizzy bubbles overflowed their rims. Chloe set the cheese and crackers down on a small boulder.

"A toast," said Augie. "To Rose's successful surgery."

"And to us," added Chloe, with a smile.

They raised their glasses and sent them on a collision course. The polycarbonate encounter made more of a dud than a clink.

"To us," echoed Augie.

They sat on the riverbank, propped up by a smooth knee-high rock. When the wine was drained, Chloe shifted to a supine position and laid her head on the cowboy's lap. Augie cautiously ran his fingers through her dark, silky hair. Three digits followed the smooth strands along her scalp and down the back of her neck. Her heartbeat slowed while the cowboys rose.

"I think I fell asleep," said Chloe as she slowly sat up. "That was lovely."

Yes, it was, thought Augie.

"What's—" Augie's question was interrupted by the most delicious lips. Coconut and a hint of wine convened, delivering a delicate kiss.

"I hope that was okay. I was—" This time, it was Chloe's question that was arrested by passionate lips.

The cowboy found her familiar tongue, holding her cheeks softly in his calloused palms. She blindly reached for his Stetson and set it gently on the bank. Her fingers located the buttons on his cotton shirt, and one by one, they were released. She felt the aged, raised scar on his chest, courtesy of a drunk wielding a folding knife.

Augie nibbled on her ear and untucked her flannel shirt as she nimbly worked his button-fly jeans.

God, I hope no rafters are coming down the Snake, he thought.

"Chloe," he whispered nervously. "It's been a while, so I'd like to temper any preconceived notions about expected performance, and—" Chloe put a finger to his lips.

"Shhhh," she murmured.

They made passionate love, with the river and wind conducting a symphony. The water reached a crescendo, and the breeze seemed to slow. They lay in silence with Chloe's head on his chest, rising and falling with each of the cowboy's shallow breaths. He ran a finger down her cheek, detecting a tear.

"Chloe, is everything okay?" She smiled.

"Everything is more than okay, Augie. I'm just really happy to be here, at this moment, with you."

"Ditto," replied the cowboy predictably.

"I see you haven't progressed in sharing deep feelings," she said, pinching him playfully.

"I guess I haven't. In my defense, this life is full of solitude, though. Some days go by with little to no interaction with another living soul, especially when Mr. Lawson is in Texas. Add to that, I'm not the most trusting person on the planet, so I keep a lot of things to myself. Winston does get to hear some of my deepest thoughts, but as far as I know, he's never shared those." He looked toward his horse. "Have you, Winnie?" Chloe shook her head.

"Chloe, I can't tell you how glad I am that you showed up in Jackson this summer. Having you here at such a difficult time has been a godsend." Augie looked at the river. "I mean that personally and professionally. How you've helped out and been there for all of us during one of the most challenging times we've seen on the ranch."

"Are you sharing your feelings, cowboy?" Chloe beamed. "Well, it's a start."

As Augie loaded the empty wine bottle, glasses, and zip locks into his saddle bag, Chloe finished tucking in her shirt. He helped her onto Copper, admiring her elegant beauty just a little too long. She winked at him. Mounting Winston, he immediately broke into a canter and looked back at Chloe.

"Last one to the cottonwood tree makes dinner," he yelled back.

Chloe transitioned from a walk to a gallop in a matter of seconds. They raced along the gravel riverbank, throwing up dust clouds in their wake. Chloe leaned forward, rising slightly from the saddle, her arms working in rhythm with Copper's forward and back head motion. She closed the gap to one length as they turned the bend, the cottonwood in sight, and crossed the imaginary finish line in a photo finish. Chloe declared herself the winner due to Augie's head start, and the cowboy conceded. He would be preparing dinner that evening.

They returned to the barn, washing and brushing out the two quarter horses for half an hour. Chloe brought a bag of carrots from the house and held a carrot top. She let Copper bite off the tip of the sweet treat, drawing a neigh from Winston, then moved to his stall and hand-fed him an orange root.

"Any requests for dinner, Chloe?"

"Duck a l'orange sounds good," she replied.

"Uh-huh," said the cowboy.

Augie texted Mr. Lawson. *Any idea how to make something called duck all orange?*

The cowboy's phone rang.

"I think you mean duck a l'orange. I've had it before at the Four Seasons in Teton Village but never cooked it myself," Lawson said. "Why do you ask?"

"I owe Chloe dinner tonight, and she said she wanted that."

"Are you sure she was serious, Augie?"

"That, I don't know," he replied.

"Well, I have an idea for you. There's a restaurant at Powderhorn and West Broadway. I used to stop in there at least once a week. The manager is a cute girl, a real hippie, and she'll help you. Stop by and see her."

"I'm leaving now, sir." Augie jumped into the Super Duty.

An hour later, he pulled into the parking pad on the ranch, exited the Ford, entered the front door, and deposited a plastic carry-out bag on the kitchen island.

"Dinner is served," he said.

Chloe set her book down, stood, and eyed the sack of food suspiciously. A cute black and white panda sat in the middle of a red-and-white circle.

"Panda Express, Augie? Really?"

She moved to examine the contents of the Styrofoam container.

"It's chicken? What happened to my special request?" She smiled.

"Apparently, they don't serve duck a l'orange at the Panda Express, so I got the next closest thing—orange chicken. But I also picked up these packets of duck sauce." He held the small, translucent orange pouches in the air. "Which we will put on the chicken, thus transforming it into orange duck."

Chloe leaned over and kissed him on the cheek.

"Well, thanks for trying. I'm sure it will be delicious."

Augie served up the carry-out and set two plates on the kitchen table.

"I don't know if duck a l'orange has ever been served on paper before," said Chloe.

"That's how they suggested it at the restaurant. What can I say? Also, the sommelier there said to pair it with a nice Pinot Noir."

"They have a sommelier now at the Panda Express?" asked Chloe with one eyebrow raised high as Augie popped the cork.

"Did I say *sommelier*?" Augie said. You may have misunderstood me, Chloe. The manager's name tag said, Summer Ray. She was the one who suggested the wine."

They finished dinner, made quick work of post-supper cleanup, and moved outside to the edge of the pond. Augie set the bottle of pinot down on the broad arm of an Adirondack chair, and the air was soon filled with the discordant croaking of boreal chorus frogs.

A soloist coyote joined the symphony, howling in the distance and checking in with its pack. Finally, an invisible conductor cued the rubbing of cricket wings, and a melody of chirping joined the concerto.

Augie detected a shiver from Chloe and walked to the patio storage bin, returning with a flannel blanket, which he draped over her.

They talked about the past and the present, but while on both of their minds, there was no conversation about the future. Chloe moved toward Augie and gently sat on his lap, covering them with the blanket. She snuggled into his chest as the cold mountain air arrived with the rising moon. He held her tight and hummed an old tune he had written.

(Scan to play)
As I stand right here I often wonder
Where she is and why she went under
She walked away in mid-July
Never said a word, not a goodbye
She was much too young to look that old
As she walked all alone down the red dirt road
Those brown eyes close and her smile disappears
Takes her back to those childhood fears
She sees her mother in a faded gown
Daddy's nowhere, nowhere to be found
Beaten and broken all those years
Wondering how she held back tears
Sees her sister in a ray of light
Daddy's nowhere, nowhere in sight
Then she saw it written in the skies above
Out of mouths of babes must come love

> *Ten years later after all that hate*
> *Forgave that much much too late*
> *All those years wishing and crying*
> *Could have been spent living not dying*
> *She walks back to a sea of love*
> *And a little town called Lonesome Dove*
> *She's much too old to look this young*
> *As the red dirt road brings her home*
> *The neighbors stare and her mother starts to run*
> *As the red dirt road fades in the sun*
> *She ran away from a sea of love*
> *And ended up undreamed of*
> *Undreamed of…*

Chloe had fallen asleep in the warmth of the cowboy's embrace on the Adirondack chair. Then, when the frogs had been tucked in for the night and the Wyoming evening air had turned cold enough for Augie to see his breath, he capitulated. Rousing Chloe as gently as he could, she woke with a yawn, a shiver, and the predictable fog of confusion.

"What time is it?" she asked in a husky voice.

Augie turned to the oversized bronze metal clock hanging on the home's exterior wall.

"Eleven thirty. Come on, let's head inside."

They walked hand in hand across the flagstone, through the rear door, and up the staircase, pausing at the landing. His interim room was to the right, and Chloe's was to the left. Augie turned right with Chloe in tow.

CHAPTER TWENTY-THREE

Chloe stirred as the east-facing bedroom absorbed the rising sun. With her eyes still closed, she extended her arm across the bed, searching for Augie. Feeling nothing but fine Egyptian cotton, her lids fluttered open, squinting against the assailing light. She spotted the silhouette of an airplane resting on his pillow, rolled onto her side, and reached for the paper plane, unfolding it to reveal a message. *Breakfast? Meet me at the hangar when you are up.* The cursive note was followed by a simple blue-ink heart.

Peeking out the door of Augie's bedroom and finding no sign of Mr. Lawson, Chloe scampered down the hall through the open doorway and into her room. She pulled on black yoga pants and a gray Teton Gravity Research sweatshirt and headed downstairs.

"Good morning, Chloe," said Mr. Lawson, sitting at the kitchen island reading the paper.

"Good morning to you, Mr. Lawson."

"You were certainly up early today, weren't you?" he said.

What is he talking about? she thought.

She didn't respond.

Oh, God. I know exactly what he's talking about.

Lawson's bedroom was next to Chloe's; he would have walked directly past it when he woke. With the door ajar, he would have seen a perfectly made bed and no trace of Chloe.

She poured a quick cup of coffee and headed out toward the barn. Augie had rolled the Super Cub from the hangar and was sitting on one of its large tundra tires, draining the last of his java.

"You ready?" he asked.

"Ready for what?"

"Well, breakfast, of course. Didn't you get my note?"

"Yes, I did, and it was adorable. I don't see any bacon and eggs out here, though."

"I thought we'd fly to breakfast," he said. "You up for it?"

"I haven't been up in a small plane since the last time you took me fifteen years ago," she replied.

"I'll take that as a yes. Climb on in."

She took a big swig from her mug and set it inside the hangar before entering the cockpit.

The wheels departed the grass runway, and they climbed to one thousand feet above the ground on a southerly heading. Alpine was twenty miles to the south, had one of Augie's favorite diners, and Alpine Airport sat less than two miles north of the quaint downtown.

Fifteen minutes after departing, the Super Cub entered the airport traffic pattern on a right downwind leg for runway 13. They paralleled the landing strip, maintaining one thousand feet, before descending and banking into a right base. Another ninety-degree turn, and they were on final approach, passing over the Palisades Reservoir, which glittered in the sunlight. The Cub touched down with plenty of runway remaining and taxied to the end, where they found transient parking and a tie-down spot.

A four-seat golf cart pulled up next to the Cub as they exited the cockpit.

"Good morning, Augie!"

"Hey there, George." The men warmly shook hands. "I'd like you to meet Chloe. Chloe, George Flynn. We played ball together at Wyoming. I've arranged for George to give us a ride to the Silver Dollar Diner."

"Pleased to meet you, Chloe. Hop in, and we'll switch this ride out for my pickup."

He pulled the golf cart onto the runway and headed north one hundred yards before swinging into a driveway.

"Wait, you live at the airport, George?" Chloe asked.

"This here is what we call a fly-in community. There are over seventy hangar homes at Alpine Airpark."

They exited the golf cart and walked past an open hangar housing a Cessna Citation.

"That's your jet?" inquired Chloe.

"It is indeed. It allows me to live in a somewhat remote area like this and still be able to quickly access the cities where my restaurant and hotel developments are. I truly am blessed."

They climbed in a gray Chevy Silverado, pulled out of the neighborhood, crossed the Snake River, and arrived in downtown Alpine.

"Just text me when you want me to come back for you, Augie."

"You got it. Thanks again, George."

Walking through the Silver Dollar Diner's doors was like stepping back in time. They were greeted with a black and white checkerboard floor and red vinyl booths, each having its own jukebox. Staring at the man behind the lunch counter with his starched white shirt and black bow tie, Chloe couldn't help but picture her grandfather. He had been a soda jerk in the 1940s at a diner in Illinois. As a child, she loved looking at the black-and-white photos of him in his youth and hearing the stories of those halcyon days when things were far less complicated.

The hostess seated them at a booth. Augie handed her a five-dollar bill and asked her to change it into quarters as Chloe scrolled through the retro jukebox catalog.

"This thing must be fifty years old," she said. "And most of the songs are as well."

The woman returned with the quarters, and Chloe began feeding the music player. Patsy Cline's "Crazy" was first in the lineup.

Chloe flipped through the extensive breakfast menu, going back and forth between several possible choices before narrowing it down to chocolate chip pancakes or banana walnut flapjacks.

"I'm sure they can do a couple of each, Chloe."

The server arrived right out of the 1950s, wearing a short-sleeved light blue dress with a large, starched white collar. Cinched around her waist was a stained white apron. Setting a pot of coffee on the table, she removed her notepad and asked if they were ready to order.

"I have a question," said Chloe. "Can I do two of the chocolate chip pancakes and two of the banana walnut?" The waitress nodded, still looking at her pad.

"And for you, sir?"

"I'd like the bison huevos rancheros and a side of scrapple, please."

Johnny Cash's "Ring of Fire" began to play. Chloe tapped her finger to the beat on the hardwood table as a parade of servers walked by.

"Augie, do you find it odd how many employees have walked by looking at us over the past few minutes?"

"I thought the same thing. Maybe they think you're a movie star, Chloe."

"Yes, I'm sure that's it," she said, shaking her head from side to side with a sly smile.

Elvis moved between his tenor and baritone voices as "All Shook Up" played.

They discussed Rose, considering what her care would look like over the next few days and weeks. Augie asked how Chloe liked working for Mr. Lawson and then about life on the West Coast. He reached across the table, capturing both of her hands as she talked about the friends she deeply missed from Portland.

Two servers interrupted the conversation, setting down collapsable stands and food trays. One waiter set a plate of eggs and scrapple in front of Augie, while the other placed four plates of hotcakes on Chloe's side of the table. She looked on in confusion as the second set of banana walnut pancakes was delivered. Each plate contained four enormous cakes, two chocolate chip plates, and two banana walnut plates.

"Excuse me, but why are there sixteen hotcakes here?" Chloe asked the server.

"You requested two orders of chocolate chip and two orders of banana walnut, ma'am."

Patrons turned their attention to the booth, not because of the order but due to the volume of laughter from the cowboy.

"She meant two pancakes of each, not two orders of each," he said, still chuckling. "Look at her. Do you think she could possibly eat sixteen pancakes?"

"Oh, I'm so sorry," the waitress said, covering her mouth. "I misunderstood. I'll just leave it, and you can eat what you like. I'll make sure only one order is on your bill. You'll have breakfast leftovers for days."

"Well, that explains the line of employees coming by to get a look at the woman who was going to try to scarf down four orders of hotcakes," said Augie.

The server dropped the check, and Chloe mindlessly traced the gold foil-debossed *Thank You* on the front of the leather check holder with a finger as Augie piled the leftover pancakes into a Styrofoam box. She withdrew three twenty-dollar bills from her small purse and set them neatly inside the folder.

"Chloe, I'll get that," said Augie, reaching across the table.

She playfully slapped the top of his hand.

"Breakfast is on me, cowboy."

"Thank you…I see you are still a big tipper."

"I'll always have a special place in my heart for service staff…especially at diners. It reminds me of my grandfather."

As they returned to the airport, Chloe took another long, envious look at George Flynn's Citation sleeping in its hangar. The Chevy was traded for the golf cart, and they made their way down the runway to the Super Cub. Ten minutes later, Augie announced their departure on the common traffic advisory frequency and banked the Cub into a climbing, northerly turn.

The wind had picked up, and with it, the turbulence, as waves of choppy air blew over the mountain range from the west, resulting in nerve-racking, unpredictable bumps.

"How you doin' back there?" Augie said through his headset.

"So far, so good. I'm not a big fan of turbulence, though. Should I have told you that before we departed?" she said with a nervous laugh.

"If you have to puke, please climb out on the wing. It'll make cleaning the plane easier."

Augie turned back and smiled at her.

"I'm going to descend to five hundred feet and see if it's any smoother down there. We only have ten minutes remaining. You're doing great."

The sensation of speed increased as they lost altitude. Wyoming's rugged beauty was on full display as pastures, rivers, and wildlife presented ever-changing scenes below. Augie pointed out landmarks, some of them complete fiction, in an attempt to distract Chloe from the lively invisible bumps they randomly encountered.

Circling the ranch and surveying the windsock, Augie lowered the flaps and lined up from the north. The plane touched down smoothly, and they taxied back to the hangar, where Chloe promptly removed herself from the Cub and theatrically kissed the ground.

"It wasn't that rough up there," Augie said, shaking his head. "I'll button her up. Why don't you call Mr. Lawson, let him know you didn't vomit in his plane, and see what the latest is with Rose?"

"Will do. Thanks for breakfast, cowboy."

Chloe walked in through the rear door, carrying three Styrofoam containers.

"How'd our pilot do?" asked Lawson.

"You're home," said a surprised Chloe.

"I needed a shower and something other than hospital cafeteria food. I figure we can all head back over in a bit to collect Rose."

"As far as our pilot, he did pretty well," said Chloe. "If he could just see and avoid the bumps, that would be lovely. It doesn't seem that difficult to me." Lawson smiled.

"Any updates on Rose?" Chloe asked.

"Doctors said she had a good night. No sign of infection or anything else troubling."

"That's great to hear…If you haven't eaten, I brought some leftovers," Chloe said as she opened the three containers.

Lawson shifted his gaze from the considerable amount of hotcakes to her face.

"You have a dozen leftover pancakes?" he asked with a hint of confusion.

"A simple misunderstanding, Mr. Lawson. But yes, we do have about a dozen cakes."

"Okay. Well, plate me up, please."

Lawson was one stack in when his cell phone vibrated on the kitchen counter. Chloe looked at the screen, carrying the phone toward him.

"It's Dr. May," she said.

Chloe stared anxiously at Lawson, only able to hear one side of the conversation. Augie walked in, and she mouthed *hospital* as he ended the call with the physician.

"She's still on schedule to come home this afternoon. Dr. May said a nurse would call us around noon with an exact time."

Chloe breathed an audible sigh of relief.

"Should we put some decorations up?" she asked tentatively, unsure if it would be appropriate.

"I think it would be okay to do something if you and Augie want to run into town," said Lawson.

The pair returned from the party supply shop and set up three-foot-high yard sign letters spelling WELCOME HOME. Chloe had purchased four additional letters to personalize the yard stake greeting, as well as a few decorative signs.

The hospital called back and indicated Rose would be ready to be discharged at 3 p.m., prompting Chloe to collect a set of sheets from the linen closet and convert the family room sofa into a temporary bed. To prevent a potentially dangerous fall while navigating the stairs and minimize Rose's exertion, the nurse had advised them to set up a bedroom on the ground floor for the first forty-eight hours.

Arriving at Jackson Medical Center at 2:45 p.m., they pulled into a visitor spot out front. Mr. Lawson completed the discharge paperwork as Dr. May reviewed protocols for the next several days. She indicated Rose might have a little pain from the procedure and would most likely have some fatigue, but unlike a craniotomy, she could return to normal activities within a few days.

Rose greeted the threesome with a big smile. Her eyes were alert and back to life after the effects of the anesthesia had worn off. From her bed, she extended both arms wide, signaling that a group hug was in order. Once the reunion was complete, Augie produced her white Stetson, triggering a wide grin.

The cowboy remembered my hat.

Two nurses helped Rose transition from the hospital bed into a wheelchair. She set the Stetson on her head and waved to the hospital staff like a queen riding in a chariot as Augie pushed the chair through the hallways. Many of the staff were aware of Rose's condition and had made an effort to line the parade route and salute her courage.

As they approached the exit doors, Rose scribbled quickly on her notepad. *Again.*

"Sorry, Rose. Only one lap is allowed. These folks need to get back to work," said Augie.

Augie held Rose by the elbow as she slowly moved from the wheelchair to the back seat of the Super Duty. He buckled her belt, and Chloe slid in on the other side. Rose lowered her window and tried to recall the hello or goodbye greeting signal Augie had used while driving home from the rodeo. She remembered it just as Augie put the truck in gear, closed her fist, and extended her middle finger toward the remaining hospital staff.

"Rose!" Chloe quickly grabbed the girl's hand, forcing it inside the vehicle.

Mr. Lawson turned around and asked if everything was okay.

"Everything is fine. Rose was just waving goodbye and putting the window up at the same time. I was just worried she might catch her hand."

What is she talking about? Rose stared at Chloe, perplexed about what had just happened.

"We don't give people the middle finger, Rose," Chloe whispered. "I'll explain later."

On the ride home, Mr. Lawson explained in no uncertain terms to Rose that she needed to take it easy for the next few days. He told her about the temporary first-floor bed and that she was not to use the stairs for forty-eight hours. Lawson knew the next part might draw some ire.

"And there will be no horseback riding for a few days, honey."

They waited for the predictable arms-crossed scowl. But it never came, as Rose simply nodded.

Augie turned the truck into the drive and watched the rearview mirror for the redhead's reaction to the yard sign.

What is this? That's my name!

She climbed slowly from the parked truck and inspected every letter carefully. Each one had its own color and pattern. Additional decorative signs were cut out to look like flowers growing in the yard, and she knelt before one resembling a daisy, tracing its outline with a finger before turning back to the party of three and popping a bright smile.

CHAPTER TWENTY-FOUR

Augie was the first to rise the following morning and quietly descended the staircase. He checked on Rose, who was still sound asleep on the sofa, skipped his morning coffee for not wanting to wake her, and headed to the barn, where he saddled Winston.

Pinks and blues surfaced on the eastern horizon as the sun considered rising. He rode his usual loop around the ranch and found himself distracted for the first time in a while. His thoughts wandered along a route as unpredictable and winding as the river he rode beside. Three months prior, the solitary cowboy's life was far from complicated, but his world had become labyrinthine in the past ninety days.

He hadn't tasted deep emotion in some time. The introduction of Rose, almost losing Lawson, and the all-but-forgotten love of his life walking toward his bar stool at the Whiskey Wheel had unlocked something inside him.

In his younger days, he would have been more than content letting things play out as life intended. At fifty, he now needed to know how the script would end. If he could foresee the future, he might influence the present. His self-talk began to run rampant as he catastrophized the outcome of all three relationships.

What if Rose's tumor ends up untreatable?

What if Mr. Lawson's heart gives out?

What if Chloe ends up being a casualty of me just not being enough?

He had worked himself up into a restless constellation of anxiety and queasiness. Dismounting Winston, he walked to the river's edge, dropped to his knees, and allowed the cold water to pool in his hands as he performed his cleansing ritual. The jolt of the frigid river grew more tolerable with each splash upon his face. He breathed in the crisp mountain air deeply through his nose and exhaled forcefully. With the calming sound of the expelled breath, his tension began to release.

Winston neighed, impatient with the routine currently underway. After three more breaths and corresponding splashes, Augie stood, dusted off his knees, mounted Winston, and continued his trek around the property.

He spotted Rose making her way through the wildflowers and galloped in her direction.

"Rose, you're supposed to be taking it easy. Where are you going?"

She pointed north toward Augie's cottage.

"The hitching post?" he asked. She nodded.

"I don't think you should be walking that distance. How about Winnie and I give you a ride?" She nodded.

"Do not tell your grandfather you were on a horse. Understood?"

A smile fell his way, backed by a short, warm nod.

"Hang on just a minute. I will text him and let him know you're with me."

He reached down with one arm and easily lifted the small girl into the air. Then, sliding back slightly on the saddle, he situated her in front of him and wrapped an arm around her waist. She looked back at him several times during the first few minutes of the ride.

"What is it, Rose?"

She hadn't brought her notepad, and her facial movements did nothing to help the cowboy understand her desires. The redhead decided to take matters into her own hands as she flared her legs away from the horse's belly, then retracted them, heels first. Winston didn't respond, so she tried again.

"Rose, are you trying to make him gallop?" She nodded.

Yes, cowboy! This is far too boring.

"It might be my last day at the ranch if you fall off, so we'll keep Winston at a walk. And that goes for your Sleeping Indian drill as well. I'm going to need to stay with you."

Boo! I'm nine years old. I'll be double digits next year!

They arrived at the hitching post, and Rose removed the lasso from the saddle's horn before being lowered to the earth.

"What do you need that for, Rose?"

She pointed to the cedar beam, then wrapped the lasso around her body.

"You want me to tie you to the beam instead of staying out here with you?"

That's exactly what I want.

"You cannot be serious, Rose. Wait here while I grab the headdress."

She shrugged and walked toward the hitching post. Augie returned, lifted her to a seated position, and handed her the bonnet. She removed her Stetson and progressed through the mirroring routine, with Augie spotting her from the side.

When satisfied with her facsimile, Rose slowly sat up and allowed Augie to help her down. She rubbed her right temple.

"Headache?" Augie asked. She nodded stoically.

"It doesn't mean the procedure didn't work. It could be just an after-effect from surgery."

Rose didn't respond and led Augie by the hand back to Winston.

Halfway to the ranch, Rose pulled on the reins and pointed down. Augie dismounted and lifted her from the saddle, unsure of what she wanted. The redhead took her time appraising the individual residents in the meadow of wildflowers. She settled on three blue-violet blossoms, eventually discarding one of them. Rose removed her hat and slipped a stem behind the black band on the left side of her Stetson. Then she pointed to Augie's hat.

He dismounted and offered it to her, and she did the same with the second flower, tucking it into the cream band. The redhead patted the saddle, and Augie deposited her on Winston's back. Rose planted her heels in the horse's side, and this time, he responded, breaking immediately into a trot.

"Rose!" Augie yelled, running behind them.

She pulled on the reigns, bringing Winston to a stop.

"Rose, you know better than to do that."

She pointed at the equine, eyebrows raised.

You should be lecturing your horse, cowboy. Not me.

Augie climbed aboard, and they headed for the lodge with Rose staring straight ahead, hiding her devilish smile.

"When you get back to your notepad, I have a question for you." She turned her head ninety degrees and nodded.

The pair returned from the ride, finding Chloe and Mr. Lawson working through another set of leftover hotcakes. Rose was exhausted from the simple excursion. But, before slipping under the blanket on the sofa, she picked up her pad, drew a question mark, and pointed the notepad toward Augie.

"Yes, my question. I'm curious why, when you walk through the fields, are you so careful about where you step?" he asked.

Flik, she wrote and turned the paper toward the cowboy.

"That's why you walk through the fields the way you do? Augie asked. She nodded. "I don't get it. Who's Flik?"

Chloe joined the conversation. "Are you talking about Flik, the misfit ant?"

Rose pointed at Chloe, nodding.

"I still don't get it," said the cowboy.

"*A Bug's Life*, Augie. You know? The animated movie? A colony of ants? Bullying grasshoppers? None of this sounds familiar?"

"No, it doesn't," he replied blankly.

"We'll have to watch it sometime," said Chloe. "Rose must pick her way through the fields to not crush any ant hills. Is that it, honey?" Her head moved up and down.

"What were you and Rose up to this morning?" Lawson asked. "Wait. Let me guess. The Indian?"

"The Indian," Augie answered. "I get the feeling Rose isn't quite as committed to following the doctor's orders to take it easy over the next few days. So maybe I'll stop by the county jail and see if the sheriff will loan me one of those ankle monitors we can attach to Rose. That way, if she gets loose, the police can locate her for us."

Augie winked at Lawson.

"That sounds good, Augie."

The blanket slowly lowered, revealing a set of emerald eyes.

Surely, they aren't serious.

The green polyester fibers reclaimed her.

For the next several days, Rose was on her best behavior. She passed the time primarily by drawing, sleeping, and brushing Scarborough. The orange bucket had mysteriously appeared at the dinner table one night, but no one seemed to know how it arrived.

"Rose, any idea who moved the pail from my den out here?" asked her grandfather.

What pail? she wrote.

"The large orange one you can't miss, sitting directly on the table where the centerpiece used to be."

She feigned surprise at having just noticed it.

"Honey, we want to wait until you are cleared for activities before we pull more slips of paper from the bucket. I'd hate to get your hopes up on something and not be able to let you do it. Your follow-up appointment is in two days. I'm sure Dr. May will update us on what you can and can't do then."

Forty-eight hours later, Mr. Lawson and Rose drove to the Jackson Medical Center, where Dr. May's physician assistant inspected the surgical site on Rose's scalp. The wound was healing nicely, and much to Rose's displeasure, she would now be allowed to shower.

Rose looked at her grandfather with a gentle pout.

Allowed. She didn't say I had to.

Dr. May came into the room and asked Rose several questions about how she was feeling, what activities she had done, and how her appetite had been. The redhead wrote out some basic answers.

"Good news, Rose. I'm going to allow you to return to moderate activity. I don't want you doing anything too strenuous, though. We are still in recovery, okay?" Dr. May said.

Rose sketched a quick horse and flashed it toward the physician.

"Do you have a helmet?" she asked.
Rose nodded.

"Okay, only if you are with one of the adults. And nothing faster than a walk. Understood?"
Another nod.

"In four weeks, we will start the second treatment phase to help you feel better. It's called radiation, and the best part is that we will not need to make any incisions in your head."

"Mr. Lawson, I'll call you next week to fill you in on the specifics of the IMRT treatment."

Rose raised her hand, looking at the doctor.
"Yes, honey."

She drew an orange bucket, followed by a question mark.

"I'm not sure what you're asking, Rose," said Dr. May.

"She's talking about our bucket list," said Lawson.

He was about to explain when Dr. May interrupted, alarmed.

"You all have a bucket list for a nine-year-old?" she asked incredulously. "Can I speak with you privately for a moment?"

"No, no, it's not what it sounds like. Sorry, I shouldn't have led with that part. We all put notecards of fun activities or things we want to try in a bucket, then remove a card every few days," explained Lawson. "We've put those on hold as some may require exertion. Rose wants to know if we can resume pulling cards."

A relieved Dr. May replied, "Yes. I'll leave it to your discretion. Again, some moderate activity is fine. Let's avoid climbing fourteen thousand feet to the top of Grand Teton," she said, smiling.

Returning home, Rose pranced through the front door, eager to resume the activities that had been postponed. She headed directly for the den and sprung from the door, holding the bucket.

"After dinner, Rose," said her grandfather.

A thumb emerged from her closed fist, pointing straight up as she ran toward the back door, headed for the barn.

At dinner that evening, Rose ate faster than usual. Her eyes darted between the casserole before her and the orange pail on the floor. She began trying to clear plates before anyone was finished.

"Rose, people are still eating," said Augie.

Oh, I hadn't noticed. I'm just trying to be helpful.

She returned to her seat and began tapping her fingers on the hardwood.

Why does it seem like the cowboy is eating in slow motion?

In actuality, he was. She sternly shook her head at him, drawing a devious smile from Augie.

"I'm sorry, Rose. It's just that I like to take my time when I eat," he said with a slightly hidden smirk.

What! You usually eat like a steam shovel.

Augie playfully asked for seconds, then changed his mind after a glare from the redhead.

"What shall we do next?" asked Lawson. "Maybe go for a walk?"

Chloe and Augie played along, both exclaiming the virtues of post-dinner exercise.

No, no, no. There will be no walking.

Rose loudly deposited the bucket on the dining room table.

"Oh, that's right, we were going to do the bucket list tonight," said Mr. Lawson.

Augie peered inside. The notecards had multiplied like rabbits over the past several days, and he was sure none of the additional cards were from anyone over the age of nine.

"Rose, why don't you draw a card for us?" said her grandfather.

Two days prior, when the adults thought she was sleeping, Rose had snuck into the den and marked the back of *her* cards with a small blue dot.

All she needed was a quick glance into the bucket to identify one.

She stole a glimpse just before turning her head and closing her eyes. The redhead had identified a card on the right edge of the pail, and down her arm went. She snatched the paper between her thumb and forefinger, then lingered in the bucket, moving cards from side to side before revealing her find.

"It's one of yours, Rose!" said Chloe.

The redhead brought both palms to her cheeks in a failed attempt at surprise.

She showed them the card. *Stay at a nice hotel.*

They all had the same thought. The last time she had been at a hotel, she had watched her mother's murder. Supplanting that memory could be therapeutic in the little girl's recovery. Chloe and Augie looked at Mr. Lawson.

"The Four Seasons it is!" he said. "Chloe, would you book us three rooms? Or will we only need two?"

Oh, boy. She looked at Augie. *He knows about us,* thought Chloe, uncertain if this would be an issue.

Augie saved them. "Mr. Lawson, I don't know if I can spend the night at the hotel with Aurora. I'll come by in the evening for dinner, though."

"I'll see when they can get us in," said Chloe as she headed for the den.

Rose opened her sketchbook and titled one of the columns *Packing list for the hotel.*

Deep in thought, she tapped the end of her pencil on the table before writing a question and showing it to Augie. *What do I bring to the hotel?*

"I would think you would want to bring a nice dress for dinner."

Rose added that to her list, then looked up with sad puppy-dog eyes. She slowly shook her head from side to side.

"What? You don't have one?" Augie asked, earning another shake of the head.

Mr. Lawson interjected, "We'll take care of that tomorrow, Rose."

Augie continued, "And there's a world-class spa there. Maybe your grandfather will let you get a manicure, pedicure, or facial. Do you know what those types of spa treatments are?"

She pointed to her fingers, then her toes, and nodded. Touching her face, she shrugged with uncertainty.

"Chloe had me get a facial fifteen years ago. I can't really explain it, but I'm sure you would love it. Also, you should get a robe. I always picture fancy guests at the Four Seasons spending a lot of time lounging around in their robes."

Rose was giddy, barely holding down her excitement as Chloe returned from the den.

"I reserved a two-room suite for the day after tomorrow. Also, Mr. Lawson, you may have to call in a favor as the five-star restaurant stated the only seating available was at 8:30 p.m."

"Thank you, Chloe…Apparently, some spa services are in order for you and my granddaughter, as well as a shopping trip tomorrow. I'm going to head upstairs and read before bed. Augie will fill you in on what you missed."

Rose hugged her grandfather goodnight and then requested, via her sketchbook, a viewing of the second Harry Potter movie.

"I'll make the popcorn," said Augie.

"Rose, wake up. Time to go shopping!" Chloe yelled up from the first-floor landing.

The redhead appeared in her doorway, already dressed for the outing.

"Come on down. We'll get you some breakfast and head into town."

Please tell me there are not still leftover pancakes, thought Rose as she walked down the steps.

"How do pancakes sound, honey?" Chloe winked at the redhead and pointed at a box of Cheerios.

Cereal. Thank goodness.

Rose was all smiles on the drive into town. Their first stop would be Terra River Boutique, just off the square. The redhead wove through the aisles in the children's section, transfixed by the overwhelming number of designs and textures. She rubbed the satiny material of a leopard print dress between her fingers, lost in the mesmerizing pattern, before a nude pink gown cascading with ruffles and lace caught her attention.

Hanging elegantly on a mannequin was a teal blue sequined dress. *Queen Elsa!* Rose closed her eyes, envisioning herself in the *Frozen*-inspired gown.

Chloe chatted up the owner of Terra River as the redhead pranced through the aisles.

"Let us know if you want to try anything on, Rose," said Chloe.

She waved Chloe to the back of the boutique, took her hand, and led her to some of her favorites. An employee followed them diligently, collecting each potential finalist. When her arms were full, Rose agreed she had a fine selection of choices and retreated to the dressing room.

One by one, she modeled each gown for the attentive audience. At nine years of age, there was little chance three adults would sway her. She tried every dress on three times before the owner eventually lost interest and politely slipped away to answer a phone that wasn't ringing.

Rose emerged from the dressing room, proudly raising the winning garment above her head.

This is it!

A long white silk chiffon gown draped from its hanger. The sheer fabric shimmered under the fluorescent ceiling lights.

"Is that silk?" asked Chloe. The employee affirmed.

This is going to be an expensive outing, she thought as Rose returned to the dressing room, intent on wearing it home.

Chloe took a more frugal approach to the bathrobe purchase. They stopped at Target on their way out of town, where Rose made quick work of the limited choices in the kid's section. She went with a pink hooded plush fleece robe and wrote on her pocket-size notepad. *Can I wear it home?*

"On top of your new dress?" Rose nodded.

"Honey, I don't think that's a good idea. People might get confused if you are a debutante or are homeless."

Upon arriving at the ranch, Rose dashed from the truck. Bursting through the front door, she searched for her grandfather and Augie. She found Mr.

Lawson in the den working on the computer, and he lowered his glasses from the bridge of his nose as Rose twirled in her silk gown.

"Bravo, Rose!"

She performed a version of a curtsy she had seen recently on a special about the Queen of England.

"You're a real stunner in that dress, kid." She ran from the den toward the back door. "Where are you going, Rose?"

The redhead pointed toward the barn.

"The barn?" She nodded, grabbing her notepad from the counter.

I must show Scarborough, she wrote.

"Now, Rose. We don't want to ruin that fine gown. So let's not wear it except for special occasions, okay?"

Grandpa's probably right.

She headed upstairs and changed into her new robe, suspending the dress with care on its hanger. A curl of contentment sat on her lips.

CHAPTER TWENTY-FIVE

Check-in at the Four Seasons was at 3 p.m., and they arrived punctually, as Rose intended to maximize what she presumed would be a glamorous experience. A fancily dressed man in an immaculate gray suit wearing a matching cap resembling that of a train conductor loaded their bags onto a cart.

"Your luggage will be waiting for you in your room, sir," he said to Mr. Lawson.

Lawson shook the bellman's hand and slipped him a twenty-dollar bill before briefly conversing with the valet. Another twenty and a parking slip exchanged hands. His next stop was the concierge desk, and after a short conversation and phone call, a twenty-dollar bill slid across the desk to the appreciative staffer. Rose watched all of these transactions with a degree of confusion.

"They found an opening for us at 6:30 for dinner," said her grandfather.

"Perfect, I'll text Augie and let him know. But he should be stopping by anytime to say hello," said Chloe. "…And Rose and I have a mani-pedi scheduled at four."

The front desk attendant handed Chloe an envelope with the room keys and provided directions and special instructions on accessing the suite.

They boarded the ornate glass elevator, and Chloe slipped the magnetic strip into an access slot reserved only for the top two floors. Rose watched, her face pressed against the glass, as the lobby disappeared below.

The lift chimed, and the doors slid open, revealing the opulent eighth-floor concourse. Following the signs to the Presidential Suite, they wound through the hotel's corridors, arriving at a set of carved wood double doors adorned with gold leaf trim.

Classical music filled the room as Chloe used the keycard to open the door. A scarlet and coral-blue Persian area rug greeted the guests as they crossed the threshold, and thick hardwood beams dissected the vaulted ceiling rising above them. Rose ran past her grandfather and planted herself in the middle of the spacious family room, spinning in circles with her arms wide until she collapsed with dizziness.

She walked in an uneven line toward the sliding glass door. The mountain view room looked out onto the snow-barren slopes of Teton Village Ski Resort, where a high-speed gondola whizzed by, carrying summer tourists to the summit of Rendezvous Mountain. A spec in the distance grew larger as it headed from a peak toward the hotel.

Is that an eagle?

The odd creature gradually came closer into view and appeared to be a sizable sail. Rose ran to Chloe, tugged on her shirt to follow, and pointed out the sliding door at the oddity. Now, clearly visible were two people sitting in chair harnesses suspended under a nylon wing.

"Those are paragliders, Rose. A pilot operates the parachute like an airplane, but there's no motor."

Rose grabbed her notebook and swiftly scribbled, *When are we going?*

"*We* are not going, and I doubt your grandfather will let *you* go," said Chloe.

Now it was her turn to drag the patriarch to the door. Once she pointed out the paraglider, she formed prayer hands and looked longingly at her grandfather.

"I don't know, Rose. It seems kind of dangerous," he said, rubbing his chin.

"It's safer than an airplane, as long as it's not too windy." They turned toward the door.

"Hey, Augie," said Chloe.

"I used to instruct new paraglider pilots here at the resort. If the weather is good, it's perfectly safe, Mr. Lawson."

Rose pointed at the cowboy.

Yes. What he said.

"Let me talk to Augie about it, and I'll let you know," said Lawson.

"Come on, Rose. I'll show you to our bedroom, and we can get ready for the spa," said Chloe.

The two girls departed the suite for their 4 p.m. appointment, leaving Augie and Lawson alone on the balcony, admiring the scenic view around the hotel.

"Is something going on with you and Chloe, Augie? And you can tell me if it's none of my business."

"Why do I think you already know the answer, sir?" Augie said with a smile. He continued, "Would it be a problem if there was?"

"Of course not. I think the world of Chloe, and it warms my heart to see you both seemingly so happy. The way you two nurture Rose …I wish you had stayed together…I'm sorry, Augie. It's not my place to say that."

"It's fine, sir…I do think of what might have been, but this life can be incompatible with a family." The men watched in silence as another tourist took to the Wyoming sky. "It's just complicated, Mr. Lawson. Chloe is supposed to be leaving at the end of the summer, which, by my account, we are at, and—"

Lawson interrupted, "It's only complicated because you are making it so in your head and because we both know you aren't the best communicator when it comes to relationships. Talk to her about what she wants and what you want. I think you'll find it's much simpler than you believe."

The cowboy's gaze drifted from Lawson to the mountain, then back. He nodded.

Lawson continued, "She's afraid."

"Chloe? Afraid? Of what, sir?"

"Look at it from her perspective. She shows up here in your town and is now living on the property you work at. She's probably walking on eggshells, trying not to interrupt the life you've created here. Chloe isn't a mind reader, and I would guess she is pretty unclear about what you want and where things are going. That could be terrifying for her."

"When you put it like that, sir…I think you're probably right."

"You do what you want, Augie. I've probably already inserted myself where I don't belong. I think you two were great together way back when, and if something is to be rekindled, I'd be the first to offer my blessing. Not that it's needed."

Lawson put his hand on Augie's shoulder warmly.

"Thank you, sir. I've got to return to the ranch for a few things, but I'll be back for dinner."

"Sounds good. And bring your appetite. The restaurant here does it big."

Rose finally settled on Cherry Bomb for her manicure color. The nail technician finished cutting and shaping and was now furnishing the redhead with a hand massage. She was giddy with excitement as the first deep-red stroke crossed her pint-sized fingernail. Her eyes were glued to the brush as she was transformed from a nine-year-old into a beauty queen. After the second coat dried, the manicurist brought out a bottle of vibrant yellow paint, and on each index finger, she carefully drew five petals.

A sunflower!

Once the design was finished, Rose waved her hand toward Chloe.

"Wow! She gave you a sunflower, Rose. That's beautiful."

Rose pointed at Chloe, then at her own index finger.

"You think I should get one too?" Rose nodded frantically.

"Okay. A sunflower it is."

When the time came for pedicures, Rose and Chloe followed the technicians to a small aquarium sitting on the floor, where dozens of tiny Garra rufa fish darted back and forth in the tank. Rose stood, looking quizzically at Chloe as she took a seat and set each foot in the water.

"Rose, this is a fish pedicure. These little guys eat the dead skin away. It will give you softer feet."

No, thank you. My feet are soft enough.

"Come on, Rose. Just try it with one foot. If you don't like it, we'll move on to the rest of the pedicure."

With pursed lips, the redhead deliberated thoughtfully. Chloe patted the seat next to her.

Okay. One foot.

She sat and slowly lowered her left foot into the pool of water, cringing as if it were charged with an electrical current. The fish attacked. Water splashed from the tank as Rose quickly withdrew her foot.

"You aren't scared of a few baby fish, are you?"

No. She shook her head.

Rose tried a second time. The tingling quickly turned to a tickle, and water again exploded from the aquarium as she yanked her foot from the tank. A single fish flopped on the floor momentarily before the tech scooped it up and deposited it back into the container. Rose committed both feet to the bath and held tightly to the chair's arms as the tiny creatures worked their sorcery. She squealed and splashed and, when she could take no more, removed her feet from the tank, shaking her head in defeat.

The nail tech wiped each foot dry and escorted her to the pedicure station for more trimming, shaping, and tickling. Rose stuck with cherry red for her toes. Once her nails were dry, the technician brought out bottles of white and green polish, and tiny dots of bright white were applied to her big toe.

A ladybug?

On the distal edge of the nail, slender green shapes took form.

Leaves?

The manicurist looked up and smiled at Rose.

A strawberry!

A matching berry was painted on her other big toe.

As they lingered in the salon, waiting for their pedicures to dry, she couldn't take her eyes off her fingers and toes. Stretching her hands out before her, she admired the nail art.

"Is this your first mani-pedi, Rose?" She nodded, then pointed at Chloe.

"Nope. I've had too many to count. But I do remember my first one. It wasn't until I was fourteen." The redhead's eyebrows rose, and her eyes opened wide.

"I know, right? My mom didn't think it was virtuous for a little girl to wear polish. If it were up to her, I would have had to wait until I was in college, but one Saturday morning, when my mom was shopping, my dad took me to the nail salon. We picked out a light color for my fingers to not bring too much attention to them for my mom to notice. Do you know what it was called?"

She shook her head.

"Bubble Bath," said Chloe. Rose smiled. "For my toes, we went with mint green. My dad said if my mom noticed, I should tell her it was to honor our family's Irish heritage. He thought that might save me."

Chloe looked at her watch. "Well, I think it's about time to go."

What! Finish the story.

Rose turned both palms up, raised her brows, and dipped her chin as she leaned toward Chloe.

"What is it, Rose?"

The redhead pointed to Chloe's fingers, then toes, and made small, rapid circles with her hands in front of her face. The universal sign for *keep going*.

"Oh, I bet you want to know if my mom caught me." Rose nodded feverishly.

"Well, she never said anything, but she knew. She asked my dad that evening why I looked so angry. I had been walking around the house with my fists balled so my nails didn't show. He had to come clean." Chloe chuckled, shaking her head.

She settled up with the salon, and Rose watched as more twenty-dollar bills changed hands. Later, she would need to ask why they handed out so much money.

Rose curtsied. This had become her new way of combining a thank you and a goodbye. She felt it was regal and perfectly appropriate for such a high-end hotel.

Returning to the room, they found Mr. Lawson asleep in a high-back lounge chair. They tiptoed into their bedroom and put on the TV. Rose flipped through the channels until she settled on a cartoon where a school teacher was chastising an obese boy in a red jacket and a blue hat.

"I don't think so, Rose," said Chloe. "Keep searching."

This drew a *but why*? gesture from the redhead.

"If your grandfather wakes up and finds you watching *South Park,* we are both in big trouble. Besides, you need a shower before dinner. And, as he would say, that's not a suggestion."

Rose tucked her arms to her side and rolled to the edge of the bed before dropping to the floor and heading off as if to the executioner. Chloe removed their dresses from the closet and laid them on the bed, then poked her head into the bathroom and saw Rose, fully clothed, standing outside the shower, attempting to tilt in just enough to get her hair wet.

Chloe leaned against the doorframe and waited. Then, shutting off the shower, Rose reached for a towel and dried her hair. Chloe cleared her throat, and Rose turned.

Chloe stared, having decided to go with a silent interrogation, as this always made people crack. Rose was up to the challenge and gazed back.

I can do this all day, Rose thought.

Chloe realized her futile mistake of having engaged in a stare-down with someone suffering from selective mutism.

"Rose. A shower, not a hair rinse."

She obliged with a soft sigh, stripping out of her jeans and T-shirt.

"And don't forget to wash behind your ears!" yelled Chloe from the bedroom.

The redhead washed herself more carefully than ever before. She worked hard to keep her newly polished toes and fingers out of the stream, unaware that the paint would suffer no damage from the water. She finished showering, towel-dried off, and walked to the mirror. Leaning in as close as she could, she attempted to fold the cartilage of her ear lobe forward in a vain attempt to see behind her ear. Each time she would turn her head sideways to find the right angle, her eyes would be forced away from the mirror. Ultimately, she threw up her hands, hoisted her bottle of Camile perfume, and doused herself.

"Well, don't you both look…and smell stunning," Lawson said from the lounge chair when the two girls emerged from the bedroom. "Two of my favorite scents—vanilla and bergamot."

"You clean up pretty good yourself," Chloe replied.

"Rose, come over here. I have something for you," said her grandfather.

He reached into the breast pocket of his navy blue blazer and pulled out a gold chain. Attached to the end was a 28-karat gold coin bezel pendant holding a Morgan Silver Dollar. Lawson slipped the necklace over Rose's head. She ran to her notepad and wrote, *It's beautiful!*

Her thumb slid over the raised profile of a woman with a crown on her head.

"Lady Liberty," said her grandfather.

She pointed to the numbers on the bottom of the coin.

"That's the year the coin was produced. 1893."

Rose's eyes danced left and right, up and down, as she was trying to do the math.

One hundred twenty-nine years old.

She flipped the coin over, revealing an American eagle with outstretched wings.

Eagle!

"Look closely at the bottom, under the eagle. Do you see any letters?"

She squinted, eventually nodding. She wrote, *CC.*

"So that means it was minted in Carson City, Nevada. It also means that this particular coin is very valuable."

Chloe whispered to Mr. Lawson, "Can I ask how valuable?"

"If it were in mint condition and in a case, it would probably sell for over five thousand dollars," Lawson said.

Rose raised her hand.

"Yes, Rose?" asked her grandfather.

She scribbled on her pad a question about why they handed out money to the employees at the hotel. Mr. Lawson explained that it was called tipping, and if a hotel employee did an outstanding job with something, they might be tipped.

"Augie is meeting us downstairs, so if everyone is ready, let's go," said Chloe.

Rose checked her look in the mirror and placed the white Stetson on her head. She adjusted the medallion around her neck, turning the eagle side to face out.

The maitre d' greeted Mr. Lawson by name and escorted the party of four to a semi-private table in the rear with a spectacular view of the mountain resort.

"Best table in the house, sir," said the man in the black tuxedo.

Rose thought she saw another twenty-dollar bill change hands.

Many menu items were foreign to the redhead, so she pointed to words, and Chloe translated. Caviar, foie gras, and calamari were explained, and all received the same wrinkled nose and loose lip response—the universal sign for disgust.

"Let's start with the Teton Tower," said Mr. Lawson to the server.

Rose scanned the menu, looking for her grandfather's selection.

Main Lobster Tail, Jumbo Shrimp, Oysters, Tuna Tartare, Crispy Wonton.

She pointed a finger at the word "tuna." "That's raw fish," said Chloe, drawing more repulsion.

"But you'll like some other things, honey."

Rose raised her glass of lemon-lime soda with a splash of grenadine and directed it toward her grandfather.

"Yes, a toast," said Mr. Lawson. "To our family of four. To our health and happiness."

"Cheers," said Augie.

They clinked their glasses and drank.

The colossal appetizer was delivered to the table with much fanfare. It climbed three feet in the air, each level containing a different delicacy.

Rose's eyes studied the grand dish quietly from top to bottom.

Chloe set a wonton and a single shrimp on Rose's plate and added a dab of cocktail sauce. Rose cut into the Chinese dumpling first and cautiously took a bite. Sweet and salty combined in tasty goodness, the redhead nodded her approval to Chloe. Next, she picked up the shrimp by its tail, dragged it carefully through the cocktail sauce, and bit into it. By the second chew, she knew this would be a problem. The texture and taste repulsed her. She fake-chewed the third and fourth bites while trying to calculate a plan for disposing of the prawn.

If only Aurora were here.

Bringing her napkin to her mouth, she released the shrimp into the cotton cocoon and, in one motion, brought it down to her lap, opened it, and let the shrimp drop to the floor. No one seemed to notice.

There must be a dog around here somewhere.

"Did you like the shrimp?" asked Chloe before depositing an oyster on Rose's plate.

A firm side-to-side head shake left no doubt about her position on the shrimp.

The oyster shell hadn't been in contact with the porcelain dish for more than a few seconds before Rose returned to its home on the tower's second level.

"No?" asked Chloe.

Rose shook her head and watched with repugnance as Augie slurped an oyster from its oval exoskeleton, chewed once, and swallowed.

"Would you like to try a lobster tail, honey?" asked her grandfather.

So, you want me to try a much larger version of the thing I just spit out and that is now on the floor? Uhm, no, thank you. She stared at him.

"I guess that's a no," said Lawson as he took a bite.

A paraglider launched from the mountain. Rose pointed out the window and flipped both palms up, looking at her grandfather.

Did you decide?

"Rose, are you sure you want to do it? It seems scary for a little girl," said Mr. Lawson.

She wrote on her notepad, *Yes! Please.*

"Well, Augie seems to think it's perfectly safe, so if they have an available slot tomorrow morning, you can do that instead of your facial." Rose formed prayer hands and bowed ever so slightly.

Augie was on his third oyster when the maitre d' appeared at the table and asked for a private word with Mr. Lawson. They stepped away for a moment, shook hands, and Lawson returned. He walked to where Rose was seated and looked down toward the floor. Her bare feet peeked out from below the dress's hem.

Uh oh, he knows about the shrimp.

"Rose, did you forget something when we left the room?"

Okay, it's not the shrimp.

She shook her head.

"Are you sure?"

He didn't give her time to answer.

"Chloe, would you mind escorting Rose up to the suite where she can finish getting dressed? It seems she has forgotten her shoes."

She picked up her pencil and quickly wrote, *No one will be able to see my strawberry toes.* The sentence was punctuated with a sad-face drawing.

"Honey, five-star restaurants have certain requirements, and shoes are one of them."

Give the guy another twenty dollars.

"Come on, Rose, let's run upstairs," said Chloe.

Dinner was being served when they returned from the suite. Rose only nibbled on her citrus-grilled chicken, as she was much too excited about paragliding the following day to eat. That all changed when the dessert cart rolled to the table.

All of that is for us?

"What looks good, Rose?" asked Augie.

She pointed to the chocolate raspberry mousse, the tiramisu layer cake, and the lemon soufflé.

"You get to choose *one*, honey," said her grandfather.

She presented two fingers. He reached out and folded her index finger back into her palm before it slowly uncurled.

"One," he said.

The chocolate raspberry mousse triumphed, but Mr. Lawson's dessert stole the show. A waiter appeared with a cart transporting a burner, a frying pan, and the essentials for bananas Foster. Butter, cinnamon, and sugar were warmed in the pan, and Rose watched as if a magic trick were being performed. A banana was quartered and set in the skillet. Rum was the last element to participate, resulting in an eruption of fire, a squeal from the redhead, and panic from the table. It was too much rum, and the bursting flames caught the waiter's tie on fire.

Augie was the first to react as he reached for his goblet of ice water and threw it at the waiter, missing the tie but soaking the horrified server from the neck up.

What fun!

Rose had no idea there were restaurants like this. She grabbed her Shirley Temple and slung the mixture in the waiter's direction, dousing his trousers before looking at Chloe.

It's your turn.

The funny man in the black tie dropped to the floor, compressing his chest to the carpet while wriggling forward.

He's trying to do the Worm. No, no, that's all wrong.

Rose lowered to the ground next to the frantic waiter, planted her hands under her shoulders, and kicked her legs up and backward. Then, arching her back, she rocked forward on her stomach, completing one cycle of the breakdancing move.

"Rose! What are you doing?" asked her grandfather. He received no reply.

The general manager had witnessed the incident from across the dining room and moved as quickly as possible without alerting the entire restaurant. When he arrived at the table, the frightened server was on his knees, shaking. The little girl was writhing across the floor, encouraging the waiter to follow her.

"Is everyone okay?" asked the GM. "I'm so sorry."

"I think so," said Lawson, looking at the horrified server.

"Please tell me she's not on fire," said the manager as he pointed toward the redhead.

"No, she's fine," replied Lawson.

"Sir, your dinner will be on us tonight."

"Thank you, but that is not necessary. Maybe we could get our dessert to go?"

"Of course, Mr. Lawson."

They walked to the elevator with their sweet treats in a to-go bag.

"Rose! Where is the coin from your pendant?" her grandfather asked.

Chloe answered, "It must have come out while she was on the floor."

She shook her head a happy no.

"Well then, where is it, honey? It's very valuable," asked Lawson anxiously.

She wrote on her notepad, *I tipped the funny man in the black suit with it. He did a great job.*

"Augie—"

"I'm one step ahead of you, sir," said Augie as he immediately turned back toward the restaurant.

Rose was already awake and dressed when Chloe's 7 a.m. alarm sounded, breaking the silence in the suite. Augie had arranged for the concierge to schedule a paragliding flight for her at 8 a.m. He cut his morning ride of the property short, having promised Lawson that he would meet the paraglider pilot and be a second set of eyes over the flight's preparation.

Chloe, Rose, and Mr. Lawson exited the hotel and walked to the tram's base. A representative from Teton Paragliding directed them to a counter, where Lawson signed the required legal documents. He tried to skip over any sections where *death or dismemberment* were used. When all potential legal recourse was sufficiently eliminated, he signed a final time and slid the papers across the desk.

A man in a navy blue fleece with the image of a paragliding sail embroidered on it arrived at the counter.

"Charlie here will escort you to the launch point, Mr. Lawson. Augie is already up the mountain," said the woman behind the desk.

Lawson and Chloe were far too nervous to enjoy the spectacular mountain scenery zipping by below. Chloe shuddered in response to the twenty-degree temperature drop as the ten-minute tram ride ended, having gained 4,100 vertical feet of altitude.

Rose spotted Augie on the side of a grassy hill and ran ahead.

"Good morning, Rose. You ready for your big day?" said the cowboy, earning an excited nod from her.

"This is Jenny. She's the best paragliding pilot around."

Rose waved.

"Hi, Rose. We are going to have big fun this morning! We should be ready to fly in about fifteen minutes."

The redhead watched in wonder as they continued inspecting the canopy, risers, and harnesses. Dozens of colored lines led from a backpack to the edges of the enormous nylon wing.

"Okay, Rose, let's get you in your harness, and we'll go flying," said Jenny.

Leg straps, carabiners, chest straps, and helmets were all double-checked.

"Here's what's going to happen. I'll inflate the big wing behind us. We'll run a few steps and be airborne in seconds. Sound good?" A thumbs up from Rose confirmed she was ready.

Mr. Lawson held Chloe's hand as two pairs of feet left the grass-covered hill. A shriek announced their departure, and the earth dissolved below them. Tops of aspens, willows, and cottonwoods passed beneath as Jenny gently banked the glider to the right, giving Rose a look back at the launch point where three small hands waved in the distance.

They lazily followed the mountain's contour down toward the valley, and as they picked up speed, the wind screamed through the vent holes in Rose's helmet. Jenny performed a steep 360-degree turn to the left, drawing another shriek from the redhead.

"Ready to land, Rose?"

No, no, no.

Just before touchdown, Jenny pulled on the brake lines, allowing the pair to settle gently into the grass field. She turned and gave Rose a high-five before detaching them from the gear. A staffer from the paragliding outfit corralled the giant golden wing as the valley breeze attempted to send it back into the Jackson sky.

Rose gazed up the mountain, visually tracing the route down. She closed her eyes, sent her arms wide, spun three complete circles to the left, back to the right, and then pointed at the employee stuffing the wing into a carry bag.

Why is the man putting the big sail in a bag? Don't we need to fly back up?

Jenny tried to comprehend her non-verbal question but was lost as Rose motioned to the top of the mountain.

"Your family? They'll meet us down here," said the pilot.

Rose shook her head. She stretched her arms out like wings, simulated flying, and pointed again at the launch point.

"You want to fly back up?" She gave a sharp nod.

"It doesn't work that way. Do you know what gravity is?" Jenny continued, "We would need a motorized paraglider to fly from the valley floor to the top."

When the gear was collected, they made the short walk from the field to the base of the tram, where Augie, Chloe, and Mr. Lawson had just arrived. Rose ran to the threesome and gave each a lower-body hug.

"How was it?" asked her grandfather.

The rosy-cheeked redhead spawned a double thumbs up with a wide smile.

CHAPTER TWENTY-SIX

It had been four weeks since Rose's surgery. Chloe was fifteen days into a Rosetta Stone program, learning Italian courtesy of the orange pail. Augie spent the last few weeks on one of his bucket list items, learning to play chess on his lunch break. As a young boy, he had watched people of all ages compete on Saturdays in the town square, relishing how the participants seemed lost for hours in their matches. Worldly concerns were temporarily put on hold as they focused on scheming offensive and defensive maneuvers.

Mr. Lawson had pulled one of his cards from the bucket that said, *Learn to draw*. Rose had been working with him in the evenings and had determined early on that he had little to no talent for this, but she worked patiently with him nonetheless. His apples were improving ever so slightly. She had him try a horse, but this proved too complex. So she switched him back to drawing apples.

The hospital had called to schedule an appointment one week before beginning Rose's radiation treatment. During the visit, Rose and Mr. Lawson met with Dr. Maher, a radiation oncologist, and learned how Intensity Modulated Radiation Therapy (IMRT) worked.

Are they going to cut my head open again? was Rose's first and only question.

"No, Rose," said Dr. Maher. "This is what we call non-invasive. A three-dimensional image of the tumor will be taken ahead of time. Exact coordinates are then entered into a computer program. The computer then guides a linear accelerator, which delivers radiation beams. I know, too many big words, right? Follow me."

Dr. Maher led the pair to a vacant treatment room.

"See that big machine on the far wall?" They both nodded. "That's a linear accelerator."

It looks like a giant bathroom sink faucet, thought Rose.

"You'll be lying on the table in front of it, and we'll slide you back toward the treatment head, where the X-ray beam will work on destroying the cancerous cells. Believe it or not, the human body comprises over 100 trillion cells. Each cell is a living building block. They make up everything in your body. Unfortunately, some of these cells are abnormal, growing and spreading very fast. Bad cells end up causing headaches and some of the other symptoms that are not fun for you."

He continued, "I know your most important question, Rose…The answer is *no*. It does not hurt at all. The machine will make sounds, but you won't feel anything."

"Will she have any side effects?" asked Mr. Lawson.

Dr. Maher turned toward Rose. "Some patients have no negative reactions to the treatment, while others may experience headaches, nausea, diarrhea, hair loss, or dermatitis. I'm telling you this not to make you nervous, but so you know it's normal if it happens."

Rose fought back tears. All she heard was *hair loss*. The shaved patches from the prior procedures were bad enough, but potentially having her hair fall out was unimaginable for the nine-year-old.

The first treatment was scheduled for Monday of the following week. Rose would need to arrive at 8 a.m. each day, and the procedure itself would take about fifteen minutes.

Dr. Maher explained that they would be there a little longer on the first visit as Rose would need to be fitted for a mesh mask. This would ensure her head stayed still and assist the X-ray beam in targeting the precise location.

"Rose, I need to speak with Dr. Maher about some logistics. We are going to step outside for a minute," said her grandfather. She nodded slowly, having no idea what *logistics* meant, as they walked into the hallway.

"Doc, when will we know if the radiation is working?"

"I wish I had a simple answer for you, Mr. Lawson. The truth is radiation therapy does not have an immediate effect. It can be days, weeks, or months, as the cancerous cells can continue to die well past the end of the first treatment cycle. This initial series of treatments will last four weeks, and then we will pause to assess its effectiveness and to give Rose a break from potential side effects."

"I'm not sure I want the answer to this next question, but I need to ask it," said Lawson. "What is the success rate in cases like Rose's?"

"As I'm sure Dr. May has informed you, glioblastoma is a nasty and resolute form of cancer, and it's difficult to treat, but the good news is that the prognosis is better for children than adults. Unfortunately, we won't know if the remaining tumor is shrinking until we conduct an MRI after the radiation."

Mr. Lawson nodded calmly; inside, he was anything but. His prayers and wealth seemed useless against the evil disease growing inside Rose as he stood by helplessly, on the verge of possibly losing another one of the most important people in his life. His wife, Marie, had drowned in front of him. Dennis was locked away for murder.

Things come in threes, he thought.

He swallowed the notion of a third tragedy, forcing it into the shadows of his consciousness. Powerless for the first time in a long while, he turned his head and wiped away a tear before returning to the room to collect Rose for the drive home.

That evening, Mr. Lawson brought the orange bucket to the dinner table. With the uncertainty surrounding the possible side effects from the radiation that would begin the following week, he was intent on getting Rose through more of her notecards.

Chloe had prepared a kid-friendly menu—hot dogs, tater tots, and brown-sugar-glazed carrots. Following dinner, the redhead dove deep into the pail and showed off the winner. Chloe struggled to read the card, as it had been one Rose had written quickly and secretly added to the bucket the day prior. She could make out the words "swim" and "pool."

"Brilliant!" said Lawson. "That will count for our after-dinner exercise. So put your suits on, and we'll meet in the basement lap pool."

Rose arrived first, wearing jean shorts and a tank top, carrying the Home Depot bucket in one hand and the previously drawn index card in the other. Mr. Lawson appeared in the same outfit as Rose. Augie showed up in a pair of gym shorts, and Chloe stunned in a two-piece lemon and light blue floral print bikini. It would have made for an outlandish family photo opportunity.

"No suits?" Augie asked Rose and Lawson.

Rose shook her head.

"I'll be honest. I've never once set foot in this pool in all the years I've owned this property. Can you believe that? I do have a bathing suit, though. I'm just not sure where it is."

"I'm with you, sir. I think the last time I went swimming was at the campsite at Jenny Lake when I was ten. Remember that Fourth of July when we had all my cousins there?"

"I do, Augie. As I recall, you had a mishap with your swim trunks." Augie smiled.

"I did indeed, sir."

"What happened?" asked Chloe as Lawson grinned.

"All the adults were parked in lawn chairs on the water's edge. Some of my cousins and I were about twenty feet from the shore, cooling off in the lake, when one of us—I'm not sure who—thought it would be funny to remove our suits. I raised mine above my head and spun it on a finger like pizza dough. The only problem was that it slipped off into the dark water.

"I was sure I could find it, but I got tired after ten minutes of diving to the bottom. Meanwhile, my cousin Matt laughed so hard that he appeared to be in the initial stages of drowning. I couldn't get out of the lake with everyone on the shore, and none of my cousins would get me a towel; they thought it was hilarious. Eventually, I bribed one of them with the promise of not telling my uncle that his son had shoplifted a candy bar from the campground store earlier in the day. He swam to shore and brought a towel out to me."

"Well, don't get any ideas of a repeat performance," said Chloe, dipping a toe in the pool.

Assured that the heater was working properly, she sat on the edge and slipped in. Rose followed Chloe's lead and promptly disappeared under the water, sinking to the bottom.

"What's she doing?" asked Chloe to no one in particular.

Augie dove in after her. Rose's limbs flailed eight feet down as the cowboy wrapped an arm around her chest and kicked hard to the surface. The redhead coughed up water as she held firm to the pool wall.

"You can't swim?" her grandfather asked. She shook her head sideways.

No. Did you not read my card?

Mr. Lawson helped her to the deck, where she beelined it for the chair on which she had placed her index card. She pointed dramatically at the first word on the card as she displayed it to her grandfather.

"Rose, I can't make out that scribble. I see *swim* and *pool*."

She reached for her colored pencil and rewrote the first word more clearly: *LEARN*.

Chloe took Rose to the shallow end, made her stand and lowered her face into the water. They progressed from blowing bubbles through her nose to turning her head and breathing. Over the next half hour, Augie watched from the pool's edge in admiration as Chloe patiently guided the redhead step by step. The lesson culminated in a five-body-length swim from the wall to Chloe, and Rose let out her trademark squeal upon completion.

Standing in the shallow end, she drew back her arm and drove it forward, skimming along the water's surface. The wave exploded from the pool, sending a sheet of water toward Augie and her grandfather.

The cowboy went in after her, chasing her playfully as she ran, the resistance of the water slowing her to a walk. Upon catching the redhead, he grasped Rose under her armpits and launched her skyward. Another squeal. She returned to Augie with her arms wide.

Again!

CHAPTER TWENTY-SEVEN

With the first radiation treatment scheduled for the following day, Sunday evening brought silence and mixed emotions to the dinner table. Mr. Lawson flipped back and forth between hopefulness and periods of disquiet.

How is any parent prepared to go through this? he thought.

Augie broke the silence.

"Hey, Rose. If you're feeling up to it after your doctor's appointment tomorrow, I'll come by the lodge at lunch, and maybe we can make a special exception for you to pull one of *your* cards from the bucket."

She looked up and slowly nodded.

I pull one of my cards every time, cowboy. Haven't you caught on yet?

Lawson methodically cleaned up the evening meal, washing each plate twice before setting it in the dishwasher. The scrubbing provided at least a short-term distraction, and when he was finished, he retired to the lounge chair and a recently purchased book, *Man's Search for Meaning*. The 1946 classic was Viktor Frankl's inspirational story of finding hope during his three years in Nazi concentration camps. Lawson's most powerful takeaway from the book was that it doesn't matter what we expect from life. What matters is what life expects from us. This was about to be tested on an unimaginable scale.

"Anyone want to watch a movie?" Chloe asked, looking expectantly at Rose. The redhead gazed up, shook her head, and continued to draw.

"Augie, would you mind bringing me my tea?" asked Mr. Lawson.

He circled the kitchen island, wound behind the sofa, stole a glance at Rose's drawing, and set Lawson's cup on the side table.

"What's she sketching?" whispered Mr. Lawson.

"Looks like a sink faucet." His answer sounded more like a question.

Lawson nodded.

"Why is she drawing a faucet, sir?"

"It's not a faucet. It's a linear accelerator."

"That was going to be my second guess," said Augie. "And what exactly is a linear accelerator?"

"Hopefully…it's Rose's savior."

"Rose, it's about time to hit the hay. How'd you like a bedtime story tonight?" asked Augie. She slowly nodded. "Okay, I'll meet you upstairs in five minutes."

"Snug as a bug, I see," said Augie as he entered her bedroom. Rose offered a faint smile.

Sitting on the end of her bed, he flashed the cover of *Where the Sky Never Sleeps* toward Rose, who yanked her arm from under the comforter and pointed at the yellow Piper Cub on the front of the book jacket.

"I know," said Augie. "It looks just like your grandfather's plane, doesn't it?" She nodded. "This is one of my favorite books. It's about family, the wilderness, and adventure. You're going to love it. Ready?" Her head bobbed excitedly.

Cody wiped the sweat from his brow with the dirty sleeve of his tattered green sweatshirt. He was carefully balanced on a narrow branch of the tall spruce tree. Just fifteen feet below him, a gray wolf lurked, circling the base of the tree in silence. As Cody shifted his weight, the quiet was broken with the sickening sound of the spruce branch snapping.

Rose's tired eyes grew wide as Augie paused dramatically. He continued, glancing up occasionally, expecting the redhead to have drifted off. At the end of the third chapter, her eyelids grew heavy, fluttered, and finally shut.

The cowboy kissed her gently on the forehead, turned the bedside table light off, and flicked on a unicorn nightlight.

Chloe sat cross-legged, cuddling into a nook of the couch with her latest Lucille Lovewell novel.

"Mind if I join you?" asked Augie.

"C'mon, cowboy. Aren't we past that?" she said, breaking into a big smile.

"Hey, there's no one more gentlemanly than a cowboy. I'm just trying to uphold the standard," he said with a wide grin.

She patted the cushion, and he sat down and reached for her free hand. His heartbeat quickened. Augie's thumb found a groove and slowly brushed back and forth over the top of her hand as she lowered her head onto his shoulder.

"I've been meaning to tell you about a conversation I had with Mr. Lawson when we were at the Four Seasons," he said. Chloe looked up.

"He asked if anything was going on between us." Chloe set her book down and removed her glasses.

"Don't worry. He was very supportive. I know he really likes you, Chloe, and wants us both to be happy."

"So he didn't have a problem with *us*?" she asked, furrowing her brow.

"No. Absolutely not." Chloe was relieved.

"I think he knows I've stayed in your room, Augie," said Chloe with a sleepy yawn.

"I think you're right." The cowboy smiled.

"He alluded to admiring our parenting skills and said he wished we had stayed together," said Augie.

"The way you are with Rose, I completely agree, Augie. I've watched you balance empathy, empowerment, and discipline. You're a natural."

He squeezed her hand and contemplated her comment.

Is her agreement with Lawson only about the parenting skills, or was it also about having stayed together? he thought.

Her breath grew heavy as he reflected on their time together fifteen years ago.

"Chloe?" he asked softly. She didn't stir.

He gently roused her and whispered, "Chloe, we have a big day tomorrow. Let's get you to bed."

Apprehension hung in the air Monday morning as the foursome went through the motions of breakfast. Mondays always seemed to bring a sense of uneasiness to Augie—the start of the week. Lists of things around the property that needed to be attended to, but this Monday had a different degree of anxiety.

A platter of bacon and eggs sat untouched on the kitchen island. Lawson watched through the window as Rose walked sluggishly toward the barn for a final conversation with Scarborough before beginning her treatment.

"Are you sure I can't come with you, sir?" asked Augie.

"No, but thank you. We'll see you around lunchtime. Chloe will pick up a sack of sandwiches from Pearl Street, and we'll see what the bucket has in store for Rose."

Augie walked out to the barn, where he found Rose on her tippy toes, whispering in Scarborough's ear, unaware of the cowboy's presence. The horse's head raised and lowered in understanding. Rose was pleased that they were in agreement, as she had changed her mind about the radiation.

We will leave immediately, Scarborough.

She opened the stall door and led the mare to the mounting block.

I guess I can ride bareback.

"And where do you think you're going, Rose?"

She pivoted, grabbed a thick tuft of mane, and twisted it around two fingers. Then, with her free hand, she simulated brushing the equine.

Can't you see, cowboy? She has a knot.

"You were going to brush her?" She nodded.

"Rose, you weren't thinking of riding off to avoid treatment today, were you?" She shook her head.

"Honey, it's okay to be scared about all of this. You've gone through more tough stuff in a few years than most adults will experience in a lifetime. It's perfectly normal to be frightened, especially for this first session at the hospital, because you don't yet know what to expect. Does the machine you were drawing last night scare you?"

She slowly nodded.

"Let me ask you this. Do doctors help people?"

Another nod.

"Well, think of that big faucet as an oversized doctor who just forgot to put on his lab coat."

A small smile began to appear.

Augie lifted her from the mounting block, and she threw her arms around his neck, collapsing into his hug.

"Run inside and get ready. I'll put Scarborough away and see you at lunch. You'll do great today."

Mr. Lawson and Rose rolled slowly down the driveway and turned east toward the medical center. After more paperwork and a quick change into a hospital gown, Rose was ready to be fitted for the mesh mask. The radiographer situated her in a supine position, then momentarily soaked the mask in warm water before placing it over the redhead's face and attaching its edges to the table. Several marks were made on the surface of the mask, which would help line up the accelerator before each treatment. It was then removed for a short time to harden.

Dr. Maher entered the room and greeted Rose warmly. He reassured her that she would feel nothing and that they would be done in about fifteen minutes. Then, pointing to a booth with a thick piece of glass, he told her that's where he would be while overseeing the treatment. Two medical assistants adjusted Rose's position on the table and secured the mesh mask.

Maher's voice came over the room's intercom. "Okay, Rose, here we go. You are going to hear some clicking and a few other noises. Just close your eyes and stay still for me."

The machine turned on, and the X-ray beams began targeting the tumor. Rose picked up on an unpleasant odor; a cleaning agent her grandfather's housekeeper used had the same scent. She briefly opened her eyes and saw flashing lights above her head.

"You're doing great, Rose. We're almost done," said the voice over the intercom.

Then, everything went silent. She felt the table sliding away from the giant faucet.

"That wasn't so bad, was it?" asked an assistant as she removed Rose's mask.

"You feel okay, Rose?" asked Dr. Maher. She nodded. "Let's get you changed out of this gown and find your grandfather."

Lawson was in the waiting room, pacing, when they walked in. She walked over to him, and he enveloped her in a warm embrace.

"She tolerated it well. As I mentioned last week, she may or may not have any side effects develop today or in the next few days. Don't be surprised if she has a bit of fatigue. Partly due to the treatment but also due to the stress of the first day."

"Thanks, doc. We'll see you tomorrow morning," said Mr. Lawson with a handshake.

Rose's head hung out the open window of the Ford on the ride home, and Mr. Lawson feared the side effect of nausea.

"Are you going to get sick, honey?"

What? No. She shook her head.

When they turned off Route 22, Rose was still hanging out of the window, trying to clear the chemical smell from her nostrils.

Chloe was setting up a small buffet on the kitchen island as they pulled into the drive, with Augie and Aurora following in the Kubota.

"Lunch is served," said Chloe as they entered the lodge.

Chloe handed Rose a paper plate, and she chose half of a turkey and cheddar on a sesame bagel, then poured a handful of potato chips from the open bag onto her plate.

She paused mid-bite, scrunching her eyebrows. *Why is everyone looking at me?*

All eyes quickly returned to their respective lunches. No one was quite sure what to ask.

Augie broke the silence. "How was it?"

Mr. Lawson responded, "The doctor said Rose did great, and there have been no immediate side effects as far as we know."

Rose set her sandwich down, walked to the den, and returned with the Home Depot bucket.

"I almost forgot," said Augie. "And I did say you could pull one of your own cards, so, without further ado." He motioned for her to proceed.

She reached into the pail and withdrew a slip of paper.

"It says, *Drive the truck,*" said Chloe.

"What do you mean exactly, Rose?" asked her grandfather.

She put her hands at ten and two, took her left hand off the imaginary wheel, made a fist, and shook it out the window at an unseen driver. The redhead capped it off by extending her middle finger toward the offending vehicle.

"Rose!" Chloe said firmly. "I thought I told you that is not nice."

The redhead pointed toward the cowboy and raised three fingers.

I've seen him do it three times.

Her grandfather spoke, "Rose, if you would ever like to pull another card from the bucket, I don't want to see that gesture again. As Chloe said, it's not appropriate for you to be doing… And how are you even going to drive the truck? You can't reach the pedals."

"I could have her sit on my lap and steer, sir," said Augie. "We've probably all done that at some point growing up."

Mr. Lawson pondered the request. Rose's prayer hands did not help him hold a firm line.

"Fine. But, Augie, let's keep it under ten miles per hour and, of course, only on the property."

"Rose, grab the key. It's on the counter," said Augie.

She ran to the kitchen, quickly scanned the marble, and returned, arms out, palms up, empty-handed.

"I just saw it there, Rose." She shook her head.

"I might be of assistance," said Lawson. "I believe she thinks she is looking for a *key*. Rose, see if there is a small black remote control on the counter."

She went back into the kitchen and returned holding a fob in the air. Rose waited for a sign confirming this was somehow being considered a key. Her grandfather nodded.

She walked to the front door and removed an actual key from the deadbolt, holding both up side by side.

One of these is a key, people.

"Sorry, Rose. I should have been more specific. Most cars nowadays use key fobs, like the one you are holding in your right hand," said the cowboy.

She waved Augie toward the front door.

Enough already. Let's go driving.

"I guess we're going for a ride," said Augie as he headed for the door.

He climbed in the Ford, adjusted the driver's seat to provide additional room, and helped Rose into the cab. She pointed to the seatbelt.

"We're going to drive slow, Rose. It's okay." She crossed her arms and added a firm headshake, indicating no.

"Fine."

He tugged the shoulder strap across their bodies, secured it with a click, and started the truck.

"Hands on the wheel, Rose." She complied. "Here we go."

They accelerated slowly down the drive, with the redhead making tiny corrections left and right. Rose rocked her body forward and back and turned her head toward Augie as far as possible. She wanted more speed.

Augie applied slightly more pressure to the gas pedal, and Rose watched as the needle moved close to fifteen miles per hour. They wound down the driveway, paralleling a section of the split-rail fence.

Suddenly, Rose jerked the wheel hard to the right, leaving the pavement behind. Augie quickly slid his foot over to the brake, and they skidded to a stop in the damp grass no more than a foot from the fence.

"Rose! What did you do that for?"

She turned and pointed at the cowboy and then at the fence. She placed her hands together in front of her face and quickly separated them in a dramatic fashion. He knew exactly what she was referring to.

"Rose, I drove through the fence that time because I thought you were in danger of being trampled by a mama moose. We don't just do that for fun. Things can get damaged, and people can get hurt."

She shrugged.

It was only fifteen miles per hour.

CHAPTER TWENTY-EIGHT

Rose was already up the following morning when her grandfather appeared at the top of the staircase. She had slid a kitchen chair over to the pantry door and was perched upon it holding a red marker, drawing an X across the wall calendar's Monday square; she marked off the first treatment.

Nineteen more.

"Good morning, Rose." She nodded.

"Can I get you anything for breakfast?"

She shook her head from side to side while dragging the chair back to its proper place at the table.

"We'll leave in about twenty minutes. Make sure you're ready," said Lawson.

Rose followed her grandfather to the driver's side of the Ford, and as he stepped up and into the truck, he noticed her behind him. She pointed to herself, then moved her hands to the ten and two o'clock positions.

"You want to drive?" A nod.

"Okay, but only to the end of the driveway."

She smiled as he helped her onto his lap. Rose lightly slapped her grandfather's hand, resting at six o'clock on the wheel.

I can do this.

"I think it's best I keep a hand on the steering wheel in case you have any sudden urges to deviate from the gravel.

She turned quickly and looked back at her grandfather. *The cowboy snitched!*

As the driveway curved to the right, she raised the turn signal lever on the left side of the steering column.

"Excellent, Rose. Anything else you know how to use?"

She began randomly turning knobs and additional levers.

The redhead jumped slightly in her seat when the wipers suddenly came on at high speed, followed immediately by an unexpected splash of blue fluid on the windshield. Her hands ignored her steering duties as she tried to provoke the vehicle to perform more tricks.

"Let's go ahead and get you situated in the back seat. We are almost at the end of the driveway."

With the truck still in motion, she unclipped the belt, scrambled between the driver and passenger seats, and launched into the spacious confines of the cab's rear compartment.

"Not safe, Rose. Not safe."

They arrived at the hospital and completed her check-in significantly faster than on day one. She was taken back to the treatment room, the mesh mask was fitted over her head, and the linear accelerator came to life. Within half an hour, she was walking hand in hand with her grandfather back to the truck.

By Friday, Rose was experiencing noticeable fatigue. She napped for three hours after the week's final day of treatment and woke with Chloe sitting at the foot of her bed.

What day is it? she wrote on her notepad.

"It's Friday, honey. You finished your first week of treatment and did great."

She slowly wiggled out from under her blanket and swung her legs over the edge of the bed. When she summoned the strength, she dropped to the floor, took Chloe's hand, and led her down the stairs to the pantry door, where she proudly marked off the week's fifth and final X.

"We need to celebrate, Rose," said Mr. Lawson, who had watched the calendar ritual from a stool at the kitchen island.

She turned toward her grandfather.

"How about a sunset picnic ride tonight? I'll show you something magical that few people ever see." She nodded.

"Chloe, can you tell Cassidy to have four horses ready at about 6:30?"

"Yes, sir."

"How does a bucket of KFC sound?" he asked next.

"Sounds great, Mr. Lawson, but I don't think your cardiologist would agree."

"Good point, Chloe."

"How about I run to Whole Foods and pick up a few things, sir?"

"Splendid."

Cassidy prepared a quarter horse named Sunshine for Mr. Lawson, and he would join Copper, Winston, and Scarborough for the ride west toward Mount Glory. An insulated saddle bag hung from Augie's mount.

Chloe removed three chorizo and sweet potato tamales from the steamer and quickly wrapped them in foil. Lawson watched with disappointment, knowing which meal was for him as tomato, basil, and mozzarella were layered onto a French baguette.

"Too much lard, Mr. Lawson."

"I didn't say anything, Chloe," he replied with a smile.

"But I know what you're thinking," she said. "Your doctor would prefer you have a Caprese sandwich."

"My cardiologist won't know."

"Yes, but I will." Chloe grinned.

A quart of Mediterranean pasta and a small container of mango salsa were pulled from the refrigerator, and both were set in a fabric shopping bag. Disposable cutlery, plastic wine glasses, a corkscrew, a bottle of zinfandel, four bottles of water, and one lemon-lime soda were positioned neatly in the sack.

"Let's get a move on. We don't want to miss the show," said Augie from the back door.

Rose was already in the barn playing tic-tac-toe in the dirt with Cassidy when the rest of the family arrived. She sprung to her feet, eager to discover what this adventure entailed.

"Honey, are you wearing adult riding chaps?" asked her grandfather.

Brown suede chaps at least five sizes too large hung from her waist. The bottom eighteen inches drug behind her as she moved toward Mr. Lawson.

"I tried to tell her she wouldn't be able to ride in those, but she insisted on trying them on," said Cassidy.

"Where'd she find them?" Lawson asked.

The horse wrangler pointed to an open door next to Scarborough's stall as Rose wriggled loose from the chaps and returned them to the closet. She emerged with a new prop.

"What are you planning on doing with that?" questioned her grandfather.

Rose simulated sitting on a horse, reached behind her with the newfound riding crop, and mimicked lightly whipping an imaginary equine.

"Absolutely not, Rose." Lawson pointed back to the closet.

The early evening sun was low on the horizon as the group departed the ranch in a single file line, with Augie leading the pack. Scarborough was tethered to Winston, followed by Copper, and Sunshine brought up the rear. A grove of aspens swallowed the cluster of four as they made their way west along Trail Creek.

They stopped at a small waterfall and allowed the horses to drink. The liquid tumbled over a large boulder, pooled, and then drizzled down upon the rocks, where the stream continued its tranquil journey.

The horses' breath grew louder as the trail abruptly rose before them, the rise giving way to a clearing bursting with wildflowers and a small pond. On the far side of the glade, the Tetons resumed their dramatic rise into the Wyoming sky.

Augie brought the pack of horses to a stop and dismounted. He pulled a rope from his saddle bag, reached above his head, and secured each end to a pair of cottonwoods fifteen feet apart. Then, with the highline complete, he and Mr. Lawson tied the four horses to the horizontally running rope.

Chloe removed a large red blanket from her bag, laid it on the ground, and set the tamales and Mr. Lawson's sandwich down, along with the wine, plates, pasta, and Rose's soda.

Augie pointed west to where the mountain began to rise.

"Rose, do you see that barren spot that looks like rock? The one with no trees around it?" She nodded. "That's the entrance to an old mining cave. As the sun begins to set in the next few minutes, keep an eye on that area."

Chloe popped the cork on the bottle of zinfandel, and the rock face came to life.

What is that? thought Rose.

A small cloud of brown myotis bats emerged from the granite, darkening the sky as thousands poured from the cave. Rose looked at Augie confusedly and flashed her notepad toward him, displaying a question mark.

"Bats. And they're coming this way."

The redhead dove for cover beneath the picnic blanket.

"Don't worry, Rose. They don't want to eat you. Each one will consume over a thousand insects in the next hour."

Emerald eyes peeked out from under the fabric as the swarm converged over the pond and began diving in uncoordinated hysteria. Moths, flies, and mosquitoes were devoured by the hundreds in minutes.

When she was confident that the colony did not have a certain redhead on the menu, Rose crawled from under the blanket.

"Do you know that bats are blind, honey?" asked her grandfather. She nodded.

"Do you know how they don't crash into each other?"

She shook her head sideways.

"Echolocation. A bat emits a sound wave that bounces off objects nearby and is reflected back to the bat. This is how they know where other colony members are and where their prey is."

Rose pointed to her ear.

I don't hear anything.

"The sound they make is too high of a frequency for humans to detect."

They watched in silence as the bats danced across the silky orange sky.

Augie broke the collective trance. "Time to pack up. We want at least a little light left for the first part of our ride through the forest."

When the last picnic supplies were secured in the saddlebags, Chloe helped Rose onto Scarborough, and they departed the meadow for home, with Winston leading the way through the darkness. Ten minutes later, they emerged from the timber and rode the final mile through the moonlit valley.

Cassidy met the riders as they dismounted at the barn and loosened the cinch of each horse. Augie helped the wrangler as they removed the tack and led the equines to a watering trough.

"Thanks, Augie. I'll get them put up from here," said Cassidy.

He tipped his hat and headed inside.

Rose was rubbing her neck, grimacing in what appeared to be an attention-seeking performance.

"Everything okay?" asked her grandfather.

Rose shook her head as Chloe moved closer to inspect the source of the redhead's discomfort. She removed her right hand from her neck, revealing two small red marks.

"Oh, my," said Chloe. "What is that?"

She continued, "Mr. Lawson, there are two red dots on Rose's neck."

Her grandfather walked toward the pair.

"Let me guess, Rose. You got bit by a bat?" She nodded a stern yes.

"Show me your left hand, honey." She didn't react. "Rose?"

Slowly, she uncurled her fingers, exposing a small red marker.

"Very funny, Rose. Very funny," said Lawson as he turned away, shaking his head.

CHAPTER TWENTY-NINE

It had been four weeks since beginning radiation treatment, and other than fatigue and headaches, Rose had managed to avoid a plethora of possible side effects. Augie, Chloe, and Lawson gathered around the pantry door as the redhead proudly drew the final red X of the first treatment cycle on the calendar.

"Dr. May and Dr. Maher said you get a week off before resuming the radiation, Rose. So what will you do at seven every morning since you won't have to go to the hospital?" asked her grandfather.

She brought both palms together in prayer hands, then slid them to her right ear and rested her cheek on the back of her left hand.

"I don't blame you, Rose," said Augie. "If your grandfather would let me, I'd sleep until ten every morning."

"I've known you too long, Augie. You know damn well you enjoy the dawn. You could never sleep until ten," said Lawson.

The cowboy smiled. "You're probably right."

"Do you know where we should take Rose to celebrate, sir?"

Lawson shook his head.

"Church," said Augie.

"The megachurch we visited a few weeks ago?" asked Mr. Lawson.

"No, no, no. Church at the Whiskey Wheel on Sunday night."

"Rose, can you square dance?" queried her grandfather. A look of puzzlement crossed her face as she shook her head.

"That's okay. We have one of the best teachers in Wyoming right here on the ranch. Chloe, how about giving Rose a lesson this weekend?"

Chloe had spent countless hours at the Whiskey Wheel on Sunday nights when she had previously called the valley home.

"Yes! That'll be so much fun! You better be ready to get your do-si-do on, Rose."

Do-si-dos! I love them! She nodded in Chloe's direction.

Rose had spent most of the first grade as a Daisy in the Girl Scouts and fondly recalled the spring cookie drive. The oatmeal peanut butter Do-si-dos were her favorite, followed closely by Thin Mints.

Yes, square dancing it will be.

"How does tomorrow morning at seven sound, Rose? We can get started with your first lesson then."

She held up both hands, flashing Chloe ten fingers. Chloe gave the redhead a double high five.

"Seven it is."

No, no! That means ten o'clock. Rose shook her head furiously.

Chloe smiled. "I know, 10 a.m. I was just kidding, honey."

"Mr. Lawson, I'm going to take Rose into town this afternoon to get the proper attire for her big Sunday, if that's okay with you."

"Of course, Chloe."

Saturday's square dancing lesson began on time. Chloe explained that typically, eight people participate in the dance, but Rose could learn the calls solo. The music started, and she began with the most basic of calls—circle left. Next, allemandes, promenades, and sashays were gradually introduced. Augie and Mr. Lawson walked in at precisely the wrong time.

"Boys! Perfect timing. We could use your help, and I know you can both square dance with the best of them," said Chloe. Augie rolled his eyes.

Rose danced toward the cowboy, hooked her right arm in the crook of his, and practiced her elbow swing. Augie spun 360 degrees, and to everyone's surprise, he shuffled to Chloe and performed a sashay with her.

"Now we're talking," said Lawson.

The foursome shimmied through a half dozen calls.

"How about some Do-si-dos?" asked Chloe.

Rose had worked up an appetite and rubbed her stomach with anticipation. Chloe faced Augie; they stepped past each other, their right shoulders brushing as they passed. Then, without turning, they moved to their right, passing behind one another. Each then stepped backward and returned to their starting position.

Rose tugged on Chloe's denim shirt and nibbled on her tiny fingers.

What about the cookies?

"We'll get something to eat after the lesson, honey."

Rose snatched her notepad from the kitchen island and wrote, *Do si dos.*

"Yes, that's exactly what we are doing. Let me see you try."

The redhead extended her arms out to her side, palms up.

I'll gladly try one. Where are they?

Exasperated, Rose looked at her grandfather, then at Augie.

Cowboy, I know you heard Chloe say we were having cookies.

Rose disappeared into the kitchen pantry.

The parking lot at the Whiskey Wheel was already jammed with vehicles when the Super Duty pulled in Sunday evening at 6:05. They could hear the band warming up through the Wheel's open windows.

"Let's go. We're late for church," said Mr. Lawson.

"You can't be late for this kind of church, sir," Augie replied, shaking his head.

An octogenarian's thumb and first two fingers worked double-time on a banjo, picking the intro to a lively folk tune. Drums, bass, acoustic, and electric guitar joined in as the crowd's hands came alive, finding the rhythm and coming together on the second and fourth beats. Cowboy boots stomped on the aged, wide-plank pine boards, rattling the Wheel's tables.

They found a high top away from the stage and took in the sights, sounds, and smells. The scent of leather and dust mingled with stale beer. Most men wore a dark shade of denim jeans and western-style button-down shirts. Neckerchiefs and bolo ties decorated many of the outfits. For the women, circular skirts, petticoats, and colorful blouses prevailed on the dance floor.

Chloe tapped her foot, antsy to let her body move with the music.

"Are we ready?" she asked.

Rose slid from her stool as the others stood, took one final glance down at her red bandana print dress gussied up with white lace, tugged nervously at the hem of her sleeve, and followed Chloe into the swarm of dancers. They paired off, Chloe with Augie and Mr. Lawson with Rose, and warmed up with some basic moves.

When the song finished, the group joined another set of four dancers and formed a proper square. The caller spoke in an ear-pleasing sing-song voice, matching the cadence of the music. Rose confidently improvised as a swing call gave way to a half sashay; her headache was replaced with euphoric dizziness as she spun and twirled around the room.

"Face your partner and do-si-do," wailed the caller.

Here we go again with the cookies. She looked pitifully at the dancers in her square. *If they only knew, there would be no cookies.*

After half an hour, Augie waved his hand in defeat and signaled toward the high top. They returned to the table, minus one redhead skipping her way through random dancers, snagging elbow swings wherever she could.

Augie ordered two Jenny Lake Lagers and a vodka cranberry from their server as Chloe and

Lawson struggled to converse over the sound of the band. Augie turned his attention back to the stage.

"Chloe, can you collect everyone's favorite redhead?" asked the cowboy.

The band's drummer had given Rose a drumstick, and she was unabashedly smashing the polyester skin of the high tom.

"At least she's keeping the rhythm," Chloe said with a smile.

She returned to the high top with Rose in tow.

"You've been busy making friends, it appears," said her grandfather. She nodded fast.

The server returned to the table. "Anything for you, young lady?"

Rose pointed to the vodka cranberry in front of Chloe. The waitress hesitated, glancing at the adults.

"Honey, that's not a Shirley Temple, if that's what you're thinking," said her grandfather. "She'll have a Shirley Temple," he told the server.

They returned to the floor for the second round of dancing. The group of eight sporadically dwindled to seven when Rose exited an allemande and continued toward an adjacent troupe of dancers. Patrons eagerly welcomed the only nine-year-old on the floor into their group. Then, the band broke for a short break, and the dance floor was temporarily abandoned.

Mr. Lawson smiled as he reminisced about all the Sunday nights he had spent at the Wheel. *So much change in the valley over five decades.* Yet one thing had evaded time and stayed the same—the Whiskey Wheel. Progress had stopped somewhere short of the parking lot, and this sacred place had been frozen in time, from the band members to the oak bar to the decor. The clock's hands had ceased to turn.

He retired from his contemplation and returned to the present as Rose fled the table's boredom and searched the bar for someone or something more interesting. She found it in a game of rock-paper-scissors with the only other preteen in the Wheel.

"Don't you talk?" asked the eleven-year-old Native American girl. Rose shook her head.

That was enough of an answer for her new companion.

"I'm Lolotea, but everyone calls me Lolo." Rose held one finger in the air.

Be right back.

She dashed to the high top and grabbed her notepad and pencil.

Rose, she wrote, then handed the pad to the brown-skinned girl with two long braids.

Unsure of what the redhead wanted, she shook her head in confusion. Rose pointed to her own name on the pad, then to Lolo. She nodded and wrote, *Lolotea*. Rose carefully examined the odd sequence of letters.

"It means *gift from God*," she said. "I'm Arapaho Indian."

Rose took the pad back and wrote, *Very pretty*. A smile flickered across Lolo's face.

"Do you live here?" she asked Rose. A nod.

The redhead pointed back at her.

"No, we live on a reservation." Rose's eyebrows scrunched.

"Arapaho and Shoshone Indians live there. It's about two hours away. We drive over here one Sunday a month. I think my parents secretly love square dancing as much as they like our Native American dances. Do you know what a powwow is?" asked Lolo. Rose shook her head.

"It's so much fun. We dance and sing and honor old traditions. You should see all of the beautiful outfits we wear. There are more colors than a rainbow!" Rose nodded excitedly.

"We have our fall powwow next weekend! You need to come!"

Yes! I must come!

Rose grabbed Lolo by the hand, dragging her to the high top. She directed her new friend to tell the strangers about the powwow.

"Hi, I'm Lolotea. You can call me Lolo."

"Hello, Lolo." Mr. Lawson spoke first. "I'm Rose's grandfather, and this is Augie and Chloe."

Enough with the introductions. Tell them.

Rose scribbled, *Wowpow.*

"It's *powwow*," said Lolo, smiling. The redhead rewrote the word.

"Can Rose come to a powwow on our reservation next week?"

"What reservation do you live on, honey?" asked Augie.

"The Range River," she answered.

"When I was about your age, Rose, I attended my first powwow. Do you know where it was?" Mr. Lawson asked.

The redhead pointed at Lolo.

"You would be correct, young lady. It was early July at the Range River Reservation, and boy, was it hot. I can still picture the dancing and the colorful regalia."

"BRB," said Lolo as she left the table.

She returned quickly with an adult in each hand.

"These are my parents."

Tonya and Dakota warmly greeted the family as Augie extended his hand and made introductions.

"I hope Lolo hasn't been bothering you," said her father, a slight reservation accent discernible. "She's not shy," he added with a laugh.

"It seems my granddaughter wants to go to the powwow next weekend," said Lawson.

"It's the reservation's second largest, and it certainly is spectacular," said Dakota. "Have you ever been?"

"I was just telling my Rose, I went a long, long time ago."

"We would be honored to host you," replied Tonya.

Rose tugged at the hem of her grandfather's denim jacket.

Please, please, please!

"I think we could probably make a day trip out of it. What do you think, Augie?"

"Sounds good to me. Chloe?"

"You know I'm up for it," she replied.

Rose hugged Lolo as her grandfather exchanged numbers with Dakota.

Saturday morning of the powwow, the Lawson clan rose before the sun and piled into the Super Duty for the two-hour trip to the reservation. Chloe pulled up powwow videos in the backseat, and Rose watched eagerly.

"Knock it off, honey," said Augie from the driver's seat.

His headrest had become a makeshift drum, with Rose matching the beat of the current YouTube video being played.

You're no fun, cowboy.

Rose pulled her notepad from a drawstring backpack and wrote out the alphabet. They passed a Workers Ahead road sign. She quickly circled the A and spelled *Ahead,* then handed the pad and pencil to Chloe, pointing to the B.

"The alphabet road trip game," said Chloe with a smile. "I haven't played this in a while."

They paralleled the Snake River, heading north as Chloe searched for the next letter.

"Beaver Creek!" she exclaimed, motioning to a green road sign and circling the B.

They reached the letter L as the Ford climbed to 6,800 feet, passing the tiny town of Moran and turning east. The redhead grew bored and laid her head on Chloe's shoulder.

"If anyone is hungry, I packed some snacks in the cooler," said Augie.

As they came around a curve, brake lights filled the windshield. Two dozen vehicles were pulled over on the shoulder.

"Bear jam?" queried Augie, looking at Mr. Lawson.

"I would say so," he replied.

Rose hurriedly wrote, *Bear jam?*

Please tell me the cowboy didn't make jam from a bear, and it's now in the cooler.

"It's like a traffic jam, Rose; only the reason everyone stops is that they have spotted a bear," explained Chloe.

"Pull over, Augie. Let's see if we can show Rose her first bruin," added Lawson.

As Rose locked her door, Augie tucked the Ford in behind a VW camper van.

"Honey, it's fine. We aren't going to get close to it," Chloe said, patting the redhead's hand.

They exited the Super Duty, minus one, who had relocked herself in the truck. Augie clicked the key fob, reentered the cab, and pressed the button for the moonroof, sliding it open.

"Stand on the center console, Rose, and stick your head out the opening. You'll be able to get a good view and stay safe. Okay?" She nodded.

Chloe stood in the truck bed, pointing fifty yards to the east. A grizzly sow with two cubs foraged in the field as wildlife photographers scrambled to find the perfect shot while ignorant tourists tried to close the distance to the family of three.

"I think that's bear three ninety-nine," said Mr. Lawson. "Rose, you are looking at the most famous bear in the world. She has over twenty cubs and grandcubs."

The sow stood tall on her hind legs, drawing immediate shutter clicks and a muffled uproar from the assembled masses.

For twenty minutes, Rose was captivated watching the simple act of the sleuth gorging their way through a copse of chokecherry shrubs. The threesome eventually disappeared into a thicket, and the crowd slowly returned to their vehicles to thumb through the photos on their digital cameras. Each tourist was hoping to have captured the next Thomas Mangelsenesque iconic shot.

Rose slept as they wove through the arresting scenery of Bridger-Teton National Forest. Traffic began to back up a half mile from the entrance to the reservation, and Chloe nudged Rose awake as a flagman directed them to a parking spot in a field stuffed with cars and trucks from around the region.

Lawson glanced at his watch. "Let's get a move on. We're meeting Dakota at ten by the main arena."

Rose climbed out of the Super Duty and was immediately greeted with the *thump, thump, thump* of a drum circle in the distance. They followed the sound up a small grass hill, and Rose's world exploded with color as she gazed toward the open-air arena. Eagle feathers adorned intricately fashioned vibrant regalia as Arapahoe and Shoshone Indians staged for the Grand Entry.

Rose felt momentarily dizzy as she absorbed the kaleidoscope of color.

"Rose!" Lolo scooted her way through the swarm of people and embraced the redhead.

"Come on! The Grand Entry is about to begin. My parents have seats saved in the bleachers."

They hurried to the arena and slid onto the metal bench beside Dakota and Tonya. Shaking hands, Dakota signaled for them to stand as the announcer began to speak. The drum circle beat out the entrance song as an elder led the flamboyant dancers into the arena. Chanting momentarily replaced the rhythmic pounding before ceasing with a final drum beat, and the public address announcer began to speak. He welcomed distinguished guests, dancers, tribal members, and visitors.

"And remember, there are no spectators. Everyone is a participant here today," he concluded.

Following the invocation and prayer, the drum circle returned to life, and the men's traditional dancers negotiated their way back into the arena. Dakota interpreted the dance as the men—complete with war paint and a bustle of eagle feathers—told the story of a battle through movement.

The ceremony continued with the men's fancy dance, followed by the men's grass dance.

Girl dancers? wrote Rose, showing the notepad to Lolo.

"They're up next. Wait until you see the jingle dress dance," said Lolo excitedly.

Two dances later, the jingle dancers entered the arena, each covered with hundreds of metal jingles sewn onto their dresses. The rattling rows of cones added a unique depth to the drum beat and chanting.

"What's the meaning of the bells?" asked Chloe.

"Legend has it," Tonya began, "that a small child was healed after her father had a vision about designing a dress like the ones you see here. The jingles are thought to heal both the mind and spirit. The individual dresses are each unique and are a source of great pride for our people. Look closely if you have a chance later. There is so much intricate beadwork and color combinations. Just don't touch a dancer's dress without permission."

"Did you hear that, Rose?" asked her grandfather. She nodded.

The redhead closed her eyes and allowed the drum, chanting, and jingles to enter her soul as her head moved to the sound. Then, suddenly, the drumbeat stopped, triggering a smattering of applause for the dancers, and Rose's trance was broken.

"Any interest in checking out the food and art vendor tents?" asked Dakota.

A collective nod later, they abandoned the bleachers and headed for the tent village north of the arena.

Rose licked the sugary sweet remnants of kettle corn from her fingers, then looked at Chloe and pointed toward an adjacent jewelry vendor tent. Chloe followed her and Lolo inside and through rows of tables displaying handcrafted jewelry.

"We can customize any of these pieces here with your name or a message," said a Native American woman standing behind the counter in loose blue jeans.

Rose carefully surveyed the items on the table before reaching for a necklace with an alternating pattern of three gold and three red beads. Chloe nodded her approval.

"What's your name, young lady?"

Rose pulled out her notepad and wrote.

The woman turned toward a hardware storage box, slid open a small drawer, and removed an *R*. She did this three more times, withdrawing four beads, each in the shape of a different letter. Then, taking the necklace, she removed a clasp at one end and carefully slipped half the beads off before threading the four new spheres onto the string and replacing the gold and red beads.

"There, what do you think?" she asked Rose.

The redhead smiled. She turned to Chloe and wrote on her pad. *Can we get it?*

"How much is it?" asked Chloe.

"Twenty dollars," came the reply.

Chloe pulled a bill from her cross-body purse and handed it to Rose, who proudly passed it to the vendor.

After more dancing, a closer inspection of the drum circle, and a short presentation for non-Native Americans on the powwow's significance, Mr. Lawson indicated it was time to head back to Jackson. Hearty thank-yous were exchanged with Dakota and Tonya, the Ford was loaded, and they departed the reservation headed west.

CHAPTER THIRTY

Monday meant the start of the second four-week round of radiation. Aspens and cottonwoods boldly revealed their brilliant yellow and gold leaves as fall officially descended on the valley. While the winters were harsh, the falls were unpredictable, and the explosion of color would prevail until the first snow brought a blanket of white to Teton County. Mornings now always had a chill, and the threat of the season's first flakes grew more certain as September faded.

The redhead fiddled with the beads on her necklace, ensuring the four letters were properly aligned as Mr. Lawson and Rose drove into the rising sun. They pulled into a visitor parking spot, and Rose led the way through the hospital entrance. She knew the drill well by now and had even advised her grandfather that she could drive herself if he left her the keys to the Ford.

"Good morning, Lawsons," said the receptionist.

Rose smiled and reached for her necklace.

"I see you have some new jewelry. I like it."

The redhead grinned, sauntering from the desk to a loveseat in the waiting area.

"Mr. Lawson?" said the receptionist. "I have an additional piece of paperwork for you today."

He approached the desk.

"Dr. May has requested a blood draw from Rose. It's standard after the first cycle of radiation. Just take this to the lab after today's treatment. It will only take a few minutes. Also, he would like you to set up an MRI on Wednesday. I've highlighted the phone number for the imaging center scheduler, and you can call them while you're waiting for Rose." Lawson nodded.

A familiar nurse in pale blue scrubs emerged from the double doors, scanning the room before finding the redhead sprawled on the small sofa.

"Rose, you ready to come on back?"

She looked up at the nurse with sealed lips.

Not really.

She slowly rolled from the loveseat and marched toward the doors.

When Rose returned to the waiting room, Mr. Lawson had just folded up the USA Today.

"How'd you do, honey?" he asked.

She flashed a thumbs up.

Wash, rinse, repeat. Just like the shampoo bottle says, she thought.

"We need to stop at the lab, and then we can head home."

Rose shrugged and followed her grandfather down the hallway into another white, sterile hospital room.

She watched the needle enter her vein, and the cherry-red blood began filling the tube. Mr. Lawson could hardly observe the process transpire on someone else, let alone himself. He thought it odd that a nine-year-old could stolidly watch this procedure being performed on herself.

The nurse removed the tourniquet, then the needle, and held pressure with sterile gauze before wrapping the site with a compression bandage and sending the redhead on her way.

"You're such a brave girl, Rose. Needles and blood make me queasy," said her grandfather. She smiled.

On Thursday afternoon, Lawson's cell phone rang. It was Dr. May with the results of the blood draw and MRI. He stepped outside, leaving Rose to watch an old episode of *Baywatch* by herself; she would be depositing a new card in the orange bucket. *Go to the beach.*

Based on the chemical markers in Rose's blood work and the imagery, the tumor was growing. After a long pause, Lawson spoke. "I've held off asking this, but what stage is the tumor, doc?"

"Brain cancer is graded from one to four, but glioblastomas are always classified as grade four brain cancer. This is due to their aggressive nature."

Lawson's voice shook. "Can you operate again?" he asked.

"Technically, we could, but the tentacles growing from the tumor are intertwined with some extremely sensitive areas of the brain. Surgery would most likely have a significant adverse effect on Rose's cognitive and neurological functioning." Dr. May paused before continuing, "I would like to start her on temozolomide, a chemotherapy drug. It works by stopping cancer cells from making DNA."

"I assume there are similar side effects to other chemo drugs, doc?"

"Each patient reacts differently, but, yes, there is the possibility for hair loss, nausea, diarrhea, fatigue, loss of appetite. The list goes on." She continued, "Temozolomide is administered as a capsule, once a day for five days, so there is no needle in a vein as with traditional chemotherapy."

Lawson pondered his final question, uncertain if he wanted an updated answer.

"I'll ask the same thing I did when Rose was first diagnosed. With the information you have now, is this a death sentence?"

The line was momentarily silent.

"In an adult, I would say with a high degree of certainty that it is. I'm less confident providing the same answer in Rose's case, but that is a highly probable outcome. It really comes down to how long we can prolong her quality of life. Eventually, the glio will win."

"Dr. May, I need to go."

Lawson felt the blood leaving his head. He reached for the waste basket under his desk as the contents of his stomach rose through his esophagus and out of his mouth. He curled into a fetal position on the floor and shook.

Dr. May was waiting at the reception desk when Rose and her grandfather arrived for Friday's treatment. After she was escorted back for radiation, Lawson spoke.

"Sorry for the abrupt end to our call yesterday, doc. I suddenly felt unwell."

"I could tell. You never disconnected the call." Dr. May gave a faint smile. "You don't need to apologize, Don. Your family is going through a formidable and terrifying experience."

"So what happens next, doc?"

"My assistant, Meg, will sit down with you and Rose today and explain how the medicine works. Meg is great with kids. She'll answer any of your questions and give you a script you can fill here at the hospital pharmacy. Rose should start the temozolomide today, and she'll take it at the same time for the next five days, then stop for twenty-three days before beginning it again." Lawson nodded.

"Keep my staff posted on any side effects Rose has so we can manage those symptoms. If we can't stop the tumor's progress, you will most likely notice some signs of its growth, such as weakness, memory loss, drowsiness, headaches, and possibly seizures." Lawson's head bobbed slowly.

Dr. May's pager vibrated on her hip. She slipped it from the waistband of her blue scrubs and quickly read the message.

"I need to go prep for surgery. If you need anything, please don't hesitate to call." Lawson mouthed *thanks,* but no sound surfaced.

Two weeks after her first dose of temozolomide, Rose slunk down the staircase and into the kitchen. She raised a closed fist toward Chloe and opened her hand. A tangled ball of red hair rested in her palm. Fatigue, frustration, and melancholy competed for expression. She slid open a kitchen drawer, withdrew an Elmer's glue stick, made her way to the large wall mirror in the living room, and popped the top from the tube. Chloe watched Rose run the stick across the offending bald spot on the side of her head.

"Rose, honey, I get you're disappointed about losing your hair, but that won't work. It's just because of the pills you took. That means they're doing their job."

The knotted ball of red filament adhered momentarily to her scalp before succumbing to gravity and floating to the floor. She grunted and plodded to the sofa, where she covered herself completely with a blanket. Sniffling was followed by short audible inhales. Chloe walked toward the couch, gently lifted Rose's outstretched legs, and slipped under them.

"Hair loss is a side effect of your treatment, and it's just temporary."

Rose yanked the blanket down to her chest, revealing her red and puffy eyes. She pointed to the bald spot, her quivering lower lip pressing for a fix. Sadness and frustration soured into anger as she reached for a black pencil and scribbled furiously until the tip snapped off under the pressure; rabid coal-colored lines formed unintelligible shapes among protruding fragments of damaged pulp.

Chloe reached to her left and pulled Rose into her own body, the back of her head resting on Chloe's chest. She held her snugly as Rose's once-heaving chest settled into a controlled rhythm.

Fury was replaced by melancholy as tears fell unabashedly from her swollen eyes. When the sobbing ceased, Chloe tore the marred paper from the notepad and handed it to Rose.

"Crumple it up and throw it across the room as far as you can." She stared, her head cocked slightly to the side.

"It's okay. I'll pick it up later." She sat up and did as instructed. Her head remained still as her eyes darted left and right, searching for any sign of her grandfather and a scolding.

"Good job. Now, draw me a face that shows how you are feeling."

A fresh pencil traced a tightening and lowering pair of eyebrows, followed by a set of pressed lips with the bottom one pushing up.

"Mad?" Rose nodded slowly. "At the cancer?" Another nod followed. "Me too, honey…I know, it's not fair…but…" Chloe thought better of it and withheld the familiar parental sermon on life not being fair.

"Tear that one out, crumple it up, and toss it toward the other." Rose fired the paper, and it tumbled into the first one lying in the foyer.

"How about drawing me a picture of how you *want* to feel?"

A bald head grew a wide smile, and welcoming eyes took shape.

"That's good, but aren't you missing something?" Rose reached for a lock of her red mane and twisted it around her forefinger.

Chloe pulled a copper colored pencil and handed it to Rose, who begrudgingly began adding layers of hair to the profile, leaving one spot still bald.

"I have an idea, honey. I'll be right back."

Chloe took the stairs two at a time and returned carrying a floral print red cotton bandana. Retaking her seat, she folded the cloth in half, creating a triangle, laid the bandana over Rose's hair with the triangle's tip toward the back, then tied the two loose ends behind Rose's head.

"Look how cute you look!"

Chloe took Rose's hand and led her to the mirror. The redhead wiped a fresh tear from her cheek and slowly produced a faint smile.

"What do you think?"

Rose nodded.

"You could wear a different one each day, and the options are endless," she said excitedly. "I'll pick up a couple more for you when I'm in town today. How's that sound?"

Rose leaned in for a hug and held it longer than usual. After freeing Chloe from her grasp, she formed prayer hands, held them to her cheek, and walked toward the sofa.

"You need a nap? But you just got up."

Chloe regretted the comment as it exited her lips.

"Meg did say there could be lingering effects of fatigue after taking the pills. I'll make you some breakfast once you get up, okay?"

Rose picked up the notepad on the end table and wrote, *Not hungry,* followed by a heart. Then she disappeared back into her cocoon.

Chloe sat in silence. Visions of what should be for the little girl played out. She saw Rose sitting proudly, high in the saddle, being presented with a blue first-place ribbon. She saw herself, Augie, and Mr. Lawson dropping Rose off for the first day of high school, the redhead turning back with a mix of excitement and nerves. She saw her with anxious enthusiasm, tearing open her first college acceptance letter.

Chloe walked laggardly toward the kitchen faucet, allowing the cold water to hit her fingertips before gently patting the puffy bags under her eyes. Her head hung low over the sink as she slammed her fists on the granite counter.

The back door creaked open, revealing a bootless cowboy in black jeans, waterlogged from the waist down. Chloe's pained silhouette slowly turned, distress apparent on her face. Augie moved wordlessly to her, opening his arms and swallowing her in a strapping embrace. He rocked her slowly, feeling her heartbeat against his chest before speaking.

"Chloe, what's wrong?" Augie asked softly.

"This is just so cruel," Chloe began in a whisper. "And not fair. I'm trying so hard to be strong for Rose…but my heart is crushed."

Augie drew in a breath, and his lips parted as if to speak before reconsidering. He let out a languid sigh. She could cry as long as she needed. Chloe slowly untangled herself from his cradle, her palms moving up his body and settling on his cheeks as his sandpaper stubble slowed their journey.

"Thank you," she said, kissing him gently on the lips.

"For what?" he asked.

"For being you…And, Augie, you are enough."

It took him a moment to recall the context of her words.

The night at the Whiskey Wheel, with the pickleback shots, he thought.

"Should I ask why your jeans are wet and your boots are missing?"

"The Kubota and I had a misunderstanding crossing the creek," murmured Augie.

"I thought we should go straight, and the ATV decided to pull right. Unfortunately, the tires on the right side dropped into a low spot in the creek, and

I got stuck. I ended up needing Mr. Lawson to bring the front-end loader and some chains out to assist. Anyway, how's Rose?"

"She's asleep on the sofa. She had some hair fall out overnight and is understandably upset. I found a solution, though, and I think she'll be okay."

Augie eyed the glue stick on the counter.

"Tell me your solution wasn't Elmer's."

"No, of course not. That was your favorite redhead's idea."

"Well, I'll give her an A for creativity," said Augie.

"My solution was a head scarf, and she seemed open to it." Augie nodded.

"I'm going to get this creek water off me, and then I'm meeting a work crew out at the south pond."

"What's the pond project?" asked Chloe.

"Mr. Lawson is building a dock and putting in a beach. The lumber was dropped off yesterday," replied Augie.

"A beach? As in sand?"

"Yes, as in sand. I know he misses the warm Texas weather this time of year," explained Augie. "He's been kicking the idea around for the past eight months or so. I think the timeline sped up after he secretly went through the notecards in the bucket and saw Rose's wish to go to the beach."

"On a different note, how about Luna Blu tonight, Chloe?"

"Are you asking me out on a date, cowboy?"

"I guess I am. Pick you up at six?" Augie smiled and bounded up the stairs.

Aurora was chasing ducks from the pond's bank when the Moran Marine Construction crew arrived half an hour late.

"D.W.," stated the boss, extending his hand.

"I'm Augie," the cowboy said, returning the handshake.

"Sorry for the delay. A timber lorry overturned coming down Teton Pass. Lost part of its load around one of the curves."

"Glad you made it. So, what's the plan?" asked Augie.

"This should be a two-day job. It's a short pier and a pretty small dock platform. Worst case, we may need an extra half day. As I understand it, the landscaping company is ready to bring the sand in once we are done," said D.W.

"That's what Mr. Lawson is aiming for. But there already is a delay with the sand delivery, so we're waiting to see how many weeks out they are now."

"Got it. Let me organize my guys, and we'll get started."

"Sounds good. I'll check back later this afternoon and see if you need anything," said Augie.

The two men shook hands again; Augie and Aurora climbed in the Super Duty and headed for his cottage.

Augie slid the patio door open and stepped inside while the husky lapped from a water bowl on the deck. He walked to his sparse closet and began sliding hangers along the rod. Luna Blu was a four-star restaurant, and he was determined to find something that, at minimum, met their dress code. His patience waned as he scanned his finite inventory of apparel. He settled on a white button-down, a black blazer, and gray slacks—his only dress pants aside from his suit.

The cowboy owned three ties, all of which had been gifts. He rubbed the smooth silk of a diamond-patterned silver tie but thought better of it as there was little chance he could recall how to create a proper knot. Laying the garments on his bed, he released a mist of Febreze over the clothing before pulling his black Laredos from the closet floor.

It was early evening when Augie swung by the pond to check in with the crew from Moran Construction. Eight pilings rose from the dark water. Bolted-on stringers connected the large pilings leading to a partially finished small platform at the end of the embryonic pier. The foreman set down his drill and approached the Super Duty.

"Looks like progress," said Augie through the cab window.

"So far, so good. We're about to wrap up for the evening, but at this point, I feel confident we will be able to finish tomorrow," replied D.W.

"Mr. Lawson will be happy to hear that. I'll leave you and your crew be and see you in the morning."

Augie returned to his cottage, pulled the guitar from the wall, and finished writing a song he had been working on.

(Scan to play)
Powers and prayers don't go far
In the final moments, you'll know where you are.
Elvis is there and opens the gate
Holds out a hand just a little too late
I think it's May or maybe July
A girl in the clouds starts to cry
She knows too well it came too soon
He reached out a hand on the 6th of June
Back to those powers and back to those prayers
Ain't doing much good for us down here
In the shadows of life, silence calls
Just loud enough to reach us all

Time has passed and hasn't healed us all
Matter of fact, we're still waitin' the call
From the spirits that lie awake each night
And cry for an angel to make things right
Silence brings something strong
With some courage we might find right in wrong
Tomorrow don't care what's washed away
Closing our eyes, we might hear her say
I'm waiting for you somewhere near
Just around the corner, the corner from here
I'm waiting for you, somewhere close
Just around the corner when you need
me the most.

CHAPTER THIRTY-ONE

Augie fed Aurora, showered, and primped in the mirror. Then, satisfied he had transformed from a ranch foreman to a gentleman, he gave the Laredos a quick spit shine and slipped on the boots.

He pulled into the front drive of Lawson's house right at six and parked next to an Amazon delivery truck.

"The Lawsons?" the driver asked, holding up a small box.

"That would be us," replied Augie, taking the package.

Augie stepped through the front door, removed his Stetson, and set it on the entry table.

"I'll be right down," Chloe yelled from the threshold of the second-floor bedroom.

Mr. Lawson emerged from the den, and Augie handed him the brown box.

"I hear Luna Blu is the destination tonight, Augie," said Lawson as he tore the packing tape.

"Yes, sir. Very much looking forward to it."

Rose yawned from her familiar spot on the sofa, turned on her side, and watched as her grandfather approached.

"I have a present for you, honey."

He held the cardboard flaps open as she reached in and withdrew a silver handbell. She peered intently at it; her confusion was evident.

"You ring it when you need something from us, Rose. For example, if you want a glass of water, ring the bell, and one of us will attend to you. If you need help getting to the bathroom, just—" Her hand shot out toward her grandfather.

I don't need help going to the bathroom.

Lawson smiled and pulled his thick buffalo leather wallet from the back pocket of his jeans. He removed three one-hundred-dollar bills and waved them toward Augie.

"Dinner's on me tonight."

The cowboy raised his hands defensively.

"No, sir, I can't accept that."

"Come on, Augie. You and Chloe have done so much for Rose and me over the past few months. It's the least I can do."

"Much appreciated, but you pay me well enough to afford a nice dinner out, sir."

"Okay, whatever you say." Lawson disappeared out the front door.

Augie sat on the sofa beside Rose and rubbed her stocking feet softly before the redhead slowly made her way to a seated, then a standing position. He watched as she shuffled over to the wall hanger holding her grandfather's Gibson guitar. Returning, she handed it to Augie.

"You want me to play something?" Rose nodded and refound the warmth of the fleece blanket.

"Well, this one I wrote a long time ago. I was inspired by a certain lady who is currently upstairs, making us late for our reservation." Each of his final words grew exponentially louder.

"I heard that," Chloe yelled down. "It'll just be another minute."

Augie slipped the capo on the third fret.

"Now, Rose, to give you some backstory on this song, it's not exactly historically accurate, as they say. I wrote it based more on a feeling when I first met Chloe; she seemed a little lost and sad." With that, he began to play.

She's calling out to spirits, you know she never sees

And looking for answers, she's looking to me

Well the storm is coming, I've seen it in her eyes

And tears start falling as she begins to cry

The mirror refuses to tell her the truth

She's wondering what's happened to her youth

So she sits with a novel in the corner of her room

Just reading by candle and light of the moon

*She's built herself a wall, it grows
stronger every day*

She'll only let you in if you promise to stay

And the angels they wonder what's become of her

Such a pretty girl in such a lonely world

*So won't you take her from this carnival, this
carnival tonight*

Take her to the other side, the other side of life

The other side of life

So she picks up her Martin and begins to sing

*It's an old song she'd written when he'd taken
back his ring*

She sings love will come, and love will go
And love is the only thing you never really know
You never really know
And she's running from this
carnival, this carnival tonight
Never looking back, and she's only 25
She's only 25
And she's calling out to spirits,
you know she never sees

Chloe stood at the top of the staircase, recalling the first time Augie had played "Carnival of Life" for her. It was late summer, and they had been sitting across from each other around a rock fire pit on the shore of Jenny Lake as the twilight arrived. She could still see the uncertainty in his eyes as his gaze turned from the fire toward her, and he rested his hand on the guitar's body. *I love it*, she had said. Augie had sighed. *Thank God.*

The sound of weak clapping brought Chloe back to the present.

"Thank you for the applause, Rose," said Augie. "Did you like it?"

The redhead pointed toward Chloe as she made her way down the stairs.

Did she like it?

"If you want to know if I liked it, Rose, I did very much so then and even more now."

Augie turned to see her gracefully descending the steps wearing an emerald sequined dress with a deep slit. The cowboy swallowed hard and stood, unconsciously adjusting his blazer.

"Stunning," he said faintly. Rose nodded in agreement.

"I could say the same about you, Mr. West."

He took her right hand softly as she reached the final step and lifted it over her head, coercing her into a twirl to her left. This drew another round of hushed applause from Rose.

"We better get going before they give our table away," said Augie. "Rose, we'll see you in a few hours. Don't wait up for us."

The couple walked to the front door hand in hand, and Augie reached for his hat. He shook his head and chuckled. In the band of his Stetson were tucked three one-hundred-dollar bills.

The hostess led the pair to a candlelit table in the corner of Luna Blu, where Augie slid the dark red upholstered chair back from the table and seated Chloe. Opening the foil-stamped leather cover of the wine list, he methodically ran his index finger down the roster.

"Good evening. Welcome to Luna Blu. I'm Liz, and I'll be taking care of you. How are we doing tonight?"

"Very well, thank you, Liz," said Augie.

"Have you two dined with us before?"

"It was a long time ago," replied Chloe with a smile.

"Welcome back. Our menu has probably changed, but I think you'll find the same exquisite attention to culinary detail as you did the last time you joined us. Do you have any questions for our sommelier about the wine list?"

"I don't think so. We would like a bottle of Brunello di Montalcino," said Augie.

"Excellent choice, sir."

"That's a mouthful," quipped Chloe. "Italian, I presume?"

"Yes, Tuscany," answered Liz. "I think you'll enjoy it. I'll leave you to the menu and be back with the wine."

"See any apps that look good, cowboy?"

"I do. I'm just not sure if I can pronounce them properly to ensure we get the right thing."

"You choose. I'll order," said Chloe, smiling.

Augie pointed toward a mussel dish as well as a sautéed shrimp plate.

"How do these two look?"

"I'm good with anything," answered Chloe. "No escargots for you?"

"Those are snails, right?" asked Augie.
Chloe nodded.

"No, thank you. Disgusting. Repulsive. Who would even—"

"I get it, Augie. It's a hard no for you."
Chloe smiled.

The server returned with a bottle and two glasses. She uncorked the wine and poured a small taste into Augie's glass. He swirled the deep red liquid clockwise and drew in a mouthful. Augie swallowed and nodded at Liz, who then filled Chloe's glass.

"I'll give you two a few more minutes to look things over," said the server.

"Cheers," said Chloe. "Here's to unexpected reunions."

"To unexpected reunions," replied Augie. They clinked their glasses.

He momentarily held Chloe's gaze, wondering what their future might hold, before returning his eyes to the relative safety of the menu.

"Would you two like to put in an appetizer order?" asked Liz when she returned.

"How about the cozze e vongole possillipo, an order of gamberi napoletana, and the lumache alla luna," said Chloe.

"Excellent. I'll get those right in."

They spent the next ten minutes reminiscing about how different life in the valley was even just fifteen years ago. Outside money fueled progress, and progress, it was agreed, had disrupted the cowboy town long ago. The beauty was still there, but it seemed to have lost some authenticity since it was surrounded by miniature golf, T-shirt shops, and a Ripley's museum. Chloe had just begun reciting her favorite attractions at the museum of oddities when a food runner arrived with their appetizers.

Augie eyed the third plate suspiciously. "You ordered the snails, didn't you?"

"Oh, come on. Just try one. They aren't much different than the mussels." She hid her amusement behind a tight-lipped smile.

"No chance, Chloe. They're all yours."

Augie deposited a serving of shrimp, tomatoes, and Kalamata olives on his side plate while Chloe cut into her escargot puff pastry.

"This is so good, Augie. It has the perfect amount of slime, and when those big eyes—"

"Enough. If I vomit, they will kick us out, Chloe."

The entrees appeared as Chloe washed down the last mussel with a sip of wine. She stared at the massive tomahawk steak resting across the table.

"Are all cowboys such a cliche, Augie?"

"What's that mean?" he replied.

"How about salmon Wellington or a watermelon salad with duck? If it's not from a cow, a can, or an Idaho farm field, it's not on a cowboy's menu," said Chloe playfully.

Augie contemplated for a moment before shrugging his shoulders in agreement.

"What can I say? We like what we like."

Augie sawed away at the steak while Chloe picked daintily at her Quail Foie Gras.

He leaned to his right, looking under the table.

"Drop something?"

"No, I was seeing which purse you brought. Aurora would love for me to bring this rib bone home."

Chloe glared at the twelve inches of bone attached to the remaining fat and gristle.

"That is definitely not going in my purse."

"Well, it's too big for my pocket," Augie replied with a smile.

Their plates were cleared, and two steaming mugs of medium roast decaf were set on saucers. Chloe tapped her fingers nervously on the table.

"I have an opportunity…to return to Portland, Augie."

His eyes darted from the table back to Chloe.

"One of my clients is offering me a full-time graphic design position, and they would like me to start next month."

"So you are seriously considering it?" questioned Augie, looking away.

"I am…" Chloe started. "I mean, it's a great opportunity with a good benefits package, and I was only supposed to be in Jackson for the summer. But it's complicated. I certainly don't want to leave Rose. And then there is you and I, whatever we are and will be…and…I love you, Augie."

If you have anything to say, now is the time, cowboy, thought Chloe.

After a long pause, Augie spoke.

"Chloe, we both know I'm not the best at sharing my feelings."

The understatement of the year, she supposed.

Augie continued, still staring blankly out the window. "And I certainly don't want to interfere with your career."

"Let me worry about my career, Augie. I want to know what *you* think about us."

He turned his head back toward her.

"I was getting there, Chloe. This is a lot to process with everything going on and all. Things are good with us. You need to do what you need to do."

"I need to do what I need to do? That's all you have for me?" Augie looked away.

Chloe scanned the room for the server and raised her hand, giving the universal signal for *the check*.

"What are you doing, Chloe?"

"Getting our bill. I need to go."

"Chloe, don't be like that."

"Be like what, Augie?"

They drove home in uncomfortable silence. Chloe lowered her window and let the chilly valley air blow through her hair as Augie fidgeted with the radio. The lodge was dark when they pulled into the drive. Chloe exited the Ford before it was in park and walked purposefully toward the front door.

Mr. Lawson sat in the lightless den, his face faintly lit by the blue glow of the computer screen, as Rose slept on the couch.

"How was dinner?" he asked, continuing to stare at the monitor.

"Fine," was Chloe's answer as she made her way up the staircase, disappearing into her bedroom.

Lawson looked up from the screen expectantly at the front door. Then, after several minutes with no movement, he closed his laptop and walked toward the entryway. Through the sidelight, he could see the cowboy sitting on the third step, his silhouette outlined by the front walkway light, his

Stetson shuffling between his hands. Lawson slowly opened the front door.

"Care to talk about it, Augie?"

"Did Chloe say something, sir?"

"It's more like what she didn't say," Lawson replied. "What happened at dinner?"

"Everything was great until it wasn't…I'm a bit out of practice regarding relationship talk. She has an opportunity to return to Portland, and I think I missed my cue to tell her how I feel."

"Missed your cue or saw it and raised the flood walls, Augie?"

"Possibly the latter, sir."

"I've told you before; it's much simpler than that head of yours makes it. I know you. You are probably catastrophizing what could happen if things don't work out. Do you want Chloe to stay here in the valley?"

"She's never left my mind in fifteen years, Mr. Lawson."

"I believe that's your answer, Augie. I'd suggest heading inside, taking the stairs three at a time, and busting down her door before she gets any ideas about packing."

The cowboy nodded, processing the twists and turns over the past hour. He knew Mr. Lawson was right, and he also knew he had been a coward for not telling Chloe how he felt. He stood.

"And one more thing. Be vulnerable."

Augie kissed Rose gently on the forehead as he came inside, circled the sofa, ascended the steps, and rapped on the bedroom door.

"It's open," said Chloe.

"Hey. So…sorry about that back at the restaurant," he said. "Can I sit?" She nodded, and he joined her at the foot of the bed.

"I've never told you this, but I showed up at the church the day you married Steve. I didn't have a well-formed plan, but I intended to stop the ceremony."

"What…why…would you do that?" she stammered.

"Because I knew I made a mistake letting you go." She reached for his thigh and covered the back of his hand with her palm. "This, Chloe," he said, raising a hand and motioning around the room. "This feels like *home*. And it feels that way because of you."

Her hand left his thigh and drifted up to his cheek, where she wiped away a lone tear. He leaned in and found her warm, soft lips. His tongue slipped inside, finding hers. She grabbed a handful of his button-down shirt, rose from the edge of the bed, and gently pushed him away.

"I choose you, Augie, and this life here. I just need to know what you choose before it's too late."

She headed to the bathroom and closed the door behind her.

He sat motionless on the bed, staring at the floor, thoughts squirming out of control in his head, and it felt like an internal clock was ticking. His time to move a chess piece was up.

He could hear the sink running as he knocked softly on the bathroom door. The brushed nickel handle slowly turned, and the door cracked open.

"Stay. Chloe, I want you to stay. I've never stopped loving you."

The nightstand alarm clock displayed 1:42 a.m. when Augie woke. He wove through a maze of garments lying scattered on the carpet and slipped out the bedroom door in nothing but boxers. Quietly descending the stairs, he headed for the kitchen and rested a tumbler on the water dispenser's ledge. He pressed the glass against the paddle, releasing a stream, before training his eyes on the bundle nestled in the middle of the sofa. Something wasn't right.

He set the glass down on the island and walked toward the couch. A throw pillow and blanket rested where the nine-year-old should have been.

"Rose?" he whispered. "Rose?" he said, louder this time.

Augie moved quickly toward the hallway restroom, then to the den, finding no sign of the redhead. Panic began to set in. He bounded up the stairs and searched each room before arriving at Mr. Lawson's. He knocked.

"Mr. Lawson. Mr. Lawson."

A groggy voice came from behind the door. "Come in. What is it, Augie?"

The cowboy cracked the door open. "It's Rose. I can't find her. Is she with you, sir?"

"No. What do you mean you can't find her? She's not on the sofa?"

"No, sir."

Lawson sprang from his bed as quickly as his septuagenarian frame allowed him to. Chloe's head poked from her bedroom door.

"What's going on?" she asked.

"It's Rose. She's not here," said Augie.

"Rose!" yelled Mr. Lawson, pulling on a pair of jeans.

Augie hurried down the stairs, turning on lights as he worked through the house's first floor. There were more unanswered calls for the redhead.

Lawson threw open the front door and hollered for Rose as Chloe searched the second floor again. Then Augie saw it. A light was on at the barn.

He slid the stingy red door open, confirming his suspicion. It was an odd sight. Scarborough was lying down with Rose draped across her back.

"Rose." She stirred. "Honey, you scared the heck out of us. What are you doing out here?"

She slipped from the horse and aimed a finger out the large stall window toward the sky.

"I don't see anything out there, Rose. What are you pointing at? Let's go back in, okay?"

With a big yawn, she opened her arms wide toward Augie.

Carry me.

The cowboy swooped her up and hauled her back inside.

"I found her!" he yelled as he entered the rear door.

Rose did not understand all of the fuss over the middle-of-the-night family reunion.

"Rose, you can't leave the house after dark. That's not safe," said her grandfather.

She pointed Augie toward the sofa and fell asleep again in a matter of minutes, curled snugly under her blanket.

"I'll stay down here for the night," offered Chloe.

Augie kissed Chloe on the cheek and followed Lawson up the stairs.

CHAPTER THIRTY-TWO

The following morning, Augie snuck down the stairs, finding Chloe and Rose still fast asleep on the sofa. A creak grew from an irritated hinge as he slowly coerced the heavy front door open, permitting the brisk darkness to penetrate the foyer. He stepped outside, gingerly released the knob, allowing the latch to nest in the strike plate quietly, and moved to the Super Duty, headed for his cottage.

A mosaic of oranges surfaced to the east and reflected in the sliding door before disappearing as the glass entry glided open. He walked to his Martin guitar. A jumbled collection of lyrics had been swimming in his head since the talk with Chloe, and he knew from history he would need to put pen to paper before they evaporated.

An hour later, he had written the first iteration of "Just One Kiss."

Quiet lives of desperation
Leave him with no explanation
Wonders where he ought to go
Watch her now as she dances slow
Her eyes are closed she'll never see
Just how much he wants to be
The one whose arms reach around
And hold her close without a sound
She fills a glass with pink champagne
Stands alone in the acid rain
Waiting for the tears to fall
They never do as she recalls
Recalls a time long ago
Indian skin aglow
As her heart falls and breaks below
Every time he found the words
He only got them out in thirds
Caught somewhere beneath his lungs
He might as well have been speaking in tongues
She fades away to an apparition
Wonders where he'll find salvation

Turns and sees a cloud of thunder
Walks into it and stares in wonder
He's got her song finally done
Filled the pages by the midnight sun
Into her heart, he'll collide
Hoping she's still inside
Sees her in that flower dress
Decides it's time to confess
Walking slow to her door
To tell her she's the one he adores
She whispers back with quiet lips
You're the one I've always missed
And seals it with just one kiss

When Augie returned to the lodge, Chloe and Mr. Lawson were sitting at the kitchen island, cautiously sipping their steaming coffees.

"What exactly was Rose doing in the barn last night, Augie?" asked Lawson quietly.

"Not sure, sir. She was lying on top of Scarborough. I asked her, and she just pointed skyward out the stall window."

Lawson slowly shook his head from side to side.

"I'll talk to her this morning. It's dangerous enough for a child to be in that stall, let alone Rose in her weakened condition in the middle of the night," said Lawson. "I've got a call with my contractor in Fort Worth in ten minutes. I'll be in the den. Let me know when she wakes up."

Chloe reached both hands across the island and took Augie's.

"Rose is going to die, isn't she?" Chloe whispered.

Augie looked through the kitchen and into the family room.

"We're all going to die," he answered softly.

"You know what I mean, Augie. The radiation and chemo aren't going to stop the cancer, are they?"

"Mr. Lawson has been filling me in after each appointment, and from what he understands, no, they aren't going to stop the cancer."

Chloe squeezed his hands tighter.

"This just doesn't seem real," she said, a tear streaking her cheek.

"This is as real as life gets, Chloe." He returned her squeeze as she stared out the back of the lodge.

"It cannot end like this, Augie," she said softly. "I know…this is going to sound selfish…and Rose isn't mine, but…I can't lose three daughters." Her voice broke as she spewed the final word.

Augie's forearm muscles clenched as he tried to quiet the trembling stack of their hands.

"It's—" he started.

"Please don't say, 'It's going to be okay,' Augie."

He nodded, and they sat in silence.

The clapper inside the silver handbell connected with the bell casting and ringing reverberated through the first floor of the lodge.

"I guess Rose is up," said Chloe, walking toward the sofa and etching a faux smile on her face.

"Good morning, Rose. What can I get you?"

She shook her head. *Nothing. I wanted to see if this really worked and if someone would come.*

"You don't need anything?" She shook her head again.

"Okay. Your grandfather wanted to talk to you. Let me see if he is off the phone."

Chloe peered through the glass panes of the den door, and Lawson looked up from his computer.

Rose is up, she mouthed.

Mr. Lawson set his reading glasses on the desk and headed into the family room.

"How are you feeling, Rose?" he asked. She nodded slowly.

"About last night…What were you doing in the barn?"

She reached for her notepad and wrote, *Shooting stars.*

"You were watching for shooting stars?"
Another nod.

"Did you see any?"

She wrote, *All the time.*

Lawson paused.

"What do you mean, *all the time*? Have you done this before?"

She didn't respond.

"Rose?"

She rang the handbell.

"Honey, the bell isn't going to get you out of this. Have you snuck out to the barn other nights?"

She looked at Augie, then Chloe, eventually nodding.

"Rose, that is very dangerous," began her grandfather. "No one knew where you were. Please don't do that again. How about we make a deal? If you really, really want to go out to watch the stars, ring the bell, and one of us will take you out there. Okay?" A weak nod was followed by a finger pointing to the orange bucket on the floor.

"I guess we are due for a card from the bucket," said Mr. Lawson.

Several days prior, he had secretly removed all of the notecards that were not Rose's. Her grandfather carried the pail to the redhead, who immediately withdrew a card. *Tea with the Queen.*

"What exactly does that mean?" asked Lawson to no one in particular.

"I think I know," said Chloe. "Rose and I watched *The Princess Diaries* last week. She's probably referring to the scene where Amelia is having tea with the Queen of Genovia and finds out she is actually a princess."

Rose pointed to Chloe, shaking her head up and down.

"It's settled then. At four o'clock today, we will have tea with the queen," said Lawson. "Chloe, you better start going through your closet to find something queenlike."

No, no, no. Rose shook her head rapidly, immediately regretting the quick movement. She paused, then pointed to herself.

I'm the queen.

"I take it you will be the queen?" asked her grandfather. She confirmed with a commanding nod.

"Chloe, in that case, see what you can do regarding a wardrobe fit for a queen."

"I'm on it, Mr. Lawson."

Augie watched as Chloe rummaged through her closet, finding nothing suitable to convert into a queen's gown. She signed aloud.

"You could tear down one of Mr. Lawson's fancy drapes and turn it into a costume like Julie Andrews did in *The Sound of Music*."

"I'm sure he would love that, Augie."

"I have a perfect solution for you," he said. "The Halloween costumes are already out at Target. I'm sure you can find something fit for royalty there."

"That's a great idea! Why didn't I think of that? I'll run out now."

Chloe's hands worked the hangers along the costume rack, and after two false alarms, she found it. The outfit had an underdress of ivory brocade topped with an overdress of satiny pale blue material. Bell sleeves flared widely at the wrists and were ringed with faux fur. The packaging mentioned a crown, but that appeared to be missing. A gold plastic scepter completed the royal look.

Perfect! thought Chloe as she held it up for a final inspection.

She stopped at Whole Foods on her way back to the ranch and picked up prepared sandwiches that she would cut into smaller portions suitable for tea time. A half dozen chocolate croissants, two lemon custard bars, and a pair of tiramisu cake slices were deposited into the shopping cart, along with an eighteen-ounce bottle of sweet iced tea.

"Look what I found," said Chloe as she returned to the lodge and entered the foyer.

Rose looked up from her semi-permanent position on the couch, threw off the blanket, and moved at a speed evocative of a pre-glioblastoma Rose. She bounced on her toes as Chloe held the regal blue gown above her head.

"Well, look at that, would you?" Augie had just come in the back door.

"What do you think, cowboy?" said Chloe. Rose looked at him for his approval.

"It's fit for a queen. That's for sure," he said. "It looks like we will have one queen and one chambermaid."

"I'm nobody's chambermaid," replied Chloe, removing the scepter from the dress's hanger. "Here, Rose," she said, handing the gold staff to the redhead. "Cast a spell on Augie or do whatever you do with this thing for his rude comment," ordered Chloe with a smile.

Rose approached him and, using her empty hand, gave the same signal he did to command Aurora to lie down.

"You want me to lay down, Rose?" She shook her head and pointed to his knee.

"Oh." The cowboy took the cue and went down on one knee in some type of royal greeting he presumed Rose had witnessed.

Thwack! The scepter descended and made solid contact with the top of Augie's thigh.

"Rose! W-what did you do that for?" he stammered as the sting persisted. He rubbed his thigh, eyeing her in disbelief.

The redhead immediately pointed to Chloe.

She made me do it.

"Rose, I told you to cast a spell on him, not attempt to break his leg." She continued, "Augie, you're fine. Get up."

He playfully limped toward the patio door.

"I'll be back at four for tea, Your Royal Highness. And you, chambermaid," he said, pointing at Chloe. "Have my bathroom clean, and my sheets washed when I return."

Rose looked at Chloe, who nodded in her direction. The redhead raised her scepter high and chased the cowboy as he escaped out the back door.

At precisely 4 p.m., Rose emerged from the den dressed in her new costume and waited expectantly for whatever greeting she may receive. Augie was the first to notice her.

"Greetings, Your Majesty," he said, bowing his neck.

Yes, that's more like it.

"Don't you look queenly," added Chloe as she folded sticky notes into intricate triangles.

Rose pointed a finger to her head, made a circle, then turned her palms upward.

"Your crown, I know. It was supposed to come with one. I'm putting the final touches on it now," said Chloe. "Two more of these, and I'll have a makeshift coronet ready."

She taped ten sticky notes together in a row and, when she had them properly folded, connected the two ends. Then, theatrically, she placed the crown on Rose's head to applause from Augie and Lawson.

"Mr. Lawson, where would your three-tiered serving stand be?" asked Chloe as she cut the sandwiches.

"My what?" he replied. She repeated the question.

"It's probably with my bread maker and egg separator."

"Okay, where are they?" she asked.

"Chloe, I'm a bachelor. I don't have any of those things."

"Her Highness is expecting a certain royal standard," said Chloe. Lawson laughed.

The tea kettle blew a long whistle from the stovetop as Chloe put the final touches on the perfectly cut mini-square sandwiches. She dropped a tea bag in each porcelain cup and filled them with boiling water.

"Afternoon tea is served, Your Majesty," called out Chloe. "Be careful. It's hot."

Rose went right for a lemon bar, a slice of tiramisu, and a chocolate croissant. Next, she performed her one potato, two potatos routine to determine which dessert would be devoured first. Unhappy with the outcome, she went through the game again.

Yes, the tiramisu!

A dollop of mascarpone hung from Rose's lower lip as she warmed her hands over the steaming cup of tea.

"Your honor," said Augie, pointing to his own lip. She shook her head at him as her tongue found the offending creamy morsel.

That's not what you call a queen.

Rose brought the cup of liquid to her mouth and took a small sip. Her face wrinkled.

"Too bitter, honey?" asked her grandfather. She nodded.

"I thought it might be, so I took the liberty of picking up some sweet tea at the market," said Chloe, heading for the refrigerator.

She returned with a clean teacup and poured the ginger-brown liquid. Rose took another small swig, paused, and nodded her approval. After finishing half of each dessert, she raised her scepter and gently tapped all the tea party attendees on the top of their heads.

"What was that?" asked Chloe.

"I think she just knighted us," said Augie.

Yes. She pointed to the cowboy and motioned for everyone to stand. Next, she curtseyed and waited patiently for the requisite display of respect from her subjects. When that didn't happen, she turned her ire on the cowboy and swung the scepter at him. Augie saw it coming this time and managed to step out of its path, drawing a growl from Rose. It took her three bows for the trio to understand what was being requested of them. When the acts of reverence were complete, Rose returned to her makeshift bed on the sofa and quickly fell asleep.

CHAPTER THIRTY-THREE

In the past several weeks, Rose's condition had deteriorated quickly. Seizures were a daily occurrence, as were occasional losses of consciousness, and the doctors had stopped Rose's treatment and set up an in-home hospice team. The hospice nurses had coached Augie, Chloe, and Mr. Lawson on having honest conversations with Rose about death and dying should she directly or indirectly bring it up.

Stairs had become too difficult to manage, so a hospital bed had been set up in the corner of the living room, although Rose far preferred the couch's comfort and slept there most nights. She would often wake to find her grandfather, Augie, or Chloe asleep in the bed.

This morning, it was Augie. He slipped from the hospital bed and saw that Rose was already awake, drawing, propped up on the sofa with two throw pillows.

"Morning, Rose."

A feeble smile crossed her face. She motioned for Augie to come to join her. He sat as she transitioned from drawing to writing. Then, turning her sketch pad toward the cowboy, she looked at him hesitantly.

What happened to my mom when she died?

Augie paused momentarily. "Well, she went to heaven."

She slowly nodded and began writing again. *Will I see you in heaven?*

He read it twice, loitering in his head while a question he was unprepared to answer hung in the air.

"Rose, you're not…there's still…" Augie was dazed, as if by a blow to the head. Finally, recalling the guidance of the hospice team, he surrendered the truth.

"I believe you will, Rose…someday…Do you?" She nodded. "What do you think heaven is like?"

The redhead flipped to a fresh page and slowly began drawing. Augie watched as two vertical columns were connected by a horizontal beam. Several different shades of golden honey combined to produce an astonishingly authentic hitching post. Five simple saddles were added to the piece of timber paralleling the ground before a small child found a seat and was joined by a woman. The pair held hands beneath an elaborate ten-color rainbow.

"Wow. Really good, Rose. I assume that's you?" said Augie, pointing to the little girl. She nodded. "Is that Chloe in the saddle next to you?" She shook her head, then wrote, *Mommy.*

The lump in Augie's throat ripened as he fought a sudden swell of emotion. Afraid to speak on account of concealing the certainty of a quiver in his voice, he pointed to the three empty saddles.

You, Chloe, and Grandpa, she wrote.

Augie smiled a soft smile born of sadness and situational necessity.

Underneath her drawing, she wrote, *Will my grandfather be okay when I'm gone?*

"Your grandfather…will be very sad…but Chloe and I will take good care of him. And Rose, no matter what happens, you will never be *gone.* Your footprints, smile, and soul will always be part of this land. You will live on in all our hearts until our final breaths."

Her eyes grew tired. She drew a heart, preceded by an *I* and followed by *you.* Then her eyes closed. Augie leaned over and kissed her on the forehead.

"I love you too, Rose," he whispered.

The cowboy sat motionless on the couch; when he was certain she was fast asleep, he allowed himself to weep for the first time in a long while.

Chloe came down the stairs and quietly made her way toward him. She walked behind the sofa, draped her arms around him, and nuzzled her head against his moist cheek.

"Is everything okay?"

He grasped her hand, which was resting on his chest. Chloe cocked her head, eyeing the sketch pad, and saw the three questions. She pointed toward the pad and whispered in Augie's ear.

"Did she ask you those?"

"She did," he answered softly. "She did."

"You can tell me later how that went. First, let me make you some breakfast."

"That would be nice," he replied.

She squeezed his hand, kissed him on the cheek, and walked to the kitchen.

Lawson awoke to the smell of sausage on the griddle and made his way down from the second floor. Augie was still on the sofa, softly rubbing Rose's sock-covered feet. He quickly reached for the sketch pad, flipping it upside down.

Lawson stared out the front window at a slate-gray sky, reflecting the mood overtaking Six Dawns Ranch the past few weeks. The clouds hung low and heavy, like the burden everyone was carrying.

"Mr. Lawson," Chloe said from the kitchen. "Mr. Lawson," she said again, attempting to break his trance.

"Sorry...yes, Chloe?"

"I was just wondering how you would like your eggs this morning?" she asked.

"I'll just have some coffee, but thank you anyway."

"What day is it?" he asked.

Augie looked at Chloe, who returned a head shake.

"Tuesday?" said the cowboy.

"I think it's Wednesday," offered Chloe.

"Augie, isn't the delayed delivery of sand for the beach supposed to come Wednesday of this week?"

The cowboy reached for his cell phone on the side table and opened his calendar.

"You are correct, sir. I can't believe I overlooked that. It is being delivered today, and they are supposed to arrive between ten and eleven." Augie continued, "I'll plan to be at the pond a little before ten."

"What's your phone say the weather will be like tomorrow?" asked Lawson.

Augie pulled up his weather app.

"Mostly sunny, a high of fifty degrees."

Lawson looked over at Rose, asleep on the couch.

"I think we are running out of time on multiple fronts for beach days, so tomorrow is going to have to do," said Lawson. "If the sand installation goes fine today, let's plan on a picnic at the beach tomorrow."

Augie walked to the end of the new dock a little before ten and numbly cast a fly onto the pond's glassy surface, trying to keep his mind busy with something other than impending death. He reeled in his line and was about to cast again when the peaceful morning silence was broken by the cacophony of noise from two small dump trucks coming around the corner.

Setting his rod down, he followed the short pier back to the shore. The engine's roar had been replaced with an unsynchronized beeping sound, signaling the trucks backing up. Augie approached the cab of the nearest dumper.

"Did you bring a beach with you?" he asked.

"Fifteen tons worth," replied the driver as he stepped from the truck.

"I've got stakes in the ground showing the general outline of where we want the sand," said Augie.

The driver surveyed the area and nodded.

"This should be a smooth install. We have another truck coming behind us carrying a small tractor with a front-end loader. We should have this done for you in a few hours."

The men shook hands, and Augie returned to the end of the dock to collect his fly rod and christen the new pier. He pulled a black titanium William Henry pocketknife from his belt and began carving into the dock's bench. A rough heart took shape, and letters were added inside. *RL, DL, AW, CO.* He rubbed his fingers over the carving, adding more pressure with each stroke, and eventually, he was rewarded with the prick of a splinter penetrating his forefinger. He had been numb for days and needed to feel something, even physical pain. Augie examined the sliver of wood buried just under his skin's surface.

How can such a small thing cause so much discomfort? he thought.

Pulling on the exposed end of the splinter, he slipped it from its skin shell and flicked it into the pond. A rainbow trout approached the surface to investigate the potential meal, then spun away and disappeared into the murky water as Augie sucked a drop of crimson blood from his finger and headed for the truck.

As predicted, Thursday delivered a sunny but cool early afternoon. Chloe had prepared cold cuts and a pasta salad for the beach-day picnic.

"Rose," her grandfather said. "We have a surprise for you today." Her pale, gaunt face looked up. "We are going to the beach!" Her eyebrows scrunched. He continued, "Actually, we are bringing the beach to you, honey. I had one built right here on the ranch, and we're going to take a picnic today."

She forced herself to sit up and let her legs fall over the couch cushion. Then, standing slowly, she began to shuffle toward the stairs.

"Hang on. Where are you going, Rose?" asked her grandfather.

She paused as she passed the end table and picked up her notepad.

Swimsuit, she wrote.

Lawson smiled. "Rose, it's fifty degrees. I don't think you can wear one today." The redhead's shoulders slumped, and her face turned downward.

Chloe interjected, "Mr. Lawson, she could probably put it on under her sweatshirt, just in case it warms up." Chloe knew there was little chance the forecast would change, but Rose seemed to have her heart set on the bathing suit. It represented something she no longer had—a sense of normalcy in a life turned upside down.

"Okay, Rose. Get your suit on," said her grandfather.

He looked at Chloe and jerked his head in Rose's direction. She took the cue and followed Rose closely up the stairs. The redhead had to stop twice on her way up to catch her breath. Beads of sweat had formed on her forehead when she finally arrived at the top of the landing.

"You okay?" asked Chloe. She slowly nodded.

Rose changed into her swimsuit, and Chloe helped her pull on her gray sweatpants and a sweatshirt, the redhead's thoracic vertebrae clearly visible as they protruded through her skin. She paused at the top of the staircase, eyeing the banister.

"Don't even think about it," said Chloe.

She passed on the notion of riding the railing down and settled for the traditional route.

Rose's sunken, tired eyes ballooned as the Ford approached the pond. The sand—white quartz crystal directly from the beaches of Siesta Key—was blinding. It gave way to the dark blue water, which in turn surrendered to a cloudless azure sky.

She paused on the short walk from the truck to the beach, removed one shoe and sock, and continued before stopping to strip the remaining pair off. The perfectly sifted powder felt cool under her feet, and she wiggled her toes until they were no longer visible, turned, and smiled at her grandfather.

"I almost forgot," said Augie, heading back to the truck.

He lowered the tailgate and picked up a laundry basket. Rose watched as he set the hamper down at the water's edge and, one by one, withdrew items and set them on the sand. A yellow plastic shovel and matching bucket, a mold of a castle, a kite, and a multi-colored beach ball all appeared.

"Do you know how to make a sand castle, Rose?" asked Augie. She shook her head.

He motioned her closer.

"Take this bucket and fill it with water. We need to get the sand nice and wet to make it stick together."

After several pailfuls of water had been poured, Augie took Rose through the steps of building the base. Rose was meticulous with her placement of structures that formed her newly created kingdom. The castle began to take shape as Chloe and Mr. Lawson watched from the dock. She pulled a lifeless reed from the brush and broke it into two-inch pieces that she laid out to form a staircase up to the castle's front door.

"Very creative, Rose. I love it," said Augie, drawing a small smile from the redhead.

She circled the castle three times, ensuring everything was perfect, before waving her grandfather and Chloe over.

"Wow," said Lawson. "Who lives there?"

Rose paused before pointing to each of them and finally to herself.

"Does it have a name?" asked Chloe.

She paced back and forth at the edge of the water, watching her creation as she walked. When she had settled on a name, she used a discarded reed and wrote in the sand, *RANCH ROSE*. She changed her mind, and the letters disappeared under her feet. Finding a pristine patch of sand, she drew again. *DARC RANCH.*

"Your K looks like a C," said Augie.

She drew another C below it and pointed to the letter.

It's supposed to be a C, cowboy.

"What does that mean?" asked her grandfather.

She directed the reed's tip to the D, then pointed to her grandfather. Next, Rose identified the A and focused the reed on Augie. She directed a finger at herself for the R and, lastly, aimed the reed at Chloe.

"Okay, I get it now, Rose," said Augie. "DARC Ranch. I like it. Do I get to choose my bedroom?"

She shook her head and pointed to the back side of the castle, then drew *DUNGEON* in the wet sand.

"What! Am I living in the dungeon?"

"You must have been a bad boy," quipped Chloe, chuckling.

Lunch was out on the end of the dock, and they ate in silence, broken only by a soft shriek from the redhead when a pair of eagles were spotted overhead. Once they were out of sight, she turned her attention to the water, where she dropped a piece of her mostly uneaten sandwich. A cutthroat trout made quick work of the sourdough bite.

She walked to the beach, gathered the kite from the sand, and deposited it on Augie's lap.

"Do you know what this is, Rose?" he asked. She shook her head from side to side. "It's a kite."

Augie pulled the kite from its box, laid it on the sand, and carefully unfolded the quadrilateral.

"That's as good as you could do, Augie?" said Chloe incredulously.

"There were only a few to choose from. It was this, a plain red one or one with a walrus on it," Augie replied.

"So you chose that?" she said.

"Yes. Isn't it great?"

He held the kite before him, revealing a black nylon cover with a white skull and crossbones. The design was finished with a red bandana tied over the crown of the skull.

Augie deftly tied a lark's head knot and connected the spool of line.

"A kite is a bit like an airplane, Rose. As wind passes over the material, it generates lift, making it fly. There's a pretty good breeze over the pond, and I think it'll be enough wind to make her fly."

Augie put his back to the wind, handed her the kite, and set her arms at the proper launch angle.

"Hold onto it until I tell you to let it go," he said as he backpedaled a few feet away from her, releasing string from the spool.

"Okay. Ready?" She nodded.

"Let go!"

Augie pulled the line taught as Rose released her grip, and the wind found the kite's belly. It jumped skyward, then slipped left and right. He let out more line from the spool as it tugged in an attempt to break free from the confines of the cotton string.

Rose held both hands above her eyebrows, looking skyward and shielding her eyes from the sun as the kite defied gravity, rippling high above in the breeze.

Augie walked toward Rose and handed her the spool. She hesitated.

Rose took the cylinder of thread and squeezed until her knuckles were white. The kite danced with the wind as she gradually released her grip, allowing more string to run. When her arms felt too weak to fight the tension in the line any longer, she handed the spool to Augie.

"Had enough?" he asked. She nodded with a smile, laid down on the dock's bench, and fell asleep in the afternoon sun.

CHAPTER THIRTY-FOUR

The end was most certainly near. Rose could only shuffle short distances, and her ability to prance through the grasslands of Six Dawns was gone. The image of the redhead deftly picking her way through the field to arrive at the hitching post was burned in Augie's mind. He couldn't reconcile the two contrasting pictures.

Augie struggled mightily with the concept of God being so loving and creating a universe of good, yet there was so much pain and suffering. Compound that with the distress, in this case involving a nine-year-old who deserved none of this. Chloe had given him a copy of *When Bad Things Happen to Good People,* hoping to provide a little comfort in the face of overwhelming pain. He had cracked the book, but his heart was in no position to absorb the healing message.

Augie carried Rose through the lodge's front door and to the Kubota. She had become so frail that he was worried the small bumps on the trail would shatter her fragile bones. He rested his right arm across her chest to ensure she stayed in the vehicle as he made the short drive to his cottage. Rose's face frailly lit up when Augie lifted her from the ATV and carried her to the hitching post. He had set a western saddle on the beam to stabilize Rose in her weakened condition and surmised that Rose would appreciate the sensation of mounting a saddle again.

She slowly turned her eyes east in the direction of the Indian, sat for a stretch, then touched her hat. Augie produced the headdress and helped her replace the Stetson with it. He kept light pressure on her back with his right hand, supporting her as she reclined. The saddle made for an awkward position instead of the flat beam of the hitching post. Rose only spent a moment on her back before Augie assisted her up. She turned toward him, threw both arms over his shoulders, and weakly wrapped her legs around his waist. He lifted her effortlessly from the hitching post and carried her back to the Kubota as she rested her chin on his shoulder.

"Marry her."

Augie's head jerked backward as he stared into Rose's eyes.

"Rose?"

The raspy voice materialized again, saying, "Marry Chloe."

When Augie and Rose returned from the hitching post, Chloe was pacing in the second-floor bathroom. She distracted herself temporarily with the thought of how few people had bathrooms large enough to *pace* in. At thirty seconds, she walked back to the double sink and quickly glanced down, then turned away for another half minute of exercise. She returned to the vanity, stopping six feet short and squinting at the small thermometer-looking apparatus, as if distance could protect her from reality. Only it wasn't a thermometer. Two pink vertical lines appeared in the device's window. Chloe fainted.

Mr. Lawson and Augie both heard the thud.

"Chloe!" yelled Augie. No response.

They moved quickly toward the staircase, arrived at the closed bathroom door, and Lawson nodded at Augie. He knocked. No reply.

"Chloe!" he hollered again.

Augie reached for the doorknob. It was locked. He looked at Lawson.

"Do it," said Lawson.

The cowboy took one step backward and launched, his right boot making contact just above the handle. A loud crack echoed as the latch shattered the soft pine of the door frame. Chloe was on all fours, slowly beginning to stand, when Mr. Lawson spotted the First Response pregnancy test.

"Chloe, you okay?" asked Lawson. She nodded. "Augie, I'm gonna head downstairs. Let me know if you need anything," he added.

"What happened?" asked Augie.

He no sooner had the words out of his mouth when he saw the stick on the vanity. His eyes moved from it to Chloe and back again.

"Chloe?"

"I think I'm pregnant," she said, her voice quivering.

"I'm fine doing this on my own if you don't—" He cut her off.

"Chloe, this changes nothing. I've always wanted to be with you. I should never have let you go. It's been the greatest regret of my life." He walked to her and grasped her hands.

Augie continued, "I have always loved you more than anything. You give me purpose, you can expose me, and you are my kryptonite, and that's a good thing. We are in this together."

Rose was asleep on the hospital bed in the family room when Chloe and Augie came downstairs. Mr. Lawson had already explained the commotion of the bathroom door being kicked open to the hospice nurse, who was checking Rose's vital signs.

"How's she doing?" asked Chloe.

"It's a matter of days," the nurse whispered. "She tried to write something. I think she was telling me that she saw her mom. This kind of vision is fairly common at the end of life…All we can do now is make her as comfortable as possible."

"Last night," Chloe began, "when I was lying with Rose, she wrote, *She's sitting on the end of my bed.* Was she referring to her mom?"

"I think so," said the nurse.

Chloe reached for the sketch pad at the foot of the bed and flipped to the last page.

"She also wrote this. Any idea what it means?" she asked, pointing to a second sentence.

She says to tell you thank you.

The nurse studied the words thoughtfully.

"It would just be a guess…but maybe Rose's mom was thanking you for taking such good care of her little girl because she wasn't able to. That's how I'd feel if I were her."

Chloe's eyes glistened as she slowly absorbed the weight of the suggestion. Augie reached for her hand and gave it a gentle squeeze.

"Where is Mr. Lawson?" he asked softly. The nurse pointed to the back door.

Chloe and Augie found him sitting at the patio table, dabbing at his eyes with his shirt sleeve.

"Would you like some space, sir?" asked Augie.

"No, it's fine. You two come and sit down," he answered. "I have an ethical dilemma I'd like you both to weigh in on if you don't mind…Dennis."

"What about Dennis?" asked Chloe.

"He probably deserves to know that his daughter has only days left." He paused, staring down at the ground. "I would think he'd want to speak to Rose, but there is no way I could allow that to happen. So, the question is, do I tell him now or after she's gone?"

Augie looked at Chloe, then spoke. "If he isn't going to get to talk to Rose, I don't know that it matters, sir. If you want me to, I can call the prison and relay the message to him. I suspect whoever delivers it will possibly be on the receiving end of some serious anger."

"Why anger?" asked Chloe.

"Because the last time Mr. Lawson spoke to him, he was asking about the value of the ranch. Dennis has some delusion that Rose will inherit Six Dawns one day, and then he will snake his way into millions of dollars."

"Dennis will never see a dime from this place," said Lawson. "Chloe, any thoughts?"

"I'd call the prison now and be done with it. You don't want that on your plate…" Chloe trailed off. "…once Rose has passed."

Lawson looked at his watch. The black and stainless steel Submariner indicated 9:30 a.m.

"The prison accepts calls from 7:30 to 10:30 local time, if I recall correctly. I might as well get this over with."

He grabbed his cell phone from the patio table and walked toward the barn.

Chloe and Augie watched the conversation unfold. It began stolidly but escalated quickly as Lawson gestured wildly with his free hand, and his voice grew louder. It reached a crescendo; then, all was silent. Lawson slipped the phone into the back pocket of his jeans and turned toward the lodge.

"As expected, sir?" asked Augie. Lawson silently stared into the distance.

"What does this mean for me?" said Lawson. Augie looked at Chloe, tilting his head quizzically.

"Dennis said, 'What does this mean for me?' That was his first response. It was as if he didn't hear the part about his daughter being at death's door… He is a narcissistic sociopath."

"I'm sorry, Mr. Lawson," said Chloe softly.

"He tried to recover and stammered something about requesting a temporary release to see Rose, but I don't see that happening. When I told him he wouldn't be welcome here, he mentioned legal action." Lawson put the final two words in air quotes. "That's when I ended the call."

"You did the right thing, sir," said Augie. "It's done."

Lawson drew in a deep breath and let out a heavy sigh. "That it is, Augie. That it is."

"The time is near," said the home hospice nurse as Mr. Lawson stared at his untouched sandwich and nodded imperceptibly from the kitchen island.

He stepped outside, and his hands trembled like the leaves on the aspen tree he stood under as he texted Augie the news, then Chloe, and within ten minutes, all three were surrounding the sofa. Her grandfather held Rose's meek hand as her breathing grew irregular.

"Rose, you are the greatest gift of my life," Lawson said, barely above a whisper. He twitched at the sensation of slight pressure in his fingers.

Augie leaned over and kissed her softly on the forehead.

"She's crying," murmured Chloe to the nurse.

"Those aren't her tears," came the gentle reply.

Chloe looked at Augie, who was fighting a losing battle with the rivulets streaming down his face.

"One more thing…Hug your grandmother for me," were Don Lawson's final words to Rose.

At 12:13 p.m., Rose Lawson left this earth, forever having changed the three souls weeping over her body.

CHAPTER THIRTY-FIVE

The day before the funeral, Mr. Lawson called Augie and asked him to stop by the lodge around 11:00 a.m. Augie decided to ride Winston over. It was therapeutic for him to go through the process of preparing the horse, and in the darkness of Rose's death, the carnal connection to something so powerful and alive brought a breath of life into his numb soul.

Once the bridle was secured, he mounted the horse and headed south, taking the long way, weaving through thick tree-covered trails, crossing and recrossing creeks, with the pines finally coughing him up and spitting him out just east of the lodge. He dismounted, paused, took three steps up to the porch, coerced the heavy door open, and stepped inside.

"Sit down, please," said Lawson. Nodding toward the woman on the leather sofa, he said, "You know Lynn St. James, our attorney."

"Good morning, Ms. St. James. Nice to see you."

"Hey, Augie. I'm sorry to hear about Rose. I understand you, and she formed quite the bond over the past several months."

"Thank you, ma'am. It's certainly a sad day at Six Dawns Ranch—one of the saddest I recall. All due respect, Mr. Lawson." Lawson nodded.

"Augie, I'm sorry for the timing of this meeting, but there really never is a good one. You know this property *is* my soul. There are so many memories here, but I'm seventy-five and can't do what I once did. I just don't have the energy or enthusiasm to do what needs to be done in my position.

"You do a brilliant job with the hard stuff, running the day-to-day, but the ownership piece is a devil. I guess I'm saying I'm just tired. It's time for me to move full-time to Fort Worth and manage half an acre, not three hundred."

Augie looked down solemnly at his scuffed boots. *Well, I knew this day would come sometime. I can still find work,* he thought.

Ms. St. James stood and handed a manila folder to Lawson.

"Look, Augie, you have been an unbelievable employee for Six Dawns…" Lawson began, "as was your father, and you know I think of you as family, so let me cut to the chase. At the end of the month, I'm moving back to Texas. Should you choose to stay here in the valley, Six Dawns is yours, free and clear." Augie's gaze rose from his boots to Lawson, confusion on his face.

"I have a trust set up that will pay the property taxes on the ranch for the next twenty-five years. It will also compensate you with a yearly salary of five hundred thousand dollars for the next fifteen years. In addition, there is a check in this folder for five million dollars, payable to you. At any point in time, should you choose to sell the property, you can. You will then be left with the profit from the sale, less taxes, of course." Augie just stared. "Augie?" said Lawson.

He came out of his trance, still uncertain of what had just been said. Augie had Mr. Lawson repeat everything twice. Lawson smiled as he provided the details once again.

"But, Mr. Lawson, what about you?"

"Augie, I could never go through the money, mutual funds, and oil and gas stock I have even if I lived another hundred years. I'll be fine. I'll be more than fine. You deserve this."

Augie stood and walked toward Lawson.

"I don't even know what to say, sir. I'll start with thank you."

He extended his right hand. Mr. Lawson ignored it, instead grasping the cowboy in a warm embrace.

Augie entered the den and returned with the orange Home Depot bucket and one blank notecard.

"Where are you going with that?" asked Lawson.

"There's one more card, sir, and I believe it's mine."

Augie and Winston returned to the cottage, this time using the more direct route. He stood under the hot shower, intent on depleting the warm water supply, as his emotions fought like devils and angels on his shoulders.

Had Lawson just given him a fifty-million-dollar property? Had Rose just passed? Sadness swelled in the face of joy. A wall of sorrow prevailed over any modicum of happiness. He briefly considered running away from this place with such a dichotomy of memories. But the thought of Chloe affirmed what he already knew—that he would stay. He would stay as long as this land allowed him to and as long as she would have him. Hopefully, forever. He picked up his Martin.

Maybe they're kinder southwest of here
All of those faces that fell through the years
I'll find me a freight train, moving so slow
Run like the wind and never let go.
We'll light up a candle and watch the night burn
Leaving behind those lessons unlearned
Still here we are, falling from grace
With nothing to show but these lines on our face.
His back is now turned, facing the moon
Watching it all fall away too soon
He's back on that freight train, picking up speed
With nothing he wants but all that he needs
He gave it away so long ago
Wants it all back, but it's too late he knows
That train jumps the tracks, and he does the same
Waves goodbye to those cowgirls and
southwestern plains
Stands there again, watching the tide
Searching for something that's so hard to find
His back is now turned, facing the sun
On the side of that river where this
whole thing begun
He slips back again where hearts grow cold
Dreams of those cowgirls and the stories they told
And they're so hard to find

Chloe knocked on the sliding glass door as he set the guitar back in the corner. She slid the door open and stepped into the family room. He walked to her, and she disappeared into his arms. They held each other without words for several minutes, changing the pressure but never the location of their embrace.

"Are you ready for tomorrow?" asked Chloe.

"I don't fathom that anyone is ever ready for this, are they?" replied Augie.

"I guess not," she said. "Fathom? That's a big word for you, August West."

"Only six letters, Chloe. That does not make a big word," he smiled a small smile.

He walked into the kitchen and returned with the orange bucket.

"What's that doing here?" she asked.

"There's one more notecard, Chloe. I figure, in honor of Rose, we should pull it." Augie nodded at her.

Chloe removed the final slip of paper and saw the cowboy's name on the top.

"It's yours, Augie."

"What's it say?" he asked.

Her eyes scanned the card, growing wider with each word. She opened her mouth to scream, but nothing came out. An enormous smile unfolded as the first tear started down her face.

"Yes! Yes! Yes! Of course, I'll marry you, Augie West."

"I'm so sorry I didn't ask you fourteen years ago or even fourteen days ago, Chloe."

There was joy, and there was sadness. The particular tear's emotions were not discernible, but they collectively existed. They held each other in an embrace that mutually said, *Never let me go.*

"One more thing. Remind me sometime after the funeral to tell you about my conversation with Mr. Lawson this morning."

"Is everything okay?" asked Chloe.

"I think we're going to be okay," he replied, kissing her softly on the forehead.

Augie walked toward the sliding glass door and looked out at Sleeping Indian.

"She said, *yes*, Rose…She said, *yes*," he whispered.

A representative from the funeral home stood in the cool mountain air and briefly summarized how the service would proceed. He made the hollow but ubiquitous compulsory remarks about sadness, life, and death. Then, he reminded the mourners that Mr. Lawson had arranged a gathering at the Whiskey Wheel after the service for anyone who wished to attend.

One hundred white chairs had been carefully set out in the grass in perfect rows. They were four hundred short. The valley had turned out en masse to support Mr. Lawson, Augie, and Chloe and to pay their final respects to Rose.

In the second row, an eleven-year-old, teary-eyed Arapaho Indian girl rested her head on her mother's shoulder.

The boy with brown side-swept bangs sat in the third row, wearing a blue blazer and a red tie. Maya's hand covered his.

Cassidy held the lead of a familiar gray American quarter horse as it neighed from the cemetery's southern edge.

"It's okay, Scarborough," whispered the wrangler as she patted the equine on the bridge of her nose. "I know she misses you too."

A lone figure in his Service Dress Blue uniform stood in the shadow of an aspen tree. Above the rows of colorful ribbons on his left breast pocket was the Special Warfare insignia pin—better known as the Navy SEAL Trident.

Everyone likes to believe that a funeral can be a celebration. *A celebration of life,* they call it, but there is no merriment when a nine-year-old child leaves this earth. Augie stood at the lectern dressed in the only suit he owned, the blackest of black. The brim of his Stetson did double duty, shielding his eyes from the scattered light that filtered through the pines and concealing the ever-reddening, tiny, inflamed blood vessels blooming in his eyes.

A late afternoon sun fell over the Tetons, bathing half of the small graveyard in golden rays. While the headstones furthest from the foot of the mountain were still in the light, those slightly west waited patiently in the shadows for their turn to wake, which would not come until morning.

Breathe. He gave a heartfelt eulogy, most of which centered around the past five months. Twenty weeks that had changed him forever. Prone to monosyllables, he now shared with intention. His heart hurt as he stumbled through his emotional cleansing. He had been so strong for Rose. Picturing the Jackson Lake dam releasing its stored energy in an explosion of boiling water, he felt the same.

When his final words had been absorbed by the pines, he stepped away from the lectern and withdrew a small piece of paper with a rainbow imprinted on the top left corner. He opened it, taking one last look. On it, he had used a marker and an unsteady hand to draw a thick red heart. Inside the symbol, he had penned the final lyrics— eight lines—to the song he had written for Rose. Augie watched as it was released to the forces of wind and gravity, descending six feet down and settling on the casket lid. Inside, the redheaded girl lay peacefully in a white silk dress, brown floral cowgirl boots, a whittled owl at her side, and a Blackfoot Indian eagle-feather bonnet proudly adorning her head.

Turn your head now
Try not to stare
Close your eyes slow
Pretend she's not there
Hope as we might
Angels still send
Wings for us all
For racing the wind

EPILOGUE

Rose Marie West was born at 5:43 a.m. on June 6, exactly a year to the day Rose Lawson had arrived at Six Dawns. Air sped past her vocal cords producing a wondrous cry as tears streamed down the cowboy's face. She weighed in at a diminutive five pounds ten ounces and had brunette hair and striking emerald eyes.

Chloe was the first to notice the scent, and her brow furrowed as she searched the hospital room. Augie drew two short breaths in through his nose and looked at Chloe, then at Mr. Lawson, who was smiling. Vanilla and bergamot crept through the air—Camile.

Lawson walked to Chloe. She held Rose Marie, who was swaddled, on her chest. He bent down, gently kissed the infant's head, and whispered, "Rose says 'hello.'"

Scan the QR code below for a recording of the last eight lines of Augie's song for Rose.

ACKNOWLEDGMENTS

First, I need to thank my wife, Jen. She has provided insight into all of my books but never more than this one. Her feedback on changes, concepts, and plot was invaluable. *Racing the Wind* would not be what it is without her. To my beta readers, Debbie, Teri, Leigh, Kasey, and Barry a heartfelt thank you.

To my sister Kara, thank you for the feedback and for responding to the endless stream of texts and emails with random grammar questions.

To my brother Mike, who has overseen a property for two decades that this book was partially inspired by.

To J.M. Matos—an amazing chef and friend—turned inspiration for the novel. He read my book *Where the Sky Never Sleeps* and challenged me to attempt a novel. Twelve months later, here we are.

As an avocational singer-songwriter, the lyrical verses in this manuscript are all original songs I have written.

ABOUT WOODY

Woody Sherwood grew up just outside of Washington D.C., in Rockville, Maryland. He graduated from Xavier University in Cincinnati, where he earned a Bachelor of Science in Psychology while playing NCAA D1 soccer. Sherwood also received his Master's Degree in Education from Xavier. After two decades coaching college soccer, he started two businesses, UCARE-ED (www.ucare-ed.com) and WOODYSPEAKS (www.woodyspeaks.com.) His UCARE-ED program targets high stressors and provides students with coping skills for dealing with anxiety, setbacks, and failure. His WOODYSPEAKS program is geared toward providing tools for creating better employee engagement and building a championship culture. He is the author of the non-fiction books *Cope, Rise, Thrive!* and *Engage, Excel, Exceed.* He has also written a children's/MG book (which many adults have also loved!), *Where the Sky Never Sleeps.*

Additionally, Sherwood is an active, instrument rated pilot, having earned his pilot's license in 2007.

Woody can be reached by email at info@woodyspeaks.com.